Praise for
and Sea Glass Summer

"Soul-stirring...A sweet, sensitive charmer."
—*Publishers Weekly*

"*Sea Glass Summer* was all romance and heart. I already can't wait to read it again!"
—FreshFiction.com

"Liasson aims straight for the heart in this book and does not miss. There's so much depth of emotion, so many layers for both Kit and Alex to navigate. I shed tears with them, laughed with them, and happily celebrated their hard-won love."
—TheRomanceDish.com

"Filled with themes of loss, grieving, strength, longing, hope and love, *Sea Glass Summer* is the perfect feel-good, summer beach read. Beautifully told with characters that charm and steal your heart, I loved this novel."
—SimplyLoveBooks.com

"A heartfelt, uplifting tale...A charming, hopeful, romantic read by Liasson that is a fantastic addition to a series, Seashell Harbor, which I absolutely love and highly recommend.
—WhatsBetterThanBooks.com

"There's nothing sweeter than diving into one of Miranda's books. A wonderful read for the summer. Nothing less than expected from one of my favorites."
—WhatIsThisBookAbout.com

"*Sea Glass Summer* by Miranda Liasson is just the kind of adorable beach read I love to curl up with. It was the perfect book to read while on vacation!"

—ConfessionsOfABookAddict.com

"Once I started reading this beautiful and heartbreaking story, I could not stop! I was instantly emotionally invested in all of the characters from page one, and I cannot wait to read more by this wonderful and heart-tugging author."   —SusanLovesBooks

"After reading *Sea Glass Summer*, I purchased the first book and look forward to the next book in the series. I also confess to crying "happy tears" at the end of the story. I highly recommend this heartwarming story to other readers."   —LindasBookObsession.blog

"I love how Alex and Kit find each other in their shared grief. It's heartbreaking and sweet all at the same time. If you enjoy sweet romance, I highly recommend this one."   —MomWithaReadingProblem.com

"I always enjoy picking up a book by this author. I adore this unique grouping of friends and am eager to see what happens in the next installment."

—BooksandBindings.com

"What a touching story! I love how this story showed how deeply Kit loved her husband, but how she allows her heart to open for Alex..."

—RobinLovesReading.com

Sea Glass Summer

Also by Miranda Liasson

SEASHELL HARBOR SERIES

Coming Home to Seashell Harbor

ANGEL FALLS SERIES

Then There Was You

The Way You Love Me

All I Want for Christmas Is You

Sea Glass Summer

MIRANDA LIASSON

FOREVER

New York Boston

Copyright © 2022 by Miranda Liasson

Cover design by Daniela Medina
Cover images © Shutterstock
Cover copyright © 2022 by Hachette Book Group, Inc.

Forever
Hachette Book Group
1290 Avenue of the Americas, New York, NY 10104
read-forever.com
@readforeverpub

Originally published in trade paperback and ebook by Grand Central Publishing in June 2022
First Mass Market Edition: July 2024

Forever is an imprint of Grand Central Publishing. The Forever name and logo are trademarks of Hachette Book Group, Inc.

The publisher is not responsible for websites (or their content) that are not owned by the publisher.

The Hachette Speakers Bureau provides a wide range of authors for speaking events. To find out more, go to www.hachettespeakersbureau.com or call (866) 376-6591.

Forever books may be purchased in bulk for business, educational, or promotional use. For information, please contact your local bookseller or the Hachette Book Group Special Markets Department at special.markets@hbgusa.com.

ISBN: 9781538736272 (trade paperback), 9781538736289 (ebook), 9781538759363 (mass market)

Printed in the United States of America

BVGM

10 9 8 7 6 5 4 3 2 1

For my mom

Chapter 1

OLIVER WENDELL BLAKEMORE looked like a cute, round marshmallow as he stood at home plate, the bright May sunshine bouncing off his helmet, a cartoon shark grinning on his bright white jersey. His teammates sat on the nearby bench, a few watching, others, being five-year-olds, wiggling and laughing and fooling around and earning a semi-sternish look from their coach.

"Go, Ollie, go!" Kit, his mother, gave a whoop and a big thumbs-up as she watched nervously from the stands. The warm day, with the promise of many more to come, and the vision of the sapphire-blue ocean sparkling in the distance beyond the baseball field belied her anxious feelings. She'd made certain her son had everything he needed. Helmet, *check*. Striped socks, baseball pants, and glove, *check*. Cleats, *double check*. She'd even studied the rules of Tee ball on YouTube so she'd understand what was going on. And bought herself a glove so she could practice with him.

She'd wanted Ollie's first team sport to be a big success, even if his dad wasn't here to cheer him on.

I miss you, honey, a little voice inside of her whispered. She felt the familiar heart squeeze that she felt every single time she thought about Carson. Which was only about a hundred times a day.

"Don't forget to cheer," Kit said to her best friend Darla, who was sitting next to her. "Do you think I should go sit with the dads?" She glanced down at the front row, where said dads lined up, yelling out occasional tidbits of advice and encouragement to their sons.

"Only if you want to make the other moms angry," her other best friend, Hadley, said from her seat on the other side of Kit.

"Why would I make them angry?" Kit asked.

"Because you're gorgeous," Hadley said, brushing Kit's long ponytail back, "and while you mean well, they might interpret it as flirting."

"It's not right that that bench is just for dads. Also, I don't even remember what flirting is," Kit remarked as she smiled widely and hiked another big thumbs-up to Ollie. "And I've been too busy to get a haircut. And I think I have chocolate icing on my shirt from the brownie I grabbed this morning on the way out the door."

"I can barely see the icing," Hadley said. "And maybe you'd better remember about the flirting quick because Coach Bryan keeps looking at you."

"Coach Bryan is newly divorced and *hot*," Darla said as she poked Kit with an elbow. Most people would think at first glance that Darla, who was barely above five feet tall with curly blond hair and pretty blue eyes, was demure and unassuming, but her friends knew that she was about as subtle as her elbow nudges.

The three women were as different in personality as in physical characteristics—Kit's hair was nearly black, Hadley's was light brown, and Darla's was blond—but they'd been bound together as best friends since the age of five, their parents calling them the Three Musketeers.

"And his little boy is on the team. That's sweet," Hadley said.

"You're missing the point," Kit said. "I don't want to flirt with anyone. I just want to make sure Ollie has some representation down there." Not that she would do much since she barely understood the rules, but she was learning. Should Tee ball be this stressful for a parent?

Maybe when you were a single one, it was.

A dark-haired, well-built man walked up the bleachers to join them, smiling, joking, and fist-bumping with people on the way.

"Here comes your guy," Kit said to Hadley. For the past year, Hadley had been dating former pro footballer Tony Cammareri, or "Cam" as they all called him. And was blissfully happy.

"My guy is currently on my Z list," Hadley said. Okay, make that blissful *most* of the time.

"How come?" Darla asked.

"We're having wedding stress," Hadley confessed. "Tony knows *so many* people—football players, coaches, owners, managers, sportscasters—and he considers *all* of them friends."

"Cam's always had a big personality," Kit said. "He does tend to like everybody."

"Plus, with his new restaurant," Darla added, "he probably knows even more people."

Hadley threw up her hands in frustration. "If the guest list grows any more, we're going to need a bigger backyard."

"Oh, you've decided to get married in your own yard?" Darla said. "That will be amazing." Hadley and Cam's backyard was...on the ocean. Enough said.

"Maybe we'll just elope," Hadley said. *A little wistfully*, Kit thought.

Cam sat next to Hadley and kissed her solidly on the lips. "Eloping is like fumbling the ball on the ten-yard line. We've come this far—we just have to agree on a few more things."

Hadley smiled sweetly. "You're not going to make it over the finish line if we can't get this resolved."

Cam chuckled good-naturedly.

"Oh, you two are so perfect for each other, it's sickening," Darla said.

"Ollie's up." Kit pointed to home plate. Down on the field, Ollie shuffled his feet, his eyes darting around. She made sure to send him an encouraging wave. "He looks nervous," she said as she sat on her hands so she wouldn't bite her nails.

"Go get 'em, Tiger!" Cam yelled. "I mean *Shark*. Go get 'em, Shark!"

That got a little smile out of Ollie. And a few envious glances from the other boys, who well knew that Cam was a legendary football player, born and raised right here in Seashell Harbor, their quaint Victorian beach town in south New Jersey.

Kit cast him a grateful smile. Her friends and family had done all they could to make the past two years as normal as possible for her and Ollie after Carson's death in action as an air force fighter pilot. She was lucky to have such a wonderful support system.

Ollie wound up his bat, focusing on the ball perched atop the tee, which seemed bigger than he was.

He swung wildly, the bat hitting the tee with a reverberating *clang*.

A few of the kids tittered. So did one of the dads, which Kit instantly took note of. Maybe she would have to head down there after all.

"Easy, Kit." Darla grabbed hold of her elbow in case she followed through on her obvious impulse. "Look. Bryan is walking over to Ollie."

"It's okay, bud," the coach said, replacing the ball on the tee. "Try it again."

Ollie whiffed the air.

"How many strikes in this game?" Darla whispered. "Is it like regular baseball?"

"They get seven tries," Hadley answered.

"*Seven*?" Darla exclaimed, her eyes wide.

Yes, Kit confirmed with a nod. Seven excruciating strikes.

That realization made her nerves jangle. Not only because she'd wanted Tee ball to be a fun, confidence-building experience for her boy but also because it was slowly occurring to her that Ollie might be terrible at it. And if Ollie had inherited *her* athletic ability instead of his dad's, they were in for *big* trouble.

"What's the Admiral think about all this?" Hadley asked, nodding to the bleacher seat a few rows down from theirs, where Kit's parents sat. Her dad, a four-star navy admiral, sat with his arms crossed, assessing.

"He made him do drills last night to get ready."

"What kind of drills?" Darla asked.

"I was making dinner, but when I looked out the window, Ollie was doing sprints across the yard."

"Oh." Darla made a *yikes* expression.

A few more painful flails, and it was finished.

Ollie had made the third out. The game was over. And while there was no score in Tee ball—the game simply went an hour and then it was called—the kids still *knew*.

One of Ollie's teammates said something to him as he passed. Ollie scowled and then pulled off his helmet, tossing it to the ground, where it rolled to a stop in a puff of dust.

All Kit had wanted was for him to have fun, make friends, and fit in. Especially lately when he'd suddenly become aware of his long-standing lisp, which she'd always regarded as sweet and adorable. It never occurred to her that this could make things worse.

Kit met him near the front of the now-emptying bleachers, where he plopped himself down in the third row. "I'm not playing anymore," he huffed, crossing his arms and sticking out his lower lip. The combination of his summer buzz cut, deeply knit brows, and soulful blue eyes all gave Kit another pang in her heart. How would she ever stop grieving Carson when their son looked exactly like him? Ollie's bat clattered into the aisle, bumping its way down the metal steps and falling underneath the seats.

She chose not to scold him for dropping the bat into no-man's-land because she wasn't sure what was going on.

Carson would have known exactly how to handle this and maybe even why Ollie seemed unlike his sweet, happy self lately. *Help*, she sent up silently into the ether, squinting at the bright yellow sun shining so cheerfully over the seaside park.

Be brave, Kit imagined she heard back. That's what Carson would have said. With a wink and a jaunty smile that would have made her melt a little. And she truly wanted to be brave, for his sake, because he'd been all about brave. Carson had died on a mission over Afghanistan. He'd known the dangers, yet he'd gone gallantly and done his job.

So she could do hers.

All the five-year-olds were disbanding, gathering equipment, and talking excitedly with their families. Except Ollie, who sat there very grumpily.

Darla reached under the bleachers and fished out the fallen bat, casting a reassuring smile in Kit's direction. "It's okay, Ollie," she said in a soothing tone. "Everyone has bad days."

Kit's mother, who looked perfectly pressed in spotless white tennies, white pants, and a crisp tailored shirt, patted him on the back. "Maybe Tee ball's just not your thing."

"This is just the first game, Mom," Kit said, a little more firmly than she'd intended as she sat down next to her son and gave him a little squeeze. Besides, she thought a little wryly, Ollie couldn't quit yet. It had cost a small fortune to buy those special cleats and pants and a glove *and* sign up for the league. More seriously, Kit understood that making things easy for Ollie all the time wasn't right, even though her own family had done that—for her as well—often during these past two years.

"It takes a little while to get the hang of it," she amended, trying to convey that it wasn't time to jump ship yet. Her parents had been a godsend to her and Ollie. But sometimes she longed to simply do things the way she saw fit.

It wasn't their fault that they were trying to lighten the load. They'd swooped in to rescue her many a time, like in the beginning when her grief was so weighty that she could barely get out of bed, let alone take care of a toddler. Kit often felt that she was still slogging through the fog of sadness, but at least she was functional now. More than functional. But she sometimes wondered how much her grief had allowed her to give up her independence and lean on her loved ones a little too much.

As she rummaged around in her bag for her car keys, her fingers caught the stiff edges of a folded flyer she'd grabbed hurriedly from the library a few weeks ago during her lunch hour. She'd been drawn to it first because it was bright green. And second because its message seemed eerily targeted straight at her.

It was just a notice from the local community college making a pitch for next semester's classes, which would start in the fall. And announcing transition help for adults who'd been out of school for a while, like her. Which included taking a summer class or two with some reorientation guidance and support along the way.

Right before Carson died, she'd signed up for classes to complete her college degree in psychology, planning to become a mental health therapist. But then her entire life suddenly derailed.

And so had her drive to finish her degree. Not to mention the means to finance it.

She was busy enough with her job as the front-desk person at Seaside Auto Body, and thank goodness she had Ollie, who she was determined to be a good mom for. But lately the numbness she'd felt for so long had been blossoming into a deep unrest. And while she would never be envious of her friends, she couldn't help noting that Darla was a successful author of bestselling thrillers, and Hadley had found her happiness opening an animal rescue downtown. And that bright green flyer kept poking at her. So much so that she found herself scribbling a list of things on the back. Dreams, goals, wishes.

On her better days, she thought maybe that was a good thing because it meant she wasn't numb anymore.

And on her bad days—well, she didn't want to talk about those.

"Aunt Darla is right," her dad said in his firm but gentle way to Ollie as Kit gathered up his sports bag. Her friends hung out nearby, waiting to walk out with them. "You just had an off day. That doesn't mean we give up, right, buddy?" Her dad playfully knocked Ollie's shoulder. The lip jutted out more. "We'll just practice harder. Do some fun drills."

Oh geez. For her dad, fresh air and calisthenics was the cure for . . . just about everything.

Cam, coming to the rescue, put a big hand on Ollie's little shoulder, which sent another wretched pang to her heart. Cam was kind and so good with Ollie. He really made an effort to be an important male influence. But even an innocent, thoughtful gesture like that sent up an unnatural wellspring of anger inside of her. Why wasn't that *Carson's* hand on his son's shoulder? Something they'd all been robbed of.

"What do you say we practice some this week, huh, buddy?"

"I bought a bat and ball," Kit offered. She'd tried

to practice throwing with Ollie but she probably needed someone to help hone her pitching skills more than her son did.

"I think we might have one of those little stand thingies in our garage," Hadley said.

"It's a *tee*, Aunt Hadley," Ollie said, and went back to his slumped-down position. Because of his endearing little lisp, her name came out *Hadwey*.

Ollie's lisp gave her mother's heart another prick. Now that he was about to start kindergarten, she feared that it would make him a target with the other kids. Plus their pediatrician had recommended speech therapy twice a week, and Ollie wasn't very happy about it despite their therapist trying to make it fun and positive.

Kit had tried so hard to protect him these last few years from the perils of life. But life had a way of creeping in anyway, even for a five-year-old.

For the millionth time, she catalogued yet another way she was falling short. Of course she was, because trying to be two parents made her feel stretched thinner than a Fruit Roll-Up.

That almost brought her to tears. Sometimes it didn't take much, at the most unwelcome times. But she forced herself to think of something to distract herself. It was a beautiful day, the promise of summer in the air. That meant beach days, barbecues, and giving Ollie the best summer ever—summers like she remembered, growing up in Seashell Harbor, a magical place, with long, lazy days playing in the sand and running into the waves and the salty taste of ocean water in your mouth. Finding shells and sea glass and creatures and enjoying clambakes and fires on the beach. A place where the stars were so bright at night they looked like tiny diamonds.

That's what she wanted for Ollie. A carefree, happy childhood. And she'd do anything for him to have that.

As for herself, her goals were more short-term. She just wanted to survive Tee ball. And maybe curl up at the end of the day with a good romance novel...which happened to be the only thing she was curling up with lately.

"I hate Tee ball," Ollie said with passion as he walked side by side with her dad as they all headed to the parking lot. "I want to quit."

Hadley put an arm around Kit as they walked off the field. "There you go," she said, placing the fallen strap of Ollie's bag back on her shoulder.

"He's like Carson," Kit said, unable to shake her worry. "Once he makes up his mind, it's super hard to reason with him."

"Ollie will be fine," Hadley said. "This is just a little bump in the road."

"Hey," Darla said, jogging up beside them. "Don't forget, we're knocking on your door at seven tomorrow morning. Be awake. And wear your running shoes."

"I've changed my mind," Kit said. "I'm tired from work this week, and Ollie's upset and..." She knew exactly what her friends were doing—staging an intervention. Something that she'd taken part in at various times in their lives for both of them too. But she hated being on the receiving end of one. "...and I'm meeting Carol Drake to discuss the house at nine."

The house, known in town as the McKinnon house, was the big, behemoth train wreck that was Carson's inheritance—aka the Ball and Chain.

"No excuses," Hadley said. "You pinkie-swore."

"That was after two glasses of wine." Why had she mentioned that flyer to her friends? Because she was a glutton for punishment, that's why. One whiff of her unrest and they were off to save her. *Note to self: no more wine!*

"We'll be done way before then," Darla said. "Don't forget to bring your list." She glanced down at Kit's hands. "And why aren't you wearing the ring?"

Oh no. Last summer, they'd found Darla's great-great-grandmother's ring hidden in the toe of an old sock when they were helping her move. The ring looked like a precious stone but was actually a Seashell Harbor "diamond," made from bits of quartz that washed up on the beach after a long journey down the Catskills. Most of them made their way into local tourist shops. But Darla's courageous ancestor had used hers to fake a marriage and buy an old property on the outskirts of town where unwed mothers could learn life skills.

Pretty amazing for 1906.

"Oh, I'm sorry about that." Kit slid her hand along her empty finger. "I meant to give it back."

"No, you're supposed to be wearing it," Darla insisted. "All summer long. That was the deal."

"Look, it's big and I'm constantly getting my hands in cookie dough or washing the dog or—"

"Hadley wore it last summer and look what happened." Darla was referring to the fact that Hadley had reconnected with her first love and was now engaged.

"It can't hurt, Kit," Hadley, always the optimist, chimed in. "Of the three of us, you've always been the romantic. So wear it and see what happens."

Kit *used* to believe in true love and poetry and romance. But the truth was, her romantic well was…bone-dry, thanks very much.

She was about to just tell her friends that fine, she

would wear it to get them off her case, when Ollie's best friend, Corey, and his mom, Cindy, passed by. Corey, who had freckles and a mop of curly red hair, ran up to Ollie and put his arms around him. "It's okay, Ollie. You'll get a hit next time. You want to come over and play Transformers tomorrow?"

Kit loved that kid and so, apparently, did Ollie, as his face brightened immediately. Kit smiled at Cindy. "How is it you have such a wonderful child?"

She shrugged. "Yours is pretty wonderful too. Can Ollie play? It's my turn to host the Saturday playdate."

"Sure," Kit said. "Thanks."

"Would you mind hosting next weekend?" Cindy asked. "My finals are coming up, and I could use some study time. Or nap time." She chuckled. "I'm not sure which one I need more."

"I'd love to have the boys over tomorrow," Kit said. "And next weekend, too, so you can study. Just plan on that. If it's a nice day, I'll take them to the beach."

"You sure you wouldn't mind?" Cindy wore that sudden look of relief that moms know well.

"Not at all." Kit shook her head incredulously, in awe of her friend. "Full-time job, full-time student, full-time mother. What's your secret?"

"Caffeine," Cindy said. "Anger helps too." She gave Kit a squeeze. "Don't be so hard on yourself. Not that I'm an expert or anything, but an idiot ex is probably a lot easier to deal with than losing a great guy you genuinely loved."

Oh geez, there Kit went, feeling like she was going to tear up *again*. "Thanks," Kit managed. "And good luck with the studying." As they all headed off the field, she felt even more unsettled.

Kit used to be a go-getter like Cindy. Determined. Hardworking. A goal setter.

Used to be. That was a terrible way to define yourself.

As she rummaged in her purse for her car keys, the flyer poked her again. Reminding her of her shortcomings, no doubt.

Hadley touched her elbow. "Hot single dad alert," she whispered in a singsong voice. "*Don't* turn around."

Kit froze. She would've brushed off her friends' teasing as bluster except that Ollie's coach *had* been making a lot of eye contact with her. And she was awfully rusty at the dating game, but she wasn't dead, and she'd definitely noticed him too. "Who is it?" she asked, hoping it *wasn't* Bryan Dougherty. He was…unsettling. Handsome. A male. *Single.*

All the moms joked about how good-looking he was behind his back. And some of them blatantly flirted with him. Like Astrid, a mom who never showed up in shorts and a T-shirt, always had a fresh manicure, and who happened to be frowning at her from twenty feet away right now.

"Someone tall, dark, and athletic," Darla said with a grin. "Former college hockey star, with a gorgeous smile. All teeth present and accounted for."

Kit gave Darla a puzzled look. "Teeth accounted for?"

"It's a hockey joke," Darla said.

"A bad one," Hadley added.

Darla hurriedly tidied Kit's flyaway wavy hair, a staple of living by the ocean. Hadley pulled out her tinted lip balm and nudged her to use some.

"I'm not putting that on," Kit said.

Hadley persisted. "Chapped lips are *not* attractive," she said.

Kit rolled her eyes and took the offering, swiping it over her lips and then rubbing them together. "You haven't done that since high school," she said, but Hadley's response was a quick backward wave as she turned to go.

"See you bright and early." Darla gave a knowing nod as they both walked away.

"Hey, don't leave—" Kit dearly loved her friends, even if they were sometimes pushy and annoying. Like now.

"Hey, Kit." Bryan combed back his stylishly longish hair, which might require too much work for some men but looked great on him. "How are you?" His deep blue gaze swept her up and down in a way that should've flattered her but instead just made her feel more jittery. Yep, she was *waaaay* out of practice.

"Hey, Bryan," she said. "Do you have a second?" Maybe if she talked first, he wouldn't ask her out. Which she feared might be on his mind. Not that he wasn't cute but…she wasn't ready. The way her heart was beating like she was having a heart attack told her so. Maybe she'd never be ready. But right now, Ollie was foremost on her mind. As he should be. Right?

"For you, I have two," he said with a chuckle.

"I'm a little concerned about Ollie," Kit said.

Bryan scratched his very attractive stubble. "Hmmm, well, he is a little shy and cautious. He just needs to toughen up a little, not be afraid to take a little hit." He playfully knocked her elbow to bring home his point.

"Oh." A thousand questions flew through her mind. Including the phrases *toughen up* and *not be afraid to take a little hit*, both of which made her a little uncomfortable. Carson would probably laugh and tell her that it was okay—even necessary—for Ollie not to be overly sensitive. *You can't pad the crib forever*, he'd say with that wonderful laugh as he gathered her into his arms.

She couldn't protect her son from all the bumps and bruises of life. Or the fact that his dad wasn't here to help him—or her—through this.

"I'll look out for him next practice," Bryan said. "Don't worry."

"Okay. Thanks." There. That wasn't so bad. Maybe that's why he was approaching her. To discuss his concerns about Ollie. She turned to go but his voice made her turn back. "Say," he said, suddenly at her side, "I had a crazy idea."

He was smiling in a nice, easy way. Her guy radar, rusty as it was, sensed what was coming. "Oh. What was that?"

He dropped his voice. "It's actually not about the boys. I was wondering if you'd like to grab some dinner sometime. Whatever you can work out with your babysitter."

Kit's stomach churned. She imagined Carson standing behind her shoulder, chuckling softly. *I don't trust him*, Carson would say. *His teeth are too perfect.*

She wished he *was* standing behind her.

If she was ever going to get a date, she had to stop picturing her dead husband laughing at the guy who was asking her out.

And that almost made her laugh. Starting over seemed impossible. And she was an absolute disaster.

"Kit?" Bryan flashed a winsome grin. "Did I say something wrong?"

"No, not at all." She took a breath and smiled. Yes, that was how it was done. A nice smile and *say yes*.

She managed the first part. But the words did not come. They both stood there, the silence stretching on.

"I...That was sweet of you. Let me...check my schedule." She felt like someone could fry a hamburger on her cheeks. "That's really nice of you to ask," she added.

"Well, I really hope you can," he said. "I'll catch you tomorrow at practice, okay?"

"Sure, great." Her family and friends still stood down the field a ways, waiting for her.

She didn't want to be stuck forever. She didn't want her friends feeling sorry for her. She wanted her life back.

People could help her with a lot of things, like watching Ollie and forcing her to wake up early on Saturday to go jogging, but the hard work of living she would have to find the courage for all by herself.

"Bryan," she called after him.

"Yeah?" he said, turning around.

"I'd love to go out."

"Terrific." He walked over and asked for her phone, which she gave him to add his number. "Text me a potential day, okay?"

"Great," she said, but she didn't feel great. Or excited. She felt terrified.

But she did feel that she'd accomplished *something*. Because if she wasn't brave, how could she ever expect Ollie to be?

Chapter 2

"DID YOU JUST say I *don't* have a reservation after tonight?" Alex de la Cruz asked the clerk at the Seaside B and B, a big, historic inn right on the waterfront.

And... he was screwed. He could tell by the clerk's face.

Actually, he'd known that already, even if he had a place to stay.

Not that Seashell Harbor wasn't a beautiful, unique place to grow up, and not that his childhood hadn't been great, ever since he was adopted into a big, loving Hispanic American family with plenty of love to spare. It was just that he was constantly reminded of the best friend that he had lost. Every street invoked memories of cheeseburgers they'd eaten, balls they'd thrown, good times they'd had. The memories were as inescapable as the ocean that churned a steady rhythm alongside their picturesque town.

His heart was wrung out with sadness. Both he and

Carson had set out as air force fighter pilots to do their patriotic duty, but only Alex had come back. He couldn't imagine being here without Carson.

He couldn't imagine being anywhere without his best friend. Now a little boy was fatherless, and Carson's wife was left on her own.

Your fault, a voice within him whispered.

The deep pain in his heart made him rub his chest in desperation, but it would not be erased.

He tucked his LSAT study book into his bag. That was Part 2 of his post–air force discharge plan. After he took care of Part 1. Which had to do with Carson.

The kindly gray-haired clerk glanced up at him over her rhinestone-studded spectacles. What was her name again? She used to volunteer with his mom over at the county mental health and addiction recovery center. "Our system says you booked one night, sweetie." She smiled, and he remembered her name was Lina Amari. "That's it."

He called up the confirmation email on his phone, swearing he'd booked the room for the entire weekend. His heart sank as he discovered she was right. "Mrs. Amari, any chance you've got a room for the next two nights?" That might be enough time to find a more permanent arrangement for the two months he planned to be here.

Again, the look. Kind but with a touch of *Are you sure you're from here?* "It's the season. Every rental on the island is booked. But let me see what I can do."

He wasn't going to get a room. He knew that. This was not the usual way he operated; as his mother would say, *Siguiendo los indicadores del gluteus maximus*.

Which translated to *Leading with your butt instead of your head.*

He always had a plan. Plus a backup. He kept lists, obsessively filed on his phone. His middle name was Control.

Actually it was *Constantino*, but close enough.

He never thought he'd be the one to spearhead the renovation on the turreted, old Queen Anne that Alex used to often tease Carson about.

"There's a house behind all that mess?" Alex had asked one time several years ago as they both stood looking at it.

"This is a gem," Carson had said, pride—and maybe a touch of insanity—in his voice. "Four bedrooms and a wraparound porch. Right on the harbor. If you're nice to me, Alex my man, maybe one day I'll let you come and watch the Fourth of July fireworks from my backyard."

"You mean that overgrown jungle back there?"

He smiled at the memory. Carson had always looked on that house as an opportunity. He'd had a clear vision of what could be.

Alex, in contrast, had never been able to see it as anything but a disaster, a teardown on a great piece of property. It knifed him, knowing that his closer-than-blood-brother would never be here to fulfill his dream. Or watch his son grow up. Or be reunited with his wife.

His wife, Kit, who was surely going to kick him out as soon as she laid eyes on him. She'd already warned him not to come.

But he'd come anyway. Because Stubborn was his second middle name. Actually it was Sebastian but... whatever.

He hadn't asked his old buddies about a place to stay for fear it would get back to her, preferring the forgiveness-rather-than-permission route. He had, however, scouted all the Airbnbs in Seashell Harbor. But every single one was full.

"I'm sorry, Captain de la Cruz," the clerk said. "We're all booked up. But I can put you on a wait list. Also, can't you stay with your mom?"

Actually, she'd been his very first stop when he got back in town. She'd hugged him until he couldn't breathe, said many tearful prayers of thanks for his safe return, and filled his belly with delicious Puerto Rican food. "She's staying above the art gallery for the summer," he said. Lots of folks rented out their quaint old homes for the season. Since his dad had passed away from cancer back when he was in college, his mom had made a great profit staying in the little efficiency apartment during the summers. It funded her extended visits back to Puerto Rico to visit their family.

He didn't want to worry her about his arrangements. If worse came to worst, she'd find him a place in a heartbeat with one of her many good friends, his adopted *tias*. But he really didn't want anyone knowing his business.

"How long is the wait?" For the first time, Alex noticed the polished wooden desk with its intricate carvings. It smelled faintly of lemon oil. Which was the other reason he'd chosen this place. He'd wanted to see the restoration work. And it was all first-class.

"You'd be fifth in line. It's possible something could open up."

Alex's gaze wandered around the lobby of the meticulously renovated hotel. It boasted a grand staircase with a gleaming oak banister, a giant fireplace just made for cozying up during a chill, and killer views of the ocean through enormous floor-to-ceiling leaded glass windows that people had been gazing out of for a century and a half.

Unlike a lot of the Victorian buildings in their town, this one was light and airy. And not too pattern-crazy. That's what he was going to aim for in his own work.

If that was what Kit agreed to. If she didn't boot him out on his aforementioned *gluteus maximus*. She disliked him, something he'd cultivated on purpose over the years. Except that wouldn't serve him very well now. "Did the Cammareris do the renovation?"

"They're the best," she confirmed.

Growing up, Alex had worked with the Cammareri brothers, Nick and Cam, and their dad for three summers and counted them among his good friends. He'd spent the past months before his discharge studying journals and blogs, watching YouTube videos, and keeping an online file of photos.

He was going to make that old house shine until it brought in a price big enough to provide a nest egg for his buddy's widow. So she could send their kid to college or get herself a house or a car or whatever it was that she needed.

And maybe then the awful anvil of guilt would leave his chest. He doubted it, but he hoped it would make the weight a little more bearable. At least, that was what his therapist had recommended. She'd also told him not to isolate himself, something he'd also been pretty good at doing since the accident.

"I know you're military," the clerk said, "and I'd do anything to help you, but we're completely full. I can call around to a couple of people who might be willing to rent a room if that would help."

"Sure, thanks." As she began writing something down, he added, "You wouldn't know of anyone in town offering a short-term rental? Like, for a couple of months?"

The cheaper the better, he almost added. He wanted to invest his capital into the project, not in his own accommodations.

That was the idea. Fix up the disaster and recoup his expenses for materials when it sold. Kit would rather die than take charity, but even she would have to admit that was a fair deal to cut.

"Here you go, Captain." The clerk scrawled down some names and handed him a piece of paper. "Those are the names of a few other B and B owners off the beaten track. Good luck."

Alex thanked the clerk, pocketed the information, and left. Tossing his duffel bag into his car, he walked the few blocks to the McKinnon property and set eyes on it for the first time in a very long time.

His stomach plummeted, a feeling of foreboding seeping steadily into his veins. Carson had talked about this place like it was fricking Tara. In the front stood a couple of raggedy, half-dead pines instead of a stately allée of grand old oaks, and the great big porch was sagging so badly it wouldn't support a tall pitcher of iced tea let alone a bevy of wooden rockers.

What he saw was a turreted, old, wood-framed Queen Anne, every inch peeling, its chimney crumbling. The stone steps leading up to the porch were as crooked as a six-year-old's front teeth. The grass was cut but the flower beds were unruly. And the landscaping...ugh. Shrubs and once-decorative small trees had grown into a tangled, matted mess that obliterated most of the forlorn exterior.

Carson, buddy, what were you thinking? Of the two of them, Alex had been the dreamy, poetic one. Carson had been firmly grounded in reality. What on earth had he seen in this train wreck?

He tried to focus on the fact that you could see the historic Seashell Harbor lighthouse jutting out from a cove in the near distance—a million-dollar view.

Ha. And a million-dollar reno job.

A memory jolted him then. Kit running around the side of the house and flinging herself into Carson's arms while Alex carefully averted his gaze. The two of them had been crazy and silly and totally in love. The tragedy of that lost happiness hit him hard.

Alex would conquer this house. He would beat it into submission with every muscle in his body. He would restore and renovate and tear out and rebuild.

He would do it from the depths of his anger and his grief at losing his best and oldest friend. It would be the last thing he could do for Carson. He'd put his heart and soul into this project. And then clear out of here as fast as he possibly could.

Decided, he turned his back on the house. And prayed that the spell that Kit Blakemore had cast on him long ago had faded with time.

* * *

Kit dragged herself into her parents' kitchen at 6:30 a.m. that Saturday to find her parents sitting around the table drinking coffee, her dad reading the newspaper—in his preferred form, paper—and her mom reading a library book. The gentle *tick-tick-tick*ing of the oven filled the air, as did the warm and welcoming smell of cinnamon. Ollie, who usually had no trouble following after the early rising habits of the Admiral was, surprisingly, nowhere to be found.

Kit poured herself some coffee and sat down, blowing

on it so it would be cool enough to mainline. Unlike her parents, she tended more toward the night owl side. Ever since Carson died, all her anxieties seemed to get chatty when the house was settling into quiet, preventing a good night's sleep. So, down the hatch.

"Mom, you made cinnamon rolls?" Kit stared at the plate of steaming pastries with icing melting and dripping down the sides. "How long have you been up?"

"Well, Ollie loves them," she said, closing her book. She was already dressed, in a cute shaker sweater and jeans. And did she have lipstick on? "And he had a hard day yesterday."

The vision of Ollie's distressed face at Tee ball came rushing at her. As did the realization that her friends might make her jog five miles this morning, but just inhaling that buttery, cinnamony smell was enough to undo all her willpower.

"Why are *you* up so early?" her dad asked over his spectacles. He really couldn't understand why anyone would want to waste the morning by sleeping past 7:00.

Kit stifled a yawn. "I'm going for a jog with Hadley and Darla." She tried, but failed, to put some levity in her voice.

"That right?" her dad said, assessing her more thoroughly this time. Maybe he was checking to see if he'd heard right.

"It's a crisp spring morning." Her mom sipped her coffee. "I'm sure you'll have an invigorating run."

"It's thirty-nine degrees," her dad reported. He knew the weather better than their local meteorologist, thanks to having minute-by-minute updates from three weather apps on his phone, so Kit totally believed him. "Better dress warm."

"I will," she said automatically, feeling a little bit like a teenager in her parents' home. Then she tapped her nails nervously against her mug. *Might as well just come out with it, Kit,* she told herself. "Mom and Dad, I've been thinking of making a few changes."

That made her mom look up. "Do you mean taking up jogging? That's wonderful, dear."

"Yes. Physical fitness clears the mind," the Admiral said, his newspaper rustling as he flipped a page.

"Actually, I-I'm thinking it's time Ollie and I moved out." Both of their heads jerked up. "It might be time to get our own place."

"Why on earth would you want to do that?" Her mom's stone mug hit the table with a definitive *thunk.* "We love having you and Ollie here."

"It's been two years," Kit said. Not to mention she was thirty-five. "I think you both have taken care of Ollie and me for long enough."

"Nonsense," her mom said. "You've both been through a tremendous trauma. We'd never want you to go through that alone. That's what family is for."

"Your mother is right." Her dad put his paper down and folded his hands. "Now that we're retired, we enjoy having you and Ollie around. And living here has helped you save up for your future."

She grabbed both her parents' hands. "I love you both so much, you know that. And I'm so grateful for everything you've done. But I think it's time for me to get my life going again."

"What do you mean?" Her mom seemed genuinely puzzled.

"Yes, so, about that," Kit said. "I…I was thinking about signing up for this new program the community college is advertising for nontraditional students. It would involve taking a summer class or two to get back into things and see how I do."

Her dad's thick gray brows knit down, the first subtle sign of disapproval that Kit knew well.

"Maybe Ollie should be your first priority," her mom said, not unkindly.

When was Ollie *not* her first priority? "Do you mean because he's been a little anxious lately?"

"Well, there will always be anxieties," her mom said wisely. "But he's just going to be starting kindergarten in the fall. And how on earth are you going to move out on your own and take college classes and work full-time?" Her mom patted Kit's hand. "I know you must be restless. But changing everything all at once seems hasty."

"I have to agree," her dad said. "But being restless is a good sign. It means you're taking steps to move on."

Her mom nodded. "There's no need to try to do everything on your own when you have a great support system right here."

"But what about you two?" Kit asked. "Now that Dad's retired, you two should travel. Join clubs, volunteer. Have fun." Last year, they'd talked about traveling to Greece for their anniversary but stayed. Surely they wanted their house and their life back?

"Ollie is a joy," her mom said. "Right, Hal?"

"Absolutely." Her dad nodded.

So many times over the past two years Kit had accepted her parents' sage advice. And their help. It had been easy to do when she'd felt so unsure and unsteady and...sad.

But Kit could see herself years from now, still leaning on them like a pair of crutches while all her friends lived their very full lives. She needed to plan a solid future for her son, and all she had was a decrepit old house that hadn't sold in forever and a boss who hated when she left for lunch and grumbled every time she asked if she could go to one of Ollie's preschool programs, even though she was a stellar employee.

Was it selfish to put some of her needs before Ollie's? Sometimes? She wasn't sure if her mom ever had. A military wife, she'd quit teaching school long ago and had devoted herself to volunteer projects, being a classroom mom, making amazing Halloween costumes, and always having healthy snacks and making great dinners every evening.

Kit helped all she could around the house, and insisted on helping with expenses, but her grade as a mother, split as she was in seventeen different directions, always seemed to pale in comparison.

"Just think about it," her dad said. "You'll figure out the right thing to do."

Now didn't seem to be the time to ruffle more feathers. But what was one more teensy-weensy, slightly more upsetting detail? She took a big breath and plunged in. "I've been looking at small houses and duplexes to rent."

Her mom and dad exchanged a grave parental glance. "Oh, Kit," her mom said.

Uh-oh. Her mom hadn't used that tone since she and Carson announced they were marrying at twenty-one. Her dad put down his paper *and* his glasses, an equally bad omen.

That did it. She was definitely going to chuck the jog and all this stress. Just as she lifted a big gooey roll to her lips, there was a rap on the back window.

Hadley and Darla walked in, making themselves at home as they had for the past thirty years.

"Hey, Mrs. Wendell, hey, Admiral," Darla said.

"Have a seat, girls," Kit's mom said. She'd probably still be calling them *girls* even when they were eligible for AARP membership. Her dad pulled out a chair.

"We can't sit," Darla said.

Kit's mom nodded to the empty chairs. "Sure you can," she said. "Come chat for a few minutes."

Hadley took the cinnamon roll from Kit's hand and returned it to the plate. "Later," she said, pulling her up. "Grab a sweatshirt. It's a little chilly."

"And a hat," Darla said, then examined her hand. "And while you're at it, get the ring."

Before Kit could protest, her mom said, "Darla, your hair's getting long." Today Darla wore it pulled up in a high ponytail.

Darla tugged on it. "Finally. It's been a year and a half."

What she didn't say was *from the chemo*, which she'd had for Hodgkin's lymphoma and was successfully cured of. Thank God.

"It's so pretty." Kit tugged a little on her ponytail. Darla's hair was a shimmery shade of pale blond that Kit had always envied, very different from her own dark hair.

Tugging on Darla's ponytail suddenly brought a strange thought to Kit's mind. Fixing a little girl's hair. Would Ollie ever have a brother or sister? Being an only child was...lonely; she could attest to that. And Ollie was a sensitive soul, loving books and art. While she did all she could to help him have friends, she worried about him having too much alone time.

As her friends chatted about Hadley's upcoming

wedding and the newest thriller Darla was writing, Kit felt the same unsettling tug inside herself. The one that told her there was more out there for her and Ollie. How was she going to open up the possibilities of anything happening in her life if she didn't go out and look for them?

Darla, always the taskmaster, glanced at her watch. "It's almost seven," she told Kit. "You ready?"

Kit had no choice but to run down the hall to the mudroom and grab Carson's old Air Force Academy sweatshirt and the first hat she found. And yes, she fished the old-fashioned filigree ring with the diamond-like stone out of her purse. No, she wasn't ready, but she was presentable enough as she let her friends hustle her out the door.

Chapter 3

AN HOUR LATER, Kit stood bent over and panting, fresh from a jog up the beach and to the point. "Jog," in quotes, as she found herself slowing multiple times with her merciless friends pushing her onward anyway, both of whom barely seemed out of breath at all. Now she stood with them in the backyard of the Ball and Chain, their breath showing up as little puffs in the chilly spring air. The house seemed to be winking at them lopsidedly, its windows looking like eyes and the askew gingerbread trim like maligned eyebrows.

The day was cloudy, mist gathering over a choppy sea. The house looked as foreboding as the House of the Seven Gables. Its plank exterior had faded to a peeling poop-brown, and weeds in the beds had risen to the size of mid-July corn, emboldened by the spring sun.

And that was only the back.

Kit checked her watch. They had twenty minutes before Carol Drake, Realtor extraordinaire, was due.

Hadley carried the fresh coffee and the bars they'd just picked up from Mimi's Bakery. Mimi made a special bar every day—today's was chocolate chip sea salt blondie—but Darla quickly put the kibosh on that. As they took seats on peeling Adirondack chairs on the wraparound porch, Hadley said, "See how well you did, Kit?" She held out the bakery bag. "Have one."

"Darla picked the healthiest bar." Kit was sneak-breathing, pretending not to pant but failing epically.

"Even Mimi said not to get them." Hadley wrinkled her nose. "No sugar, no fat, nothing but...fiber."

"No fun," Kit said, examining the bar carefully. Where were the cinnamon rolls? The bear claws? The glazed donuts?

"The seniors' books and wine club volunteered at the shelter the other day," Hadley said, referring to her animal rescue called Pooch Palace, "and Eva Doyle told me she thinks Mimi puts Metamucil in these."

"Oh, so *that's* why all the seniors were buying it." Kit didn't want to hurt Darla's feelings, so she took a tiny bite. "The coffee's really good," she said.

"Hey, we couldn't ruin all the results of our run." Darla dug in way too cheerily. "Hadley's right. Good first effort."

"Don't pretend to be nice. I'm out of breath and out of shape."

"Well," Hadley said, "I only run because I date a fitness-crazed ex-athlete."

"And I run mostly because I'm a writer and I burn no calories." Darla pulled up a chair and sat too. "And studies show that sitting all day is the equivalent of death."

"Darla, don't lie," Hadley said. "You love running."

"Okay, fine." Darla could barely suppress her endorphin-generated smile. "But I was afraid you both might hurt me if I admitted that."

Kit worked out a side cramp by walking—well, make that more like limping—over to what at one time must have been a beautiful bulb garden. Giant-sized irises in deep blue and yellow still grew stubbornly among grass, thistle, and other tall weeds. "Look," she exclaimed, pointing to a beautiful pink and maroon iris she'd never seen before.

"This place is a diamond in the rough," Hadley said, looking around at the gorgeous harbor view.

"With the emphasis on *rough*," Darla added wryly, taking a bite of her bar. "Which is why I bought a new house."

"Well, we've done a lot of work in the past year to our place." Hadley was referring to the century-old cottage she and Cam were in the process of renovating. "And I can honestly say, they don't make houses like they used to. And, Kit, you actually *own* this one."

"But I can't afford to fix it up."

"I know you don't want to hear this," Darla said, "but maybe you shouldn't have blown off Alex de la Cruz."

"I don't want to feel obligated to him. Plus, he's such a grump. He makes me...uncomfortable." He'd made no secret over the years that, while he loved Carson like a brother, he couldn't stand Kit. The thought of having to work with someone like that made Kit glad she'd said no.

"Well, don't take it personally," Hadley said. "Everyone *else* loves you."

Darla, always the agitator, remarked, "Maybe he hasn't given up yet."

"What do you mean?" Hadley asked. "He hasn't been back here since last summer."

Darla shrugged. "Alex always struck me as the type that doesn't give up easily."

Kit gave up trying to eat the bar and began to look for a place to quietly stash it. "When I saw him at the benefit last July, I made it clear I didn't need his help. I think I scared him off."

Darla shook her head adamantly. "Kit, you have a heart-shaped face and giant green eyes. You're about as scary as a kitten."

"Speaking of kittens," Hadley said, "anyone want one? I've got them in the shelter in every color."

Darla held up her hands. "Not a pet person, remember? I've never even owned a goldfish."

"I can fix you up with one of those too," Hadley said with a grin. "Any time you're ready. Kit, how about you?"

"Rex is plenty to handle. I swear he still goes around every night looking for Carson before he curls up in his bed. And every morning, there he is, on Carson's side of the bed. It breaks my heart because he just looks at me like, *Where is he?* He tolerates me, but it's Carson he loved."

"Black Labs are so sweet," Hadley said. "He might just need a friend." She wiggled her brows.

Both of them ignored that. Darla took her coffee and a seat and stretched out her other arm, holding out her palm. "So hand over your list," she said to Kit.

"It's such a nice morning," Kit said, even though storm clouds were building in the distance. "Let's just relax and enjoy the water." The wind was whipping the waves into white latte foam and slicing straight through their clothes. Nothing like on warm, sunny days where kids' laughter carried on the gentle breeze and hundreds of tourists flocked to their beautiful beaches.

Darla surveyed the yard and the bay beyond. "It is a killer view. But we can contemplate beauty another time."

"Wanting to solve every dilemma as fast as possible might help you write crime fiction," Kit said, "but in real life, it makes you a pain in the butt."

"At least I'm a *concerned* pain in the butt," Darla said.

"Show us," Hadley prodded. "Maybe we can help."

"Said the people who define 'help' as dragging me out for this jog." Kit clutched at straws as she reluctantly fished her list out of her sweatshirt pocket. "My list...is really personal."

"We know almost everything about you," Darla said. "Including how long it's been since you had sex."

Kit rolled her eyes. "Okay, my list is not *that* personal." Actually it was, in ways she couldn't quite articulate. "But I feel awkward discussing it."

Darla plucked the list from her fingers. A small folded rectangle of a paper remained, which Kit carefully tucked back into her pocket. It was one of Carson's letters that he'd sent to her from overseas. It, like all of his letters, contained inspiration and advice, and sometimes funny anecdotes that still made her laugh. It made her feel a little like he was still here, talking over the little problems and the difficulties of life. Above all, the letters showed her how much Carson had loved her. And made her feel certain she'd never find that kind of love again.

He'd written so many comforting things, and she'd

memorized them all. Like in her favorite letter, where he said, *Whenever you look at the water, think of me. No matter what happens, I'm like that ocean, always there, always with you, always wrapping my love around you.*

He'd understood what it was like to grow up in their beach town, how the beauty of the ocean and its constant ebbs and flows became a part of all of them. It was the exact perfect thing to say.

Darla looked at the first item on the list. "'SELL THE HOUSE!!'" she read. She waved the paper in front of Hadley. "In all caps and two exclamation points." She looked up and grinned. "Sounds like you want to sell the house."

"Don't make fun," Kit said in a mock-warning voice.

"But hasn't it been on the market?" Hadley asked. "Like, for two years?"

"I pulled it off in the fall to make some improvements," Kit said. "Dad and I tried to clean the landscape up a little, and I had the broken windows replaced."

"Oh," Hadley said carefully as she scanned the dilapidated structure.

Her tone told Kit the improvements were about as noticeable as a pebble in the sand. "I'm going to ask Carol how much more money I should sling at it before I put it up for sale again."

Hadley was squinting at the house—would that make it look less awful?—and shaking her head. Darla was biting her lower lip, a clue that she was holding back what she really thought. Kit knew exactly what they were seeing.

Not the ever-changing ocean, the wide-open sky, and the potential for spectacular sunsets over the harbor with the old lighthouse twinkling in the distance. Not Ollie at age two, laughing and chasing Rex while she and

Carson sat on this very porch. Not the small, glittering pieces of sea glass that uniquely washed up here on the point that Ollie used to have a fascination with and collect in his little red pail. And not the majestic old beech tree Carson vowed to hang a swing from. Or the promise he'd made that one day they'd both sit here and watch fireworks explode over the harbor every Fourth of July with family and friends, their own private front-row viewing spot.

Well, none of that uniqueness, none of that potential, mattered anymore. Carson was gone, and Kit couldn't envision a life where she could ever enjoy this place without him.

"Look," she said, "I know it's a train wreck. But I keep hoping the right person will come along. Maybe a family will fall in love with it. It's finally spring, and that's when houses sell better, right?"

Her friends were extremely quiet. Because they knew as well as she did this would be the *third* spring that the house would be up for sale.

"I need to sell it if I'm going to be able to do the other things on the list," she said softly.

"Oh yes, the list," Darla said, a mischievous look in her eye. "Sorry. The large-scale potential for disaster distracted me for a second."

"Ha-ha," Kit said.

"Keep reading, Darla," Hadley said.

"Here goes," Darla said. "Number two. 'Get my own place.'"

"You're going to leave your mom and dad's?" Hadley asked.

"Well," Kit said, finally breathing regularly, "I've been looking, to tell you the truth. But Ollie's been a little anxious lately, and I'm not sure it's a good time. So far I've seen a duplex and a little two-bedroom apartment on the upper floor of a house."

"So you're pretty serious about this," Darla said.

Kit shrugged. "I went to see them over my lunch hour a couple of times. On impulse."

"Give me your phone," Hadley commanded.

Kit surrendered it, and Hadley typed in a number. "You know Seymour, my ornery old rescue cat? Gran adopted him."

"That's nice." Kit bit back a *So what?*

"The cat's just now starting to come out of hiding, and it's been a month. Gran and Paul just bought a new house, and she's afraid to move the cat again." Hadley's grandma had married Paul Farmer, the kindest gentleman on the planet, who owned the local ice cream shop, Scoops, next to Pooch Palace. And best of all, he adored Hadley's grandmother.

"Good for her," Darla said. "About moving, I mean."

"My point," Hadley said, "is that she wants to rent out her bungalow. But not to just anybody. She's lived there for fifty years. And she'd like the cat to stay."

Kit's heart sped up a little at the mention of the adorable little house right on the ocean. The three of them had spent many a sun-drenched day swimming at the beach and many nights having sleepovers, Hadley's gran teaching them to play euchre and Monopoly, and of course feeding them really well. Real treats. Without Metamucil.

"We have so many great memories of that place." Kit paused for a while. "My parents don't think that now is the right time for me to move, especially since I'm thinking of signing up for a college class. And my dad thinks paying rent is a waste of money. But if I wait until I can actually buy a house, I'm going to be fifty and still living with my parents."

"It's okay to want space of your own," Darla said. "I mean, we're not kids anymore." She shot Kit a poignant look. "And you're right. You're not getting any younger."

"I'm not that old," Kit said. "Am I?"

No one answered that. "I agree," Hadley said, "that independence and space are important. And renting is a good way to try out a house and see if you like it." She rubbed her hands together in a plotting-something kind of way. "Besides, if you get your own place, maybe you can take one of my cats too."

"Okay, ladies." Darla checked her watch. "For the sake of time, I'm going to vote that you check out Hadley's gran's place. Now for the next item, and it's a fun one…" She looked around, gearing up the anticipation. "'Say yes to a date.'"

"Check," Kit said, a little proudly. Finally, a box she could tick off. To show her friends—and herself—that she was serious about this list. About changing her life.

"You said yes to a date and didn't tell us?" Hadley sat forward, looking fake-offended.

"Do I have to tell you two everything?" Kit asked innocently.

"Yes," Darla said. "Those have been the rules since we were five. So Hottie Coach Bryan finally asked you out?"

"After Ollie's game. And I said yes." Even texted him that next Friday would be fine.

"I knew it!" Hadley said.

"Single dad, nice coach, has a kid Ollie's age…plus

he's good-looking." Darla was scratching something out and then writing vigorously on the paper.

"You carry a pen in your running jacket?" Hadley chuckled. "That's definitely a writerly thing to do."

"And sticky notes," Darla added, still scribbling. "When inspiration strikes, it's like lightning. And if I don't write it down right away, *poof*—it's gone."

Kit leaned over. "What are you doing to my list?"

Darla held up the paper. She'd crossed out *Say yes to a date* and had written *GET LAID* in big letters.

Hadley laughed and high-fived Darla.

Kit snatched the paper back. "Okay, I knew this was a dumb idea. And I'm not looking to get laid," she protested. "I mean...maybe that would be nice but I'm just not the kind of person who would have sex just for sex's sake. I'm just...I'm just trying to force myself to go out on a date, okay?"

"I get what you're saying," Hadley said. "I think you're brave to put yourself out there."

"And if that involves getting laid, that's okay too," Darla said.

Kit squeezed her eyes shut. "The truth is, I can't imagine sleeping with anyone else but Carson." There, she'd said it. Sometimes she kept what she thought were more odd thoughts to herself but...this one weighed heavily on her mind. Because she feared she'd *never* get over him. And even if she met someone she really liked, how would she ever be brave enough to love again after all this pain?

"Oh, honey." Hadley reached over and squeezed her forearm.

"I've never really imagined being with anyone else. Except maybe Chris Pine, when I got mad at Carson."

Her friends were silent, but she caught Darla elbowing Hadley, who was struggling not to laugh.

"What's wrong with Chris Pine?" she asked.

"Nothing, nothing," Darla said. "I'm more amazed at the fact that you don't imagine being with anyone else."

"I'm being honest," Kit said. "Also...it's not like when I was younger and carefree. My decisions impact Ollie now. I would never casually get involved with someone."

"When I met Cam last year," Hadley said, "I was getting over Cooper. I never dreamed I'd fall in love. So you never know."

"That's right," Darla concurred. "I think Bryan the Hot Dad is a good place to start."

Kit finished her coffee and glanced at her fitness tracker. "Oh, wow, it's nine fifteen. Wonder what happened to Carol?"

"I've got to get home and shower," Hadley said. "Cam and I are volunteering for the Fourth of July Tour of Homes committee, and we've got a meeting in an hour."

"That sounds like something your gran signed you up for," Kit said.

"How'd you guess? They wanted our house to be on the tour this year, but it's not going to be done in time. But we decided to help out with the other homes anyway. It's a great fundraiser for the pier-renovation project." She turned to Kit. "Sorry I can't stay. You going to be okay?"

"Of course." Something suddenly dawned on her. "You two dragged me out of the house and brought me here because you know how I feel about going inside the house, didn't you?"

"Of course we didn't," Hadley said a little too adamantly.

"No way," Darla said at the same time, exchanging a quasi-innocent look with Hadley.

"Okay, we sort of did." Hadley sighed. "We wanted to be here for moral support. But Tony will kill me if he has to go to this house tour meeting alone. The committee is ninety-nine percent my grandma's friends, and they fawn all over him."

"Cam loves that," Darla said.

"Even he has his limits," Hadley said.

"I just got a text from Carol," Kit said. "She's dealing with something, and she's going to text me back in a few minutes."

Darla looked a little restless.

"Get going, both of you." Kit shooed them off and pulled out her smartphone. "I'll just sit here and read until she gets here. I'm in the middle of Darla's latest book."

"You sure you don't mind?" Darla asked. "I've got a deadline Wednesday for the next one, and I still don't know who the killer is."

"I'll be fine," Kit lied. "Thank you for worrying about me. And for doing this for me. And for not laughing about Chris Pine—too much."

"We'll finish your list next time," Hadley said.

"If you need me, just text," Darla said. "Promise?"

"I promise." She hugged her friends goodbye and sat down again, alone. But she didn't open her Kindle app. The harbor was a steely gray, a shade darker than the sky, the waves tossing tumultuously. Trying to summon her courage, she pulled out Carson's letter, heading straight for the part she needed right now.

I've never met anyone more confident, brave, or strong than you, Kit. I'm just asking you to keep

*the faith until I can get back to you and we can
be together. When you feel overwhelmed, just
take every day a half day at a time. And all those
half days will add up to the one day I can finally
come back to you.*

Kit read the words again. *Confident. Brave. Strong.*
Carson had believed in her. She had to remind herself
because she didn't quite believe it herself. Somehow she
had to dig deep and muster those qualities that he knew
were inside of her.

The wind was making her eyes water. Or maybe those
were tears—again. "How can I be any of those things
without you, honey?" she whispered, but her voice got
lost in the wind.

Just then, her phone buzzed with another text from
Carol.

Hey, Kit, Ben is throwing up and has a low-
grade fever and Dave had to suddenly run into
work so I'm headed to the pediatrician's office.
Sorry to cancel, will call u later. xo

She was just texting back Hope Ben feels better
soon when she heard pounding.

Harsh, metal-biting-rock kind of pounding. The distinct, sharp *chink* of a heavy implement repeatedly
splitting stone, echoing through the early morning quiet.
Kit rose from the peeling old chair and carefully walked
down the crooked back porch steps, along the side of the
house and around the tangled, overgrown shrubbery and
low-hanging tree branches. All of which gave her plen-
tiful cover as she cautiously rounded the front, hovering

her finger over the final 1 in 911, just in case. What she saw made her gasp.

A shirtless man was taking a sledgehammer to the already-crumbling steps. And the sight stopped her dead in her tracks.

It wasn't the awful steps that drew her attention or the enormous sledgehammer glinting in the morning light as he ripped out the old mortar and cracked sandstones that were scattered all about.

A flush of heat rose all through her as she noted the fine smooth lines of tensing muscle, the elegant movements, his lean but strong build. Whoever this man was, he moved with a confident fluidity, with a grace akin to a dancer, and it was mesmerizing.

Lift the hammer, swing down hard—*chink* went the stone. Another lift and repeat.

No wonder his shirt was off. He was probably burning a thousand calories a minute. Bet his friends didn't have to drag *him* out of bed to force him to jog five miles on a chilly morning.

Also, he was way too hot to be cold.

She laughed at the silly joke. It wasn't like her to be giddy. Well, the old Kit would've been, for sure. A sense of relief rushed through her that maybe her old self really was in there somewhere.

Also...her ovaries were still clearly functioning.

Suddenly, the man straightened up. She watched as he ran the back of his hand along his forehead. Then he turned, his expression foreboding, brows drawn down over dark eyes.

Busted.

A shock reverberated clear through her as recognition hit. His pitch-black hair was wavy and longish now, grown out from the high-and-tight military cut when she'd seen him last. And his skin wasn't tan—that illusion came from his natural Latino coloring. She forced herself to look directly at him. But the intensity of his dark gaze wasn't any less calming.

Alex de la Cruz. Here, working on Carson's house. Despite the fact that she'd told him *thanks but no thanks*. A quick scan showed a shiny black pickup sitting in the driveway. She hadn't seen it since they'd jogged along the coastline and approached from the backyard.

He took in her leggings, Carson's old sweatshirt, and her multicolored knit cap with dual pom-poms, a gift from Ollie last Christmas. She saw the moment recognition widened his eyes—and he looked about as pleased as she was.

"Hello, Katherine," he said, his voice deep and as calm as if they met passing on the street. It sounded mocking because no one had called her Katherine since she'd gotten detention in high school for passing notes in Lit class.

Come to think of it, he'd been the one she'd gotten in trouble with for that. They'd also been chem lab partners, and they'd joked around and had fun. In the days before he'd developed a branch up his butt.

He might as well have called her *Mrs. Blakemore* for all the formality brimming in the deep baritone of his voice.

He'd always been a little odd. When Carson was around, Alex rarely even glanced at her, giving the air of barely being able to tolerate her. She'd written it off as him being one of those men who simply didn't "see" women—as equals, anyway. Still, she'd put up with him because Carson had loved him.

Anger welled up. Because besides ignoring the fact that she'd told him not to come, he was doing things to Carson's house uninvited. Actually, worse than that. In *defiance*.

"Hello, Alex," she managed as she struggled to choke down her fury. "What are you doing here?"

Chapter 4

ALEX DE LA CRUZ prided himself on his unflappable demeanor. It's what had gotten him into flight school and made him a basic training honor graduate, an elite designation based on test scores and physical fitness. Calm control wasn't just his redeeming quality, it was who he was.

But calm under the gaze of a woman wearing a bright knit cap with two sock-like appendages drooping down either side of her head, each topped with a pumpkin-orange pom-pom? Not so much.

He hadn't seen Kit since he'd been on leave last summer to see his mom.

In most cases, people's memory of faces grows dim with the passage of time but not for him. He remembered the curve of her cheek, the dip of her hairline into a peak on her forehead. The tiny little mole on her neck.

He remembered too clearly, despite not wanting to at all.

Kit was more beautiful than ever, even in that silly hat. And still just as out of reach.

He quickly switched his gaze—and his thoughts—back to the lopsided steps and forced himself to focus. "I wrote you about this," he said carefully.

"And I responded," she volleyed right back, drawing her full lips into a tight, straight line, every feature determined and set. She was dead serious, but it was nearly impossible to take her seriously with that ridiculous hat.

He averted his gaze to the unruly trees that surrounded the house. They were bursting with new leaves. Birds were raising a riot. He used to love this time of year, but instead he felt heavy, gray, and weighed down. Carson should be the one out here tearing out these steps. Raising his son. Being with his wife.

"Didn't you get my letter?" she asked, planted there in front of him in full battle formation.

"Yeah, I got it." He leveled his gaze on her. The crazy colors of her hat brought out the green of her eyes. A pure, mossy green, undiluted by brown. It reminded him of spring. New beginnings. Something he desperately needed to find.

He reminded himself of why he was here. To ensure that his best friend's wife could sell this big, lugging mess of a house to secure her and her son's future.

Then he might feel a little closer to forgiven. Not that the ache over Carson's death would ever go away.

And then he would move far away from Seashell Harbor and start over again.

Alex pulled himself up to his full height and grabbed his flannel shirt, which he'd draped over an overgrown yew.

"Okay," Kit said, her voice indicating a strain on her

patience. "If you got my letter that said *please don't come*, then why are you here?"

He sighed, his own way of keeping control. He'd *known* she would say no. Plus she was stubborn. Really stubborn. He knew that from the letters Carson had insisted on sharing with him.

Not that Alex had wanted to know. The guys in his squadron had jokingly called him the *Poet*. The colorful sayings of his Puerto Rican heritage, drilled into him by his mother and abuelita throughout his childhood, had given him a flare for writing that had come in handy helping his fellow pilots make their letters more feeling, better written. Unfortunately, Carson had asked for some of his assistance as well.

Kit, however, didn't want anything to do with him. "Just because you don't want my help doesn't mean you don't need it," he couldn't stop himself from saying.

"I beg your pardon?" She crossed her arms. "Did I say I needed your help? I don't think so."

"Well, I don't think you'd ask for *anyone's* help unless someone was twisting your arm."

She'd refused help before. When she was in labor and Carson had gotten stuck on the highway during a snowstorm, Alex practically had to carry her to his truck to get her to the hospital. And Carson had told him that she'd watched YouTube videos and taught herself how to fix toilets and change filters in her car to avoid spending extra money.

But now he needed her to understand that he didn't have a choice. He had to do this. For Carson.

"I know why you're here," she said, as if reading his mind. "And I want to release you from any debt you might feel to Carson. Ollie and I are doing great. In fact, I've decided to put the house back on the market. We really don't need your help."

She couldn't wait to get rid of him. She thought that he was curt and unfriendly, that he didn't like her. Which was exactly what he'd intended.

Trust me, he almost said. *I don't want to be here either.*

He forced himself to face her again. "Look," he said, choosing his words carefully. "Carson wouldn't have wanted you to sell the place like this. If by chance someone would be crazy enough to buy this nightmare of a DIY project, you'd make no profit. And let's be honest, people aren't exactly mowing each other down to see it."

"It's a diamond in the rough," she said stubbornly, but her eyes shifted from him to the house, and he knew what she was thinking.

"It's a *disaster*, Kit. We both know it."

Jackpot. Her tiny flinch let him know he'd hit a nerve. And he saw something else in her eyes. Grief, bottomless and endless. He knew it well himself. "He would want you to get top dollar for it." He found himself unable to say Carson's name as he broke eye contact. "You know he would. And I can help you."

"I appreciate what you're trying to do," she said, hands on hips now. "But...I don't have the money to renovate it. I've got to sell it as is."

She hadn't shied away from meeting his eyes as she told him the truth. But he'd known she'd say this. "I have the skills and the training," he said. "And I would only charge you cost for all the materials after the house sells." He'd been thinking and planning for months. He had anticipated every protest, had every angle covered.

Except for the curve ball that being in her presence was throwing him.

She was already shaking her head, her long ponytail swishing. "That's a lot of money to front. I could never ask you to do that."

He shrugged. "I wouldn't offer unless I meant it." She still looked wary.

"I know you loved him too," she said softly, as if she couldn't quite bring herself to say Carson's name either. "And I appreciate your wish to honor what he wanted. But—"

He cut her off. "That's exactly right. I'm here for Carson," he said bluntly. "And this is the *only* thing I can do. To honor his memory." He hadn't meant to sound desperate, but he couldn't control the crack in his voice.

It was the right and honorable thing to do. And the only thing that might give him some closure about Carson's death. "So how about we just go slow. Take it a half day at a time?"

"A half day—" Kit backed up a step, losing her footing amid the broken chunks of concrete. Maybe his desperation had thrown her.

"You okay?" he asked, reaching out to steady her.

She steadied herself without his help. "I...I haven't heard that expression in a while."

"My abuela used to say that a lot. When things were overwhelming, that was her way of making them more manageable."

"Carson wrote that to me in a letter once," she said, her voice almost a whisper.

That threw him. "He must've heard me say it." Alex fought the urge to wince.

She paused a long time before she said, "I need to think about this, okay?"

He nodded toward the heavy, scarred door. "I can show

you that it's bad in there, but maybe not as bad as you think." It *was* as bad as she thought. Worse, even. But he had no intention of telling her that.

"How did you get in?" She looked around as if she suspected he'd broken one of the windows. "I'm the only one with a key."

He raised a brow. "It didn't take much." He bypassed the steps, hopping up to the porch, and offered her a hand.

She hesitated. Actually, she did more than that. She took a big step back. She couldn't have moved faster if an animal had suddenly jumped out of the overgrown shrubbery. "I...um...I can't," she said quickly. "What I mean is, I-I'm late for an appointment."

"Okay," he said. She hadn't acted like she was in a hurry, but now she seemed absolutely panicked. "Is it all right if I keep working?"

"If you insist, but it's not necessary," she finally said, turning toward the street. "I'll call you...later." She got a few feet away before she stopped in her tracks and retraced her steps, walking toward him again. "I...I don't have your number," she said, her face coloring.

He nodded, took her phone, and punched it in, taking careful measure not to react to the fact that he'd grazed her hand, which was soft and warm. Or the fact that she smelled like vanilla cupcakes, sweet and delicious. As soon as he handed back her phone, she was gone, the rusted iron gate creaking as she jogged off down the street.

Maybe he shouldn't have come home at all, he thought as he picked up his discarded sledgehammer. But he felt sure he'd have not an inkling of peace until he did. It was as if Carson himself had willed him to come, unable to rest until his wife and son were well taken care of. Alex turned back to his work, but after a few minutes, unable to concentrate, he abandoned the sledgehammer and walked to the back of the house to clear his head.

The house was huge, complete with a big turret, a wraparound porch, and a third story. It was the kind of wonderful, quirky house filled with nooks and crannies—with real personality and beautiful woodwork. Not to mention the drop-dead gorgeous water view. The potential was obvious.

Otherwise, it was a complete wreck—rotting wood, leaky ceilings, and asbestos-lined pipes. It was also wired for the last century. If Kit had known the full extent of it, she'd have sent him packing yesterday.

As Alex turned the corner, he stopped in his tracks. The wind off the sound was a little chilly, but despite the cold making his eyes water, the harbor spread out in front of him, filling the little bay and making its way out to the ocean. Waves lapped against the sand, just a few feet from the grass. And that yard—it was a dream backyard for kids and adults alike.

Looking at water used to fill him with peace. He'd always dreamed of living near it someday. Growing up in a beach town did that for you. But lately there was nothing he could do or say to feel that way again.

As he went to sit in a beat-up old chair, a bright green square of paper winked at him from the warped porch floor.

It was a flyer from the local community college, advertising classes starting in the fall.

Been out of school for a while? No problem! Call the number below for a career counseling appointment

*to find the classes that are best for you. We have
weekend and night classes and a full online curric-
ulum for busy adults. Don't wait—plan your dream
career now!*

On the back, more interestingly, a list was scrawled in
feminine handwriting along with a little note on the side
that read *Pick up Ollie's prescription.*

Hmmm.

SELL THE HOUSE!! Was the first item. Followed by

GET MY OWN PLACE
TAKE *ONE* CLASS
~~SAY YES TO A DATE~~ *GET LAID*
LEARN HOW TO PLAY ~~BASEBALL SOFT-
BALL~~ TEE BALL

An arrow was drawn from TAKE ONE CLASS to
SELL THE HOUSE. A phone number was scrawled next
to GET MY OWN PLACE. And GET LAID was written
in bright purple marker and circled three times.

It was a list of things someone would make who was
trying to find a way to begin her life over. And that
someone appeared to be Kit.

Alex let go of the paper like it was on fire and blinked
hard to erase the purple-marker message imprinted on
his brain.

Alex was here to do a job for his best friend. He was
hoping it would bring him forgiveness.

And the thing he had for his wife...it was best forgotten. Because it could never be.

Chapter 5

KIT WAS HYPERVENTILATING, and she couldn't even blame it on running all the way back downtown because she'd been sitting on a bench overlooking the ocean for the past ten minutes, trying to calm down. The park was empty except for a few joggers winding their way past her to the trails that led to the beach.

As she ran the back of her hand against her sweaty forehead, the cool band of Darla's ring hit her skin. The ring had done her no good so far. It hadn't given her any sudden courage. And it hadn't helped her avoid a very annoying man.

She was literally running away from facing up to that stupid house.

And she'd lost her flyer. Well, no matter. It had probably blown right into the ocean along with her silly list.

Thank goodness she still had Carson's letter, tucked

safely inside her sweatshirt pocket. But even that wasn't giving her much comfort now.

Instead of putting up a calm, authoritative front so Alex would understand that she did not need his help, she'd panicked.

How could he have known that the last time she'd been inside that house had been on a sunny fall day two and a half years ago. Carson had held two-year-old Ollie. The three of them had walked from room to room, imagining a time when Carson would be stateside for good and their life together could really begin.

They'd planned where Ollie's bedroom would be, where they'd sit and have coffee, and the best arrangement for the kitchen. Afterward they'd headed out for apple cider and a hayride at a local farmer's market, enjoying Ollie's enthusiastic reaction on seeing hundreds of pumpkins lying in the fields. They'd had no idea at the time, but it would be the last weekend they would ever spend together.

Tears blurred her vision. She swiped at them as quickly as they formed, fearing that in their small town, someone she knew could pass by at any moment. And she'd gotten enough *Poor Kit* glances to last her a lifetime, thanks very much.

She never wanted to go into that house again. She just wanted to sell it off and be done with it for good.

Except she had to contend with a cranky ex–air force captain who thought he knew exactly what to do. Who came out of obligation to Carson, and who'd shown up despite her telling him *in writing* not to.

Having grown up with the Admiral, Kit understood the military mindset well enough, and Carson had told her stories. Alex had pushed himself to the limit to be at the top of their class. As a pilot, he'd always been the first in their squadron to volunteer for the riskiest flights.

Kit believed Alex was the kind of man who took charge, knew what he wanted, and was determined and stubborn. Basically, he was a royal pain in the butt.

Except for one thing that had hit her straight in the gut. In those dark, unsettling eyes of his, he carried the same exact pain she did.

She'd seen the pleading. She'd heard the crack in his voice. Whatever his reasons for coming here, he was dead serious about his mission. And he wasn't about to give up without a fight.

Meanwhile, she'd been unable to even take a step inside. And that lame excuse she'd offered—anyone could see straight through it. How could she gather the courage to go back in there?

Her phone rang. It was Hadley. "I'm at the meeting, so I only have a second. Gran says she might have a renter who wants her place. But she'd rather have you. Any chance you're free to see it? She's heading over there right now."

"Thanks, Had, but I'm going to have to pass."

"Okay, sweetie. But if you change your mind, she's going to be there all morning."

Kit hung up and sat there, the wind and cold seeping through her sweatshirt.

She twirled Darla's filigree ring, watching it catch the plain, dull light from the cloudy day and turn it into a rainbow of colors. But it gave her no easy solutions, and no magical dose of strength.

Even though Darla's great-great-grandmother had been divorced and alone, she'd moved forward and made a great life. Kit didn't want to be terrified to do something as simple as walking into an old house because of the pain she'd feel. She was tired of not being courageous enough to make decisions on her own.

And she was tired of having a hole in her heart.

The only way to the other side is to slog through the pudding. That was in one of Carson's letters too. *This separation is our last hurdle. All we have to do is keep moving forward, and one day soon we'll be standing on the other side with all this behind us.*

So slog she did, and somehow found her legs carrying her toward the beach. Five minutes later, she was knocking on the front door of a little teal-green bungalow with magenta shutters.

"Good heavens! Kit? Is that you?" she heard from inside. A kind-looking woman with gray hair and bright blue eyes came to the door. "Hadley and I were just talking about you."

"I was nearby," she said to Hadley's grandmother. "Actually, Hadley called about your house. But I haven't made up my mind yet about moving. I just...walked over."

Maddy Edwards—now Maddy Farmer—opened the door but her bassett hound, Bowie, squeezed past her and poked his nose out first.

"Hi there, sweet boy," Kit said, stroking the dog's velvety ears. "How's Bowie doing with the newest member of the family?"

"Ah yes, Seymour. He's hiding. As usual." Maddy ushered Kit in, Bowie happily trotting at her side as they entered the kitchen.

"Well, that's to be expected, isn't it?" Kit asked. "New environment and all that?"

Maddy dropped her voice as she put on a kettle. "To tell you the truth, my sweet Bowie is actually not so sweet with Seymour. Apparently, Bowie is just a tad on the jealous side. And Seymour has had a very difficult life so far, I'm afraid. He's not inclined to be very cordial either." She grabbed two heart-shaped pot holders and pulled the oven door open. "You're just in time. I made banana bread."

"Oh, lucky me." Kit gave a little clap. Somehow, a piece of banana bread was just what she needed after Darla's no-sugar, no-taste bar that she'd secretly left for the birds. Besides, bananas were fruit. Anyway, it was rude to say no, right?

Maddy took a seat at the scarred oak table. Despite the cloudy day, the kitchen felt sunny, probably because of the buttery yellow color of the walls. A philodendron in a pot next to the sink wound its way up and around the window, which was framed by a curtain with orange and yellow flowers. And Gran's plates were full of pink, orange, and blue flowers too. "I feel better just sitting here," Kit said. Between the cheery room and the scent of warm banana bread, she could feel the tension between her shoulders uncoil a little.

"Oh dear," Maddy said. "That means something's wrong."

"It's a long story. I'm really fine." Kit tapped her fingers nervously on the table and decided to change the subject. "Now that you're married, do I need to call you Mrs. Farmer instead of Mrs. Edwards?"

Maddy smiled. "Well, I decided I'm too old for a name change. And I think it might be time for you to start calling me Maddy."

"I love you like my own grandma," Kit said, "but I

can't really see myself ever calling you anything else but 'Mrs. E.'"

"Well, getting married was a big leap for me—and Paul understands that a person can only take so much change at one time. And I do dearly love this house and all my memories here, but I've come to the conclusion that it's time to create new ones in a home that belongs to both of us." She poured chai tea into cups, added milk, and blended it with a little hand blender. "A new recipe for a latte. You're the first to try it." Maddy glanced at her new smartphone. "Oh, I just missed a call. I think my potential renter left me a voice mail about wanting this place."

"Oh," Kit said, a little crestfallen. "I'm too late." Oddly, a heavy weight seemed to settle into her stomach that she recognized as disappointment.

"Of course you're not," Maddy said with a conspiratorial look. "I haven't answered it yet." She cut the bread and handed Kit a piece. "What's wrong, dear?" she asked kindly.

Maybe it was Maddy's sympathetic tone, or the delicious snack, but somehow Kit's worries poured out. "I keep having crazy ideas—about moving out, about going back to school—but I can't seem to make up my mind about anything. I think my parents are a little horrified, to tell you the truth. They think I'm in the best situation right now with them."

Gran gave a little frown as she cut herself a piece too. "What do you mean, the *best* situation?"

"Ollie's always cared for with my folks around. And I'm saving a ton of money."

"It is hard to get moving when everything seems fine as it is."

"I mean, they're probably right." The banana bread

was delicious. And it felt good to confide in Maddy, who understood more than anyone what it was like to lose a husband. But Kit knew that the answers she needed would have to come from within herself.

"The hardest decisions in life are the ones you make going against the tide." Gran rotated her teacup, which read BEAUTIFUL DAY. "But they can also be the best. Because you truly make them on your own. That means you really *want* them."

Maddy wasn't trying to talk her out of moving. Or talk her into it, for that matter. Both of which were comforting. "Did Hadley tell you about Alex de la Cruz being back in town?"

"Oh, I just talked to his mom," Maddy said excitedly. "Gloria's so proud—and so glad to have him home for a while."

"Last summer, I told him I did *not* need his help fixing up that old house on Gardenia Street, and guess where I found him this morning? With a sledgehammer and his shirt off, hacking away at the front steps!"

"His shirt off? Oh my!" She flapped her hands in front of her face and chuckled. "He's a hottie."

Maddy's expression changed from her usual reassuring and wise look to one that was a little mischievous. Reminding Kit that last year, she'd secretly arranged for Hadley to work with Cam for the whole summer, and of course they fell right in love.

"He's also a grump. To me anyway," Kit added so Maddy wouldn't get her matchmaking antennae up.

"Well," Maddy said, "I can see how you might feel all twisted up." She took a sip of tea and a bite of banana bread, seeming to choose her words carefully. "I was sixty when I lost my Charlie. You remember him, don't you?"

"Of course. He taught us how to shell pistachios. And go crabbing. And all those songs he taught us on the beach at night."

"He did love his guitar." She smiled a little wistfully. "Anyway, sixty might seem old to you. In some ways, I felt our life together was just getting ready to begin again. He was almost ready to retire from the post office. His dream was to start a coffee business. Can you believe that? Our kids were grown, and we wanted to travel and do so many things. But we never got the chance to do any of it."

"Oh, I'm so sorry."

Maddy patted Kit's hand and gave a slight smile. "Kit dear, I'm not mentioning all of this to make you sad. I think I'm trying to say that grief hits you like a ton of bricks no matter how old you are. And recovering takes time." She paused. "I also think *recovering* is the wrong word. It's more like *accepting*. Because we never stop loving the person we lost. We never 'get over' them. We just sort of accept that we have to live a different life without them."

"It's been a blessing to have my parents there for Ollie and me. I feel very lucky."

Maddy set down her mug and turned her sharp blue gaze on Kit. "But?"

"But I just miss...I miss who I used to be. I see other people doing amazing things in much harder circumstances, and I feel that I fall very short. I'm having such a hard time making decisions. I can barely manage to look a guy in the eye who wants to ask me out. It's like it takes all my energy just to exist."

"Can I ask why your parents object to your moving out? You're thirty-five, after all, not eighteen."

"My folks think I have enough on my plate, so why add more trouble, like classes and another place to live? And I need to save my money if I'm ever going to finish my degree and dump that old house. I mean, maybe they're right. I just feel so . . . restless." She stared down at her tea and then looked at Maddy. "I guess that's why I came here. You figured it all out. You met an amazing man, and you're starting your life over. How do you do it?"

"Well, I'm going to give you the advice I wish someone had given me. You can't allow fear to call the shots. Because fear has a really loud voice, and it will always talk you out of things. And listening to it will make you feel better, for a while. But then time passes and you see that you're still exactly where you were before—stuck. Except suddenly you find that you're a lot older and still haven't accomplished what you really want."

"Stuck." Kit nodded. Because that was what she was.

"Exactly."

"So, you're basically saying that being afraid is a good thing?"

"Yes." She took a sip of tea and grinned. "It's the best."

Kit looked around at the little kitchen, with white cabinets, soapstone counters, and a wide farmhouse sink. Off the kitchen was a tiny sitting area with a brick fireplace, with a cushy floral chair. Next to the chair sat a basketful of yarn and a pile of library books. The little bungalow was a gem. If she was in Maddy's place, she wasn't sure if she'd be able to leave.

A loud *meow* had them both turning to the sink. There, tucked into the little alcove between the sink and the bay window, was a very fluffy cat sitting among some potted plants. It was white and black with a gray splotch over its right eye.

Sweet Bowie, who was sleeping on a rag rug in front of the little fireplace, woke up with a start and growled. Seymour bolted down from the window and disappeared around the corner in a flash.

"*That's* Seymour?" Kit said.

"Well, I guess it *was*," Maddy said with a laugh. "I've only seen him once in the past week."

"He's very...fluffy. From the second that I saw him, that is."

"Yes."

"And the reason you have him is...?"

"I'm a sucker for my granddaughter? She practically begged me because he's used to being the top dog, if you'll excuse the expression. His owner died, an elderly woman who doted on him. And he does *not* like sharing his space with a dog. Even before he came here, Hadley said he was very nervous with the other dogs and cats in the shelter. He was causing a little bit of mayhem." Gran glanced at her phone. "Why don't you go take a peek at the bedrooms while I listen to my voice mail?"

Kit walked through the living room, which had a bigger fireplace and a killer ocean view, and headed down a small hallway. The second bedroom was small, with a twin bed tucked under an angled dormer and a little bookshelf built into an alcove, which brought a smile to her face. All that was missing was a rug in front of the bookshelf, and it would be perfect for Ollie to read and play. She could just see his superhero figures lined up on the bookshelf looking out the window, ready to guard the East Coast from mayhem.

The place was a well-loved little dollhouse, complete with a stone patio and bright pink *Mandevilla* vines climbing a trellis on the side. In the distance, the bright blue ocean peeked out beyond little dunes topped with beach grass.

Maddy caught up with Kit, showing her outside where a path made of rounded stones led to a detached garage. She led her up a set of stairs to a small one-room apartment, simply furnished with a bed, a gold couch, an old TV, and a chair.

"Charlie and I had plans to make this into an apartment but we never finished it out. It doesn't have an oven or a dishwasher. It's probably not practical for you to use as an office with Ollie being so young but I wanted you to know it's here."

Back in the living room, crazily thriving plants filled the space in front of the slider door. Gran ran her hand along the top of an oak rolltop desk. "There's no study but I always felt that sitting here overlooking the water was all the space I needed to think."

"No, this is the perfect spot." Kit could see herself making tea and settling down at this desk to work when Ollie was sleeping.

Whoa. What was she doing? How could she just pick up and move Ollie out of her parents' just because this place was adorable and on the beach—like her own personal Airbnb? It seemed…frivolous. And she'd be…on her own.

And maybe she longed for some freedom, but was picking up and moving what was best for Ollie?

She should just start with the college class. Maybe her parents were right. Better to start slow and ease into change. Not shake her whole life up all at once.

The same fear she felt at going inside that stupid house came roaring back.

At the very least, she'd need more time to think on it, right? And not be impulsive.

Impulsive was what had gotten her pregnant just before Carson had shipped out the first time.

She had to be measured. Careful. *Adult*.

"It's adorable, Maddy, but I-I'm just not sure I'm ready to make such a quick decision."

"Oh," Maddy said, her face falling. "My voice mail people want to stop by and take another look. They fell in love with it."

"Who wouldn't?" She gave a wistful sigh.

Maddy gave her a squeeze. "It's okay. You'll know when things are right for you." She looked Kit over with that sharp gaze of hers. "You know, you could just live here with Ollie for the summer and watch over the place for me. I wouldn't even charge you."

Kit shook her head adamantly. "I'd never prevent you from taking advantage of the rental money for beachfront property."

"If it was all about the money, I'd rent weekly. But renters are hard on a place, and I can't bear that. All I really want is for someone to love the place like I do and care for it while I decide what to do with it permanently."

"It's so adorable, I know you'll find the right person." She gave Maddy a hug. "Thanks for the banana bread. And the talk."

"I love talking with you," Maddy said as Kit made her way to the door. "Don't get down on yourself," Maddy called out. "Give yourself some time."

Kit sent up a wave as she glanced out the window at the round-stone walkway that led away from the beach. Back to reality.

"Oh yes, hello," she heard behind her. "This is Maddy

Edwards. You said you're still very interested in the rental?"

Kit stood at the salmon-colored door, her hand on the knob. On her finger, Darla's ring caught a beam of sunshine, splitting it into a rainbow of prisms.

Which wasn't magic, but it did have the effect of making her stop and think.

The little place, under the open sky, with the backdrop of gently rolling waves, just felt like somewhere she could...think. Plan her future. Not to mention the massive sandbox for Ollie right in the backyard. And crazy or not, she wanted that with all her heart.

She ran back to the kitchen, waving her arms wildly to get Maddy's attention. "I'll take it!" She pointed with both thumbs to herself. "Me!"

Suppressing a grin, Maddy said into the phone, "I just wanted to tell you that I'm so sorry. I just rented it this morning!"

Kit grinned back.

Maddy hung up and hugged Kit hard. "I'm so happy. We'll just do the summer, okay? Then you can reassess."

"But I'll pay you what you were going to charge that person. To be fair. Okay?"

"How about half that? I really can't see myself charging you more."

"Just treat me like a normal renter."

"Okay, normal renter." Maddy paused thoughtfully. "Except for one small issue."

"Anything. You name it." In her excitement, the words tumbled out before Kit could think about it.

"Seymour needs an opportunity to meet his full potential," she said in a serious voice. "He'll never reach it with

Bowie around. And I hate to rehome him. He's had such a hard life."

"You have a deal." Seymour hid all the time, right? How difficult could he be?

Maddy sealed the deal with another hug. "You can move in as early as Saturday."

As Kit walked along the stone path back to the road, she couldn't help wondering, what had she just done? She'd just got herself a house and an ornery, overweight cat. And if she was going to suddenly move, she'd have to postpone her date with Bryan.

But she caught herself smiling.

Then she chuckled out loud. If this craziness was what endorphins from jogging had caused, she'd make sure in the future to avoid it at all costs.

Chapter 6

AT SEVEN THIRTY on Monday morning, Kit kissed Ollie goodbye, thanked her dad for offering to drop him off at school on his way to run errands, and headed over to the McKinnon house.

She didn't know why she was here, exactly. Mostly because of a niggling feeling that she could do better than to shrink away because she was afraid. And it seemed wrong to leave Carson's house, as much as she disliked it, in someone else's hands. Or maybe it was simply because she'd already made one crazy decision this week, so why not make another?

She held up her hand. Darla's ring seemed to twinkle at her as if it were saying, *See all the trouble you're getting into? You should never have put me on.*

The driveway was empty of Alex's black Ford F-150, which made her exhale a sigh of relief. She stood at the base of the front steps—well, the used-to-be steps, since they were completely crushed to smithereens now—and looked up at the house.

She noticed that the piece of gingerbread trim that had been dangling over the front porch had been taken down. Probably by the hand of Alex, no doubt. But overall, the house still looked like it had been through a couple of World Wars. Which, actually, it had.

And it had survived, but just barely.

Kit took a deep breath and hoisted herself up. *I'm going in*, she told herself. Out loud she said, "You don't scare me. You're just a house. And memories aren't scary, right?"

Remember the last time we were here, honey? Carson's voice said inside her head, stopping her in her tracks.

"Yes, I remember," she whispered as she stood in front of the heavy wooden door, key in hand. He'd been so excited—about the big porch, the long-planked wooden floors, and the built-in sideboard in the dining room.

We dreamed of making that big front room into a family room and opening up the kitchen, remember?

Okay, now she was hyperventilating again, the ghosts of what-could-never-be kneecapping her before she'd even made it through the door. Kit gathered up her bag and what was left of her sanity and prepared to jump down the stairless front stoop and head straight to work. But then she remembered her list, the paper copy of which was lost now but still lived on inside her head.

"I'm going to trade you for a college education," she told the house. "So if that means I have to go in, then I have to go in."

That was the ticket to the future—for her and Ollie. She had to get rid of this house to get her life going.

Carson would want her to have a say in what went on

with this house. If Alex was willing to do the work, then she had to be Carson's eyes and voice.

And maybe that was enough to tolerate Mr. Grump for a while. Kit couldn't say she liked him, but she could at least appreciate that he was willing to do all of this for them.

Because she *did* need help.

And she would pay him back as soon as the house sold. So it wouldn't be like she was accepting his help for free, right?

"You can do it," she cheered herself on. "Just start with the key."

It dawned on her that she'd been talking to the front door, which also made her notice that it was actually beautiful, or rather had been at one time. Made of dark wood, maybe walnut, a grapevine was carved into it, running all around the perimeter. Complete with tiny little bunches of wooden grapes. On closer inspection, it looked like the grapes had actually been painted purple at one point, the vines a dark green. Through the decades, dirt had accumulated in the crevices, and the stain had peeled off most of whatever color hadn't faded into a worn, beaten brown.

Beautiful. Worth restoring. There was Carson's voice again, which Kit promptly shook off. "Being sentimental about you is not going to change what I have to do," she said to the door. "I'm sorry." Okay, what was worse, talking to herself, Carson, or the door? Before she could guess, she turned the key and pushed the door open.

The sun had just come up, but the light inside was wan, dust motes floating in the air. It occurred to her that she should've brought her dad or someone else along in case she fell through a rotted floorboard, never to be heard from again.

Once her eyes became accustomed to the darkness, she found that the foyer, although dusty and full of cobwebs, was actually very solid, paneled in rich, dark wood. The floor was made of beautiful old encaustic tiles laid in an intricate green and salmon design. The floorboards beyond the foyer were a little worn and creaky but nowhere near rotted.

Directly in front of her was a stunning oak staircase with a thick wooden banister and many spindles. The staircase took a turn, and at the turn was a window. Or used to be, for now the space was boarded up. At one time it must have been striking, walking in the front door and seeing the grand staircase and that window, which must have overlooked the harbor.

The damp chill made her shiver. On impulse, she flicked on a switch. She almost jumped when an overhead fixture in the foyer actually turned on, although it shed only a dim light the color of watery lemonade.

A tall, sturdy ladder stood in the middle of the draped floor. Tools sat on top of the floor covering. And what looked like construction drawings.

"There," she said, her hand still on the switch. "Just an old house, see? Nothing to be afraid of."

Beyond the ladder, a large fireplace with an arched wooden façade stood lined with old green tiles, with a hearth to match. Another drape covered an object in front of the fireplace. Just as Kit was trying to figure out what in the world *that* was—a rolled-up rug, maybe?—the lump moved. Actually, it stirred and sat up, a man's dark head emerging from the stark white of the sheet.

Kit screamed. The man nearly fell over as he abruptly

stood up, his legs tangled in the material. She willed herself to move, to head for the door, to dial her phone, *anything*, but her legs felt mired in mud. It seemed like minutes later when she finally made it to the door. But just as her fingers met the knob, a masculine hand grasped her arm. Before she could choke out another scream, he spun her about, forcing her to look at him.

"Kit, it's okay," he said, now grasping both her shoulders. "Just me." The deep, soothing notes of a low baritone rumbled through her. *Alex.* Through the fog of adrenaline rush, her brain registered his worried expression—and his thick, rumpled hair, which made him look strangely vulnerable and . . . very human. "I'm sorry I frightened you."

She managed a nod, still unable to form words. As her pulse fell a little, her fear gradually became replaced by another feeling entirely—that of being held by strong, corded arms and being near a hard, muscular body that smelled like . . . mothballs.

Yep, he smelled like Hadley's grandmother's linen closet.

Besides the tussled hair, his stubble was overgrown and bristly, and his clothing was wrinkled. Seeing him so out of control for the first time was . . . interesting. And he was clearly worried. Which made her see a much different side to the stone-faced person he showed to the world—or at least to her.

An even more disturbing thought registered over all the panic. Unbelievably, it occurred to her that this was the first time anyone besides her family or her friends— that is, a *man*—had touched her in over two years.

A powerful, heady awareness rushed through her, along with the sensation of being hot and cold, flushed all over, and suddenly shaky on her feet. "I'm okay," she managed. But she really wasn't. For other reasons entirely. "You...you can let go now." And he'd better, because his touch was sending little darts of heat shooting all through her.

Alex dropped his arms, suddenly looking uncomfortable as he raked his hands through his hair. "I'm sorry." His voice still held its ever-present edge. "My reservation in town got messed up, and every other place is booked, so I just worked late and then crashed on the floor."

"Your reservation?" She was confused. "I thought maybe you were staying with your mom."

"She's renting out her house for the summer and staying in an efficiency over the art gallery."

"Oh." Okay, that made sense. A lot of people did that. But...he was choosing to sleep on the floor rather than ask for help from anyone? Like, did he have friends? "Your truck wasn't in the driveway."

"I parked it in the back."

"Oh." As Kit calmed down, she noticed slanted rays of sun shining in through the paned windows, highlighting thick layers of dust and cobwebs. And where there were cobwebs, there were spiders, the one thing she feared nearly as much as setting foot in this house. She needed to get out of here. But more importantly, he did too. The man was sleeping on the floor in front of a stone-cold fireplace. In a place with creepy-crawly...

She shuddered. "It's too cold in here to sleep."

He shrugged. "I thought about starting a fire in the fireplace but I didn't think that was wise." He rubbed his neck and then flicked his dark gaze straight at her. "I should have asked your permission to stay here. I'm sorry."

She opened her mouth to tell him that she appreciated

everything but he should go—somewhere else, wherever that might be—but something in his eyes stopped her. He looked miserable. Exhausted. *Driven.* She saw it in the set of his square jaw, in the determination in his eyes. What had made him take time away from his life to do this?

What was it he'd said? *I'm here for Carson. This is the only thing I can do. To honor his memory.*

She got that. She really did.

"There's nothing to be sorry for." She turned toward one of the long, floor-to-ceiling windows, too many emotions racing through her.

He was here out of love for Carson. She could tell he was broken up about Carson's death too. It occurred to her that there were just a few people who could share that unwelcome bond.

And just two of them who could realize Carson's vision for this house.

She turned back and faced him. "I should've thought to ask you yesterday where you were staying but frankly, I...I got a little panicked when you asked me to come in. I haven't been in here since...since Carson. Well." She cleared her throat and struggled to keep her voice on an even keel. "That's why I came back this morning. I wanted to prove that I could do it."

She didn't know why she told him that except that seeing him like this made her want to tell him the truth. And if she could connect with Alex at all, it would have to be through the truth.

Strangely, she saw something in his eyes soften. Even the lines between his eyes smoothed out. Compassion. She saw it for the first time. He got it. He got the grief. And actually when he wasn't frowning, he was very...handsome. Could it be that his tough, cranky façade was a mask?

Doubtful. Because he'd been cool to her long before Carson died. For nearly as long as she'd known him, Alex de la Cruz had always been serious, focused, and dismissive.

Well, if they were going to work together on this house, that would have to change.

"You don't need to come in here at all if you don't want to," he offered. "I've got everything covered."

Something inside of her prickled, which surprised her, considering just how much it had taken to simply walk into this house. But now that she'd done that, she didn't want an easy out.

"Now that I'm here, it's not so bad." Except for the dust. And the spiders. And were those mouse droppings on the floor? *Ugh.*

She forced a little smile. To show him she wasn't overwhelmed. "At least I won't need any coffee this morning."

To her surprise, he gave a little chuckle. Actually, it was more of a grunt, but his mouth definitely turned up a little.

Maybe she preferred sullen Alex. Because that bare hint of a smile softened all his hard features in a way that was far too appealing.

Alex walked over to the drop cloth in the center of the room and bent over to examine a bunch of stuff laid out...bathroom faucets, a really ugly light fixture that looked like it came out of a medieval castle, a pink toilet seat.

A pink toilet seat? He'd better not tell her that was fashionable in a midcentury modern sort of way because—no.

This beautiful, old house that had been beaten down by so many things had survived, only to be desecrated by a pink toilet seat?

Unacceptable.

"I have to get to work," she said, checking her watch, "but is there a time I can come back? To walk around and get an idea of all the work that needs to be done." And find out where on earth he planned to put that ungodly relic.

"Look," he said, a determined expression on his face, "I've got everything planned so it will all run on schedule. I'm going to visit some renovation supply companies, talk to the Cammareris, contract with some services that I can't do on my own." He picked up a legal pad and flipped through pages of scrawled lists. "You really don't need to trouble yourself."

"You sound very busy," she said, undeterred, "but can we schedule a half hour? I can come back right after work. If you need me to come later, I'd have to bring Ollie or arrange for someone to watch him."

"Okay," he said reluctantly. "If you really want to." He sounded as happy as if she'd suggested he choke down some poisonous berries from the yew bushes outside.

"Great." She nodded and headed to the door before he changed his mind.

Well, it looked like Alex was going to stay and work on the house. But maybe what he didn't know was that he wasn't going to do it alone.

He didn't seem like the kind of man who enjoyed a lot of input from others. And he was clearly on a mission to get this done and move on. And he clearly thought she didn't want to have anything to do with this.

Actually, she'd thought that too. As recently as this morning.

Once Kit was outside, she breathed in a big lungful of fresh spring air and smiled. Because her little act of resistance felt good.

She could handle a sullen, cranky man who didn't like her even if he sometimes gave off a very masculine vibe that was a little bit disturbing. She *knew* she could handle this—and him.

And that was the first time she'd felt like that in a very long time.

Chapter 7

AS SOON AS Kit left, Alex walked over to his toolbox to grab a tape measure. He spied something in a bright green wrapper that looked like it would probably glow in the dark. It was a Fruit Roll-Up, and next to that, a granola bar— which Kit must have somehow left for him. He scarfed both down in about ten seconds, as grateful as if it were a steak off the grill. Well, maybe not *that* grateful, but still.

He felt her kindness physically, and that was the problem. She was this complicated mix of stiff upper lip and vulnerability that made all his protective instincts kick in. Which was the last thing she wanted and the last thing he needed.

If she wanted a rundown on all the projects the house needed, he'd give it to her. She'd see how overwhelming it was and how much he had to accomplish in a relatively short period of time. Then hopefully she'd go back to not caring what he did.

But he had a feeling it wasn't going to be that easy. It was clear she didn't want him here. And if their conversation just now was any indication, she was going to make it as difficult as possible for him to do the job.

A man with any sense might decide that, as much as he loved his buddy, this was a crazy idea. And he had lots of better ideas on how to spend his summer.

The Fruit Roll-Up was actually more delicious than it looked, but he needed more food, so he headed into town. The sun had chased away the chill, and today the weather was behaving more like a May beach day with the promise of many more to come. Petunia Street was already bustling with people getting coffee, visiting the bakery, and strolling past the art gallery.

"Well, look who's back." George Teeter stopped sweeping in front of the hardware store to say hi. He embraced Alex and thanked him for his service. "You here to stay?"

Alex greeted his old boss with a hug. "Not sure. How come you haven't retired yet?"

"I'd rather be here and crotchety." He grinned good-naturedly. "Besides, who else is going to tell all these young people how to fix these old homes up? We can't have them ruining all that character. Heard you're taking on a little remodeling project, by the way. Stop by if you need some help."

"How did you know that?" Did everyone in this town know everything he was up to? Of course they did.

"The Cammareri brothers."

Alex had worked one summer at Teeter's Hardware, and then three more with Nick and Tony Cammareri and their dad, who owned Cammareri Vintage Home Remodeling, the gold standard remodeling business in Seashell

Harbor. "Well, I'm definitely going to need all the help I can get." And supplies. So far, all he'd done was rip out steps with his own tools and make lists of everything he'd soon be shopping for.

George ripped a flyer off the hardware store's front window and handed it to him. "You've still got time to enroll the place in the Fourth of July home tour."

Alex shook his head adamantly. "That train wreck will never be ready by then." He was hoping to make it salable by August. Making it a part of the most popular tourist event of the season was another thing entirely.

"With some help, it might be," George said. "Besides, if you can get it on the tour, it might just sell. Plus they're raising money to redo the pier."

Alex took the flyer, just to be polite.

George pounded him on the back. "Glad you're back, son. Come see me, okay? I'll set you up for all your projects."

"Thanks, George," he said. "Great to see you."

Alex walked the line of shops, all of which were decked out with urns of flowers, window boxes, and hanging pots blooming in all colors of the rainbow. He had to admit that his hometown shone at its charming best in summertime. He passed Scoops; Pooch Palace, the pet rescue; the realty office; the florist; and the Cranky Crab, a popular bar. Most of the locals preferred the Sand Bar, which was a few blocks away from all the tourist commotion.

For a town that looked like it had jumped straight off a Monet seaside painting, Alex's destination, Seas the Day, was reassuringly simple. Pleasantly crowded, with a faint buzz of conversation and the stomach-grumbling smell of a combination of pancakes, coffee, and bacon, it had always been one of his favorite places. The booths were lined with red vinyl seats, and a big chalkboard behind the counter advertised the specials in plain English. It was the kind of place where you could order something pronounceable. And filling.

He'd barely picked up the menu when an older woman with blond hair and a blue apron walked up to his table. "Hey there, handsome," she said. Her face crinkled up with lines when she smiled, which somehow put him right at ease. "Look who the tide washed up."

"Hey, Loretta." He smiled at the longtime waitress. "I see you're still flattering your customers."

She laughed. "Keeps 'em coming back."

She poured him some nearly black brew that had the consistency of molasses. "Thank you, ma'am," he said politely, careful not to make a face at the questionable coffee.

"Oh, so you're *ma'aming* me," she said saucily. "They teach you that in the air force?"

He smiled and picked up his cup, toasting her with it. "Yes, ma'am."

"You get that in the air force too?" She pointed with her pen to the tip of the thunderbolt peeking out from the rolled-up sleeve of his flannel shirt.

That was the symbol of their fleet. Another reminder of Carson, who'd had one too.

"Well, our girl Kit could sure use a helping hand. Glad to see she's got two strong ones to help her out. So what'll you have to keep up your strength, Captain?"

If only she'd give him a second to look at the menu before she mentioned Kit. Or any other town gossip. But right now his stomach felt like it was gnawing on itself, despite the Fruit Roll-Up. "How about a little bit of everything?"

Her face lit up. "I have two questions. Are you hungry, and do you trust me?"

"Yes?"

"Great. You won't leave here that way." She tucked her notepad in her apron pocket. "Anything else to drink?"

"Maybe just some cream?" Hopefully that would make it drinkable.

"Sure thing. Sit tight." With a pat on his shoulder, she took off, tennis shoes squeaking.

One sip of the coffee confirmed his worst fears, but he forced down a few gulps anyway and picked up the paper that was neatly folded between the salt and pepper shakers and the wall. It was a local weekly with a long list of rentals in the back.

He needed regular access to food and a bed. He didn't need a pool, a view, or a quaint Victorian atmosphere. Except even the prices of the less flashy places were exorbitant. It appeared that, if you happened to own any type of four-walled structure within a five-mile radius of the beach, you were set for the season.

His stomach grumbled, confirming the *access to food* part. But three phone calls later told him what he already knew—every place was already rented.

The voice of a child from the next booth drifted over to him. "Can we see the puppies and kitties after breakfast, Aunt Hadley? *Please?*" Except Hadley came out "Hadwey."

Alex snapped to attention, even though the partition between the booths was high, and no one could see him. Hadley Wells was one of Kit's good friends, and she'd turned the local dog boarding place into a pet rescue. So the little kid had to be...

"Of course we can, Ollie," came a feminine voice.

"You don't have to be at school until after lunch, so we'll have plenty of time to visit Pooch Palace."

That little voice with the cute lisp unquestionably belonged to Ollie, Kit and Carson's son, who by Alex's quick calculation would be exactly five years old. He felt like he shouldn't be eavesdropping, yet he sat frozen, holding his breath for more.

"What do you want for breakfast?" a masculine voice asked. That had to be Tony Cammareri, whom he knew dated Hadley. "How about some bacon to grow those Tee ball muscles?"

"I don't like Tee ball, Uncle Cam," Ollie said. Except it came out "wike."

"Oh," Cam said, sounding at a loss. Alex had to smile because he couldn't recall a time Cam ever met a ball he didn't like.

Hadley cleared her throat. "How about we talk about breakfast instead?" she said hurriedly. "What would you like, Oliver?"

Suddenly Alex recalled the hastily scribbled LEARN TO PLAY ~~BASEBALL~~ ~~SOFTBALL~~ TEE BALL on Kit's list.

"I want a cheeseburger," Ollie said. Alex could hear a grin in his voice.

Now Alex was certain that kid *had* to be Carson's son. Because Carson used to eat dinner food for breakfast all the time. He could down a cheeseburger any time of the day or night.

Alex didn't know whether to laugh or cry. To show his face or slip out. But his stomach insisted on waiting for his food.

"How about pancakes?" Hadley offered. "Or bacon and eggs?"

"A cheeseburger and French fries," Ollie said. "And a milkshake!"

Definitely Carson's son. A flair for embellishment. Always pushing the limits. And clearly a comedian. Alex nearly grinned himself.

Cam laughed. "Okay, we'll see if they'll make us one at eight thirty in the morning."

"Kit might kill us," Hadley said in a low voice.

"Would your mom be angry if you had a cheeseburger for breakfast?" Cam asked.

"No!" Ollie said. "Because it's got pwoteen."

"You're pretty smart," Cam said. "How do you know about protein?"

"I *am* smart," Ollie said. Alex heard a zipper unzipping.

"Wow. What have you got in that book bag, buddy?" Cam asked.

"My books," Ollie said. "There's one on bugs, and one on seashells, and one on flowers. I'm going to scare my mom with this one."

"*Spiders of North America*?" Hadley read.

"Mommy hates spiders." Alex heard a shuffle, and a faint thump as a book hit the floor.

After a little pause, Hadley said, "This is a reader book. Does your mom read it to you?"

"*I* read it," Ollie said proudly.

"That's terrific, buddy," Cam said. To Hadley he asked, "Do five-year-olds read?"

"Smart ones do," Hadley replied.

"Mommy says reading makes you smart." Rummaging noises ensued. "And this is my glow ball."

Glow ball?

Something clattered over plates and silverware. Alex couldn't help chuckling as he took another swig of coffee.

This kid was cracking him up, just like his dad had. And he loved to read... like his mother, who'd always had her nose in a book for as long as he could remember.

"Let me see that ball for a sec," Cam said. "Oh, wow, look, I just pulled it out of your ear."

Giggles.

"Hey, bud," Cam said. "I think we better put the ball away until we leave the restaurant, okay?"

There was another clatter and a crash. Out of the corner of Alex's eye, he saw a boy scramble down the aisle. A mop of dark hair and a flash of blue jeans rushed by.

"Did you say you wanted a few of those?" Alex heard Cam ask while Ollie darted under an empty table across the aisle for the ball.

"A few of what?" Hadley asked.

"Kids," Cam said. "Because they sure look like a lot of work."

"Maybe the girl version sits still better," Hadley said. "Ollie," she called, turning around. "Come back here, stinker."

Full of life. Knows what he likes. Smart as a whip. *Carson's son.*

Doesn't love Tee ball. Loves books. Sweet-natured. *Kit's son.*

"Hey, Oliver," Cam said. "How about we put the glow ball back into the book bag?"

"But it's fun, Uncle Cam," Ollie protested.

Just then, an object sailed over the booth and landed in Alex's mug with a splash, sending coffee splattering over his shirt. As he dabbed at the stains with a napkin, he caught sight of a clear ball with sparkles floating in his coffee. His first thought was that he was grateful for an excuse not to have to finish it without seeming impolite.

Suddenly he felt the dig of little fingers into his shoulder, poking him like a restless kid behind you in a church pew. He turned to see a head full of dark, curly hair appear over the red vinyl booth. His heart nearly stopped as he peered into eyes the exact same shape as Kit's, although they were blue instead of green. Except the thick head of hair, the cowlick, and the mischievous expression were all Carson's.

What a strange twist life could throw at you.

As Alex met the boy's gaze, Ollie's expression turned wide-eyed and wary.

Alex eyed Hadley and Cam, looking on. Both seemed to release breaths of relief when they recognized him. "I asked for cream in my coffee," Alex said, nodding to them and shooting Ollie a smile. "I didn't expect to get a glow ball."

Ollie frowned. "Where is it?" His gaze finally lighting on Alex's mug, he giggled and pointed. "It's in your coffee!"

Alex plucked out the ball, wiped it off on his napkin, and returned it to its owner.

"I'm Alex," he said, eyeing the child carefully. He noticed a huge stack of books on the table, not two or three like he'd imagined, one with a giant black spider front and center. "No school today?"

"The pipes blew up!" Ollie made a sound effect and demonstrated an explosion with his arms.

He was a bundle of energy, for sure. Carson was always in motion, just like his boy. How proud he'd be.

That stabbed him straight in the heart. And brought back the fateful events that always lingered right at the edge of his mind. It had been Alex's turn to fly, but a bout of stomach flu had grounded him. It had been the first time he'd missed a flight in his entire career.

And that fateful event had led to...this. Coming home and staring into the eyes of a kid who would never know his dad.

He winced. Suddenly he realized Hadley was talking, and he'd missed part of what she'd just said. "...your daddy's best friend, Captain de la Cruz?"

"Just Alex, please," Alex rushed to say.

"You're my daddy's friend?" Ollie exclaimed. Except it came out "fwend." The kid was cute as pie but he definitely had a significant lisp. Which wasn't so cute when kids began to notice you didn't talk like them.

"We flew jets together."

The little boy's eyes grew wide. "My daddy was very brave," he said solemnly.

"Yes, Oliver, he was very brave." Alex found himself smiling. "I can tell you all about him sometime."

As soon as the words were out of his mouth, he knew he shouldn't have said them. How on earth would he manage to tell this kid stories about his dad when he could barely even think about Carson without choking up? Couple that with his rogue feelings about his mother and yeah. He wouldn't be doing that anytime soon.

"My mom's getting us a new house," Ollie announced, back to playing with his ball. Cam, who was sitting next to him, gently tugged it out of his hands and offered a car he'd dug out of the book bag.

When Ollie gave him the stink eye, Cam said in a teasing tone, "Better to play with the ball later so it doesn't end up in somebody's soup next, okay?"

Alex couldn't help but notice the loving, easy way

they had with Ollie. Like they were close. Like they loved him. Good people.

"'Kay, Uncle Cam," Ollie said. He grinned as he began to run the car along the back of the booth.

Hadley exchanged a glance with Cam that indicated she just might be counting the minutes until breakfast came. Certain he'd seen that exact expression on his sister's face regarding his twin nephews, Alex nearly chuckled out loud.

"Are you excited about the house?" Alex asked, hoping to distract Ollie for a minute. And also to find out—*what house?*

"My mom says I get my own room, with a bookshelf. 'Cause now I share a room with all the yarn."

Yarn? Alex looked to Hadley for help. "Kit's mom has a craft room," she explained. "The yarn is for the Scarves for Santa project."

He nodded. "Mommy says we'll have our own yard and the ocean and maybe someday we can get Rex a fwend."

Aw geez. Rex. He knew the black Lab well. And that sent yet another pang to his heart. How could it be that Carson's dog was still around when Carson himself wasn't? "Nice," Alex said. "It's great to have your own place." Was that a dumb thing to say? Probably, but he felt so thrown. And he was worried that the car was about to land in his coffee too.

He had no idea what Ollie was actually talking about, but maybe Kit had managed to cross GET MY OWN PLACE off her list.

"Kit tells us you're starting work on the old McKinnon place," Hadley said. "That's exciting."

"I'm not sure Kit thinks so," Alex said before he could stop himself.

"If you haven't noticed, Kit hates to accept help," Hadley said. "Don't let that stop you." She looked at Cam, who had stood up and come around to greet him properly. "We don't."

"Anything that can help her to sell that old place would be a godsend." Cam shook his hand and pulled him in for a hug. "Glad you're back in town. It's been too long. Also, my brother's been dying to talk to you about that house."

"I could use a consult."

"Aunt Hadley, I have to go to the bafroom." Ollie did the universal jiggle dance in his seat.

"Let's go." Cam gave a wave as he steered Ollie to the restroom.

"Don't let Kit discourage you," Hadley said as soon as they were gone. "She would never ask for help but that doesn't mean she doesn't need it. She's got a ton on her plate."

"I...um...noticed that."

"Kit's very proud. She would rather pretend nothing's wrong than admit there was."

Yes, but Hadley was leaving out the *stubborn* part, which he was also coming to see.

"Why does Oliver hate Tee ball?" It was against his better judgment to ask, but he did it anyway.

She shrugged. "He's just learning. Kit's trying her best to teach him. Some of the kids were snickering a little at the last game when he accidentally hit the tee. Cam saw, and he's planning to help out. It's just that he's so busy with his new restaurant." She must have seen him frown because she said, "I'm sure Ollie will catch on."

Carson's son getting laughed at during Tee ball? A fierce surge of anger rose up inside him. *Unacceptable.*

Ollie and Cam returned just as the food arrived. "Here you go, Captain de la Cruz," Loretta said. Turning to Ollie, she added, "And I've got a cheeseburger and fries for you, Big Man." Ollie immediately got on his knees and started bouncing in the booth. "Just hold your breeches one second, sweetheart," Loretta said. "We're going to serve the captain first, okay?" Back to Alex. "Pancakes, eggs, bacon. And creamer. You need more, you just give me a holler."

"Thanks, Loretta," Alex said appreciatively, then nodded to Cam and Hadley. "Nice to see you both. And to meet you, Ollie."

"Bye, Alex." Ollie gave a smile and a big wave and then turned all his attention to his food.

The breakfast was everything Alex's stomach had been rumbling for, but he was too lost in thought to think much of it. Kit needed help. But she didn't want him to help her. And she wasn't going to let him do the job the way he saw fit.

And now there was this little embodiment of his friend walking around in the world getting teased for not being able to play Tee ball.

He felt himself getting tangled up. He was a doer and a helper, and there was nothing he hated worse than someone being an underdog.

Fine. He'd help as much as he could. But he wasn't here to be friendly. He was determined to focus on his tasks and stay as far away from Kit—and her son—as possible.

Chapter 8

"HELLOOO," KIT CALLED, rapping on the front door of the old house for the second time that day. There was no answer, but Alex's truck was parked at the curb and the CAMMARERI VINTAGE HOME REMODELING van was in the driveway, so she pushed the door open and walked in. The same drop cloth lay in the center of the living room. Pounding and the sound of male laughter came from the direction of the kitchen.

Alex walked into the main room, a pencil behind his ear and a clipboard in his hand, efficient and organized as usual. No sign of the rumpled, disorderly guy wrapped in a mothball-scented sheet. Although that guy had been sort of...cute.

And just like that, for the second time that day, she was having hot construction worker fantasies. Which made her wonder—how could she be having this reaction to a man she didn't even like?

"You ready for the tour?" he asked, completely unaware of his effect on her. From the kitchen, she could hear hammering and a large *thunk* as something potentially big hit the floor.

"What's going on in there?" She hiked her thumb in the direction of the noise.

"Nick and Cam came over to help demolish the kitchen," he said.

"Oh." Alex was glancing at his watch and looking impatient, so she placed her purse on a folding table covered by sheeting and a bunch of tools. "I'm ready." She looked at her own watch. "I have a half hour before I have to take Ollie to his Tee ball game."

"Want to start with the kitchen?" he asked.

"Okay, but what's this stuff?" She pointed to some shiny brass faucets lying next to the pink toilet. She told herself to rein in her criticism because he was doing all this work essentially for free, after all, and did she really care about the decisions he was making?

Actually, she realized, she did care. A lot. Which shocked her almost as much as her willingness—no, her *need*—to push back on Alex's agenda.

Not that she wasn't grateful for everything he was doing. But now that she was here, she was no longer okay with letting someone else make the decisions.

"Nick took me to a renovation supply place where you can find quality items for good prices," Alex said.

"Like gold bathroom fixtures."

He narrowed his eyes. "You've got a problem with those?"

"Well, gold's not in fashion now. And it certainly wasn't for a house this age."

That stopped him in his tracks. She could tell by his stiffened posture that he wasn't pleased by her input.

"Like I said," he said with restraint, "it's excellent quality, and I got it for a steal."

"And like *I* said," she countered, "I really appreciate all you're doing, but there's more to renovating a historical house than budget finds." She had to bite her lip to keep from saying more.

Come to think of it, had she given *anyone* pushback in the past two years? Maybe not, but this actually felt a little bit...good. Actually, a *lot* good.

And it helped fight against the unsettling feelings she was having in his presence. The ones that were making her heart pound and making her feel just a little out of breath.

She was sure her reaction was because he was so...annoying. A man who had a plan and didn't want any interference.

Well, she was going to shoot that down right quick, pardner.

Alex raised a dark, foreboding brow. "I thought you didn't really care to be a part of this. And I'm sure you're busy with Ollie and a thousand other things."

Now was the time to back down. To say *You're right* and let him be. After all, he was right—she had *pleeeenty* on her plate. He wanted to get the job done quickly and move on. She got that.

But instead, she found herself saying, "That was before I walked in here and thought about it."

"I think it would be best to just let me do what I came here to do."

Kit folded her arms and looked at him. "Just to let you know, I choose to ignore any male who starts a sentence with 'I think it would be best.'"

His other brow shot up, but he didn't say a thing.

"Maybe we can compromise," Kit said in an overly cheerful tone. "If I help pick out things while you keep working, we both win."

He sighed heavily and pinched his nose. Mr. Cool and Calm had an irritation point that she was clearly hitting the bull's-eye on. Repeatedly. She was poking the bear, but she couldn't seem to stop.

And, heaven help her, watching him get agitated was actually a little...fun.

"What's wrong with the pink toilet?" he asked with measured patience.

"Nothing, if it were 1957," she said sweetly. Just then, her cell went off. A quick glance told her it was her mom calling. "I'm sorry," she said, stepping aside. "I have to get this really quick." She pushed the answer button. "Hi, Mom." She was aware that Alex was rummaging through his toolbox but probably listening to every word.

"Gramma says to tell you we can't find my pants," Ollie reported.

Oh. "Tell Grandma your baseball pants should be on the dryer. And your Sharks jersey is hanging up in the laundry room. I think. Or else I hung it in your closet." Ollie proceeded to tell her that he had a stomachache. "Maybe have a little snack. I'll be home to help you. Very soon, okay? Bye."

"You sure you don't have to go?" Alex asked a little too hopefully.

"Everything's fine." Except she was going to have to brace herself for another terrible night of Tee ball. And she would have to use every effort to coax Ollie into going, into convincing him that this time would be better.

Alex walked back to the drop cloth filled with more

renovation treasure finds. "I suppose you're going to comment about the light fixture next," he said.

"Yes, actually..." She examined the very heavy chandelier with a circular iron ring and lights that looked like fake candles. "I was wondering," she asked innocently, "by any chance, is it from Hogwarts?"

He shook his head at that, but if she wasn't mistaken, a corner of his mouth almost-kind-of-sort-of turned up just a fraction. "Maybe we should move on." He opened a door that led from the large dining room to a very small, boxy kitchen.

As she walked past him, he said, "Look, you should trust me on this. I promise I'll use top-quality materials and the work will be done right."

As she passed, she accidentally brushed his arm. A flurry of butterflies let loose in her stomach.

Whoa. What was it about this guy? *Why him, Hormones, why him?*

"I believe you when you say you'll do high-quality work." Kit made the mistake of looking up—and he was tall, so she did have to look *up*—a move that made her notice his beautiful brown eyes, which were looking more than a little wary and displeased. "But I feel the house should look a certain way too. It has so much character."

"The kitchen is tiny," he said as they moved into the room, which was painted pink. Nick was examining a beam that crossed the ceiling, and all the cabinets had been ripped out, as had the yellow vinyl floor, which revealed the subfloor beneath.

"Hey, Kit," Cam said, waving, while Nick gave her a quick nod.

"Hey, guys."

Alex assessed the half-demolished kitchen. "Whether or not that's a weight-bearing wall determines whether or not we can knock it out with ease. If that's okay with you, of course."

She rolled her eyes but smiled sweetly. "Of course, Alex."

"I was thinking if we expanded this room into that small parlor next door, it would make a nice-size kitchen that would also be open to the main living area."

"I think that's a great idea." She peeked into a doorway that held a little butler pantry containing built-in cabinets with leaded glass doors. "As long as you don't get rid of this room."

"Agreed." He crossed his arms as he stood back and mused over the job.

"We actually agree on something?" she asked.

"So," Nick said, clearing his throat, "um, this is a weight-bearing wall after all. We'd have to put a beam across this whole area to support it, which is possible, just a little costly. We can get you an estimate."

"Sounds good," she told the brothers. "Cam, shouldn't you be at the restaurant?" He'd just opened his own Italian restaurant called, simply enough, Cam's Place, at an oceanside location, and it was drawing large crowds every night.

"Just helping out for an hour." He glanced at the ornate crown molding near the ceiling. "Great bones in this one, by the way."

That was the most hopeful thing she'd heard in years. "Thanks to both of you for coming over."

"Hey, no problem," Nick said, dusting his hands off. "We're going to grab a pizza, then head over to Ollie's game."

Kit assessed her friends. And she did have great friends. Even though Nick and Darla had married young and then divorced, she still thought of Nick like a brother. Despite Darla's relationship with him being complicated. Both Nick and Cam made a point of looking out for her and Ollie. "I really don't expect you to come watch a bunch of five-year-olds play ball."

"We want to," Cam said, flashing the Cammareri smile. "Alex, join us for dinner."

"Thanks," Alex said, "maybe another time."

"Wow," Kit said as they walked out together, "you have friends. They probably don't even mind that you're a little bossy."

"At least I'm not a lot stubborn." He sent her a pointed look.

"But it can't hurt to consider options, right?"

"Look," he said, rubbing his neck, "why don't we sit down with the Cammareris and figure out the best way forward?"

She heaved a sigh. "Sounds like a plan. Now that we have that out of the way, what do you suggest next?"

He lifted a brow. "You going home and not worrying your pretty little head?" But his mouth had definitely curved up on one side.

If the guy ever actually smiled, it would be...scary.

She crossed her arms too. "Um, not going to happen." She pressed her lips together to stay serious. "All I want is a say in the finishes you pick. The cabinets. The knobs. The paint colors." She waved her hands around the kitchen.

"Is that all?"

She remained undaunted. "You might be surprised how much faster this will go if you have help."

He looked wary, like he wondered if the *help* she could offer should be in quote marks.

"I can meet you during my lunch hour or after work," Kit said. "But my boss hates it when I leave for lunch, so if I'm a minute late getting back, he might extract a kidney for payment."

"I'm pretty efficient," he said, stopping at the big staircase. "I can do a lot with an hour or two." He glanced at his watch. "Do you have a second to see something upstairs?"

"Okay," she said warily. "As long as you don't have plans to accidentally get rid of me up there."

He let out a chuckle. "I hadn't thought of that. But thanks for the great idea."

She swept her hand in front of them. "You'd better go first."

She followed him up the great staircase, admiring the carved woodwork, running her hand along the smooth, solid banister. Its girth and solidity were comforting. This house had been around for a long time. And it might be a little battered, but it was still a gem. Or at least, they might help it to become one again.

For a family lucky enough to appreciate it.

"It's beautiful, isn't it?" he asked, watching her carefully from the top of the stairs.

She traced her hands along the thick spindles. "I bet at one time it smelled like lemon oil."

They both stopped and leaned their arms on the banister, looking down at the foyer. "Do you know anything about the previous owners?" Alex asked.

She shook her head. "It belonged to Carson's great-grandparents. That's all I really know. But I wonder who built this house right on the harbor, and did they have a gaggle of kids and a couple of cats and dogs, or were they very straitlaced and formal?" As soon as she spoke, she felt her face heating up. She'd just given him more ammo to poke fun.

Instead, he looked thoughtful, tapping his fingers together. Which happened to showcase that his arms were corded with muscle. "I'd like to think the kids who lived here slid down the banister when their mom wasn't looking."

Alex straightened and started walking down the long, paneled hallway. He'd better be trustworthy about his intentions in bringing her up here because no one would ever find her body if he wasn't. As she followed him, her phone rang again. "Yes, Ollie?" she asked with forced patience.

"When are you coming home, Mommy?" Ollie asked. "Grammy doesn't know how to dress me."

She glanced at her watch. "I'll be home in ten minutes."

"Do I have to go? My tummy still hurts."

"Finish dressing and I'll be home to check your tummy. After the game, we'll get ice cream. Doesn't that sound like fun?"

Ollie barely perked up at the mention of his favorite thing. She disconnected, knowing she had to get home.

"He plays Tee ball, your son?" Alex asked.

"Yes, but he didn't do so well the last game, and some of the kids gave him a hard time."

"No one likes to be laughed at."

"I've been practicing with him, trying to get his confidence up." She bit the inside of her cheek.

"That's tough," he said, actually sounding sympathetic. "Sometimes it just takes a little time." He jiggled the doorknob. "I won't keep you, but do you happen to know what's in here? It's the only locked door."

It was her turn to quirk a smile. "Mr. Rochester's wife?"

He let out a whoop, tossing his head back. "I certainly hope not. Do you think you might have a key somewhere?"

She didn't really register the question. Because as she'd predicted, hearing him laugh was really something else. Its deep quality resonated through her and set her to chuckling too. The look in his eyes, which always seemed to be weighed down by some unknown burdens, lightened and lifted.

Her heart felt much safer when he was Mr. Crabby Pants. "I don't know of a key, but I can definitely check."

He dug into his pocket and produced a tiny, thin screwdriver. "Mind if I have a go at it?"

She waved her hand with a dramatic flourish. "Be my guest."

Alex inserted the tool between the door frame and the jamb and wiggled it until something clicked. The door popped open to reveal a dark space with dust motes circling in the dim light filtering in from a shuttered window.

"Do you really think you should—" But he was already shining his phone light into the dark space. She looked over his shoulder, which she couldn't help noticing was broad, and also that, up close like this, he smelled good, with just a faint tinge of lingering mothball. "I'm definitely staying out here in case you—"

He glanced back, his eyes full of amusement. And he was way too close. "In case I get sucked into a portal or something?"

"I was thinking more of encountering spiders," she said. "I guess the portal *could* happen if there's an old wardrobe in there too."

He gave a small chuckle before walking in. Before them was the hulking shape of a large rectangular object—a table.

"Well, I'll be," he said, running a hand along the surface. "Take a look at this. Like my abuela's dining room table times three. And that's saying a lot because she feeds, like, three dozen of us for the holidays."

Three dozen? Wouldn't a big family tend to make a person more gregarious and social? she couldn't help wondering. "That's my family times three," she said, backing out of the room. "Well, I've got to get going," she added just as Alex dragged something out into the light. It was a chair with an intricately carved back and a red velvet seat.

Alex smoothed his hands over the dusty wood. "If I'm not mistaken, this carving matches the carving in the molding around the dining room ceiling. It must've been specially made for that room." He replaced the chair and looked around the room. "There are more leaves against the wall. We could invite the entire town for dinner."

"So what do we do with Mr. Rochester's dining room table?" she asked as he replaced the chair, shut the door behind him, and dusted off his hands.

"It might be a selling point," he said, "in a town like this where everyone loves period furniture."

"All right, then. I'm just relieved there are no dead bodies in there."

"Not yet." He gave her a pseudo-warning look, but it had the effect of making her stare at him a few heartbeats too long. For the first time, she really looked at him. He had nice eyes when he was joking around. Brown and warm and expressive.

Good thing for her he almost never joked around. She

averted her gaze and headed for the stairs. "Is that all for now? I've got to head home."

"Yes. But do we have an agreement?"

She stopped and turned. A little too abruptly because he almost ran into her and had to steady himself by placing a hand on her elbow.

"An agreement?"

"Yes. I just wanted to be clear about how involved you want to be."

It felt like a challenge, rather than permission to back down. Maybe it was Alex's orneriness, but Kit felt a sudden surprising desire to be ornery too. To not show weakness. To fight back.

She kept her voice steady and professional, although she felt as out of place as Seymour the cat. "I want to have a say in the things you're ordering. And maybe I can help you hunt some of them down. Sound okay?"

"As you wish," he said. His lips were pressed tightly together, as if there was a whole lot he'd like to say but was keeping it in. But at least he seemed to be in slightly better humor than before.

"I'll do everything I can to help you with the legwork," she said. "That way we get it done as fast as we can."

"Okay," he said, his tone resolute. He offered a hand.

She took it. The contact made her suck in a breath. Not because of Darla's ring, although it pressed a little against her finger just then. But rather because of Alex. He had a strong grip and beautiful long fingers. But it was the way he held her hand—firm, yet gentle, that somehow got to her. A little unnerved, she looked at him to find him staring at her. For an uncomfortable moment, their gazes locked.

Kit's brain emptied of all coherent thought. Including

how to move her arms, legs, or mouth. Then Alex dropped his hand, as if suddenly discovering she had poison ivy. Clearing his throat, he said, "Listen, Kit, full disclosure. I may have to spend one more night here. Is that all right with you? I got a lead on an Airbnb but it's not available until tomorrow."

Three words jolted through her mind and then rose to her lips. *The. Garage. Apartment.* She quickly bit them back. What would her dad think about her letting a man with the body of Hercules stay fifty feet away from her house? Also, it was a plain fact that no one in Seashell Harbor ever missed an opportunity for gossip. And a man who looked like Alex would definitely send tongues wagging.

But mainly, how would she handle having someone so…disturbing…as close as her garbage cans?

"If you feel uncomfortable with that—"

"No, of course not." She shifted to Plan B. "Listen, why don't you come over to my parents' place? There's a pull-out couch in the basement, and it's a lot better than this. We even have blankets."

Alex shook his head. "To be honest, I'd rather just work late and crash here, if that's all right. It's only for one more night."

"Of course. Sure. No problem." The words tumbled rapidly out of her mouth as she gathered up her purse and got herself outside.

Okay, so she'd chickened out on offering him the garage apartment. But she'd done some other things she was a little proud of. Having a say in fixing up this house was the right thing to do. She felt it in her gut. Carson would never live here, but she would make it beautiful in honor of him.

And she felt that somehow, in saying goodbye to this house, maybe she'd be able to say goodbye to him too.

* * *

A loud grinding sound made Alex run out the door, only to nearly collide with Kit, who was standing there watching a cement truck block the driveway behind her car. He had to steady himself by grabbing her shoulders, which he quickly let go of like they were on fire. Actually, he seemed to be experiencing plenty of heat—and a whole bunch of other unwelcome sensations just from being near her.

The drum of the truck was churning as it prepared to do the front step pour. Alex ran to talk to one of the men outside the truck then jogged back to Kit.

"They're going to be a while." Alex dug into his pocket for his car keys. "Hop in my truck. I'll drive you home."

"Thanks," she said gratefully, already heading to the curb.

Once he'd pulled out and things were quiet again, she said, "I'm sorry to interrupt your work, but I really appreciate the ride."

"No problem," Alex said. A brief glance in her direction showed him the worried expression on her face. "So your son hates Tee ball?" came out of his mouth before he could stop himself. Hadn't he decided *Nothing personal* was supposed to be his mantra?

Kit rubbed her forehead. "Well, Ollie's not a natural at it, and even at five years old, the other kids seem to know that. I've bought him all the equipment to practice with, but frankly I'm not much better than he is at it. And

Cam's come over to help him, and my dad, and... and I'm trying to get him through this and have it be a positive experience." She looked out the window and sighed a little. "But it's actually pretty painful."

Alex tapped his fingers on the wheel, a thousand thoughts ricocheting through his head. "Kids can be mean to other kids who are different in any way."

She flashed a grin that he felt down to his toes. "Says a guy who's probably amazing at any sport he's ever tried."

"Well, I do love sports." He was quiet for a minute, debating whether or not he should continue. "I was adopted when I was seven. I really lucked out with my family, but when you're adopted, especially that late, I think you have a healthy distrust of a lot of things. And you feel different." He did his best to flash her a reassuring smile. Mainly because she still looked so worried.

"Ollie started speech therapy for his lisp, which has never really been an issue until now, and I thought Tee ball would sort of give him some friends before kindergarten starts and some confidence and be a fun thing this summer, but it just seems to be making everything worse."

"The idea at his age is having fun," Alex agreed. "Have you talked to the coach?"

"Yes, and he said he'd look out for him. But Ollie's a sensitive soul. Maybe because he's an only child and doesn't have siblings to rough him up a little." She shrugged. "Sorry, that's way more than you wanted to hear."

"Hey, I asked, didn't I?" He liked listening to her. And she seemed to need someone to talk to. As Alex pulled up in front of her parents' little colonial, they found her dad tossing a ball with Ollie in the yard. Ollie missed a catch, dropped his glove, and came running over to the car.

"Mommy! We can't find my pants. So I can't go to my game." Ollie's lower lip was pulled out in a fake pout that looked to Alex like he wasn't very sad about it. Then Ollie looked over at the driver's seat and smiled. "Hi, Alex!"

"Hey, Oliver." Alex gave a nod.

Kit looked from one to the other. "You two know each other?"

"We met at breakfast this morning," Alex said just as her dad came walking over. Alex got out of the car to shake hands with him.

"This is my daddy's best friend," Ollie said, tugging on his grandfather's pants.

"Nice to see you again, son," the Admiral said. "Kit's been telling us you're taking on that old house."

"Yes, sir. Kit and I were just discussing it."

Kit and I. Saying that made him hyperaware of her. Of *them* together. In a way he didn't want to be.

"Well, you'll have to come to dinner sometime soon."

"I'd like that, sir," he said just to be polite. *Nothing personal*, he reminded himself.

"So, Dad, about the pants," Kit said. "I washed them and left them on the dryer yesterday. I'm sure of it."

"We've looked everywhere," the Admiral said. "Come on, Oliver," he said to his grandson. "Let's go have another look."

Kit turned to Alex. "Thanks for the ride." She started to walk up to the front door. "I'll grab a ride from Ollie's game to get my car."

"Sure, of course." He started to head back to his car and then turned around. "Kit?"

"Yes?" she asked, one hand on the doorknob.

"Maybe check under his pillow."

She blinked in surprise. As if that was the last thing she'd expected him to say. "What?"

"Maybe he hid them. Under his pillow, under the bed, in his book bag..."

"Ollie's never hidden anything before."

He shrugged. "Just a thought."

"Okay. Well, thanks again for the ride."

"No problem." Alex got back into his truck and sat there parked near the curb on the tidy residential street, watching kids play a few doors down in a front yard. Then he punched a few buttons. "Hey, Nick," he said when Nick picked up. "I think I'll join you guys for pizza tonight after all."

As he hung up and pulled away, he told himself he couldn't just sit around and watch while Carson's kid got beat up, could he? "I've got your back, buddy," he said to Carson, and tried not to think that any of his reasons for trying to help involved a pretty woman with sass and an awful lot on her plate who he wanted to strangle as much as he wanted to kiss.

Chapter 9

"I HAVE TO sit down in the front and pay attention," Kit said to her friends, hiking her thumb three rows down from where they were sitting on the bleachers. "So I can't talk."

Ollie's teammates were all sitting on the bench, but Ollie was off to the side, kicking up dirt with his cleats.

"Poor Ollie." Hadley clutched her chest. "My heart is breaking for him. Maybe I don't want to be a parent."

"Go help him," Darla said, "because we want our happy Ollie back. And say hi to the hot dads."

"They're not hot dads," Kit said. "Well, maybe some of them are, but I don't care about that. I just need to help Ollie."

Darla gave her a nudge and tipped her head toward the field. "Looks like there might be reinforcements on the way."

Kit turned to see three men walking toward the

bleachers, silhouetted by the ocean and the late-afternoon sun.

Cam and Nick and...Alex.

Alex. At her son's Tee ball game. Yikes.

Lauren, a children's librarian who was Nick's latest and longest girlfriend, was sitting with her friends a few bleachers away and waved excitedly. Nick waved back.

"Alex is staring at you," Hadley said.

Also...he was laughing and joking with the guys. Kit's first thought was how handsome he looked, striding confidently across the field with her friends. But why was he here? Was he some kind of control freak with a very misguided loyalty to Carson?

The men reached the bleachers and stood talking to the dads in the front row. Lauren raced down and gave Nick a giant hug.

"Ugh," Darla said. "I know Lauren's a loveable children's librarian, plus Nick's dated her longer than any of his other girlfriends, but I just feel that she doesn't like me."

"Maybe she perceives you as a threat," Kit said.

"Hey, everybody," Nick said, grinning in an easy way that showcased his dimples. He gave a nod in Darla's direction. "Dar, okay if I come over later and work on that backsplash?"

Next to Kit, Darla colored as she gave a quick nod. Meanwhile, Lauren slipped her hand through Nick's arm and held on tight.

At least to Kit, the tension of unfinished business between Nick and Darla was off the charts. And she'd bet her lunch that Lauren sensed it too.

"So why are you surprised to see Alex here?" Darla

asked before Kit could ask about why Nick was working on her backsplash.

Kit shrugged. "I just sort of had it out with him about the house. I told him that I wanted a say in all the decisions."

"That's great," Hadley said. "You've always had great taste. That little apartment you and Carson fixed up was adorable."

"I don't know how great it is because we're butting heads with every decision. I think he's kind of a control freak."

"Wait." Darla lifted a brow. "How is he a control freak?"

"Well, he seems to have everything planned out a certain way. But he also offered advice about Ollie."

"What kind of advice?" Hadley asked.

"When the cement truck blocked my car, he gave me a ride home. Ollie was fussing about losing his pants, and he told me to look under Ollie's pillow."

"And?" Darla asked.

"They weren't under the pillow, but they were wedged between the head of Ollie's bed and the wall."

"Clever hiding place," Darla said, "but Alex offering a suggestion on Ollie's behalf doesn't exactly scream *control freak.*"

"But he's here, at Ollie's game," Hadley said. "That's a little unusual, isn't it?"

"Maybe he's just hanging out with the guys," Darla said.

"Or maybe he's here for you," Hadley said.

"No, no, no," Kit said, extending her hands. "He can't stand me. Never has. He's just got this fierce loyalty to Carson that's now extending to Ollie too."

Kit didn't miss the look her two friends exchanged. Like they didn't believe that at all. "There's more," she said. She'd gone this far. She might as well tell them the rest. "I found him curled up in an old sheet, sleeping in the house. His mom rented out her house for the summer. He doesn't have a place to stay."

"Well, there's nothing you can do about that," Darla said, always the no-nonsense one.

"Actually, there is." Kit's stomach flopped. "I'm just not sure if it's the right thing to do."

"What do you mean there's something you can do?" Hadley asked.

"Well, you know I'm renting your gran's place for the summer," Kit said to Hadley.

"She told me, and I think that's terrific," Hadley said.

"Oh, wow," Darla said. "I love that place. Bold move."

"It has a garage apartment. Of course, I'd have to ask your grandmother if it would be okay to have Alex use it. And I don't really want to, but the whole town is booked. Plus he's spending all his own money on this house and . . ."

"My grandmother is great friends with Alex's mother, you know that, right?" Hadley sounded way too excited. "She loves the guy."

"I don't really want him living in my garage." Kit crossed her arms. "He's . . . grumpy." The honest part of her knew *grumpy* wasn't the correct word at all.

Darla laughed and gave her a look.

"What?" Kit demanded.

"It's probably always a bad idea to have a hot guy living in your backyard."

How did her best friends always put their finger right smack on the truth?

"Yes, but I would never—"

Darla interrupted her protest. "Kit, why would you

never? He's gorgeous. Those melty chocolate eyes. That super-hot bod."

"He was Carson's best friend. And...I'm obligated to him for what he's doing. And he doesn't think of me like that. He's...annoying. I'm more worried about what this arrangement would look like to everyone else."

"Who cares?" Darla asked. "You're thirty-five, not twenty." But then Darla was brave and bold, from making the decision to end her marriage, to surviving chemo, to working her way up the bestseller list. Unlike Kit, who always analyzed her decisions from every angle.

"I think it's a nice thing to offer a guy who's sacrificing two months of his life to do this," Hadley said. "Even so, I can't really see the Admiral taking it very well," she admitted.

"About that," Kit said reluctantly. "I haven't told my parents that I'm moving out yet."

Her comment was met with silence, which spoke volumes.

"Hey, Gran," Hadley called to her grandmother, who had just arrived with Paul and was taking a seat a row away.

Gran gave a huge smile and walked over to say hi.

Hadley took hold of Kit's arm and addressed her grandmother. "Gran, Alex de la Cruz needs a place to stay while he's working on the house. How about your garage apartment?"

Kit felt her face burning up, and it wasn't due to the late-afternoon sun in their eyes. She shot a glare in Hadley's direction, but Hadley seemed oblivious.

"Oh." Gran turned and waved to Cam and the guys before speaking. "I think Alex is a fine man. And I love what he's doing for Kit. It's fine with me, but that decision is up to her."

"If I do it," Kit said hurriedly, "I'd pay extra rent for him."

Maddy waved a dismissive hand. "Nonsense. The only payment I'd require is that the apartment gets cleaned and scrubbed out. Frankly, I'm not even sure if the plumbing's working."

"Well, thanks for the option, Mrs. E," Kit said, ignoring Hadley's smug smile. "I'll think about it."

Darla suddenly pointed to where the boys were gathered on the field. "Kit, look at that."

Kit was suddenly filled with dread as she reoriented herself to what was going on. She'd been so wrapped up in her own problems that she'd lost track of Ollie. She was a terrible Tee ball mom.

"That tall kid just hid Ollie's bat on purpose, and now he's laughing."

Sure enough, Ollie rose from the bench and went looking for it, searching underneath and behind it where the kids had left their equipment. In the process, the same kid tipped Ollie's hat off.

"Who is that?" Hadley stood up with her hands on her hips.

Kit's heart sank. "Oh no."

Darla answered for her. "That's Toby, Bryan's son."

"The Bryan she has a date with?" Hadley asked.

"I don't care whose son he is." Kit's voice shook with a tone of outrage she rarely used. "Or if he's the crown prince of Tee ball. I've had enough."

* * *

Alex had been chatting with Nick and Cam and a few of the dads as well as keeping an eye on what was going on with Ollie. Unfortunately, like a teenage kid watching his crush out of the corner of his eye, he also saw Kit's reaction and the moment she started barreling down the bleachers, white tennies pounding.

She'd just passed by when Alex stuck out his hand and hooked her gently by the elbow. "Whoa there, Mama Bear."

Her lips were pursed together, and her fists were balled. Everything about her spelled out a woman not to be messed with. Surprise and shock flashed in her eyes as she shook her elbow free. "That...bully—"

"I've been watching everything," he said in his calmest voice. "And I think you should hold up a minute."

"Hold up a minute?" she said, her anger now directed at him.

Yikes. If *he* felt her wrath, what would that unfortunate boy who was giving Ollie trouble feel?

"Well, you can do what you want," he continued, "but in my opinion, it's not going to help Ollie if you run out there and rescue him."

"Why not?" she asked between gritted teeth.

"Calling that kid out might embarrass Ollie in front of the other boys. A lot of them don't even know what's going on, so why make them aware?"

Kit took a breath, in what he saw as an attempt to calm down. Her fierce need to protect her kid was really appealing. Just as appealing as the fire in her eyes and the fact that she didn't care what anyone thought.

He'd hoped to find she'd become abrasive. Or timid. She was neither of those things. All this was proving to him that the woman he'd come here to forget was even better than he'd remembered.

Meaning, he was screwed.

"Okay, Alex." She was still gritting her teeth. "What do you suggest I do, let that bully torment my son while I stand here and watch?"

He crossed his arms, attempting to appear casual. "I'd suggest a two-pronged approach."

"Can you just speak plain English?"

"Tell the coach to talk to that kid. Or I'd be happy to talk with the coach if you want."

"I can handle it," she said stiffly. "What's the second prong?"

"Work on Ollie's confidence. We can talk about that later."

She scanned his face, giving him an *Are you for real?* look, and then ran up to the coach, who was helping direct a kid with a scraped knee to a mom on the bleachers who had the first-aid box. "You'll be fine, buddy," the coach said. "Dr. Simmons will fix you right up."

Alex stayed right where he was so he could hear the conversation.

"Bryan," Kit said as he released the sniffling child into the care of the doc, "I have to speak to you for a minute."

"Oh, hi, Kit," the coach said, smiling widely. Alex's heart sank as he immediately noted the unmistakable way the coach looked Kit over from head to toe. "What's up?"

"I've been watching from the stands, and I can't help but notice that Toby is causing Ollie some grief."

Bryan took off his cap and scratched his head. "What do you mean?"

"He hid Ollie's bat and tipped his hat off."

"Oh no," he said, genuinely concerned. "I was distracted by that little skinned knee. I missed that." He immediately walked over to where the kids were supposed to be sitting on the bench. But several of them were poking at ant hills with sticks. Ollie was sitting miserably by himself, clutching his bat.

"Toby, come here." Bryan directed his son over to Ollie and recapped the infractions. "What have you got to say to Ollie?"

"Sorry," Toby mumbled.

"It's all right," Ollie said in his usual sweet, forgiving tone. But he wasn't making much eye contact. Stressed for sure.

"Okay, you two," Bryan said. "Head back to the bench, okay? The game's about to start." Bryan turned to Kit and dropped his voice, but still loud enough that Alex could hear.

"Listen," Bryan said. "Toby's still taking the divorce pretty hard. We've been going to counseling. And we're addressing the bullying thing. I'm sorry I didn't catch that just now. I hope it doesn't prevent you from giving me another chance. And I really hope you still want to go out with me."

Alex's brows shot up despite himself. This guy had asked her *out*?

Kit gave him a kind smile. "I appreciate that you're aware of the problem. And I'm hopeful we can work it out. So I'm still fine with next Friday night, if you are."

The coach grinned. "Terrific. I promise you I'll work on this with Ollie and the team." He turned to the boys. "Okay, guys, leave the ants alone. Back to the game."

Alex had just turned to head back to where Cam and Nick were sitting when he heard his name.

Sure enough, Kit was walking up to him. He tried not to notice her pretty tanned legs. Even in a T-shirt and jean shorts, she looked like...like his downfall. He wished he could flip a switch and turn off the raging hormones that seemed targeted just at her.

"Thank you for slowing me down," she said. "I hate to say this, but you were right."

He chuckled.

"Why are you laughing at me?"

"Not at you," he corrected. "You actually said I was right. That's a first."

"Well, don't get used to it," she said jokingly. "I'm not sure how effective prong A was, but at least the coach is aware of the problem. It makes sense that I need to attack the problem at Ollie's level. Help him to figure this out himself."

"Kids at this age have short memories. If Ollie can stand on his own, they'll forget."

"How likely is that? I mean, with a bad start?"

"You'd be surprised." My goodness, she was a cool drink of water, with those big green eyes and that dark hair, little wisps around her face blowing about from the ocean breeze.

Something about her made him want to promise that everything would be all right. He *wanted* to make it okay.

But he knew she didn't want or need that.

"Well, thanks for helping me not embarrass Ollie," she said. "But I can't promise not to run out there and wreak havoc again on anyone who upsets my sweet son."

He stared at her a long time. "Your sweet son is tougher than you think."

There was a long pause, punctuated by kids yelling and laughing in the background. The ballpark was bathed in buttery late-afternoon sunlight that foretold of long, lazy summer days ahead.

"You *are* a little bossy," she said, shaking her head. "But honest. Maybe I've...lost my equilibrium a little, you know? Carson was always more levelheaded than I am. So...thanks for the intervention."

"No problem," he said.

Except she had a date with the Abercrombie model—oops, he meant the coach.

As he turned to sit down with the guys, she tapped him on the arm and tried to hand him an envelope.

"I don't want your money." He frowned as he stared at it.

"It's not money." She laughed. "It's a key."

"What's it for?" he asked, puzzled. Her handwriting was perfect, beautiful, and curvy. Just like her.

He shook his head of those rogue thoughts and tried to pay attention.

"I'm about to move into a rental house, and there happens to be a very basic one-room apartment over the garage." She rushed on before he could interrupt her. "My landlady told me it's mine to do with what I want, as long as I vet the person well. Not that you look formidable or anything." She chuckled as she nudged the envelope toward him. "Only when you're frowning. You aren't a serial killer, are you?"

He realized that they were both still hanging on to the envelope, which was a little weird, so he quickly let go. "You're giving me access to a garage apartment when you haven't even moved in yet?" He frowned. "And I'm only a serial killer during the full moon."

She chuckled at his joke. "Truth is, it belongs to Hadley's grandmother, and she already thinks way too highly of you. I really believe Carson would insist. And...so do I. This is the least I can do."

"I don't think I—"

She pushed his hand and the envelope toward his chest. "Think about it, okay? From what I've seen, the space is hot and dusty, and there's no oven, and I don't even know if the window air conditioner works, let alone the plumbing. After I pick up my car, I'll drop off some sheets and towels, and in the meantime, you can check it out. If you want." She paused and gave him an assessing look and a shrug. "It beats sleeping on the floor."

Before he could object, she was gone, running her very fine behind up the bleachers to her seat.

He turned his attention to the game, where Ollie had stepped up to bat, his chin set in the exact same angle he'd just seen on his mom.

Alex had come back home determined to fly solo, to only interact in ways he had to, yet he was finding himself more and more involved. Before he could think about that, Ollie struck out again, painfully. In the bleachers, Alex noticed Kit gnawing on her lower lip.

"It's okay, Ollie," Cam called out. "You'll knock it out of the park next time, bud."

"Hey, Alex," Nick said, nudging him, "we're all heading over to Scoops for ice cream later. Come with us."

"Sounds great," he found himself answering.

Involved with the troubles of a pretty widow and her little son. And he couldn't seem to help himself.

Chapter 10

"BUT I DON'T *want* to leave Grammy and Grampy's," Ollie said from the back seat of their overly stuffed twelve-year-old Ford Escort as they made the short drive on Saturday morning to their new digs.

"We're only moving a mile and a half away." Kit watched in the rearview mirror as her son ate fruit snacks amid suitcases brimming with their clothes, a box of Ollie's favorite books, and his favorite stuffed owl, Hoot, which he was holding close. Some of the other boxes came from her parents' attic, never-used gifts from her wedding that she didn't even remember opening.

There was a lesson in that. *Don't wait for life to really start.* At least, that's what she was trying to tell herself today.

"This will be an adventure," she said, pumping up her voice with positivity.

"But I liked my room at Grammy and Grampy's," Ollie

whined as they halted at a stop sign. "And we don't have a fence at our new house. What if Rex gets lost?"

In response, Rex, who was in the passenger seat, reached over and licked her face in a rare display of affection. Probably to get on her good side before he started tracking sand all over the house.

"Well, we *are* going to have to watch Rex, but he's going to be the happiest dog alive, living right on the beach. He can take a swim in the ocean every day." She turned down Gladiola Lane and drove past the line of pastel beach cottages with beach roses and lavender poking their blooms through picket fences.

Gladiolas happened to be Kit's favorite old-fashioned flower, even though they weren't quite in bloom yet. *Gladius* meant "sword" in Latin. It was a flower of strength, which she needed a lot of. It seemed fitting for now and one of the reasons this decision just felt right.

"Ollie, you'll have your own room." Kit was determined to get him to love their new place. "You won't have to share with the yarn." She didn't want Ollie to be afraid of new things. She wanted him to feel that they were both moving on with their lives. And she didn't want all her fears to make *him* fearful.

"But I like the yarn," he said just to be ornery as he looked out the window.

She thought back to the Tee ball game earlier this week, when she went barreling down the bleachers and Alex had quietly tugged her back. Which had initially infuriated her. But those few moments of reassessment had prevented her from making things worse.

She had no clue how to strike a balance between being afraid herself yet not being too protective of Ollie.

But like everything else, she was going to do her best to figure it out.

And she had no clue how to deal with Alex. The more she got to know him, the less he seemed to be the gruff, disinterested person she'd thought he was.

In fact, when he wasn't being obstinate and poker faced, he was kind of... nice.

But not *that* nice. And now he'd suddenly become her new next-door neighbor, thanks to the fact that he'd accepted her invitation. Which made her stomach feel even more uneasy.

As she pulled into the driveway, she reminded herself that she'd actually accomplished something. She'd moved her stuff out of her parents' place. Amid some head shakes and doubtful looks and a hefty dose of complaining from Ollie.

But she'd still done it.

Now she was going to make this an amazing summer for Ollie. When he started school in the fall, he was going to be relaxed and confident and excited. She'd make sure of it.

She'd already strung patio lights in the back and bought him a cute bedspread with boats on it. They'd plan picnics on the beach and build sandcastles and search for shells. She'd teach him the joys of growing up by the ocean, and she'd show him that they could have a good life, even though it wasn't one she'd ever expected.

"Here we are," she said to her son, unable to help the little tinge of excitement in her voice. Ollie must have picked up on it because she finally got a smile out of him. Rex, who was pressing his face against the window in excitement, bolted right out her side as she opened the door. Kit kissed Ollie on the head, hiked him out of his booster seat, and spun him around before setting him down on the gravel drive. The dog, certain that was a fun new game, leaped right along with them.

"Let's go to the beach!" Kit clipped on Rex's leash and ran past the house onto the sand. Scattered groups of people were sitting under multicolored umbrellas at an already sun-washed ten in the morning, and a warm, salt-tinged breeze was blowing off the water that she could only describe as the smell of home.

"Can we make sand angels?" Ollie asked excitedly. "Can we, Mommy?"

It was a thing they'd been doing ever since Ollie was old enough to plop down in the sand and wave his arms and legs.

"Sure!" A feeling ran through Kit that she could only describe as lightness. Something that loosened some of the knots that had been binding her up.

Kit kicked off her shoes and ran through the warm, grainy sand, scooping Ollie up again like an airplane until he threw out his arms.

Once the plane landed, Ollie said, "Do this, Mom!" while spinning around in circles, giggling all the way.

It felt so good to hear her son laugh. She tilted her head back and whirled, bumping into him a little on purpose to make him laugh more. She spun around one more time and bumped straight into Ollie again. Except this time it wasn't Ollie.

It was a big, hard block of a man, as she could tell by the firm, steadying grip on her arms that made her feel anything but anchored to the ground. Dizzy and still a little giddy, she turned to face Alex. "Oh, sorry!"

Alex stood there in sunglasses, swim trunks, and flip-flops, a towel slung across one shoulder. And no shirt.

Suddenly she noticed that his hand on her elbow was warm. And that warmth shot up her arm and into the rest of her body like she'd just stepped into a hot shower.

Discombobulated, she stepped back.

A glance over at Ollie found him obliviously digging in the sand. The dog bolted over to Alex, leaping and jumping, basically ecstatic to see him. "Hiya, Rex," he said, stooping to give him a rubdown.

Kit shook her head in disbelief. "I've never seen him so wound up, except with Carson."

Ollie edged over, not quite sure what to make of things. "You know my doggie?" he asked.

"Very well." Alex straightened to his full height. "I knew Rex when he was a puppy. I lived with your dad in an apartment before he married your mom." He addressed Rex. "You remember me, don't you?"

The dog sat stock-still at Alex's feet, looking up at him adoringly, his tail going a million miles an hour.

Unbelievable. Sometimes it seemed Rex preferred anyone over her.

Alex stroked the dog's silky black fur. "You remember all those movies we watched and all that pizza we ate, don't you? Well, I remember too. And you've grown into a fine dog. Yes, you have."

The dog, who had edged over to sniff his face, licked him from the chin up. Alex laughed, which made Ollie laugh.

He looked at the boy. "When Rex was a puppy, he loved to dig in the sand."

"Still does," Kit said.

Ollie patted Kit's arm to get her attention. "Can we make sand angels with Alex, Mommy? Can we?"

"Ollie, Alex probably doesn't want to get all sandy."

Alex hurriedly said, "I like sand angels." To Kit he whispered, "I think. What's a sand angel?"

He grinned good-naturedly. Which completely knocked the Mr. Crankypants version out of her head. And made her feel a little light-headed.

Ollie promptly dropped into the soft sand and started waving his arms and legs. Well, so much for keeping sand out of the house. And they hadn't even moved in yet.

"Come on, Mom. You promised."

Well, she had promised. So Kit focused on Ollie—and didn't look at Alex at all because he was so distracting—and shrugged. "I guess I did." She dropped into the sand and did the same thing, reminding herself she was doing this for Ollie and wasn't going to care about acting foolish. Then she got up, dusted herself off, and tugged Ollie up to examine their masterpieces.

"Lovely," she said as Ollie proudly inspected his angel and then Kit's.

"That's really nice, Oliver," Alex said. Then he lowered his voice and smiled at Kit. "Oh, look, yours has little horns." He put his fingers up on his head. "Maybe it's not an angel at all."

"You're bad!" she scolded. Then she frowned. "Did you just crack a joke?"

"See? The devil made me do it." Then he ran to Ollie, scooping him up and setting him down on the sand, then diving into the sand himself and flailing his arms and legs. "Is this how you do it?"

Kit stood there with her mouth agape. Because not only did he crack a joke and smile, but he was also rolling in the sand with her son, laughing.

Her mom radar suddenly picked up that Rex was gone. All because she'd gotten distracted by an amazing set of abs. How embarrassing. "Oh no, I lost the dog!" She shielded her eyes and scoured the sandy landscape where she spotted him, trailing a couple pretty far down the beach who were strolling close to the water's edge.

Alex sat up in the sand, put two fingers in his mouth, and gave a loud whistle. "Rex!" he called commandingly.

The dog froze, ears at alert, then turned and plowed full-speed through the sand back to them.

Alex, who had gotten up, clapped his hands. "Good boy! Atta boy, Rexy, come on!"

"How is this dog listening to you?" Kit asked incredulously from his side. She couldn't help but notice his tan arms. His perfect muscles. His rippled, sandy back. "This dog listens to *no one*."

Alex shrugged. His lighthearted expression made him look boyish. "Rex and I are old buds." The dog came barreling at Alex, and Alex dodged aside at the last minute, sending Rex to put on the brakes, reverse course, and scamper back for more shenanigans.

"Come on, Ollie," Kit said as Ollie headed over to join the fun. "We have a lot of unpacking to do."

"Can we go see the ocean, Mommy? Just for a minute? Please?"

It was going to take an hour to pry Ollie away from this beach and get to work. Against her better judgment, she said, "For just a minute."

"Oliver, my man," Alex said, giving him a fist bump, "you are going to *love* living at the ocean." Ollie giggled, and Alex tousled his hair. "Later, 'gator."

"Later, alligator!" Ollie replied, already running ahead.

As Ollie took off, Alex said, "I'd better be getting back."

"Ollie, wait for me," Kit called. Turning to Alex, she asked, "Is everything okay with the apartment?"

He gave a slow smile. "Beats sleeping in mothball sheets, for sure. Thank you." He leveled his deep brown gaze at her. "Do you need any help unloading? I was going to grab a quick swim and then head back to work."

"Thanks, but we've got it." He looked a little disappointed. Did the man live to serve? She walked backward toward the beach a few paces. "You know, it's okay to…relax. It's Saturday."

He looked a little puzzled.

"Don't tell me—you typically work on Saturdays."

He hiked a thumb behind his shoulder, toward town. "Well, I *was* just over at the house."

"Come on, Mommy!" Ollie cried, running ahead. Rex ran at Ollie's side, until he spied a group of college kids near the water and took off again.

"I'd better go." She commanded her feet to get moving, but her gaze got snared with his.

"See you," he said, his mouth turned up just the slightest bit.

Fifteen minutes later, Kit cut the beach expedition short when a toe-dip in the water turned into Ollie getting smacked by a wave and getting happily drenched. The only way she could get him out of the water was to promise to return later after all their stuff was unloaded.

As they reached the bungalow and walked the little pathway to the front of the house, Kit noticed that the heap of their possessions filling her car to the brim was…missing. Her first thought wasn't thieves. She looked around but her new tenant was nowhere in sight.

"Where's all our stuff?" Ollie asked.

Kit walked the dog over to the bungalow's side door and opened it. Rex beat her in, immediately circling their pile of stuff in the middle of the kitchen floor. He immediately managed to sniff out his bag of dog food.

Everything was there: the box with her toaster oven and her coffee maker, her computer bag; two large suitcases, stuffed to the brim; and a box of framed photos. Hoot sat atop Ollie's book bag. Carefully placed, not randomly tossed.

"Hoot's here!" Ollie grabbed his owl and hugged him to his chest.

Kit heard the garage door close, so she ran outside to find Alex, now with earbuds in his ears, preparing to head back to the beach.

"Hey," she called from her door.

He pushed a button on his phone and looked up. "Yes?"

For a moment, the sight of him, with swim trunks and flip-flops and sunglasses, made her flounder.

"I... Thank you for unloading our stuff, but you didn't have to—"

"Just 'thank you' is good," he said, cutting her off. Then he flashed a smile. Two in one day. And it nearly took her breath away. "You know," he said, "you really should lock your car. Because you just don't know who your neighbors are around here." Then he gave a nod and continued on his way.

Kit turned back, fanning herself a little.

"Who did it, Mommy? Did Alex do it?" Ollie asked, Hoot in one hand and a book in the other. Rex had managed to tip the dog food bag over and was happily chomping away.

"He surprised us," she said.

Yes, he certainly had.

Chapter 11

THAT AFTERNOON WHEN Alex walked up to the white frame cottage on the edge of downtown that housed his mom's art gallery, he was met by none other than Maddy Edwards, selling a watercolor of a sailboat on the ocean to a tourist. Then he spotted his mom wearing a floppy yellow sun hat and sitting under the old oak tree in the tiny front yard, painting. Blown-glass suncatchers on iron sticks poked into the grass, and others made from sea glass tinkled gently in the breeze as they hung from the front porch.

"Alex! There you are!" Maddy stopped wrapping the painting and gave him a big hug. "Home at last. We're all so proud of you!"

"Hey, Maddy." The older woman often helped out his mom in the artist co-op and gallery she owned that show-cased local artists and their wares.

His mom looked up from her painting and smiled,

her colorful earrings swaying. She'd let her hair go gray since he'd seen her last, but she was still youthful and vibrant-looking. And her deep brown eyes were just as sharply assessing as ever. "Alejandro," she said. "Come here and give me a hug." She embraced him exuberantly and kissed him soundly on the cheek. "You're even more handsome than when I saw you last."

"*Bendición*, Mami." He gave her the traditional Puerto Rican greeting, hugging her back. "But I just saw you yesterday for breakfast. What are you working on?" His mom was sweeping thick brush strokes of yellow paint across a canvas already layered with greens, oranges, pinks, and purples.

"*Díos te bendiga*," she responded with one last squeeze, probably getting paint on him somewhere, a hazard he'd lived with for most of his life.

"Nice," he said, his arm around her as he viewed the swirls and general colorful chaos of her painting.

"I'm calling this one *Jubilation*." She proudly stepped back and assessed it carefully.

"Pretty."

She laughed and set down her brush. "One day you'll appreciate abstract art, I just know it."

"It's not personal. I'm just more creative with words, not paintings."

"The meaning in art goes beyond words," his mother said. "It involves the imagination and feeling. Plus, if you slowed down a little, maybe you'd understand it more."

"I love the colors," he said brightly. He hoped that was positive enough.

"Thank you and let's leave it at that." Never stingy with affection, his mom enveloped him in another hug and patted his cheek. "I wish you would have given me warning that you were coming home. I would have stayed at the house this season."

He wouldn't have allowed his mom to lose her rental income. Before he could answer, Maddy walked over. "I heard you cleaned the apartment," she said. "I hope it's livable."

His mom's brows shot up. "Apartment?"

Maddy blushed, suddenly realizing she'd said too much. "Oh, it's just a furnished room over my garage."

"It's very nice, Maddy," Alex said. "Thank you for letting me stay there—temporarily." He purposefully glanced at his mom as he added, "Until I find another place."

"I rented out my house to Hadley's friend Kit and her son, and Kit is letting Alex use the apartment," Maddy explained. "Is everything working okay, Alex?"

"Actually, the faucet in the bathroom sink is broken," he said. "I just stopped by the hardware store and got a part to fix it. You don't mind if I do that, right?"

"No, of course not. But I've got a plumber coming to the house on Friday. Kit told me the kitchen sink is leaking under the cabinet."

"Let me take a look at that too. It might save you some money."

"Why, thank you." Maddy's gaze went to the door, where a few more tourists had just walked in and were examining some ceramic dishes. "You two enjoy lunch. I'll man the store."

"Come sit," his mom said as she led him inside to a little table by the window, already set with colorful pottery plates and napkins.

"Is there a reason you're looking at me like that?" Alex asked a few minutes later as he dug into the arroz con gandules, a traditional Puerto Rican dish made with bite-size pieces of pork, small beans called *gandules*, peppers, and sofrito sauce. He inhaled the mouthwatering smell and let the familiar flavors of the golden rice dish melt in his mouth. "Wow, this is delicious."

She stared at him good and hard. "I'm glad you like it. So, Maddy's garage?"

"No worries, Mom. Maddy's place is fine until I can find another one."

"Rumor is, you've taken on quite a project," she said.

So here came the interrogation. And here he'd thought she'd just invited him for lunch. "Yes."

"That's a lot for one man to handle." Her fingers fidgeted as he continued to devour the food.

"Nick knows some great subcontractors for the work I can't do myself."

"Still, you've set aside your entire summer to do it."

He took a bite of empanadilla, a turnover stuffed with beef. "Carson would want security for his family, and Kit can't sell a house that looks like Boo Radley lives there. And I'm taking the LSAT in September. So I'll still have my evenings to study."

She set down her fork. "I see. So you're doing it for Carson."

"Yes, Mami." He sighed. His Puerto Rican mother would pry until she uncovered something. So the key was to try and steer her off his trail before she did. "Kit was dealt a bad blow." There. That's all she was getting from him, he decided firmly.

"She's kind," his mom said.

He jerked his head up. "Kind?" His heart sank. Because that was exactly how *he* would describe Kit. The fact that his mom saw it too—and would mention it—startled him.

Her perceptive gaze swept over him. "Yes. I was in that little fender bender a few months ago, remember? And I took the car in to Seaside Auto Body. There was an elderly woman there totally distraught over the damage to her car. Kit gave her a ride home and called her daughter. Her boss didn't seem very happy about that, though."

"That's nice. And your point is...?"

She shrugged. "I like kind people. If you like someone, you should go for the kind ones." She paused poignantly.

"I'm not interested in anyone right now, Mami." He stopped eating, suddenly not hungry anymore. "It's bad enough that I made it home and Carson didn't," slipped from his lips. It was betrayal enough to be the one who survived. Dating Carson's wife would be...unthinkable. A *double* betrayal.

His mom shot him a look of concern and reached over to hold his hands. "It was a terrible tragedy. But that's just the point, *mijo*. You're the one here. Alive. Don't waste that gift."

He couldn't look his mother in the eyes. Couldn't admit to her that remorse and regret churned inside of him—sort of like those paint swirls that he couldn't ever really sort out himself.

His parents had raised him to be an honorable man. Their unconditional love and support had guided him his whole life. That's why he wanted to practice family law one day. Adoptions, child custody, helping parentless kids find families. He'd certainly hit the jackpot in that department.

His mom withdrew her hand, but not before she squeezed it. "I'm a little worried about you," she said. "You never call me."

"Mami, I talk to you three times a week."

She waved her hands expressively, which sent her earrings to swaying again. "Yes, but you don't ever say anything. You seem...weighed down. I know you miss Carson but—"

"I'm fine." He forced himself to meet her concerned gaze. What if he told her what he was really thinking? That if he had gone up in that plane like he was supposed to, maybe Carson would be sitting here with him, eating delicious Puerto Rican food and chatting up his mom.

"Also, you're thirty-five." He knew exactly what was coming next. "I want grandchildren."

"You *have* grandchildren. Four of them." And he had their photos in his wallet to prove it.

"But they all live so far away," she said.

"Amelia and the twins are just an hour away," he said.

"Too far."

A solid thump sounded against the gallery window, making them both startle a little. Alex turned to see a little nose pressed up against the glass and two hands waving wildly.

As Kit peeled Ollie down from the window, Alex's mom waved, breaking out into a big smile. "Oliver seems happy to see you," she noted.

"He's a friendly kid," Alex said.

"Invite them in," she said, tapping him on the arm.

"Mom, no."

"Oh, come on. Look at how adorable he is. He wants your attention." Without waiting, Alex's mom got up and opened the door herself. "Hi, Kit." She beckoned them into the shop. "Come in. Hello, Oliver."

"Hi, Mrs. de la Cruz," Ollie said, but he had something else on his mind. "Mom, Mom." He tugged on the canvas bag that hung from Kit's shoulder. "Can I have my books? I want to show Alex."

"Ollie, Alex is having lunch with his mom. Why don't we let them—"

"I want to see," Alex said as Ollie ran over and started to pull the books out of his bag one by one.

"There's plenty of food." Alex's mom gestured to the table. "Why don't you have a seat?"

"Thanks," Kit said. "But we already ate. We're on our way home from the library."

Alex's mom uncovered a tinfoil-covered plateful of *mantecaditos*, shortbread cookies with guava centers. "You're quite a reader, aren't you?" she said as the books just kept coming.

"My mommy only let me take out six," Ollie said. "Two picture books, two reader books, and two true books."

"What's a *true* book?" Alex's mom asked, looking from Ollie to Kit, who happened to be standing next to him.

"It's a book that's not pretend," Ollie said. "Like, this one is about the stars."

"You're very curious, Oliver," Alex's mom said.

"I know," Ollie said, sounding very pleased with himself.

"Humble too," Alex said, grinning.

That made Kit smile. Which pleased him way more than it should have.

A piece of paper fell out from between the books, which Ollie dove under the table to retrieve and then held up for Alex to see. "They're doing a play. And I want to try out. Watch me." He did a little dance. "There's singing too."

"I heard about this," Alex's mom said, laughing. "The theater guild is doing an all-child cast for Fourth of July weekend. Something about promoting healthy eating. The children's librarian—Lauren, yes, that's her name—she's in charge."

"Can I, Mom?" Ollie put his big blue eyes to good use. "Please?"

"We'll discuss it at home, okay?" Kit said hesitantly.

"Alex was in plays," his mom said.

Oh no. Alex silently begged her not to continue. But of course she did. "You were in *Beauty and the Beast*, remember?" She looked at Kit. "Alex has a beautiful voice."

"Is that right?" Kit asked. "What character did you play?"

Alex clutched his chest. "The Beast."

"You were not," Kit blurted. She dropped her voice so that only he could hear. "That explains *everything*."

"It's true," Mrs. de la Cruz said proudly. "He dances so well too."

"What happened to your acting career?" Kit asked. "I don't remember you being in any theater productions in high school."

"Cut short by puberty," he said with a shrug. "But I really was a great Beast."

"You still are," she said, smiling sweetly. Before he could reply, Kit bent down and tucked the books back into the bag while Ollie wandered over to the easel. "Mrs. de la Cruz is an artist, Ollie," she said as she gathered up the bag. "She makes beautiful paintings for a living."

"It looks like magic," Ollie said, enraptured. "Blue and green and yellow and orange."

"See? *He* gets it," Alex's mom said, clasping her chest and then giving Ollie a squeeze. "Children can slow down enough to appreciate beauty." She smiled at Ollie. "You have an artistic soul, Oliver."

"Hey, *I'm* artistic too," Alex said. "In our squadron they called me the Poet because of all the Puerto Rican sayings you taught me."

His mom rolled her eyes.

Kit looked a little incredulous at the fact that he was teasing his mom. He couldn't blame her. He'd tried to hide all his human qualities from her the best he could. And sometimes he just...slipped.

Surprisingly, Kit weighed in. "There's a difference between painting walls and painting a canvas, Captain."

Their gazes snagged and held. In the background, Alex heard his mom chuckle. A voice at the open door made them both turn.

It was Coach Bryan, who strolled right in.

"Hey, Ollie. How are you, bud?" he said, giving Ollie a little punch on the arm. To which Ollie reacted shyly. The guy was totally trying too hard. Ollie didn't seem very thrilled either, which gave Alex the tiniest bit of satisfaction.

He greeted Alex and his mom, then turned to Kit. "I saw you guys in here and I thought I'd pop in and ask if it's okay if I pick you up for dinner at seven on Friday? My sitter is going to be a little later than I thought. And maybe we could sit out on my porch afterward, if you want, so bring a sweater."

"Seven sounds great," Kit said.

Sit on his porch?

That was a fun date? It was more like a poorly disguised...pickup line.

He looked up to find his mom staring at him. *Busted.* She'd seen him bristle.

Bryan moved on, and Kit glanced at her watch and said they had to get going. And then Alex was left with his mom again.

She barely came up to his chest, but when she crossed her arms, she was more formidable than his lieutenant colonel. "So," she said, tapping her foot, "are you just going to stand there *pasando moscas*?"

She literally just asked him if he was catching flies. Daydreaming instead of doing.

"I'm here to fix up the house so that she can sell it and have a good life for her and her son. That's it, Mami."

She assessed him in that way of hers that always made it impossible to hide anything. But this time, his feelings were too complicated. And his distress over Carson too great to even put into words.

"Cameron que se duerme se lo lleves la coriente."

Alex knew the old saying well. *The shrimp that sleeps is taken by the current.* Or, more precisely, *You snooze, you lose.*

"Thanks, Mom," he said dryly.

Kit wasn't his. And she never could be. He just had to make sure that he kept up his guard.

Chapter 12

LATE THE FOLLOWING Thursday afternoon, Kit was in the kitchen unpacking boxes and occasionally glancing out the window into the yard, watching Ollie and Rex play ball. All week long, she'd placed a can of cat food on the windowsill above the sink, where it managed to mysteriously disappear twice a day, without any sign of who ate it except a black and white tail disappearing around a corner or under the couch. She'd just cleaned up the empty plate when she heard a rap on the door.

"Yoo-hoo," her mom said. "Can we come in?"

Her mom and dad both walked in, their arms loaded with bags.

She ran over to give them both hugs. "What did you bring us?" she asked, taking the bags from her mom. "It's not a five-course meal, is it? I thought we were ordering pizza tonight."

"Your mom's been cooking up a storm today, so we thought we'd share."

Uh-oh. Her mom only did that when she was stressed. And Kit was afraid that she just might be the source of that stress.

"Oh, you know, I just got up and felt energized to cook is all," her mom said, looking around at the half-put-together kitchen. She lifted a box that contained a fancy coffee maker, complete with an espresso machine. "Isn't this from Aunt Marge and Uncle Al?"

"We never used it," Kit said. She and Carson had used a cheap coffee maker, thinking that one day, when they had a house, they'd open the expensive one.

Ha. She'd never delay using anything again, thanks very much.

She handed the box to her dad. "Here, you two take this. I'm not really an espresso girl anyway." Kit peeked into a giant shopping bag to find a giant pan of stuffed shells, salad, a glass container full of garlic bread, and a pan of brownies, Ollie's favorite.

"Mom, this looks like enough for Thanksgiving dinner."

"Keep digging," her dad said with a wink. "You just might find a turkey in there."

Her mom swatted playfully at her dad's arm.

"Thanks, Mom." Kit gave her a grateful hug. "But I want you to know Ollie and I are fine. And I can cook." *Sort of.*

"I know," she said. "But you've still got a lot of unpacking to do."

"How's the unpacking going?" her dad asked as he poked around the scattered boxes.

"The kitchen's nearly put together, and the beds are made, so I think I'm doing pretty well." Her big accomplishment was that she'd managed to sort through some of Carson's things. The desire to start fresh was making her come to terms with a part of her past that she hadn't been able to face before.

She realized that her dad was saying something. It ended with "You really should rethink this move, Kit."

Kit held up a hand. "I know you and Mom don't exactly approve. But I'm really close by. You'll still see Ollie a lot."

"It's not that," her dad said. "It just seems like you're impulsively moving forward without a real plan. Like, you moved out just to move out."

"I do have a plan," she hedged.

Did she? A list on a bright green piece of paper that had probably floated into the ocean?

What was she doing? And why couldn't she articulate it in a way that made sense?

No matter how much she loved her parents, she was dying for space. Time to breathe. The ability to decide what she and Ollie were having for dinner, even if it was PB&J, to kick off her shoes and leave them somewhere she didn't feel bad about, to talk on the phone somewhere else besides the bedroom still painted a bright rose pink from her teenage years. But she couldn't figure out how to say that to her parents in a way that wasn't hurtful.

She led her mom to the table and made her sit down next to her dad. Then she brought a pitcher of raspberry iced tea from the fridge and poured them both a glass. On her finger, the weighty Seashell Harbor diamond caused Darla's ring to slip, subtly reminding her that there was no turning back now.

"I'm so, so grateful for everything you've done for

us." She grabbed one of her dad's hands and one of her mom's. "But I had to kick myself out of the nest. I *had* to."

Her mom looked...fretful. "You'll need money for school," she said. "How are you going to save when you have rent to pay?"

"I've saved a ton of money living with you and Dad."

"Did we stifle you?" Her mom wrung her hands. "Not give you space?"

She squeezed their hands. "You prevented me from falling off a cliff of grief. But in some ways, I used you both as a crutch. You were always there to babysit, to take care of me, feed me, cheer me up..."

"That's what families do," her mom insisted. "We enjoyed picking up the slack when you couldn't get there for Ollie."

"Yes, and you'll still see us a ton. And...you'll get your lives back too."

They both looked at each other skeptically.

"We don't want Ollie to have strange babysitters. Or go to after-school care." Her mom said *after-school care* like it was a penitentiary. "There might be mean kids there."

But being with other kids would also be good for Ollie. Wouldn't it?

"I know that being home was preventing me from facing things I've been avoiding. I just...I just need a little bit of space. Okay? I need...I need to start my life. Make my own decisions. It's time."

She tried to sound braver than she was.

"We miss Ollie already," her mom said, still wringing her hands.

"Well, he's right there." Kit nodded toward the back-yard, where she saw Ollie with his curly mop of hair fly by as he chased a ball with Rex. "Feel free to go right ahead and—"

Her dad rose and walked over to the little bay window. "Who is that man playing catch with Rex? Well. I believe it's Alex de la Cruz, isn't it?"

Man playing catch with Rex?

"We saw you talking to him at the ball game." Her mom walked over to see too.

Kit set down her glass and stepped around the boxes to peer over her dad's shoulder.

Outside the window, Alex tossed a tennis ball in a high arc to the end of the yard. Rex tore after it, tackling it, making a huge show of rolling in the grass and then getting up and trotting over to Alex to deposit the ball at his feet.

Maybe Alex didn't know it, but Rex could make a whole entire afternoon of that game.

Ollie giggled at the dog's antics.

"Okay, now your turn." Alex handed Ollie the ball. "You're right-handed, right?"

Alex stooped and took Ollie's left hand. And fitted a ball glove over it.

Kit's heart nearly stopped.

This game wasn't really about Rex, was it?

"Well, that's a nice thing to do, isn't it?" her mom said. "Stopping by to spend some time with Ollie. Alex is a quiet fellow, but I've always liked him."

Which made another thought occur. That Alex was not just stopping by...he was literally living a stone's throw away as her new tenant. Her very male, very attractive tenant.

She opened her mouth to say some version of that, but laughter and barking interrupted her. Alex was demonstrating a stance, explaining something, and Ollie ran out to try and catch a ball.

Whatever Alex was saying to him, Ollie was taking it in stride. More than in stride. He seemed happy and eager to please.

"Let's take our tea outside," her mom said.

Maybe Alex's living situation wouldn't come up.

Okay, it was bound to come up. She'd have to say something. What would be worse, the reaction from her parents now when she told them or later if she didn't tell them and they found out anyway?

She was wrestling with that when Ollie ran up to her, displaying a bright fuzzy ball smack in the middle of his ball glove. "I caught it, Mommy! I caught it!"

She did a double take. A brand-new glove, she realized, as she noticed the bright red ties along the edge.

"That's amazing!" she said as he ran out again for another catch, Rex right at his side, looking hopeful that he'd drop it.

"Gramma, Grampa, watch me!" Ollie said. "Throw it again, Alex. Again!"

Alex threw the ball in a gentle arc. This time, Ollie missed it, but Rex didn't, snatching the ball and running circles around the small yard to show off his clever catch.

Ollie looked crestfallen. Kit opened her mouth to say something but Alex beat her to it. "It's okay. Heads-up for another one."

Rex kindly deposited the ball at Alex's feet.

"Hold your glove like this," Alex said, bending his arm a little.

Ollie ran out for another catch, and Alex tossed the ball again.

"Hello, son," the Admiral said, walking up to him.

Ollie caught the ball while Alex shook hands with her dad. "Sir." Alex nodded, smiling. "Nice to see you again." He shook hands warmly with her mom too. "Mrs. Wendell."

The Admiral stood broad and tall, his posture honed from years of practice. "How's the house coming? That's got to be a lot on your plate."

Alex acknowledged Kit with a nod and a glance that lasted about a millisecond. Or less. "Yes, sir, I'm doing a lot of the handywork," he said, "but Kit's helping too. I think it will be much more salable when it's finished."

"Well, we appreciate what you're doing," her mom said. "It will be a relief for Kit to be rid of it."

"Yes, but it's a beautiful house," Kit interjected. The house might be a wreck, but it was worth their effort. "It's just that no one can tell that yet."

"Alex, are you renting a place in town?" Kit's mom asked.

That got Alex to finally make eye contact with Kit. And it was not a great look. It was a *You haven't told them yet?* look.

"Actually, I messed up a reservation I had," he said.

"Alex is staying in Maddy's garage apartment for a while," Kit blurted. There. She'd done it. And then braced for the fallout.

There was no fallout. Only dead silence. Which could be interpreted by a casual observer as a thoughtful silence, but Kit knew better.

"Just until I can make another arrangement," Alex added hastily.

"Maddy's garage…*That* garage?" her mom asked, pointing to it.

"Yes, Mom, that garage." Kit felt her face heat up.

"Is that right?" her dad said. Which was code for *I am not happy about this at all*.

"You're not staying with your mom?" Kit's mom asked.

Could this get any more embarrassing?

"She's staying above the gallery this summer." Alex smiled in a gentlemanly way, but Kit knew from experience her parents would likely see it as a big-bad-wolf kind of smile. "Kit was kind enough to let me stay in the garage apartment for a few nights until I find another place."

"Actually, I feel kind of bad," Kit said. "It's pretty outdated and very dusty."

"Not anymore," Alex said, grinning.

"Well, since Kit and Ollie are gone, you're more than welcome to stay with us," Kit's dad offered.

"Yes, totally," Kit's mom seconded. "No sense staying somewhere that's not fixed up," she added cheerily.

"Well, thanks for the offer." Alex looked at his watch. Silence loomed, uncomfortable and awkward.

"My parents brought a ton of food," Kit said, praying the conversation would move on. "Would you stay and have dinner with us?"

"Thanks, but I'm expecting a phone call. Great to see you both." Alex gave Ollie a fist bump. "Bye, Oliver Wendell." He gave a small nod in Kit's direction.

A small nod.

Which meant they were back to square one. Just when she thought they'd figured out a way to be friendly and cordial, he seemed to slam the door.

Why did he have a smile for everyone *but* her? And why did she care?

Why was he so much fun with Ollie yet poker-faced with her?

"Bye, Alex!" Ollie yelled, and then ran up to Kit's dad. "Will you play catch, Grampa?"

"Alex." Kit halted him with her voice and ran the few steps to where he was standing while her parents were occupied with Ollie. "You bought Ollie a glove?"

"His old one was vinyl. This one's leather."

How had she messed that up? "A friend of mine whose son outgrew it gave it to me. I read about the sizing online, and I thought—"

He nodded, not unsympathetically. "If it's all right, I'll toss with him once in a while."

"Sure. Of course. Thank you."

"You're welcome." He was back to looking at her as little as possible, checking his phone.

"Well, I ... I bought a glove too. So ... so I can practice with Ollie too."

Alex nodded. "Good idea."

Something crackled in the air between them. For Kit, it was probably frustration.

"Well, I'd better be going," he said with a little wave. "See ya."

She thought of asking him again to dinner but he'd already said no. But why did she even want to keep trying to engage him? Kit felt like she was talking to a giant concrete wall, expressionless and stoic.

And it made her strangely angry. That he could be so polite to her dad and so exuberant with Ollie, and yet use as few words with her as possible. Like he couldn't bear being in her presence for very long.

He tossed her an uncomfortable glance and left before she could say anything else. As if he knew her parents thought that letting him stay in the garage was just code for *carrying on a torrid affair*.

Which made her blush. But also feel irritated.

Not about the garage thing. She could handle her parents. Handle *him*.

She was just irritated at herself for wanting him to like her.

Which really shouldn't matter to her at all.

"Kit," her mom said in a low voice as the two of them walked into the house a minute later, "do you really think having him stay here is a good idea?"

"Mom, his reservation in town fell through. And he's doing so much for free. And besides, I have a date tomorrow, and it's not with him. Okay?" She almost added *I know what I'm doing*, but she didn't. She didn't at all.

"We just worry about you. All these changes at once."

"They're good changes." Kit gave her mom a squeeze. "You'll see."

But her stomach was pitching and she was sweating. A phrase from one of Carson's letters came to mind. *Fake it till you make it.*

She had no idea if she was doing the right thing— about anything. And it occurred to her that maybe this was just how life was. You *never* had any idea, but you walked up to the plate and swung anyway.

* * *

That evening, Alex went for a run, took a shower, and made a list of everything he needed for the house for to- morrow, forcing himself to stay busy and focused. He got the distinct vibe that Kit's parents—especially her dad— had not been happy about him staying here. He got it. They thought of him as a guy who would take advantage of the opportunity.

He didn't even want to think of that. Of what could happen if he ever lost control and gave in to his attraction for Kit. That's why he had to keep his distance, no matter how tempting it was to do otherwise. And he resolved to get back on the find-a-place-to-stay bandwagon tomorrow.

He shook all that out of his mind. He'd just cracked open his LSAT study book and the windows that weren't painted shut and was trying to take a practice test when there was a knock on the door.

Kit stood there in a gray T-shirt that read SEASHELL HARBOR NATIVE, shorts, and flip-flops, her hair wet from a shower. And smelling like a breath of fresh air. And just like that, everything he'd done to force her out of his mind was undone, like a pesky shoelace that never stayed tied. *Tie and untie, tie and untie.* An exercise in futility, that's what it was.

He tried to do what he always did. Hide his reaction. Not smile. Not talk. But all his techniques for playing it cool seemed to backfire when she was around.

"Hi," she said, taking a quick look around. Noticing, no doubt, the sweaty sneakers, the duffel bag coughing up clothes, and the open Cheetos bag next to his books.

"My mom made so many stuffed shells," she said cheerily. "At this point it feels like the more we eat, the more is leftover. And Ollie's become suddenly suspicious of red sauce. So I thought you might help us out and take some." She smiled and held out a paper bag. "So it doesn't go to waste," she added.

"Thank you." He held out his hand to take it. Of course their hands grazed in the transfer, which threw him even more. He felt like a ship pitching in a storm, constantly seeking equilibrium.

"Can I sit down for a sec?" she asked. Before he could make up an excuse, she walked in and made herself right at home on the beat-up couch, the only piece of furniture besides the bed, the ancient TV, and the folding table he was currently using as a desk.

She absently plucked threads on the couch's pilled surface. "It's hot in here," she said, fanning herself.

"I think it's been a while since the air conditioner's been turned on," he said. That was the optimistic version. The boxy window air conditioner was rustier than an old nail.

"I wish you would've said something," she said. "I have a fan. You didn't have to just sit up here and sweat."

"I can take care of it."

His dismissive tone didn't put her off. "I have a feeling you're used to taking care of things for everybody else," she said. "But I'm not sure how good of care you take of yourself." She reached over to the Cheetos bag and stole a couple. "I avoided telling my parents that you're staying here. And I'm sorry if that embarrassed you." She turned to face him. She had a little bit of orange Cheeto dust on her cheek that completely distracted him and also made it impossible to maintain a distant veneer. "That's all." She gave him a little smile. "I thought I should tell you that."

He leaned back in the folding chair he was using as a desk chair. "You thought they'd disapprove?"

"I knew they would. But they might as well disapprove about all my life choices at once, right?"

She got up and paced the small room. Which he'd scrubbed from head to toe but still looked pretty desolate.

Kit took a seat across from him at the table. He had no choice but to face her. One look in those beautiful green eyes and the urge to comfort her was great. But the urge to kiss her was...overwhelming.

"As far as moving out, it was time for me to leave. I love my parents dearly but being back at home made me feel like I was a kid again. And made it easier for me to coast by without making a lot of decisions."

"They want to protect you."

"Yes, but that's not always the right instinct. Not if you want to get your life going again. I'm trying to learn that lesson with Ollie." She tapped her fingers nervously on the cheap table. "In a way, I think I've stunted my parents' growth too."

He snagged a Cheeto and then offered her the bag. "What do you mean?"

"My dad retired, and they've never had time with just the two of them together. Ollie and I being there prevented that from happening. But we were in this routine, you know? Ollie's never been to day care. And my parents have almost always been available to babysit. By moving out, I've taken us all out of our comfort zones."

"Comfort zones are highly overrated." He grinned.

She blew out a sigh. "I'm not so sure that I haven't made a huge mistake. I signed up for a college class so I can work on finishing my psych degree. So then I hired a teenage girl to sit with Ollie sometimes. I hope she's nice. And I'm struggling with hooking up my Internet, and there's a leak under the kitchen sink that Maddy's called a plumber about. And my mom apparently thinks I'm incapable of cooking dinner because she literally brought me a week's worth of food. And I've been unpacking things Carson and I last used in our apartment, but if it were up to me, I'd toss everything out, but I can't afford to do that. Because even something small and stupid like a bottle opener has some kind of memory attached to it. So...basically I'm screwed. But I'm still alive. I had one moment where I sat down with a cup of tea and looked over at the yard and I felt...okay. Like maybe I needed to do this."

She scraped back her chair. "Sorry. I really did just come up here to bring you some food, not to have verbal diarrhea."

He smiled before he could stop himself. "You're not making a huge mistake."

"How do you know that?"

"Sounds to me like you're finding the rhythm of your life."

"That sounds like something Carson might say."

"Carson would say that?"

"Well, he'd write it anyway. In his letters. They were full of humor and little anecdotes, and encouraging things to keep my spirits up. Funny he'd worry about me when he—both of you—were in so much danger."

Carson *wouldn't* have said that. At least, not that way. He was a straight shooter, no metaphors or sentiment. He would have been supportive in every way, but he spoke more with his actions than with words. That was why he often asked Alex for inspiration.

"Once he wrote me a Spanish proverb that translates something like, *With patience and skill, an elephant can eat a spider*. Which I've always remembered because it's a little weird. He must've gotten that from you."

"Ha! Good one. I can't really explain that but it means little by little, step by step, if you persevere, you'll succeed." How many times had his abuela said that? One thing was becoming clear—Kit had taken those letters to heart. Which made him feel even worse. Changing the subject, he said, "Finding your own way again can't help but be better for you and for Ollie—in the long run." He sat back and smiled. "Besides, I'm a product of day care *and* after-school care, and I turned out pretty well."

She frowned and tapped her lips. "Hmmm. Wonder if your mom would agree?"

"Thanks for the vote of confidence."

"You're welcome. So we're good?"

"Well," he said, "sounds like you're fighting enough battles. Having me here…it's a complication you don't need."

She laughed. "They're just having a hard time understanding why I moved out, let alone while I have an attractive male guest living in my garage."

He grinned despite himself. "Attractive, huh?"

Easy, Alex. Watch where you're going with this.

"Did I say attractive?" she said, grinning now herself. "I meant *annoying*."

He laughed. "Well, if I had a daughter, I'd feel the same way as your dad."

"If your daughter was thirty-five, I'd think you'd back off a bit."

"Maybe," he said. "But I'll start looking around for another place ASAP."

She glanced around the plain but now-tidy room. "I want you to stay. I'm so grateful for all you've done. And I…I can deal with my parents. I'm sorry I didn't handle that better."

"Maybe they're right," slipped out of his mouth.

Her head jerked up, and she looked confused.

He stared at her a long time. He tried not to look at her lips, which were soft and pink and so, so kissable. A low, slow ache started deep in his chest.

Seconds passed. They felt like minutes. That same charged connection volleyed between them, clear and strong. With any other woman, he'd go with his gut and take advantage of it.

Who was he kidding? If he'd felt chemistry before with other women, it had been a little steam coming out of a test tube compared to this—this simmering volcano that threatened to erupt at any time. It took everything he had to tamp it down fast.

Carson's wife. Carson's. You're here for Carson. What was he doing?

"I'm just teasing," he managed. "But...I see their point. I'm planning to start looking for a place tomorrow, by the way."

"It's high season. I honestly don't think you'd find an empty doghouse anywhere in town."

He chuckled. "You just might be right about that."

She assessed him for a minute, faint frown lines appearing between her eyes. "I'll be going." She stood and walked to the door, much to his relief. But then she halted and turned back around. "Can I ask you a question?"

"Sure." But he found himself holding his breath.

She seemed to force herself to look right at him. "I...I know you don't like me very much and I'm wondering if I've done something to make you feel that way? Like, by accident? Like sometimes I think we're okay and other times I just...Anyway, if I've done something that I'm not aware of that's upset you, I hope you'll tell me."

Oh, hell. She was going to push him to his limits. That's what she did, until she got answers. She might not think of herself as bold or brave, but she was— and tenacious too. It was probably the characteristic that would save her.

It was, however, about to be the death of him.

"I don't not like you," he said, which sounded ridiculous. "I just—" He looked at her good and hard, and something inside him melted. How could he let her think he disliked her? How badly he'd hoped that being with her in person would banish this crazy obsession, when everything he learned about her only made him like her more.

"I guess being back here reminds me of Carson and that makes me...sad," he finally said. It was true in many ways. And it was the only thing he could think of that made even half a nugget of sense.

She blew out a breath. "Well, that's a relief. I was afraid I'd offended you somehow."

He rubbed his neck, thinking that anything he'd say right now would land him in big trouble. Things like, *You could never offend me. I'm trying so hard to stay away from you but I'm failing at every turn.*

"So we're good?" she asked.

"Good," he confirmed with a nod.

"Well, I better go. I was on hold for an hour with my Internet provider. Hopefully some kind customer service representative can get me up and running before my class starts on Monday." She placed her hand on the doorknob.

"Kit," he said.

"Yes?" she said, turning.

"About the leather glove. It molds better to the hand, so it makes it easier to catch." A thousand things rose to his lips. That he could teach her to catch too. And fix her Internet. That he missed Carson, too, and that yes, being back here amplified that heartache times a hundred, and how did she do it, live amid all the memories?

"Well, thank you for the glove," she said. "It was thoughtful. I've been watching YouTube videos about batting and catching. And learning the rules of the game."

How exhausting it must be to need the knowledge base of two people instead of one. "Better watch out. You get too good, and they'll have you coaching next year."

"Ha! I'm just aiming for both of us to survive the season." She opened the door. "Well, hope you enjoy the food. And I'll leave the fan in the garage. Please let me know if you need anything else."

As Alex shut the door behind her, he heard the thudding of footsteps down the wooden stairs and the crunch of gravel under Kit's feet as she made her way across the driveway.

Leaving him feeling more alone than ever.

Chapter 13

THE NEXT EVENING, Kit had just put on a flowered sundress, fastened her sandals, and rummaged around to find her jean jacket in an unpacked box before her date. Her parents had insisted on taking Ollie for the night, having big plans to take him and his buddy Corey to a drive-in movie.

Kit had just run back into her room to grab a forgotten earring when she found a fluffy ball of black and white curled up on her pillow, fast asleep.

She stopped dead in her tracks. Seymour, apparently not surprised in the least, lifted his head, giving a sleepy, nonchalant yawn. "Well, hello there," she said.

He blinked a few times and stared at her. Which was a definite improvement over his usual MO of bolting and disappearing under the bed.

"Well, now that you're here, do I look okay? I'm a little worried about the shoes." Half of her wanted to pet the poor thing, but the other half thought that this was the first baby step, and she didn't want to push her luck. She'd just sat down at the edge of the bed and reached over when a knock on the door made the decision for her. It also awakened Rex from his snooze on the family room couch, and he immediately began to bark.

"For what it's worth, it's nice to see you, Seymour." With that, the cat lowered his head, closed his eyes, and settled back in. Which she took as a good sign. "A big part of me wishes I could join you." But instead she got up, grabbed her earring, and fastened it on the way down the hall.

Through the paned windows of the back door, she caught a glimpse of the black, silky layers of Alex's hair, blowing a little in the breeze, and her stomach flipped. He was standing there, his dark brows knit down—in concentration or displeasure, she wasn't sure, glancing between the houses at the ocean.

After their talk last night, Kit thought things would be different. There had been an electric moment when she thought for sure he'd been flirting with her. But again today, Alex continued to be happy and jokey with Ollie but barely exchanged anything beyond what was necessary with her.

Which should have made her accept their relationship for what it was but instead drove her up a wall. What if he'd come now to tell her he'd rather spend the evening with her, instead of her going out with Bryan? What if this stupid date had made him a little jealous and he couldn't bear things being awkward between them anymore?

Or what if she forgot the romantic daydreaming and settled for wringing his neck instead? Which might be *very* satisfying. Kit chuckled a little and opened the door.

"I know you're going out tonight," Alex said in a no-nonsense tone, stooping to pet Rex, who was wiggling his butt in excitement at Alex's presence, the traitor. "Is it okay if I come in and work on your sink?"

Work on her sink?

"Is this a joke?" Anger welled up. And not just because she finally had the house to herself for two minutes and there he was. But because she wanted to drag him across the threshold and say, *Why are you really here?*

Except she had no clue.

Did he really have nothing better to do than fix plumbing on a Friday night?

He lifted a wrench and one sardonic brow. "Does this look like I'm joking?"

"It's just...I'm getting ready for my date."

She watched him closely for a reaction, but the irritating man was looking past her. Apparently, the kitchen plumbing problem was more intriguing than she was.

Wait. Did she want to be intriguing? To him? That shook her up a little.

She walked over to the counter and tossed Rex a dog treat, which he swallowed whole before immediately returning like a magnet to Alex's side. Oh well, nice try. She placed her hand on a box. "This is for you."

He came and examined it. "Another fan?"

"I just found it. Thought it might help a little more."

"Thanks." He didn't quickly move to the sink and get to work; he just stood there. In fact, if Kit was not mistaken, he was trying really hard—but failing—not to notice what she looked like.

Maybe because she was feeling a little sassy, she said, "You can close your mouth now. I mean, I know I don't get dressed up every day, but it can't be that shocking."

He crossed his arms but still didn't budge. "You look... nice."

"Thank you." Wow, had he actually paid her a compliment? "Well, I don't want to be late. I still have to do a couple of things." As she gathered her purse and her keys, she said, "You probably date a lot."

He frowned.

"I'm only interested because I need to ask you a question."

"Shoot."

She held out a foot and rotated her ankle. "Are these mom sandals? I don't think I own a pair of shoes with a heel over two inches. And these are pretty low but—"

He cleared his throat. "I don't think you should have any worries about your appearance."

Now it was her turn to frown. "Um, is that a positive comment or a negative one? Like, are you telling me, don't worry because there's nothing I can do about it now, or I look fine?"

His gaze flicked up and down, which gave her goose bumps, even though she was still mad at him. "Kit," he said slowly and carefully, "any man who has the honor of going out with you will have no bones about your appearance."

"Oh. Okay," she managed. Her heart fluttered. And her knees got all noodley. Even though, as far as compliments went, that was *not* really a strong one.

"Now I have a question." He was leaning against her kitchen counter with his arms still crossed, looking a little formidable. "Your date's not picking you up?"

"I'm meeting him at Cam's Place." She'd decided that would be better than having Bryan come here with Ollie around.

"Do you have cash on you?"

"Maybe a few dollars. Why?"

"In case you need to get home. You can always call me if things go south."

"Thanks, Dad," she said, which made him frown. She put a lipstick in her purse and picked up her keys. "I'm all set."

"I meant what I said," he persisted. "You don't like this guy, I'll come pick you up ASAP. Even texting a single code word works."

"A code word?" Such a strange guy. He blew hot and cold but his actions...were selfless, if overprotective. And that struck her right in the heart. Even if he was acting worse than her father before a date. "Hadley and Darla and I used to have a system like that. Our word was *LEMON*."

He roared at that. His laugh was deep and rumbly, and it made her feel...strangely happy.

"You should laugh more," she said, one hand now on the doorknob. "It sounds...nice."

Which was a dumb thing to say. To which he said nothing, just gave a quick nod.

But she never even made it out the door before it opened wide.

"You look cute," Hadley said, walking straight past her into the kitchen, Darla following right behind. Both of them paid homage to Rex, who was beside himself with all the company. Then Hadley turned to Kit, holding up some silver beads. "Here, I brought you a necklace."

"Thanks," Kit said, taking them. Not really her style, but she was touched that her friends had come to see her off. Or make sure she passed inspection—she wasn't sure which.

"Cute dress," Darla said, smoothing down her errant curls. "And I see you're wearing the ring. But we could've brought you some better shoes. Why didn't you say something?"

A side glance at Alex saw him biting back a smile. Kit flashed him a look. So much for trusting his opinion.

"Hey, Alex," Darla said, walking over to the kitchen. "What's going on?"

"Leaky pipe." He hiked his thumb toward the sink.

"Oh. Okay. Like an emergency?"

"You could say that," he said.

Hadley, rummaging in her purse, pulled out a spray bottle. Between Alex and her friends, Kit felt like she was watching a late-night comedy routine. A bad one at that.

"What is this?" Kit asked as Hadley shoved it into her hand.

"Body spray," Hadley said. "But it can also be a weapon if needed."

"Okay, this guy is my kid's coach. He's not a sociopath, is he? Because you're making me nervous instead of calming me down."

"He might be a flirt," Darla said. "I heard he dates a lot."

Hadley shot Darla a warning glare. "We're just here to wish you well. And to make sure you look nice."

"I appreciate it, but I'd better get going."

Alex stuck his head out. "Have fun," he said in a deadpan voice.

As they walked her out, Hadley asked, "Why is Alex fixing your plumbing on a Friday night?"

"Maybe because he's a workaholic and he's bored," Kit said with a shrug.

"My opinion is that he wants to *check out your fixtures*, if you know what I mean." Darla, thinking that was hilarious, chuckled. She poked Kit in the side with her elbow and whispered, "Not the sink kind."

Kit rolled her eyes. "Darla, sometimes I'm amazed you're on the *New York Times* bestseller list."

"Not for writing comedy," she said. "I was just trying to make you laugh."

"Call us if you need us, okay?" Hadley said. "We're taking my grandma to the theater in Evanston for the rom-com fest."

"Oh, fun," Kit said. "What's playing?"

"*Sleepless in Seattle* and *You've Got Mail*. You know how Gran loves Meg Ryan."

"I want to come too," Kit said a little too wistfully.

Darla gave her a little push toward the car. "Next time. We're only a text away."

"You sound just like Alex. He even asked if I had a code word I could text him if I was in trouble."

"You didn't tell him our secret word, did you?" Hadley asked.

Kit ignored that and pulled out her keys. "Even if I did, do you really think we're ever going to use that again?"

She laughed and gave a shrug. "Better safe than sorry?"

"Why isn't this guy picking you up again?" Darla asked, looking around as if she expected Bryan to pull up at any minute.

"It's better this way," Kit said. "No awkward small talk at my door."

"Do you have your purse?" Hadley asked, still in worry mode.

Kit held up the bag that was slung over her shoulder.

"Your jacket?" Hadley asked.

Kit held that up too.

"Protection?" Darla suppressed a grin.

Kit shook her head. "It's a first date, okay? That's not going to happen."

"You never know," Darla said.

"Trust me, I know," Kit said firmly.

"Well, it's been a while," Hadley said.

"Yeah. You might be…ready to ignite, if you know what I mean." Darla mimed an explosion, complete with sound effects.

"Okay, I'm leaving," Kit said as she gave her awful friends a quick hug. "Thanks for seeing me off."

Hadley held up her phone and shook it. "We're just a call away, 'kay?"

"Yeah, yeah." As she pulled out of her driveway, she tried to get excited for her date, but instead, she found herself thinking about the hot guy with the wrench who currently had his head buried under her kitchen sink.

Part of her wanted to sit him down and somehow make him talk. Find out what he was like behind all those walls she just couldn't get past.

And the truth was, she wanted to do that more than go on this date.

* * *

The Sand Bar was hopping as usual on a Friday night. Kit was early for her date, so she decided to stop in for a drink at the familiar gathering spot before meeting Bryan at Cam's restaurant.

Her hands were sweaty as she picked up her glass of wine, thanked Jack the longtime owner, and took a seat in a booth under a papier-mâché octopus. Also hovering overhead were a lobster, a crab, and a giant swordfish. It was a comforting place, kitschy and homey with a great view of the bay.

She took a sip of wine, but her nerves had rendered it tasteless. Probably because she'd calculated that the last time she'd had a first date was...seventeen years ago. She adjusted her hair and her dress and tucked her sandals out of sight under the bar stool. She was going to need a lot more help than a glass of wine to get her ready for tonight.

"Hey, Kit. How goes it?" Jack asked, leaning over and smiling. "Where's your lady friends? I don't think I've ever seen you alone here before."

"I have a date," she said.

He frowned. "Who with?"

"Bryan Dougherty."

"I think I know him. Good-looking guy, flirts a lot?" That didn't seem exactly like an endorsement. But Jack smiled kindly. He'd been a good friend of Carson's. And he was a great therapist in a pinch.

"I'm a little nervous." Actually, she was a lot nervous.

"One step at a time. Then suddenly you've eaten the whole alligator."

Kit frowned. "I don't understand."

He nodded above their heads. "My newest addition."

Sure enough, there was an enormous bright green gator floating above a nearby table. "Nice. And thanks for the wisdom, I think."

Jack rubbed his neck. "Does your date happen to have a great big white smile...and maybe a girlfriend?"

"A what?"

Jack nodded to the other side of the bar, where a couple sat close, whispering and chuckling, and...kissing.

Definitely kissing. And one half of the couple was definitely...Bryan.

And the other half was...Astrid, the mom at Tee ball who was...perfect.

Kit turned around quickly and slumped down a little, her heart drumming in her chest. She tried to say something but no words came. "I feel...I feel..." Awful. And shocked. "I was supposed to meet him at Cam's. But I'm clearly his second choice for a first date. I don't even know how to process that."

Jack sent her a kind smile. "This isn't about you. It's about him. And trust me, it's better to know from the beginning with a guy like that."

"I suppose so." She began to plot her exit. Which was going to be a little tricky because she would have to walk right by them on her way out the door.

"Oh no," Jack said, which made her blood run cold.

"What is it?" She braced herself. What could possibly get worse about this situation?

"Don't turn around," Jack said, taking a second to whisper something to the other bartender on duty. "It's progressed from kissing to checking each other's tonsils. The whole bar is watching. I just sent Owen over there to say something."

Kit turned to see the other bartender jokingly tap the bar between the couple to break them up and say something she couldn't hear. He ended up taking their drink order.

"Hey, Jack," Kit said. "Can I put in a carryout order?"

"Sure thing. What can I get you?"

Kit ordered food to go. Actually, lots of food. Because she was going home to eat a dozen Thai chili wings all by herself. And wash them down with more wine.

She absolutely would not SOS Darla and Hadley. They were in Evanston, a good forty-five minutes away. She definitely should have gone with them to Rom-com Night.

Everything okay? Hadley suddenly texted, like a mind reader.

Yes, he showed, she texted back. Which wasn't a lie. She wasn't going to ruin their night over this.

Jack passed by again. "If you want to wait in your car, I'll bring your food out to you."

"That's sweet. But that won't be necessary. I...I have to do something." She grabbed her purse and slid off the stool. This time, Alex wasn't here to hold her back from being impulsive. But she didn't care, because she was going to stand up for herself.

Who was *herself*? She wasn't completely sure. But she was about to find out.

Jack's eyebrow shot up. She gave him a little wave to show him she was...okay. Because strangely, she was.

She looked at the two canoodlers, whispering and giggling. Bryan was rubbing Astrid's back.

Ugh. She tapped Bryan on the shoulder.

Astrid saw her first, her eyes widening.

"Hey, Bry," she said pleasantly. "Hey, Astrid."

Bryan spun around on the stool.

Kit smiled sweetly. She suddenly felt calm. And good. Except for those mom sandals. A moment like this called for much better shoes. But oh well.

"How's your date going?"

"Oh, great," Astrid said.

Bryan, she was sad to see, didn't even have the decency to blush. "Kit, I...I can explain."

"I think a picture is worth a thousand words," Kit

said before he could talk. "I'm glad you're having a little warm-up for our date, but I'm afraid I'm going to have to cancel."

"Wait," Astrid said. "You have a date? With *her*?"

"I can explain," he said. "Kit, it was a babysitter thing."

"A what?" She couldn't wait to hear this.

"Yeah. I mean, you know how hard it is to get baby-sitters. I...I double-booked. I'm sorry. We can all be civilized about this, can't we?"

"Wait a minute," Astrid said. "You have a date with her *after me*?"

"In ten minutes," Kit confirmed, tapping her watch.

"Baby, I scheduled it a few weeks ago." He set down his drink and took Astrid's hand. "Before we went out."

Kit rolled her eyes. *Unbelievable.*

Bryan stood up and signaled to Owen for the bill. "Okay, Kit, listen. I brought my car, so we can drive together to the restaurant."

"No," Kit said definitively. "There's not going to be a date."

Astrid was gathering up her purse and her wrap.

"Astrid, wait," Bryan said. "Kit, you're taking this all wrong. It's not like I cheated. We haven't even gone on a date yet."

Kit shook her head, mostly because she couldn't believe her good fortune in choosing to come here first. And also be-cause Bryan was utterly clueless. "We won't be going on any dates. Because...because I only go out with men who are genuinely excited to get to know me. Not guys who...who kiss other women ten minutes before a date with me."

There. *That* was exactly what she needed to say.

Then she turned away. The bar had become silent except for a click of a glass or an occasional cough.

Kit smiled politely at everyone. She felt...well, she felt...

Not angry. And not especially hurt.

Relieved. Because she realized she hadn't really been spending much time thinking about Bryan, except to worry about this stupid date. And she definitely hadn't been dreaming about him. Or even getting excited about it.

She should have been excited. Instead, this whole thing had felt like something she'd had to do to prove to herself that she could actually go on a date.

And that was a very bad reason to do anything.

She turned back to the bar. Jack, who'd been staring at her like everyone else, quickly picked up a bar rag and threw it over his shoulder and grabbed a couple of empty glasses.

"Is that takeout ready yet?" she asked. Because she was suddenly really, really hungry for those Thai chili wings.

Jack grinned. "Five more minutes." He reached over and filled a beer glass with his tap. "On me," he said. "Because that was awesome."

"Oh. Thanks," Kit said, as he placed the ice-cold drink in front of her. "What is it?"

"A new vanilla porter. It's local. Tell me what you think."

Kit took a seat at the end of the bar to wait for her food and finally summoned the courage to look around. People had gone back to carrying on with their conversations and their meals.

She'd almost calmed down enough to enjoy the one swallow of beer she'd managed to take when her phone went off. Three bright yellow lemon emojis showed up in a text. From Alex.

She looked up to find him at a table a short distance away. Staring right at her, a corner of his mouth half turned up as he slowly picked up his own beer and raised it to her in a toast.

He'd been here the whole time, surely. Witnessing...everything.

She did a mental head slap. But then suddenly he was walking over.

And he looked heart-stoppingly handsome in a plain black T-shirt and faded jeans. The soft, worn kind that fit like a glove. Looking like...like Bryan never even existed.

"Hey," he said, "mind if I have a seat?" Kit felt his gaze on her. More like burning into her. Something flickered in his eyes, but it wasn't humor. It was...desire. She was sure of it. For a second, she couldn't look away, feeling the pull of him. The same wanting flooded her right back, causing her to go hot and cold. Making her shaky.

"Only if you used the lemon emojis as a joke. I don't need to be saved, thanks anyway."

"Maybe I'm the one who needs saving," he said as he pulled out a bar stool.

"From the plumbing problems?" she asked, trying to tamp down the furtive beating of her heart. "I did leave you under my kitchen sink."

"It was a little lonely under there. Thought I'd come have a beer." He lifted his glass to his nice, full lips. "Didn't realize there was going to be entertainment too."

Chapter 14

"BEFORE YOU GET angry, I want you to know that I meant that in the best possible way." Alex raised his glass. "Bravo for you."

She looked surprised. "You're...congratulating me?"

He took a sip of his beer and grinned. "Definitely." Except why had he said that stuff about him being the one who needed saving? He needed to focus his mind on something else. Like how badly he wanted to strangle Bryan.

She flushed just as Jack walked over with her giant takeout order and looked at her with concern. "You okay, Kit? Hey, Alex."

Alex gave a nod as Kit signed the bill. "I am now." She handed Jack the receipt and tucked her credit card back in her purse. "Thanks, Jack—for everything."

"No problem. Have a nice night."

"What's in the bag—I mean, bags?" Alex emphasized

the plural and fake-coughed. There looked like enough food for a dozen people.

"Thai chili wings. And maybe some other stuff," she hedged. "So don't judge me. Do you like those?"

"Yes?"

"Yes with a question mark?"

"I'm not sure I've ever had them. I'm more of a hot sauce guy. But I definitely like wings." He paused. "Especially if you're buying."

"Look, I appreciate your support. But I'm fine. Don't let me interrupt your night."

"I know you're fine. More than fine."

"More than fine?"

"You were amazing back there. I'm glad you didn't let him get away with that." She *was* amazing. There and everywhere.

"It was only a first date. But...but first dates are important."

"First dates are really important." He could have had one with her years ago if fate hadn't intervened.

She gave him a hard look. "Anyway, I'm headed home. With my wings. Thanks for the company." She went to pick up the bags, but his voice stopped her.

"Let me drive you." He seemed to be doing everything in his power to keep her from leaving. Part of it was that he wanted to make sure she knew that what happened wasn't her fault. That she shouldn't get down on herself. But the other part was that he just didn't want her to go.

"I drove myself, remember?"

"Let me drive you anyway."

"Look, I know you have this savior complex, but I don't want pity company now. I just want a friend."

Alex stood up from the stool. "I'd like to be that friend."

She looked a little surprised, and a little skeptical. But he read something else entirely in the way her eyes went a little soft. And in the way she smiled just a little. It told him what he already knew from all those countless times their eyes had met and one of them had looked away.

She felt it too. *It* being…whatever this was between them.

Which he should take as a warning, but he had no intention of letting her go home alone after what had just happened. "And…I really do love wings."

"*Are* you my friend? I think you feel a sense of obligation to me because of Carson."

"Is that what you think? That I'm hanging around because I feel sorry for you?"

She crossed her arms. "I wouldn't know, Alex. Because you don't exactly talk to me."

She was right about that. He hadn't let her in. Only in those rare times when his guard had slipped.

But now…now she could use a friend. And he just didn't have it in him to tell her another lie.

"I'd like to be. Your friend." His longing for her flared, but he tamped it down as always. He'd never act on his feelings. He hadn't for all these years.

She shot him a wary look. But then her mouth eased into a smile. "Well, then," she said, grabbing one bag while he took the other, "let's go have us some wings."

* * *

Once they got to Kit's, Alex unloaded the bags onto the kitchen table while Kit gathered some plates. He'd even run next door to scrounge up two IPAs from his mini-fridge to go with the food. "Thai chili wings," he read on one foam container. He read the others. "Honey barbecue wings. Sriracha. How many different kinds did you order?"

She walked up next to him and peeked in the bag. "That should be all the wings."

Meaning there was more food. Out of the other bag, he proceeded to pull out French fries, cheese dip, and something chocolate dripping with caramel sauce. "What's this?"

"Double chocolate brownie bomb," she said. "They didn't forget the ice cream, did they?"

He pulled out a container of ice cream, which she stashed in the freezer. "Have you ever had one of those?" she asked.

"Can't say I have."

She flashed a mischievous smile. "Well, you won't be the same person after you do."

He wasn't the same person since the day he'd first encountered her in front of the old house. Every day since he'd told himself that spending time with her would prove that she was just a fantasy, something his mind had somehow gotten stuck on, like a song that plays over and over in your head. But he'd never met anyone like her. Kind, beautiful, brave, and a wing aficionado to boot.

A few minutes later, they were settled on the patio, the containers of food spread out before them. A light breeze blew in from the ocean, the waves calmly lapping to shore in the distance.

He tried every wing flavor. Kit made sure he did.

"So, what's your favorite?" she asked with enthusiasm.

"Well, I know you're into the Thai ones, but I vote for the sriracha."

"I like that one too," she said, licking her fingers.

The urge to kiss her hit him hard, and he forced himself to look away. "Do you always get this excited about wings?" he asked instead.

"Well, yes." She grabbed another napkin from a pile. "But part of the fun is getting other people addicted."

They sat there eating and watching the sun set as couples and dogs walked along the beach, a citronella candle flickering in the middle of the wrought-iron table.

"For the record," she said, wiping her fingers and tossing the napkin on her plate, "I don't feel bad about catching Bryan with someone else. It was just my first date and I'm waaay too comfortable in my own skin to let something like this get to me. I would never take that personally."

"That's good," he said, taking a swig of beer and watching her barrel through some French fries.

She stopped eating and looked at him. "I'm lying. It hurt. But not that bad." She grinned and picked up another fry and her beer. "Save room for dessert." She pointed the bottle toward the double-chocolate-whatever-it-was. "Are you one of those people who doesn't eat dessert? Because if you're not going to help me eat this, I don't want to be judged."

"I have a big weakness for chocolate." And her.

"I'm a mature, confident woman. My self-esteem does *not* depend on the first guy I have a date with deciding he prefers a woman ten years my junior."

"Great attitude," he said. He was coming to suspect from the way she kept talking that she was more upset than she let on.

"But I will tell you one thing," she said, washing the wings down with another swig of beer, "the worst thing is having everyone in the Sand Bar see that."

"Yes, but you dealt with the situation. You turned it around by yourself."

"Thanks, but do you know what I'm really worried about?" she said.

"What's that?"

"What if Bryan treats Ollie differently because of this? Like, gives him the cold shoulder or, I don't know, acts disgruntled."

"Personally, I don't think he really pays that much attention to Ollie." He took a sip of beer. "And I have another opinion too."

She lifted a brow, which he took as an okay to keep going. "Bryan seems to be the type of person to think more of himself than of anyone else. So I'm not sure he would think to do anything so complicated."

She looked out over the sea, her brow furrowed, and smiled wryly. "You said that in such a nice way it doesn't even sound like an insult."

He gave a little chuckle as he sat forward, leaning his elbows on his legs and tapping his fingertips together. "Stop worrying. Ollie's getting more confident. He doesn't need Bryan to be nice to him."

She sat back in her chair and looked at him. "How do you not . . . worry about things? I spend my life worrying— what I'm doing right, what I'm doing wrong, everything I'm not doing for Ollie—"

"Ollie's a great kid. He's going to be just fine."

"I hope so. I'd sure like something to go his way this summer so he's happy and excited to start kindergarten."

"Are you going to let him try out for that play?"

Kit sighed. "I don't think I have a choice. He taped the flyer to the front of the fridge, and made his own calendar. Every day he crosses off another day until tryouts."

That made him chuckle. "Now I *know* that kid's going to be all right."

She still looked uncertain. His throat tensed with unspoken words. He wanted to tell her she was a great mom. And that he'd do everything in his power to ensure that things would be okay. But if he said something like that, she'd run for the hills. Fast.

That's what happened when you hid feelings. You had to keep hiding them or you'd shock the hell out of people.

"Thanks for your vote of confidence," Kit said. "You say it in such a calm way that I'm inclined to believe you."

"Well, I'm always glad to help." He did his best to focus on the softly rolling waves. The way the moonlight played on the water. The stars suddenly visible above. Anything but her.

"That's the funny thing about you, Captain," she said, assessing him in a way that unsettled him even more. "You are somehow always around to help."

He shrugged. "It's my military training. I'm here to serve."

"Well, I wonder who helps *you*?"

"Don't waste your worrying on me. I'm tough."

"Well, I'd like to be able to help you too—the way you've helped us. But you don't say much." She paused, as if considering that. "Maybe you're just strong."

He wasn't strong. Not at all. How could he ever tell her about the guilt he carried? It was a gnawing secret he would have to take to his grave.

She closed her eyes. "I thought I was strong before Carson died. It's funny where life takes you, you know? You think you have a plan and...poof."

"Tell me about it," he said. He'd never planned on his best buddy being gone.

"I mean, I didn't exactly plan my future very well. And I used Carson as my backup plan. I didn't finish my degree. I didn't do a lot of things I should have."

"You're too hard on yourself. You're an amazing mom. You don't give yourself enough credit." All those words had rushed out of him before he could censor himself.

"Wow." Kit looked incredulous.

"What?" Inside, he cringed. Had he been too effusive with the praise?

She held up two fingers. "You just gave me *another* compliment."

He chuckled. "Actually, I gave you *several*."

"All righty, then, I'm just going to say thank you."

"You're welcome." For a moment, everything stood still. He felt the same familiar warmth coursing through him, the same forbidden desire. The same slow but steady acceleration of his heart.

Her gaze met his, full of feeling. But she flicked it away, back to the sea. "I know you don't like to talk much, but of everyone I know, you're the one who can relate the most to losing him—Carson. You lost your best friend. And so did I."

It was like she had to force herself to say his name out loud. He knew the feeling. Once again, guilt needled him. He was the one alive and sitting next to her, not his buddy.

All the *should have*s went on an endlessly repeating loop through his mind. During their training exercises two days before Carson died, Alex should have navigated the wind better with his chute. He should have made a smoother landing into the water, where his feet ended up getting tangled in marsh grass on the riverbed. And he should've stayed calm and not let panic make him release his breath a few seconds early on the way up so he didn't choke on all that dirty river water and get sick a day later.

He should have talked Carson out of becoming a fighter pilot, way back when.

Because ultimately, Alex hadn't been able to protect him. *That* was the elephant sitting right smack on top of his chest.

"I think Carson would laugh about my date tonight," Kit said. "Tease me endlessly for not seeing the signs. And for thinking the best about Bryan. Then he'd threaten to go take care of that jerk."

Alex laughed. "I think Carson would've said it wasn't worth the skin on his knuckles to punch him out."

"Ha!" Kit stabbed the air with her finger. "You're absolutely right."

"To Carson," he said, his voice catching. He held out his bottle. She clinked it with hers. *I'm so sorry* welled up in his throat and caught there. It wasn't something he could ever say.

"To Carson," she said softly, taking a drink. Then she set down the bottle and folded her arms, leaning her elbows on the table. She had this way of moving elegantly and fluidly that had always fascinated him.

They sat there, listening to the ocean. She kicked off her sandals and put her feet up. He kicked his off too.

Kit finally broke the companionable silence. "Grief is like those waves. Sometimes I'm fine, and then suddenly, it comes. Wave after wave, wanting to knock me over. And then I think, what am I doing? Maybe my parents are right. I should've done one thing at a time. I should have had a better plan. Maybe leaving their house was best for me, but not for Ollie."

Before he could think, he grabbed her hand. He heard her sharp intake of breath. "Look at me," he said. Reluctantly, she met his eyes. He rubbed the inside of her palm with his thumb.

She gave a strange laugh. "What?"

"In Spanish, we have a saying, *Confundir la hierba con la maleza*. It means you're confusing the grass with the weeds. You've made a lot of changes in a short amount of time. Don't discount everything as bad just because of an off day."

She blinked back tears. "I just feel like I have no idea what I'm really doing."

"Well, you've done a lot. In the face of opposition. In my opinion, that makes you really strong."

"Thanks, but there's a lot of faking going on here." She gave a weak smile as she wiped her eyes.

"You *are* strong." He squeezed her hand. "Carson said it all the time. He was proud of you, Kit. And he used to tell me how he couldn't wait to be with you and Ollie. You two were his world."

"See?" she said. "That's just the thing. I can do everything I possibly can to move on except I can't do the one thing that matters—forget him." And suddenly she was crying again.

Alex cursed silently. He'd meant to comfort her but instead he'd made her more upset. Something inside of him broke. He got up and sat down beside her, placing his arm around her shoulder. It was a natural move, one he would have made for anyone in distress. Except it set off warning sirens in his head.

He tried not to inhale her scent, something fresh and

summery, and he tried not to feel how soft she was, or how she melted against him and sobbed against his shoulder. Her hot tears burned through his shirtsleeve.

He raised his hand to soothe her, to rub her back, but stopped the impulse in midair. "It's okay to cry, *cariño*." He felt helpless. But he didn't dare do more.

"I don't believe getting over someone's death means to forget them," he finally said. "We never forget them. My mom told me something after my dad died that really helped me—that you know you've gotten through the worst of grief when remembering them makes you happy, not sad."

She drew back and looked at him. She was tearful, her eyes filled with sorrow, but again he sensed that familiar, forbidden feeling between them.

No. He was imagining things. His thoughts were out of control.

The gentle rolling of the waves suddenly seemed loud and rhythmic, like a drum beating. Or was that his heart?

Seconds ticked by.

Alex forced himself to do the honorable thing. He drew back, but Kit clutched his arm. "Please don't let go," she whispered.

One look into her beautiful, tearful eyes and suddenly he was...lost. Unable to resist.

And with one brief tug, he took her fully into his arms.

* * *

Kit sucked in a breath. Because it had been a very long time since she had been held.

It wasn't the same as when he'd first moved to comfort her. This felt...a lot different.

And he smelled heavenly, a clean, manly smell.

Oh, this was not good.

"I'm sorry," she said, appalled and upset.

"For what? For loving him?"

"I don't usually fall apart in front of people." She could feel his heart against her hand. It was pounding.

She became acutely aware of being cocooned inside his embrace. Of his warmth. Of the rhythm of his breathing.

Of the fact that he was very, very male.

With that thought, she sat up straight, pulling back. "Thank you for...listening."

Solid arms gripped hers. Alex's dark gaze drilled into her. And there was no mistaking the feeling because it incinerated her insides.

"Don't be sorry," he said. "I...I miss him too."

He reached up and carefully wiped a tear from her cheek. The gentle act undid her. Kit reached up and clutched his hand, unable to look away. She pressed his palm against her cheek.

He was trembling. So was she.

And then their lips met. She'd initiated the kiss, unable to hold herself back. It happened suddenly, a burst of flame between them, a melding of grief and passion. He tasted salty, a little spicy from the wings, and wonderful. The world spun, and sparks of pleasure burst behind her eyes.

He kissed her carefully, tentatively, and then more—Kit felt him drawing closer, as if needing to comfort her, wanting to take away her grief and pain. But their first kiss was like a lit match and, once sparked, rapidly became full blown, frantic, and open-mouthed.

His body surrounded her, his mouth showing her with

strokes of passion things that neither of them could put
into words. She clutched the fabric of his shirt, gripping
it fiercely. A warm river of desire pulsed through her as
her body came alive at his touch. She pressed against
the hard muscle of his chest, stoking the connection
between them.

Suddenly his chair scraped against the stone patio floor
as he drew closer, erasing the space between them. For a
moment, the constant, boundless pain she'd lived with for
two years vanished.

As the heat of desire pulsed through her, a whimper
escaped her throat.

The sound must have startled Alex because he broke
off the kiss, the shock in his eyes evident. He started to
step back but she curled her hand around his neck. "Don't
stop," she heard herself saying. "Please."

Because she felt something. Something that was not
grief.

She felt desperate, her hands drifting anxiously along
his chest, her lips craving more. At first, she was acutely
aware that he was not Carson. Alex felt bigger, broader,
more...hungry.

His chest was heaving as he took in a deep breath.
He brushed back a lock of her hair and cradled her face.
"Kit—"

She silenced him with a kiss.

"Don't," he said. "I can't—control—"

She grabbed his wrists. "I just want to feel...I just
want to feel like I didn't die too." For a flash, she saw her
own pain reflected in his eyes. The eyes of a man who
was suffering too. They had that in common. That was
their bond.

She could see the struggle in his face. He was a good

man. A moral man. But she didn't want morals now. All she wanted was for him to hold her, to feel his hands on her, to let his mouth erase all the pain she carried in her heart that she felt with every beat.

"Please," she whispered.

Something in his eyes melted as his walls gave way. Cupping her face in his hands, he kissed her.

For a man who kept his feelings so guarded, the way he kissed was...exactly the opposite. Passionate, expressive, *feral*. But tender too.

And she was melting in his arms, overtaken by the barrage of sensations that worked their way all through her.

And in the greedy, frantic, frenzied way he kissed her back, she was finally able to forget.

* * *

Make me forget.

Alex shouldn't have done it, kissed her back. But all the pent-up emotions he'd held in for so long came pouring out and he couldn't think.

He could only kiss her on her sweet lips, down her beautiful neck. Hold her as he had so often in his dreams.

He tried to fight, but it was like fighting a current. He couldn't swim up and out of the haze of desire. A desire he'd felt for too long.

And then he was gone, lost in her. And nothing else in the world existed but her—the feel of her lips, the salty-sweet taste of her, the little sounds of pleasure she made deep in her throat. And he kissed her until nothing existed but the two of them together.

Chapter 15

THE FIRST THING Kit heard the next morning was the vibration of her phone. It was rattling against a hard surface, over and over again, the way it does when you've lost it and can hear it but have no idea where it is. She groped along the nightstand only to find Darla's ring, which she quickly shoved behind her lamp.

That ring completely sucked. Since she'd put it on, her life had been one wild decision after another.

She jumped out of bed, following the sound, only to realize...she was naked.

And she had a big, whopping headache.

"Oh no, oh no." Her voice reached a tenor it hadn't reached since Ollie was a baby. One day, he was sitting in a playpen on the patio while she planted flowers nearby and got stung by a bee. Her panicked cries brought the reverend next door running over with his Bible because he'd thought someone died.

Helpless panic flooded her as everything she'd done—*they'd* done...Alex...her...together—came rushing back in spades.

She had a very dim recollection of Alex placing a cover over her around dawn. He'd taken the time to carefully tuck it around her, like she sometimes did for Ollie.

Other memories bombarded her just-awake brain. Wild, crazy, passionate ones she tried to shake out of her head—but they just kept coming.

She grabbed her robe off a hanger and wrapped it tightly around her, sitting down hard on the bed and taking a minute to breathe.

The phone's insistent vibrations prevented her from chastising herself even more.

She tore through the house looking for it, finally finding it sitting tidily on a charging pad on her kitchen counter.

Which was odd. Because first of all, she didn't own a charging pad.

Second of all, her phone had died last night, and she'd forgotten to plug it in. Because she'd...she'd gotten busy with Alex. Grumpy, somber, deadpan Alex.

Who was actually absolutely none of those things...in bed.

Just as she was about to check her phone, her coffeepot gurgled and chugged, filling the air with a rich, strong aroma. She'd never programmed it before in her life.

She sat down on the sofa, hyperventilating, and forced herself to look at the phone screen. There was a text from *him.* I'm at the back door. Your dad is on the way with Ollie.

That made her drop the phone. Looking up, she saw

the hulking shadow of a man peering at her through the windowpanes.

She wanted to die.

But there was one thing Kit feared more than Alex's sinfully handsome face pressed up against the window, seeing her at her absolute worst. Seeing her *at all* after last night.

She'd had a one-night stand. Who *was* she?

She forced herself to open the door because…Ollie. One look at Alex standing there, shifting his weight from one foot to the other, made her realize he was uncomfortable too. But he was also showered and tidy and wearing those soft worn jeans she loved and a gray T-shirt.

And she still wanted to disappear into the sand.

Alex cleared his throat. "Um, hi. I saw your dad and Ollie pull up a little while ago, so I talked to them. They decided to grab some breakfast sandwiches before they come back."

Kit blew out a breath. "Ollie probably talked my dad into driving through that new little breakfast place on the beach." She stood up. "I have maybe ten minutes to…"

He was staring at something over her head. One swipe with her hand revealed it was her hair.

Her wanton, crazy hair. From her *one-night stand*.

She swiped a hand over it again.

"I forgot to charge my phone," she said.

"I noticed."

"Thank you."

"I couldn't find your charger, so I just brought over my dock."

Yes, he certainly had.

She blushed at that. What was wrong with her? Her mind was going places it didn't usually go.

"I never sleep in like this. In fact, I always have trouble sleeping. I'm usually up at the crack of dawn." Okay, time to stop talking now.

"Right."

"And I never..."

"You never?" His gaze flicked up, which suddenly made her forget anything she was about to say. He had beautiful eyes. Warm and brown and expressive, and meltingly tender—when he let himself show it. Which was definitely not now. But now, they sort of sparkled. With a tinge of amusement.

She shook her head. The conversation had to stop. Last night, she'd said what was on her mind and in her heart, and he'd comforted her, and things had escalated way, way out of control.

She'd started everything. He'd pulled away but she'd kissed him anyway.

My God, what had she done?

"Thanks for the heads-up," she managed, pulling her robe together. "And for..." For what? For covering her up so sweetly before he left? For charging her phone? For a night that was making her knees weak just thinking about it?

No, no, no. Well, she had to say something. Right now. To make it clear that... "I...um. We—"

Yes, that was very clear.

She was embarrassed, floored, overwhelmed, freaked out, and on an orgasm high. Which she hadn't been on for a very, very long time.

He cleared his throat. "What time is Ollie's game?"

Kit groaned.

His eyes darted over to her. "What is it?"

She pressed her palm to her forehead. "I'm in charge

of the parent snack. I was going to make Rice Krispies treats and..."

She was never an incompetent parent. *Never.*

"Do the kids mind donuts?"

"No, of course not, but some of the parents don't really like unhealthy—"

"Well, it's Saturday," he said decisively. "A treat. I can go get a couple dozen, if that's okay with you."

She almost cried. "Thank you."

He responded with "No problem" and a quick nod.

"Do you...do you want your charger thingy back?"

"Later," he said, starting to walk away.

"Alex," she called after him.

He lifted a solitary brow.

"Can you please get a couple of gluten-free ones? One of the kids has celiac. And let me grab some money—"

"Kit," he said.

"Yes?"

"I got the donuts. You do you. Okay? Everything else can wait. Including talking about last night." And then he smiled. A calm, quiet smile.

"Okay," she said, trying to take a breath.

"See you in a few." He turned and gave a quick wave over his shoulder.

Kit shut the door and collapsed against it.

She had a few minutes to brush her hair and her teeth and to find clothes and some composure.

And to try to wipe from her brain how she'd unexpectedly had amazing sex with someone she had no intention of ever doing that with again.

* * *

A little while later, Alex turned off the weed trimmer he'd grabbed from the garage to pretend like he was doing something outside so he could intercept the Admiral. He'd managed to edge about ten feet of the walkway that ran between the house and the garage when the Admiral returned with Ollie.

He turned the weed whacker off as they got out of the car. Ollie was clutching a white bag of breakfast sandwiches.

Kit's father handed him a coffee. "Nice trimmer."

"Thanks, sir," Alex said, accepting the coffee.

"That's thoughtful of you to edge the yard."

Alex smiled. "Just keeping things tidy." *Right.* His mind was a jumble as thoughts bombarded him about last night—that crazy, wonderful, off-the-charts night. That could never happen again.

The Admiral gave a big smile and looked over the edging tool with great interest. They launched into a pro-con discussion of lawn edgers, which Ollie only tolerated because he'd sat down on a nearby decorative rock to eat his egg sandwich. Alex mentally wondered how long he would have to discuss torque and horsepower, electric versus gas, to give Kit a chance to get some clothes on.

Get some clothes on.

Geez.

Last night, Kit had been fun, spontaneous, and uninhibited. Being with her had been the worst kind of crack. His plan to see her for what she was had completely bombed. Because she was everything he'd dreamed she'd be and more.

Still, he'd crossed a line that he never should have crossed. He'd made a big mistake. Huge. The *worst.*

All that wanting. Too much wanting. That's why it had happened.

Once he'd taken her into his arms, his heart had burst open, and his longing for her spilled over. Because he couldn't stand her pain. He'd comforted her and held her and ... well.

It wouldn't happen again. It could not.

Yet he couldn't stop these feelings ... these protective, awful feelings that swelled up in his chest and fogged his brain. *Those* were what had led to ... what they'd done.

He'd snuck out of a woman's place before but he'd never bothered to charge her phone and program her coffee maker. Or cover her and stare at her, memorizing all the contours of her face as she slept.

What was *wrong* with him?

"Hey, Alex, will you toss me a pitch?" Ollie held a ball in his hand. Except it wasn't a softball.

"Where's your other ball?" he asked.

"I don't know." Ollie held up a ratty green tennis ball. "Rexy likes to share."

Alex took the ball—which was a little soggy, he could only imagine why—only to have Rex bound right over and sit at attention, looking at him expectantly.

So he left the Admiral to the weed whacker and steered Ollie—and Rex—toward some batting practice.

"Okay, buddy," he said as he straightened Ollie's ball cap. "Remember what I told you about the swing."

"Hold the bat out straight, right, Alex?" Ollie bent over, his butt out, trying really hard to do what Alex had taught him.

"That's right."

After two missed tries, Ollie straightened out and asked, "Can I have a donut? The kind with the pink icing."

"After the game, buddy." Alex laughed, mostly at the attention span of five-year-olds. "Get ready," he said as he dramatically wound up for another pitch. "Here comes the ball."

"I keep whiffing it." Ollie lowered his head and kicked the sand.

"Try again. You know why?" Alex unwound his arm, which Rex took as *my turn now*, sitting up at attention, his ears on alert. Ollie glanced up, looking for something.

Reassurance and support. Encouragement. Alex got it. "Because my abuela says that the hardest battles are given to the strongest soldiers."

What was he doing? He had no idea how to talk to a five-year-old.

Ollie frowned. "What's that mean?"

"When the going gets tough, the tough get going. When you fall off your bike, you get back on. It means you're tough, and you can handle this. And...just don't give up." Weed whackers and inspirational coaching...all before coffee.

He lobbed a pitch to Ollie, which Ollie nicked with the bat. Rex promptly retrieved his ball and ran off to a corner of the yard to salivate on it some more.

"You definitely caught a piece of that." Alex went to stand behind Ollie and was showing him how to follow through on his swing when a breeze swept in from the ocean, carrying with it a sweet scent, flowers or fruit or something soft and fragrant.

And suddenly there Kit was, standing in front of him in a white T-shirt and jean shorts, her hair up in some kind of bun that probably only took a minute to fix but looked really complicated. Seeing her shattered him. Because he still felt every single thing he shouldn't—

that she was beautiful, inside and out. And sexy as hell.

His pulse skyrocketed. His lungs struggled to take in air. And his heart sank with the realization that being with her hadn't flushed his desire for her out of his system at all.

Kit, on the other hand, seemed together and composed. And she was dragging a large ice chest, which he ran to take from her.

"That was quick." His gaze swept over her before he could catch himself.

"Mom life," she said with a shrug.

They stood there for a few heartbeats, staring at each other. In that brief connection, there appeared to pass between them a lot of unspoken things.

From his end, it ran something like, *You're adorable when you're trying to blink the sleep out of your eyes and your hair is all tousled everywhere. And all I want to do is take you back to that bedroom and discover twenty more things that get you to make that little sound of pleasure deep in your throat.*

And on her end . . . well, he couldn't guess. But she had two little worry lines knit between her brows that made him try to get his head straight by heaving the whole cooler up and depositing it into her trunk, where it landed with a great *chunk*ing sound from the ice shifting.

"I filled it with ice for the water bottles," she said.

"I saw some in the garage. I'll just grab them, and we'll load them at the field." With Kit's nod of agreement, he turned to Ollie. "Want to help, my man?"

"'Kay."

Kit turned to her son. "Now, if those boys try to . . ."

"Hey, Oliver," Alex said, interrupting, "go ask your

granddad if he'd bring that big case of water over here, okay?"

As Ollie ran off, following the sound of the weed whacker, Kit put her hands on her hips. Beautiful, curvy hips he remembered well.

"Um, excuse me?" she said in an intense whisper. "You have an issue with me telling my son to be on guard against mean kids?"

"I'm sorry I interrupted," he said. "And it's your call. But it might be better to just have him focus on improving his game."

She frowned, crossing her arms. "What do you mean?"

"We keep working on his skills. And if we don't remind him of the mean kids, he won't start out feeling bad about himself. That's what I was thinking."

"Oh." She dropped her hands. "That might make sense."

He gave a brief nod. "You have my word, if one of those kids gets out of line, I'll make sure they don't get any donuts."

She chuckled, her expression softening. "Okay," she said. "I believe you. But this is the second time you've stopped me from acting impulsively to protect my kid."

He shrugged. "Maybe we complement each other."

Frowning, she asked, "What do you mean?"

"Because of you, I have a place to sleep—and friends." He didn't say that he'd gotten really good at avoiding nearly everyone in his life since the crash. Out of guilt or self-punishment or just plain sadness, or likely because of all three. "So I believe you've helped me a lot more." Actually, he *knew* it.

"Let's call it even," she said.

"All right, then."

He thought things were settled, until she touched

his arm. "Look, Alex, I—we—need to talk about what happened."

"I know." He rubbed his neck. "For right now, let's focus on Ollie and worry about last night later."

He wished he could practice what he preached. Because with those big green eyes and that thick dark hair, and with the breeze from the ocean blowing little wisps of it into her face, he couldn't think about breathing, let alone Tee ball problems. Or process what had happened between them. She gave a quick nod just as the Admiral and Ollie returned with the water. Alex helped to load it and shut the trunk.

His only chance to get out of this unscathed was to have Ollie be able to hold his own. Then he could back away. Finish the house and get out of Dodge.

Before he fell for her for good.

Chapter 16

AT THE BALLPARK, it was another perfect day, hot and sunny, filled with the familiar sounds of kids yelling and laughing while they played or headed with their families to the nearby beach. Kit set the donuts next to the cooler, which Alex had placed on the lowest bleacher. Once again, she was struggling to decide between sitting with the dads as an outsider or sitting in the bleachers with her friends.

Not thinking about last night was so hard when Alex was standing right next to her, tall and tanned and lean. She was elated, appalled, and completely bowled over. Being with him had been... well, kind of wonderful and now, in the light of day, horrifying. All at the same time.

"It's fine with me if you want to join your friends." He nodded toward the bleachers. "I'll sit with the guys and keep an eye on Ollie."

"You don't have to be nice just because we... you

know." Her stomach was churning and she was shaking a little. And not just because she'd gulped down a giant cup of coffee and forgotten to eat breakfast.

"I *am* nice," he said. "And I wouldn't offer if I didn't want to do it."

"I think moms should sit on that bench too. Every game. Not just dads."

"You might be right. But I'm just saying it's okay to take a break. I've got Ollie covered. And you can always come down when you want."

Somehow, staring into his deep brown eyes and trying to be defiant at the same time just didn't work. It made her see what he couldn't hide—that he *was* nice, down to his core. It was so easy to get lost in those eyes, in the warmth and depth of them, in the caring way he'd treated her when they'd...

Which was *not* what she wanted to be thinking about. At all.

She really needed to talk with her friends.

"I'm going to say thanks. And I'm just a little... overwhelmed, shocked, confused..." She should be playing it cool. Not running at the mouth. But she couldn't seem to help it.

"Yeah, I think we both are." One edge of his mouth tilted upward.

"I'll just be up there if anything happens." She hiked a thumb toward her friends. "And... thank you. Like, a lot."

"You're welcome." As she walked away, she heard him say, "You just agreed with something I said—again."

"Don't get used to it," she tossed over her shoulder. "That'll probably be the last time."

She heard him chuckle. Which made her smile, but of course he didn't see it.

Everything was different between them. Even though they still argued, their push-pull was packed with a...giddiness. An intimacy, despite her best efforts to be as non-intimate as possible. Even the air between them seemed crackling with current.

Kit worked her way up the metal bleachers, the tinny clang of each step unsettling as they vibrated under her feet. She'd never had a panic attack before but judging from her racing heart, her pounding pulse, and the way she was sweating profusely, she was coming pretty darn close.

Moms didn't get to pick when to have panic attacks. Maybe sometime after Ollie's game.

Frankly, it had been a relief to let Alex take this over. Not that she needed to lean on him for anything but...it was wonderful that she wasn't alone in this. And somehow she knew he had Ollie's back. And hers.

Which felt...interesting.

She collapsed next to Darla, who was chowing down on a donut.

"How did you get that?" Kit asked. "I thought those were for *after* the game."

"You two were so preoccupied, you didn't even notice that I snuck one. Okay, two." She chuckled and took the last bite, which made Kit shake her head.

On the field, the kids seemed to be doing some kind of warm-up drill where they ran around the bases. A few rows below them, Alex was talking and laughing with Cam and Nick and the other dads.

She was the only one whose whole world seemed different.

"Are you okay?" Darla licked icing off her fingers. "You look a little stressed."

She did feel like she was melting down, and not in a good way. She wiped her sweaty lip unceremoniously on her shirtsleeve. "I've just had...a morning."

"Hey, everyone," Hadley said, carrying a cardboard drink holder containing four cold drinks, the giant kind you get at the gas station for under a dollar.

"Just what I need," Kit said. "Ice and a lot of caffeine."

"Well, then," Hadley said, "today is your lucky day." She handed Kit a cup. The ice rattling was the best sound in the world on a hot late-spring day.

"I said no to the straws," Hadley said, "because I didn't want them to end up in a turtle's nose."

Kit took off the lid and took a huge gulp of Coke and then sat there fanning her face.

"What's wrong?" Hadley paused in the middle of handing Darla her drink. Over the past few years, her friends had often exchanged worried glances over her head, and Kit saw one pass between them now.

"Don't worry, Kit. Ollie will be okay," Hadley said. "Cam talked with Alex, and they're actually planning to do some informal drill sessions with the boys. They're going to mention it to Bryan after the game."

"Look, Alex is out there talking to Ollie." Darla pointed to the outfield.

Sure enough, Alex had run out onto the field. He said something to Ollie, patted him on the shoulder, and jogged back to his seat between Cam and Nick.

"Ollie's laughing, so it can't be that bad," Darla said, adjusting her pink ball cap.

"Maybe you two can come over later?" Kit asked. "I know it's Saturday, so only if you're not busy."

Darla and Hadley exchanged concerned glances again.

"What happened last night?" Hadley asked, scrutinizing her face for details.

Just then, as fate would have it, Bryan gave a wave. Kit forced herself to smile and wave back. At least it appeared he wasn't going to hold a grudge, and that was good for Ollie, right?

"Wait a minute." Darla choked on her drink. "You had a date last night. With Bryan." She dropped her voice. "You *slept* with him, didn't you?"

Kit shushed her and looked around uncomfortably, but no one seemed to be paying attention. "I did *not* sleep with Bryan," she whispered. "And please lower your voice."

"Okay," Darla said, "but if you didn't sleep with Bryan, then what happened? Like, was it awkward?"

"What's bothering me has nothing to do with Bryan," Kit said. "Oh, I need to pay attention. Ollie's up."

Hadley frowned. "What are you doing sitting with us? Don't you want to be down in the front pacing or something?"

"Alex has it covered." Uh-oh. She should not have said that.

"Oooooh," Darla said in her most annoying voice. "What else has Alex got covered?"

She shot Darla a look of death. "He's been working with Ollie so I-I'm letting him handle this. For now."

"Wow," Hadley said, looking puzzled. "What happened to 'Alex is a grump who hates me and never smiles'?"

"Hey, you two," Kit said, hoping to distract her friends from putting two and two together. "Pay attention."

Ollie wound up his first swing and promptly banged the bat into the tee with a loud *clang*. One of the boys laughed. Was it Toby? Kit leaned forward, prepared to stalk down the steps at any moment.

Just then, Alex looked up and gave a slight wave. But his look told her everything. It was an *It's only the first swing so don't panic* look.

Which made her instantly feel more at ease. He seemed to care a lot about Ollie. And from what he'd just done, he seemed to care about how she was feeling too.

She couldn't think like that. Kit shook her head and focused on the second swing.

Which was... a strike.

Kit tried not to wince, instead gripping the cool edge of the bleacher with both hands. Being a parent was... horrendous.

Third swing. "Foul ball!" Bryan called.

"Keep your eye on the prize, Oliver," Alex called out. "Nice and easy."

"Waaait a minute," Darla said in an exaggerated voice, glancing from Alex to Kit. "It's *Alex*, isn't it? Not Bryan. Something happened with Alex, didn't it?"

Just then, there was a giant crack as Ollie smacked the ball.

"Run, Ollie," Kit yelled, standing up. "Run, run, run!" She bolted down the bleachers, amid the whoops and yells of her family and friends, until she was standing next to Alex. Together they watched as Ollie hustled with all his might to first base, his hat flying off and landing in the dust.

The first baseman missed the catch. Ollie stood there, unaware that he needed to keep going. "Run, Ollie," Alex yelled. "Run some more! To second base!" Ollie paused despite Alex waving his arms wildly, signaling for him to keep going. Then, as if someone had suddenly lit a fire under him, he scrambled toward second base.

Where he promptly got tagged by the baseman.

Safe or out?

Kit suddenly realized two things. One, she was holding her breath. Second, she'd been hanging on to Alex's forearm with a vise grip.

"Safe!" the dad-umpire called.

"He's safe," Alex said, grinning from ear to ear. "Yeah, Ollie," he cheered, pumping his fist in the air.

"He's safe," Kit repeated incredulously, clapping and jumping up and down.

And hugging Alex.

Something did her in. It wasn't being surrounded by his hardness, his lean muscle, or his strong arms. Or hearing his genuine laughter at Ollie's feat. It was seeing that his reaction to Ollie's success was real and genuine. Alex had cheered Ollie on with as much enthusiasm as she had.

He laughed and gave her a squeeze. Then he picked her up off her feet, twirling her around. "He did it."

"Yes, he did," she agreed as her feet hit the earth. Only her brain was still somewhere in the clouds.

She didn't even feel let down when, a minute later, Ollie got tagged at third base. Apparently, Ollie wasn't either as he made his way back to the bench, his little face positively beaming. "I did it, Alex," he yelled. "I hit it!"

Alex. He'd wanted Alex to know first.

"Nice job, champ." Alex fist-bumped him and tapped him on the cap. "Keep it up."

Ollie ran to Kit for a hug. "I did it, Mommy. Did you see me hit the ball?"

"You did so awesome!" Kit said, hugging her son.

"*Two* bases." He held up two fingers.

"Hey, Ollie," a boy on his team called, and Ollie ran off.

"He doesn't seem to notice that he's out," Kit said to Alex.

He was standing so close, their elbows were touching. "It's not whether you win or lose; it's how you play the game."

"And?" Kit said expectantly.

"And what?"

"I'm waiting for the Spanish version of that."

He chuckled. "Um, to be honest, I'm not sure about that one."

"All righty, then," she said. "We'll have to make the English version do." She got lost somewhere in the warm brown of his eyes, and she had to rip her gaze away so she didn't lean over and kiss him. "Ollie's so proud. I can't thank you enough."

He colored a little, seeming uncomfortable with the praise. "We still need to keep practicing until he hits it out of the ballpark."

Kit shook her head, still smiling. "Such an overachiever."

He shrugged. "Hey, look on the bright side. They lost, but not because of Ollie. Plus, there are donuts." He held out the box. She couldn't help reaching for a chocolate one.

"Relax." He looked at her, calm and steady. "It's a good day. And it's going to be okay."

Kit wasn't sure exactly what he was talking about—them, Ollie's baseball career, or life in general. But she had to admit that his words were...soothing. And reminded her yet again that she wasn't in this alone.

"Thank you for helping Ollie," she said. "He likes you a lot."

"It was my pleasure." He grabbed a glazed donut.

The word *pleasure* brought everything she hadn't wanted to think about rushing back.

Kit dropped her voice, aware that a dozen little boys were now running toward the donuts. "Alex, I...I have to say last night was...well, indescribable, but it can't—it won't—happen again."

He put his hands up. "Believe me, I totally agree."

She frowned. *Believe me?* That was certainly firm and definite. Why did she feel a little put off? "That it was indescribable or that it won't happen again?" she asked.

He raised a brow. "Both."

Before she could get her balance, Ollie ran up. "Donut time!" he called.

Alex helped maintain order in the donut line as Kit opened all the donut boxes and handed them out with napkins.

When it was all over and she was gathering the empty boxes, her friends showed up. "Looks like somebody hit a home run," Darla said, holding out Kit's Coke, which she'd forgotten in the stands, wearing a smug look on her face. "And it wasn't Ollie."

Hadley pretended to cough to hide her chuckle.

"Also, we just found out what happened with Bryan in the Sand Bar last night."

"Who told you?" Kit asked.

"Like, three people. Two were there, and one heard it from someone else."

Kit took back her drink, unable to decide if she loved or hated her friends. "So how about six thirty for dinner tonight?" she asked. "I'll throw some burgers on the grill or something."

"Cam's going out with the guys, so I'm good," Hadley said. "I'll bring chicken nugget apps, okay? For Ollie."

"I'll bring dessert," Darla said. "You're not the only one who might have some things to discuss, you know."

As Kit sat down to eat her donut, Ollie ran around with a couple of kids, playing tag and laughing as the parents began rounding everyone up.

Alex, who had grabbed Ollie's glove and hat from near the bench, was watching him too. Then he glanced up, catching her staring at him *again*.

Kit hurriedly looked down at her donut. As she polished it off and began to clean up, she realized two things. First, for all the panic and awkwardness, chastisement, and fretting she'd done in the past couple of hours, she'd earned that donut. And second, for the past hour and a half, which was probably a record, she hadn't thought of herself as a grieving widow.

* * *

Later that day, Kit stood in her yard, a little pleased that she'd managed to put the coals on her new grill and not torch the house down with lighter fluid. A big feat for someone who'd never touched a grill before.

Just as she admired some shells Ollie had collected in the sandy yard and finished throwing on some burgers, Alex happened to walk by. Actually, he jogged by— shirtless, of course; did he have to show off those perfect pecs?—and came to a halt when he hit the driveway.

She tried to play it cool and pretend that she cooked on a grill every day. Which only resulted in her dropping a grill utensil on her foot.

She also tried not to notice that his chest was glistening a little. And shut down a memory of what those rock-hard pecs felt like up close, which hit her like a two-ton boulder.

Suddenly a hamburger flamed up and she tamped it

out with the grill flipper. "Well, that was Darla's burger," she said. "She's usually a vegetarian anyway."

Why did she ever think it was a good idea to let him use that garage apartment? Next time she was definitely not going to be so nice.

"New grill?" He appeared to be biting down on the insides of his cheeks.

She summoned a stern frown. "Darla and Hadley are coming over, and I was trying it out."

"Nice," he said, ignoring the burger, which had flared up again and was now a glowing charcoal rock.

"I can do this," she accidentally said out loud. She managed to flip the burgers and prevent Ollie's hot dog from rolling across the grill and suffering a similar fate.

Alex stood there, quietly grinning the whole time.

Frankly, Kit thought she'd seen him smile more since they'd slept together than in the entire time she'd known him. So at least some good came out of all of this mess, right?

"Do you cook?" she asked.

"I grew up with Puerto Rican women who love to feed people. I'm a little slow on the learning curve for cooking myself. But yes, I can use a grill."

"I have extra burgers. Would you like to join us?"

"Thanks," he said, "but I'm actually going out with Nick and Cam tonight."

"Oh, okay," she said. "That's nice."

He crossed his arms. "Want to talk?"

"Yes. Absolutely," she said in her most upbeat voice, even as she flinched inside. "Look, Alex," she said at the same time he said, "About that..."

He chuckled nervously. "When someone says 'Look, Alex,' it's not usually good."

"I think we both know what happened was a mistake." Saying that made her heart roll over. It *was* a mistake, wasn't it? She couldn't possibly be interested in him? Or he in her?

It was just that their combined grief over Carson had brought them together.

"Yes. Agreed," he said definitively.

The sense of relief she expected didn't materialize.

Which threw her. "It was an emotional moment," she said. "I got a little overwhelmed...by grief. I'm sorry if I...if I—"

"It was just as much my fault as yours," he said quickly. "Sometimes I can be a little overprotective. And that turned into an error. In judgment. That we both regret." He was rocking back and forth on his heels and staring between the house and the garage at the tiny strip of ocean that was glimmering in the late-afternoon light. Part of her wanted to take off and run to the water like she was a kid, thrilled just to have her feet be in the warm sand, thrilled to be near the sea. How did life become so complicated? "Nothing personal," he continued, eyeing her carefully, like he didn't want to hurt her feelings. "I mean, I like you. You're...nice," he said stiffly.

He seemed to have to force himself through that. She was *nice*? If she was going to be rejected by a partner after the first time she'd had sex in over two years, *nice* was not exactly inflating her confidence. "Right. Nothing personal," she repeated. "We leaned on each other for support at a very hard time. And...you don't have to worry about it happening again. We can keep our relationship friendly." She paused. "Right?"

"We have to work together on the house. So we will. We can be adults about this."

But something niggled at her deep in her stomach. And a voice whispered in her ear, *It had been so good.*

She tried to pretend like it was no big deal that she'd completely lost all sense of reason. That she'd fallen so easily into physical intimacy with him without even really knowing him.

Her feelings were in a terrifying jumble. And this little discussion hadn't exactly provided clarity.

Somehow, Alex had taken the grill utensil from her. Having rotated all her burgers and Ollie's hot dog, he stepped back. "Okay, then," he said, handing it back with his usual killer smile. "Well, I'd better be going."

"Thanks," she said. As he walked away and her friends pulled up the driveway, she tried to poke at the meat the way he did, causing the hot dog to roll across the grill and fall with a sizzle straight into the coals, where it promptly caught on fire and disintegrated before her eyes.

Which pretty much summarized everything.

Chapter 17

"WHOA," DARLA SAID as she walked over from her bright green vintage Bug that she'd just parked in Kit's tiny driveway. "Hot shirtless neighbor alert."

Kit focused on carefully rescuing the remaining burgers off the grill and putting on another hot dog for Ollie. Which fared better this time.

Darla surveyed the overdone meat and gave her a dubious look.

"Don't worry," Kit said, "I have veggie ones inside."

"I wasn't judging," she said with a wry smile. "Too much."

Kit knew that the same attitude held for her personal dilemmas too. Her friends were always there for her, and they weren't too judgmental, even though they never hesitated offering their own opinions. But knowing they would always support her no matter what didn't make it any easier to tell them what had happened.

Hadley got out of the car with a giant platter. "Cam made some chicken tenders. And they're really good."

"These are for Ollie?" Kit asked as she peeked under the tinfoil cover to find the steaming tenders laid out with three different dipping sauces.

"He got a little carried away," Hadley said. "Honey mustard, spicy buffalo, and sriracha. Oh, and a pile of veggie nuggets too."

Darla gestured toward the car. "We brought wine too."

"Wait a minute," Kit said. "This is looking like a backup plan for my cookout."

Hadley exchanged glances with Darla. "We weren't sure you were in the right mindset to take on a grill. Also, I brought you something else."

Kit knew her exuberant friend well enough to know when something was up. "Something else?"

She ran around to the back seat of the car and pulled out a pet carrier.

"Hadley, *no*."

Ollie dropped his plastic pail where he was shell collecting and ran over. Being at eye level, he was the first to peek in. "It's a kitty!" he said, jumping up and down.

"He's so cute!" Darla said, stooping next to Ollie.

"A kitty," Kit said in a deadpan voice. "You do realize that that fat little tabby you gave your grandmother is now a fixture in my house and that I have a dog, right?" Not to mention that her head was about to explode from stress.

Speaking of the dog, Rex, who was in the house, gave a bark, just to let them know he was missing out on the excitement.

Hadley set the carrier down on the driveway and reached in, pulling out a gray and white kitten with beautiful deep gray markings.

"Oh, he's pretty." Darla leaned in to examine the cat. "What kind of cat is that?"

Hadley straightened out, cradling the kitten in her arms. "*She's* a gray tabby. Aren't her markings extraordinary?"

The fact that Kit was ready to take a prisoner must have been evident because Darla grabbed her elbow and steered her away. "She's just bringing it for a visit," she said as she herded her toward the house.

"A visit, my a—"

"Darla's right," Hadley called. "I brought her for fun. One of Cam's employees found her near the dumpster at the restaurant. Fuller, the vet, said she looks like she's about three months old." She kissed the tiny thing on the head. "We call her Chaos. Kay for short."

Kit stared at her friend incredulously.

"Just for tonight!" Hadley expertly cradled the cat. "I'll keep a good eye on her, I promise. Pets are relaxing. They lower blood pressure."

"Your idea of relaxing is really odd," Darla said. "Is it time for wine yet?"

Despite everything, Kit somehow did start to relax. Ollie loved playing with the kitten, and Hadley was such a pro with pets that she handled the kitten and Rex, and Ollie too. Seymour, however, could not be coaxed out of hiding by a visit from one of his own kind.

They ate on the porch and then took Ollie and Rex for a stroll on the beach. Kit didn't even feel bad when Hadley stayed behind to babysit the kitten. The fresh air and wide-open ocean were always soothing. Ollie was in a great mood, and being with her friends finally made Kit's tension release its grip a little.

Ollie, already tired from his big day, was falling asleep practically before his head hit the pillow.

"Mommy," he said as she bent to give him a kiss. "I made a double today."

She smoothed back his curls. "Yes, you did, sweetheart. I'm so proud of you."

"I'm proud too. Now can I try out for the play?"

The fact that he was negotiating made her smile inside. And gave her hope that her old Ollie was back. "Ollie, you can try out for the play even if you don't get a hit in Tee ball. You know that, right?"

"I want to be the lemon," he said. "The lemon gets to sing a song."

"Well, you love to sing."

"I know." He nodded sleepily. "I'm really good at it."

That *definitely* sounded like the Ollie she knew.

Kit tucked the sheet around Ollie's arm. And made sure it didn't cover Hoot's head.

"Mommy," Ollie said as she turned to go, "I like Alex."

Hearing his name struck her heart.

"And Daddy did too," he continued, "because he was Daddy's best friend, right? So he's good, Mommy. He likes you, and he'd be a good daddy too."

Kit's breath hitched. *Out of the mouths of babes.*

She knew she needed to respond but her words got jumbled before they hit her mouth. *Don't get attached, he's only here for a while. No, Ollie, not him for a daddy. Because he's too...*

Too guarded, too sexy, too what?

Too close to Carson. That thought hit her straight in the chest.

"Alex is a nice friend," she finally ended up saying.

"Yeah." Ollie gave a big yawn and turned on his side. "He likes me too."

"Yes, and I *love* you." She kissed her son on his tanned

cheek. "Good night, my sweet," she said as she turned off the light.

As soon as Kit walked outside onto the porch, Hadley handed her a full glass of wine.

"Yes. Thank you." She plopped down on a recliner.

"What a great night," Hadley said, looking out over the ocean.

The water was quiet tonight. They sat and listened for a while to the gentle swishing of the waves as they churned up sand then headed out to sea again. They caught the sun's last act as it set as a perfect orange ball, slowly dimming right before it slipped below the horizon. Even Chaos the kitten curled up and slept on a soft blanket in her carrier. Finally Kit said, "This view never gets old."

"I love it too," Darla said. "So many great memories. I'm glad Ollie can grow up like we did, right near the water." She took a sip of her wine. "I like my house but nothing beats this lovely old neighborhood."

"Don't tell Nick that," Hadley said. "Isn't he redoing your kitchen?"

"He's not redoing my kitchen," she said a little defensively. "He's just changing out the backsplash."

"What was wrong with it again?" Kit asked. Darla's big, oceanfront house had all the bells and whistles, including a massive open deck right on the water, floor-to-ceiling windows—and no resident ornery pets.

"Nothing," Darla hedged. "Just that it was dark gray and wavy." She moved her hands in a wave pattern. "It reminded me of a cloudy day. Depressing."

"Darla, don't you think it's a little odd that Nick is back at your house, working on things?" Kit asked. Kit caught Hadley's eye, and knew they were both thinking the same thing. That maybe Darla, consciously or not, wanted him there. Besides, Kit thought as she took a sip of wine, the longer she kept her friends talking about themselves, the longer she could stall on bringing up her own problems.

"All I did was ask for a recommendation of a tile place," Darla protested. "He said I should go visit that artsy place in Wellington. They're local but gaining a reputation. So I did. Then he said he'd come do the job for me. And I did argue about it and tell him it was unnecessary. But he just showed up one morning with all my tile and a bunch of grout."

"I'm glad you two are finally friends again," Hadley said. "I mean, sometimes I see you catching up together at the Sand Bar."

Darla rarely looked distressed. Out of the three of them, she kept her problems the closest to her chest. But Kit could tell something was bothering her now. "We're cordial, yes. But it's weird. And definitely not like it used to be, where I could tell him anything. That got destroyed with the divorce. We never talk about anything significant." She chuckled softly. "That's probably how we're able to get along."

"Yet this is the third project he's volunteered for in the past six months," Hadley pointed out. "Your leaky porch roof, the backsplash, and didn't he install one of those wireless security systems a few months ago?"

"I know I have to put a stop to this. Also, I caught Lauren giving me a dirty look when he offered to stop by and fix my garden hose."

"Sounds like he's trying to tell you something through kind acts," Kit said.

Darla shook her head firmly. "Nothing can make up for the pain of a divorce."

"Maybe he wants to say he's sorry, but he doesn't know how. Or maybe he wants to get back together."

"What's done is done." Darla finished her wine and set her glass down on the table with a clink. "He clearly doesn't want to get back together because he's dated four different women since I moved back last year. You know how I know that? Because I can't help but see it. And do you know how I still feel when I see him with someone else? Bad. Really bad. I'm coming to see that maybe it was a huge mistake for me to move back here."

Kit reached across and squeezed her hand. "I guess it's just something that takes time."

Suddenly Kit burst out laughing.

"Did I miss something?" Darla asked.

"Just that I can't believe I said that. If I had a penny for every time someone told me *it just takes time*, I'd have enough money to fix up that old house myself. I'm sorry, Darla. You're getting advice from someone who can't practice what she preaches."

"I get it," Hadley said. "How can you get over someone when you see him every day? Especially when he's with other women. That seems like an understandable reaction."

"It's understandable but not acceptable," Darla said, "because I have to move on. It's been over a year since I finished my cancer treatments. I have a house and a stable career. I wanted to be closer to my mom and come home to the place I love, but I really think that seeing Nick all the time is preventing me from moving forward."

Darla, who seemed on the outside to be the toughest of all of them, was always extra hard on herself. But before Kit could say anything else, Darla sat up. "Enough of me. We're proud of you, Kit," she said, changing the subject.

"Don't minimize the progress you've made." She nodded toward the house. "Look what you've done."

"Burned burgers?" Kit waved her hand over the empty platter still sitting on the table.

"They were good," Darla said.

"That's because you microwaved a veggie one. I saw you sneak back into the kitchen."

"Hey, it was your first time," Hadley said. "New place, new grill, new class starting Monday. Lots of first times."

"Speaking of first times." Darla's mouth turned up in a mischievous smile.

To which Kit promptly tossed a napkin at her. Then she twisted Darla's ring off her finger.

"Oh no," Darla said, holding up her hands. "It doesn't work like that."

"Work like what?" Kit asked, trying not to be even more annoyed.

"You can't give it back just because you're uncomfortable with something that happened."

Kit held out the ring. "I agreed to wear this stupid thing, but ever since I've put it on, I've made bad, impulsive decisions."

"Okay, fine," Darla said, "I'll take it back." As soon as Kit dropped the ring into her hand, Darla wasted no time in saying, "So tell us what happened. That's what we really came here for."

Kit stalled a little longer by offering her friends some brownies. She'd made them from a mix; therefore they were basically un-ruinable. "I still don't understand what happened exactly. Alex drove me home after the fiasco with Bryan. One minute we were talking about Carson and we were both pretty emotional, and the next he was holding me and comforting me and then..."

"And then he kissed you?" Darla had a certain gleam in her eye that Kit knew as foreboding. "Because if he used your vulnerability to take advantage..."

"It wasn't like that," she added quickly. "Actually, I kissed *him*."

Hadley gave a little gasp.

"See?" Kit said, poking the air. "Even you agree. Out of character." She squeezed her eyes shut and pinched the bridge of her nose. As if anything could take her bad decision away. "What was I thinking? How could I do that?" Her stomach and her emotions in a tangle, she let out a little sob.

Hadley put a hand on her shoulder. "Alex wasn't...He wasn't mean or rough or—"

"No, not at all." He'd been kind, gentle, sexy, and passionate. "He was...amazing. And...yeah. Pretty amazing. But it should never have happened."

Darla brought the tissue box.

"How does Alex feel about this?" Hadley asked.

"We both agreed it was a huge mistake." Kit pulled out three tissues, wiping her eyes and blowing her nose.

"Why exactly are you calling it that?" Darla asked.

Kit wiped her eyes. "It was reckless."

"Reckless as in no birth control?" Hadley asked.

"I'm not *that* reckless," Kit said. "In one way, I think...well, it was pretty incredible. But in another way I feel that I've done something terrible. Alex was trying to help me. He tried to back away, and I...I told him not to. And on top of that, I'm afraid that I've messed up all my memories of Carson by doing this big, impetuous...thing."

That made her break down even more.

"Oh, honey," Hadley said.

"I think something else is going on here," Darla said.

Kit blew her nose. Again.

Darla tapped her fingers on the table. "I think you might be feeling guilty about Carson because you're afraid."

Kit snorted. "I've been afraid of *everything* for the past three years. That's why I've been trying to make changes." She dabbed at her eyes. "But changes are hard."

"You can never ruin your memories of Carson," Hadley said. "Don't even think that."

"I have a question," Darla said. "Why did you sleep with Alex? Because you're right when you said it's not like you to do that. And don't say you were both emotional and talking about Carson. Maybe you did it because you genuinely like him."

"Well, I remember we were both sharing memories about Carson and crying a little and...and he looked distressed that I was distressed. Like he was in pain too. And when we kissed, things just...ignited. Like, we had this...connection. I just forgot everything."

"Wow," Darla said.

"That doesn't excuse anything," Kit rushed on to say. "I mean, of all people, Carson's best friend? I feel..."

"Stop," Hadley said. "Alex is a great guy. And most importantly, it's okay to be attracted to him."

Kit threw up her hands. "He's staying in my garage. I mean, what am I going to do now?"

Darla gave a wide, slow smile, which Hadley poked her in the ribs for. "Okay, I have to tell you something," Darla said. "Nick told me he thinks Alex has got a thing for you."

"What is this, high school?" Hadley asked. "'A thing'?"

"He just said Alex behaves like he has a crush on you. Looks at you when you're not looking, that kind of thing."

"That's funny," Kit said, "because he's barely spoken to me for the past ten years."

"Think about this," Darla said. "If you were secretly in love with your best friend's girl, you might act like that too."

Kit shook her head. "That kind of stuff might happen in your books, but not in real life. Alex is very attractive. I'm sure he has no trouble finding women."

"It makes sense, though, doesn't it?" Darla said. "His buddy is gone but he still feels like he shouldn't want you. See? A dilemma."

"That's ridiculous."

"Okay," Hadley said, always practical. "I don't know about any of that stuff but here's what you're going to do. You're going to keep doing everything to make Ollie's and your life better. And you're going to give Alex a chance."

A chance? With Carson's best friend? Not going to happen. "No way."

"Carson's not here anymore, Kit," Darla said gently. "You have to stop feeling like you're cheating on him. You have to set aside all your feelings of beating yourself up and see if you *want* to give Alex a chance."

With that, they got up and started to stack some dishes. "Oh my gosh," Hadley said a minute later from inside the house. "You guys, come see this."

Darla and Kit ran through the sliding door into the small family room. Hadley had placed the cat carrier near the door. A fat black and white cat was sleeping next to the carrier, his tail wrapped around it.

"This is the sweetest thing I've ever seen." Hadley looked up at Kit. "Seymour came out of hiding to protect the kitten."

"That's so amazing," Darla said, taking a photo for her Facebook page, no doubt.

Kit was still freaking out. And miracle or no, she did not want another creature to take care of. But Seymour lifted his head and meowed, and she found herself scratching his head, which made him purr and headbutt against her hand for more.

"You ventured out of your shell, didn't you?" Kit said.

Rex bolted over, and for a second, Kit thought the cat was going to attack but instead he ran for the hills. But Rex stayed, sniffed around the carrier, and then, his curiosity satisfied, lay down at Kit's feet.

"Rexy, you're not jealous, are you?" Kit asked, scratching *his* head. Apparently, Rexy was an affection hog if it meant Seymour was getting her attention. Figures.

As Kit sat there and listened to her friends' exclamations of amazement at the cat, she realized that they didn't seem to think that what had happened between her and Alex was that big of a deal. Underneath all the feelings that were screaming at full volume inside her head, she recognized something else. That she liked Alex. A lot. And maybe she owed it to herself to give him a chance.

Chapter 18

ON MONDAY MORNING, Alex was waiting in his truck in front of the McKinnon house when Kit pulled into the driveway. She'd told him she had a lead on an architectural salvage place, and they planned to check it out over her lunch hour. She got out of her car, carrying a bright green tote bag with daisies on it, and climbed into his truck.

"Hello," she said cheerily, arranging the bag on her lap and placing her purse on the floor. The small cab was immediately filled with her fragrance, which he was quickly starting to recognize as part of her. And which he could only describe as something a little fruity, a little flowery, and a whole lot wonderful. It brought with it a vivid flashback of running his lips along her skin, inhaling that essence.

That made him immediately crack the window and start the car.

"I'm sorry I'm late," Kit said, rummaging through her bag. "Mr. Marfler gave me the stink eye on the way out. I swear he invents tasks for me at the last minute, just to be difficult."

"Were you asking him for a longer than usual lunch break?" She was dumping things out onto her lap—sunglasses, a juice box, one of those fluorescent Fruit Roll-Ups. He forced himself to look away from her pretty legs, peeking out from under the bright yellow print of her dress.

His mouth went dry. It wasn't lost on him that he'd been with her for less than a minute and was already on sensory overload.

He opened the window all the way.

"I got someone to cover the front desk for an extra hour, but I had to promise to clean the break room later." She must have noticed his scowl. "No worries. I'll be fine as long as I'm back on time."

He wondered how any man, even a cranky one, could fail to succumb to Kit's good-natured charm. And he also wondered why she kept a job that she clearly didn't like. But he kept his musings to himself. Because they'd agreed to...What was it they'd agreed to again? Not be lovers.

So then, what exactly were they?

He did his best to focus on backing the truck out of the driveway.

"So where exactly are we—" He was interrupted by a sandwich baggie dangling in front of his face as he put the truck in drive. "What's this?" he asked, accepting the packet with one hand.

She finished unwrapping a similar bag herself and took a bite of a sandwich. "PB and J. I figured we could scarf down lunch quick."

Again, her kindness. He ventured a quick glance in her direction, but she was busy eating and washing her food down with water from a bottle. "Thank you," he said. She nodded, produced a napkin out of somewhere, and placed it on his thigh.

He burst out laughing.

"What?" she asked. "What is it?"

"It's probably not a good idea to rub my leg while I'm driving."

"I'm not flirting with you." She tilted her head and frowned. "That was a mom move, not a . . . a sexy move. I was trying to protect your pants."

He decided not to even go near that one. "I think I'll leave that at thank you." And his heart, not his pants, was what needed protecting. He took a bite and said, "I forgot how good PB and J is."

"My kid is addicted to Hadley's grandmother's blueberry jam, so that's probably why it tastes so good."

"Smart kid." She smiled at that, which made him happy that he was able to break the tension a little. "So what's on the agenda for the next two hours?"

"I'm taking you to the largest architectural reclamation place in South Jersey. At least Nick said it was." She rummaged around again in her purse, coming up with another baggie.

"Some of the fireplace tiles are missing. I brought one to see if maybe we could find more."

"The light fixtures on either side of the front door are broken," he said. "I assume they have period fixtures like that?"

She nodded. "Maybe we could check it out, then come back another time with a real list. And we do need toilets. Preferably not pink ones."

"Hey, that was a high-quality seat," he said in defense.

"Our goal is quality at a bargain, but we have to be true to the period."

Talk like that made him shudder. He knew how his sisters shopped, endlessly debating colors, fabrics, prices, and just about anything else.

He swore she was stifling a snicker. "Don't look so horrified," she said.

"I have two older sisters. As the baby, I pretty much got dragged around on a lot of shopping trips."

"Don't worry. We just need to keep it simple and let the house speak for itself—the woodwork, the high ceilings, the moldings. I want people to look out the windows and think how lucky they are to live right on the harbor. So I'm thinking the walls inside can be a very light seafoam color, almost white. What do you think of that?" She seemed passionate, speaking with her hands.

"I like white." She must think he was an idiot. Also, what kind of color was *seafoam*?

"Nick was telling me about a client who remodeled their kitchen to look like a fifties diner, with chrome seats and a bright red table and Coke signs on the walls. It was very beachy."

"I don't picture an old home like that looking like a fifties diner."

"Well, I don't either, but it did appeal to renters." She paused for a bite. "See? You say that you don't care but maybe secretly you do."

He couldn't help chuckling. "Secretly, I'm relieved I don't have to pick out all this stuff myself."

A few miles out from town, they pulled up to a large warehouse. In a large field on the side, rows of toilets sat in an orderly row. One had flowers planted in the tank, which Kit immediately ran over to examine.

"A potential use for the pink toilet seat?" he asked.

"Ha! The flowers are clever. I wonder if they'd buy the pink one from us? They have every color of the rainbow."

They walked by endless collections of sinks, granite slabs, steam radiators, porch columns, pedestal sinks, and bathtubs.

"How's that claw-foot tub in the big upstairs bathroom?" Kit asked.

"Solid as a boulder. And Nick knows someone who recoats cast-iron tubs. Thank goodness, because I'm not sure how we'd ever move it out of there."

"I always wanted a claw-foot tub," she said with a sigh. "They're romantic."

There went his imagination again, on overdrive. Candles, bubbles, the smooth curves of her shoulders...

He forced himself to think of how badly he hated shopping instead.

"I've never seen so many windows," she said as they passed rows of them in all shapes and sizes. She stopped to admire a large palladium window lying on its side.

"Drafty ones," he noted.

She squinted in the sun at all the rows of stuff surrounding them. "I'm overwhelmed, and we haven't even gone inside yet."

"Let's just do a quick look around," he said, steering her into the place, where they came upon more collections— of fireplace mantels, crossbeams, and doors. And that was just the big stuff.

He whistled. "This place looks like an antique store and Lowe's had a baby."

Kit walked over to a table full of door hardware—knobs, hinges, and screws. "Look at these antique door knockers." She picked up a lion. "Not very welcoming."

"It's the pre-Internet version of Ring." When she rolled her eyes, he tried again. "A non-barking watch-dog?" She still wasn't impressed. "I've got it," he said, snapping his fingers. "A decorative BEWARE OF DOG sign."

She shook her head and chuckled. "I think you're having way too much fun here. Look at this creepy man with a beard and curly horns."

"That's Pan."

She examined it and set it down quickly. "The god Pan?"

He nodded. "The deity of fertility and nature."

"Oh. Why would he be on a door?"

"I'm not sure." He held up one that was shaped like a brass hand. "Also creepy."

They surveyed a pineapple, a fish, and a cherub.

"Which one do you like?" he asked.

She pointed to a brass scallop. "Simple. Beachy. Cute." She looked up, and for a second, their gazes collided in that same crazy way that he could not seem to control.

"And not scary," he added.

She opened the scallop like it was talking. "Definitely not scary," she said in a high-pitched voice.

He let out a belly laugh but then looked up a little later to find her assessing him strangely. "What's wrong?"

"Um...when you laugh, that completely wrecks my impression of you."

"On second thought, I like the creepy fist." He lifted a brow. "How's that? More in character?"

She cocked her head and examined him. "Actually, I'm trying to figure that out. It seems like you have a side you show to the world and one that's more hidden."

Not to the world, just to you, he thought. Out loud, he said, "I think you're giving me too much credit. I'm not that complicated." They moved on to a collection of stained-glass windows.

"I could spend all day here," she said. "I feel like we're in a museum."

"We kind of are," Alex said. "Take a look at these."

Leaning against a wall was a collection of Tiffany-style windows, many depicting intricately crafted scenes of dragonflies, irises, sunflowers, and even a peacock.

They both gravitated to the same one, a large, rectangular window showcasing a great old tree, its branches radiating out in all directions, the leaves different delicate shades of bright green and gold. Brilliant blue and purple birds nested near the top of the tree in a sunlit sky. Behind the tree was the ocean.

"I think it's a Tiffany-style take on the Tree of Life," Alex said.

Kit bent to examine it. "Except instead of mountains in the background, there's the sea."

Alex lifted the window and held it up. Vivid blues and greens lit up, the sea and the sun in the background sparkling with radiant pinpoints of light.

"Alex, look." Kit pointed. "The ocean is made from sea glass. It's stunning. Imagine what it would look like if the sun were streaming through it."

"Wow," he said in appreciation. Which wasn't exactly intelligent. But he was genuinely moved.

"It reminds me of a summer day by the sea." Kit gave a soft, longing sigh. "My favorite kind of day." Her face was lit up, happy. She was completely absorbed in the art and excited about it—a rare moment where she didn't seem weighted down by grief or worry.

And he got it. He completely got it. The artwork was breathtaking.

"Oh, hello," an older woman with gray hair and a flowered smock with pockets said. "I'm Angie. I see you've found the Tree by the Sea."

"That's what it's called?" Kit asked.

"Well, that's the little name we gave it. Isn't it beautiful?"

"It looks like a Tiffany," Alex said.

"Yes, it's got a tremendous amount of detail. But it was done locally. The artist was Margaret Driscoll, who did work for Tiffany for a time. She was very talented, wasn't she?"

"It's like it tells a story," Kit said.

"Well, it sort of does," Angie said. "Would you like to know?" She tilted the window forward and pointed to the wood frame near the bottom. "There's a title written down there, right near the artist's signature. She called it *A New Day*. We believe it's because your eye moves forward into the artwork, through the blossoming tree, the birds, the flowers, and then to the burst of sunshine and the ocean. It's a happy, positive piece, isn't it?"

Alex pulled out his tape measure and began measuring.

"What are you doing?" Kit whispered. "We can't afford this. It probably costs five thousand dollars."

"This is a salvage yard, and it's been sitting here awhile," he whispered back as he kept measuring.

She tugged on his sleeve. "Come on. We'd better get to the toilets."

That made him smile. *Again*.

MIRANDA LIASSON

"Let me know if I can help with anything," Angie said, moving on to help another couple.

Alex ran his hand along the top, pushing off a thick coat of dust. Then he tilted the window forward and flipped over a tag on the back. "Five hundred. Hmm. Not bad."

"Are you thinking the landing?" Kit asked.

"Just wondering if it's the same size."

"We came for white toilets," Kit whispered.

"I know." He tried to sound regretful but couldn't. The window was superb. And it looked to be very close to the size of the window on the stair landing.

She tapped him on the shoulder. "All we've done is look at animal door knockers and beautiful windows." She glanced at her watch. "We need to get out of here."

Alex pocketed his tape measure. "We don't want to make Mr. Muffler angry."

"Mr. *Marfler*." But he could see she was trying not to laugh.

As they walked out, he shoved his hands in his jeans pockets so he wouldn't take her hand, which somehow seemed like the most natural thing in the world. He had to steel himself to fight the wave of chemistry shimmering between them like sun on the ocean on a bright, sunshiny day. Or, rather like the panes of that glass.

Alex opened the truck door for her, and she said, "Congratulations. You survived your first shopping trip."

He made a fake-pained sound in his throat.

"Come on, admit it." She playfully bumped him on the arm with her fist. "It was fun, even if we didn't get any toilets."

Her hair was backlit by sunshine, displaying surprising shades of red and gold among the deep brown strands.

Lighting up his darkness. He pushed the sappy thought away. "But we saw some amazing things, didn't we?"

She nodded, her smile reaching her eyes. Which was another amazing thing to see.

He'd enjoyed the trip. A lot.

He'd been telling himself—quite a bit, the last few days—that after they'd had sex, the attraction was bound to wear off. That had been his typical experience with other women.

Because it had been, when it came right down to it, just sex. Two people swept up in grief, comforting each other.

That was all.

He didn't want to think of them having any common ground other than their combined mission to fix up this house. And a sexual attraction that was off the charts.

He *couldn't* think that way. Or he'd never be able to let her go.

Chapter 19

AS ALEX PULLED up to the house, Kit knew their time was up, but somehow she hated to go. Who'd have thought architectural salvage could be so much fun?

"Well, I'd better be getting back," she said as she climbed out of the truck. "My first class starts tonight, and I've got a new sitter coming over."

"You aren't dropping Ollie off with your parents?"

"I think your words were that it's good for him to have new experiences, right?"

He chuckled softly. "I do recall saying that."

She dug in her purse for her keys. "Well, I think you're right. I just hope Ollie likes her. Her name's Catherine, and she's the daughter of one of my work friends. She helps Hadley sometimes at Pooch Palace." Now she was rambling. But she couldn't seem to stop. "I don't know if I'm more nervous about the babysitter or my first class."

"It will be a new experience for both of you. And knowing Ollie, he'll be fine."

She nodded as optimistically as she could and headed to her car. "Thanks for the fun trip."

Suddenly he placed a hand on her elbow. "Wait," he said. "Just one second, okay?"

Alex didn't wait for her answer. Instead, he ran around the house. She followed him to the big beech tree in front of the harbor. Before she could ask what he was doing, he took a penknife out of his back pocket and sliced off a loose piece of bark from the central trunk.

She had no idea what he was about to do. But judging by the earnest expression on his face, it was going to be something touching. As he stood there under the old tree, dappled light hitting his handsome features, she felt that same familiar pull, that same desire as always.

And she wished their time wasn't up. She wanted to keep talking with him, and joking, and . . . discovering new things. He had a way of making her see things differently, more molehill than mountain, with more humor. And she wanted to learn more about him.

"Here you go." He held out the bark.

"Thank you?" she asked as she took the offering into her palm. "Are you going to say something poetic?"

"Nothing poetic." The corner of his mouth lifted. "But I am going to tell you that my father taught me that beech trees are very special. Do you want to know why?"

She fingered the bark, which was gray and raised and rough, yet also oddly smooth.

"Well, if you put it that way, of course I do."

"Beech trees are symbolic for wisdom, understanding, and knowledge. They can live to be three or four hundred years old, so they're considered to be wise, old trees.

Keeping a piece of their bark is supposed to bring a person luck in their studies."

She looked from the bark to Alex and back again, suddenly a little teary. She swallowed hard. "Thank you. I...yeah." Yep, she'd been right. He'd gotten her all emotional with a piece of bark. "Sometimes I sink back into thinking that I'm clearly over my head in so many ways." She bit her lower lip. "But you...you're just so positive." She held up the bark and tapped it against her hand. "This just made me feel a little bit less alone." She immediately tried to lighten things up. "And, by the way, that *was* poetic."

"You're not alone, Kit," he said softly.

His dark eyes burned into hers, but there was a gentleness beside the intensity. The way he looked at her was like a caress without words, without touching.

But she got the feeling loud and clear.

Then she remembered the time, and work, and the thousands of other things she still had to do.

As she walked around the house to where her car was parked in the drive, Darla's VW Bug suddenly pulled up behind her. At the same time, Nick walked out of the house to join them.

"I'm glad I made it in time," Darla said, a little out of breath.

"What's wrong?" Kit's thoughts immediately turned to Ollie.

"Nothing bad," she said quickly. "Nick called and told me to come over. We have something to tell you."

Kit eyed her watch. "Whatever it is, it better be quick so Mr. Marfler doesn't blow a gasket."

"Okay, so I was talking to Agnes Vanderhaven." Darla was talking fast. "And she said they could use another house on the tour. One of the homes isn't going to be done in time."

Kit shook her head. "Agnes is the head of the Architectural Review Board. A do-it-yourself project like ours is never going to pass muster with her."

"She walked through here yesterday," Nick said. "I hope you don't mind that I let her in. She thinks we're doing an amazing job."

"It's a bad idea," Kit rushed to say. "The amount of work we'd need to do to finish in time is astronomical. Not to mention I'm starting a class. And the Fourth of July is only five weeks away."

Alex had been standing there quietly, listening. "Actually, that's a very doable timeline," he said.

Kit shot him a daggered look. Did she say she loved his optimism? That was hasty.

"Listen," he continued, "it could work to our advantage to get the house on the tour."

"Tons of people come through," Darla agreed. "I bet the house would sell."

"She's right," Nick said. "Our company didn't do any reno work on the tour this year. So it would be good marketing for us, too, if you'd let me put our Cammareri sign and some business cards in the kitchen."

"You guys are forgetting something," Kit said. "We don't have any furniture."

Nick gave a little smile. "We've done this before, where we contract with a designer in town."

"It's short notice. Plus…I can't afford a decorator. That's why we picked out everything ourselves."

"I have a better idea," Darla said. "I bet Apoorva would help us." Apoorva Vasu ran the Ivy Cottage, a large antique shop in town. "If she agreed to let us borrow furniture, she could advertise and make some sales. And the antiques would look amazing in the house. What would you think of that?"

"Plus, we'd help you," Nick chimed in. "Obviously."

"There's just one last teeny, tiny detail." Darla pinched her thumb and forefinger together. "Agnes has to know today. The photographers have to come out and take some pics for the brochure."

"Want to talk about it?" Alex asked, motioning that they could talk privately.

"I didn't want to say this," Kit said as they stepped off to the side, "but I don't think I can handle more stress right now."

"I'll handle as much of it as I can. It's a great idea, Kit. I'd hate for you to lose a great opportunity to sell the house after all our work."

She thought about that. He looked so sure. And you know what? She believed him. Even more than that—she *trusted* him. Sighing heavily, she asked, "Is there a bark for calm?"

"No," he said with a laugh, "but I hear they make a wine out of birch sap."

She was rolling her eyes when he added, "Let me drive you back to work."

"I have my car. Why would you do that?"

He touched her arm and smiled, both of which filled her with warmth. And made her a little dizzy. "So I can be with you for five more minutes."

Kit groaned but she couldn't help smiling right back. "That's really sweet, Alex. But I think I have, like, three minutes to save my job." On impulse, she reached up and kissed him quickly on the cheek. "See you."

"See you," he said, squeezing her hand.

Maybe she shouldn't have done that. But Nick and Darla were talking and didn't even notice. But even if they did, would it have mattered? She wasn't sure.

As she said goodbye to Nick and Darla and headed into work, she found it impossible to hold on to her regret about sleeping with Alex. It had been replaced by something warm, fuzzy, and a little fizzy, something that at one time she might have called happiness.

* * *

After Kit left, Alex carted out a ladder and some supplies into the yard. He found Nick standing there, leaning his long frame against the thick trunk of the beech tree.

"Hey. How'd you like the salvage place?"

"It's a gold mine," Alex said. He dusted off his hands and walked over to the water, placing his hands on his hips as he looked out over the bay, which was sun-kissed in the early afternoon light. Sailboats with bright white sails glided by, carefree. He had to admit that spending time with Kit had lightened his mood. But judging by the way Nick was standing there, arms crossed, he got the distinct feeling that his friend was unhappy about something. "I think getting this place ready for the tour is a great idea," he offered.

"Me too," Nick said. "But can I ask you something?"

"Sure. Of course."

Nick cleared his throat. If Alex knew anything about heart-to-hearts among men, starting with throat clearing was not a good thing.

"Did you give Kit a piece of bark?"

Alex frowned. "Yes," he said honestly. "I took it from the back of the tree and made sure I didn't cut too deeply—"

"I'm not worried about the tree."

"Oh, okay. It was for good luck. She's starting class tonight." That sounded really sappy, now that he had to put it into words.

"Look, Alex," Nick cut to the chase, "I have to tell you that when I was married to Darla, Kit and Hadley became like sisters to me. I feel very protective of them."

Right. He got that. "Look, I'm not here to..." Here to do what? The truth was, he'd slept with Kit. They'd both agreed that wouldn't happen again, but if he was being honest, every minute in her presence presented a struggle to keep that promise.

Nick rubbed his neck, clearly uncomfortable. "I feel a need to remind you that Kit is vulnerable now. She's making a lot of changes, and she's trying really hard to make a new life for her and Ollie. I don't want anyone to mess with that—if you're not serious about her."

"I'm not out to hurt anyone," Alex said. "I'm not after a relationship." Both things were true. So then why did he allow himself to get close to her?

"You're misreading me." Nick pushed off from the tree and stood up. "If you want something serious with her, that's one thing. But if you're just looking for a summer thing, I'm going to have to step in. Because I don't want her to get hurt any more than she has been. You hear what I'm saying?"

"Loud and clear." Had it been that obvious that he needed a talking-to?

Alex picked up the thick coil of coated rope he'd left on the ground near the ladder and started rolling it up.

"You're putting up a swing?" Nick asked.

"I thought it would be a selling point."

Nick picked up the wooden seat and examined it. "Nice job. Oak?"

"I glued two pieces of plywood together and put about five coats of polyurethane on it."

Nick handed him the wood. "Alex, you're an upstanding guy. What I'm seeing is you acting a lot like you might be interested but you say nothing's going on. So which is it?"

So many things went through Alex's mind. How it might be nice to confide in a friend about what he was going through. And how Nick was reaching out, and Alex was, as usual, not saying much.

Which left him where he always was. Alone. Keeping secrets he didn't know how to let go of.

"You want to talk sometime?" Nick asked. "Because if you do, I'm a great listener. Especially if there's beer involved."

Alex wished he could tell Nick the truth, treat him like a real friend. Only the things he had to confess were unconfessable.

My best friend isn't here because of me. And I think I'm falling in love with his wife.

Just thinking that made him shudder. He could never say those words out loud. And he could never solve the dilemma.

It reinforced how important it was to stick to the plan.

"I appreciate how much you care about Kit," Alex said, rolling up the stray rope. "But no worries. I would never do anything to cause her more pain." Then he walked away before he said something more.

Nick was right. Giving in to his feelings would only harm Kit in the long run. He had to stay away from her for her own sake. And for his.

Chapter 20

"HAVE YOU SEEN Kit?" Darla asked Alex as she walked up to him where he was settled into a seat at the Sand Bar that Friday.

"Nope," Alex said. "I'm just meeting Nick for a beer." Nick, who probably felt bad for laying into him, but Alex had told him no hard feelings.

"You're meeting Nick?" She frowned slightly.

"Yes." He nodded toward the beer in front of him to show her he was telling the truth. "Is something wrong?"

"No." She seemed to shrug off her concern. "Of course not. I'm just...meeting a date."

"Oh." It occurred to him that she probably didn't want Nick watching her from afar. "That's nice," he said carefully. "You aren't nervous, are you?"

"Of course not." Darla gave her typical response. But then her face softened. "Okay, yes. Pretty nervous. And the fact that Nick's going to be here, too, just seems awkward."

"I get it," he said. "But don't let that stop you from having a good time."

"I'm actually excited about it. So when you see Kit walk in, would you tell her I'll be over there?" She pointed to the outdoor seating area on the water. "Don't tell her this, but my date is bringing a friend. Which could be good for her, you know?"

He couldn't prevent his brows from hiking up. Darla seemed to be carefully assessing his reaction. As if maybe she was on to everything that had happened between him and Kit. Alex had no idea what Kit told her girlfriends, but judging by how tight they all were, he would guess *everything*.

"It would be good for her to meet someone," he said carefully. "Someone who would treat her like the amazing woman that she is." There. He needed to start signaling to everyone that there was nothing between them. And he might as well start now.

Darla scanned his face, but he gave her his most impassive smile.

"Oh, I almost forgot." She reached into her jeans pocket. "Will you give this back to Kit?"

Darla handed him what looked like a giant diamond ring.

"What is this?" he asked, examining it.

"Family heirloom," she said. "She'll understand. Oh, there's Sam now." She nodded to a good-looking man who was following a hostess to a table. "I've got to go. Send her my way!"

"Good luck with the date," he said as he settled down at the bar.

Sure enough, Kit came through the door a minute later, waved to him, and headed over. She had on a strappy black dress and gold hoop earrings. And her long dark hair was down, the breeze blowing it in gentle wisps.

She looked beautiful.

"Hey," she said. The sun was starting to sink to the horizon, flaming down in shades of orange, the sky fading from blue to a deep indigo as night came on. A perfect summer night.

"I love Fridays," she said, grinning widely.

Every part of him wanted to claim her as his. Ask her how her day was. Tell her about the progress on the house. And the swing. And a thousand other things.

And it all broke his heart. Because he knew what he had to do. And it wasn't sitting and flirting with her or hanging out talking about light fixtures and brass door knockers, all of which had been surprisingly fun.

"Our little trip to the salvage yard has been making me think of more ideas for the house all week." She sounded excited and animated.

"Great," he said, chuckling. "Just what we need. More ideas."

Before Kit could respond, probably with something that would put him in his place, Darla beckoned from across the restaurant.

Kit gave her a quick wave. "Darla's meeting one of her superfans here tonight. He's read every book she's written. She met him at her last signing, and they hit it off, and he asked her out. I told her I'd sit with her, just to make sure the guy isn't a stalker. But I'd rather sit here with you."

"I'm just waiting for Nick." He took a nervous glance

at his watch, even though he couldn't care less that Nick was running late.

"Oh, that's nice." She paused, as if she were choosing her words carefully.

Before he could say something, Darla waved.

"Sorry, I forgot to tell you," he said, "that Darla came over and wanted you to know where she's sitting."

"That's okay, I see her." She stood on tiptoes to look over the crowd. "Hmmm. It looks like there are two guys with her, not just one."

"Her date brought a friend," he said.

She groaned, which secretly pleased him. "Will you be around a little later—after Nick?"

Alex's stomach churned. He knew what she was subtly saying. That they clearly had chemistry out of bed, too, and maybe their sleeping together was seeming a little less shocking. And that she wanted to spend time with him, maybe see where things would lead.

All of which made him hesitate. Made him unsure that he would be able to do what he needed to do. But keeping on the path they were on would only lead to the same thing again. And that wouldn't be good for either one of them.

The line had to be drawn in the sand. And sadly, he had to be the one to draw it.

"I'm pretty tired," he said. "Think I'll head back soon."

"Is everything all right?" She swept a concerned look over him. "Are you feeling okay?"

"Fine." He averted his gaze to his beer, overly absorbed in watching a bead of condensation trickle slowly down the side. "I think it's a good idea for you to meet the friend." *No he didn't.* He took a large swig to prevent himself from immediately taking the words back.

"I've already met the stalker—I mean, Sam. At the book signing." She chuckled a little. "I have to stop calling him that. He seems nice."

"I don't mean Sam. I mean *his* friend."

"His frien—" She scanned his face. "You want me to meet his friend, as in, someone I might be interested in?" She seemed to let that settle in.

"Yes." That little bead had almost made it down to the table. Really fascinating.

"As in, you're blowing me off?"

He forced himself to make brief eye contact. But he wished he didn't, because she looked furious. "I'm not doing anything that we hadn't already agreed on. I just think it would be best if—"

"Best if what?" She folded her arms and glared, which reminded him just how much she hated that expression.

He couldn't do it. He couldn't look her in the eye and tell her a lie. So he dropped his gaze to her feet. Where he saw she was wearing sexy, strappy sandals. Definitely not the mom kind.

"Best if we stick to friendship." He suppressed a wince. "Like we said," he added weakly.

"Oh," she said, looking hurt. "I see." She turned to leave.

But a second later she was right back at his side. Blowing out a big breath, she said, "You're sending me mixed messages. There are times when you act like you really enjoy being with me, but then you ice everything down again. I have such a fun time with you. And I thought you did too. And then all of a sudden…why this? It doesn't make sense. What's up with you?"

Of course, she couldn't just take what he'd said and not question it. Her toughness was something he admired greatly. How did she manage to see through him so clearly? And call him out on his baloney?

Just then her phone buzzed. "Darla needs me over there." She looked him over one last time. "See you around."

"Later," he said as he watched her walk away in her sexy heels and her black dress and the little purse she'd looped over her shoulder.

He ordered a whiskey straight up and checked his watch. He'd ruined that in no time. But it had to be done, sooner or later.

The whiskey didn't make him feel any less awful. He was about to toss some money on the bar and leave when Nick walked over, a beer in hand.

"Hey," Nick said. "Sorry I'm late."

"Hey." Alex nodded. "Have a seat."

"Who are those dudes?" Nick asked, his gaze drifting across the bar to where Kit and Darla were sitting.

"One of them is Darla's fan," Alex said. "Kit said he met her at the book signing."

"Darla met someone at the book signing?"

"A superfan. Apparently he's read all her books."

"He's read all her—"

Darla let out a whoop of laughter that carried across the bar. Kit was laughing too. Nick didn't look pleased that they were having fun. Frankly, Alex wasn't either.

"Look," Nick said, facing him. "Whatever it is that's bothering you, is it worth still carrying around?"

"How do you of all people know that something's bothering me? You're the one who told me to stay away from her."

Nick's perceptive gaze swept over him. "Darla thinks I'm an emotional Neanderthal—she actually called me that once." He chuckled. "But even I can tell when someone's carrying an anvil around their neck. And I want you to know I feel a little bad about the other day. Like maybe I don't know your story."

"I just want Kit to be happy. That's it. I'm pretty simple." Alex frowned on the outside, but on the inside, he felt uncomfortable. Nick was fishing, and he was getting a little too close to the truth. "Kit should meet someone nice. Who treats her the way she deserves." Maybe if he kept saying it, he'd actually come to believe it.

Nick's loud, "Oh no, look at that," made him turn. Across the way, Sam the Stalker moved next to Darla, and his friend moved across the booth next to Kit. Alex averted his eyes. He couldn't watch this anymore.

Nick wasn't letting this go. He pointed a finger. "Look at you. You can't take this either. I can tell you hate it too."

"I'm watching the sunset."

"You're grinding your fist into the table, bro."

Alex decided the best defense was a good offense. "Maybe the real question is for you. Why do you care if someone checks out Darla?"

Nick took a long pull on his beer. "I don't know. That's the honest truth. She's my ex, but part of me keeps holding on. I think part of me will always want her back. I guess it doesn't help that I'm planning on installing a brand-new floor in her kitchen."

"Why are you doing that?"

"Because she wanted one," he said with conviction. "And I can do it the best."

That was almost as messed up as Alex was. "And yet you're dating someone else."

"I'm doing everything that I can to make up for being a jerk when we were married." He tapped his fingers on his beer glass. "But being with me isn't what's best for her."

Alex groaned inwardly. Yeah, definitely messed up. But at least the focus wasn't on him. "What exactly did you do that's so bad?" he couldn't help asking.

"Be an idiot. I resented that she was driven and worked really hard to get published. We were newlyweds—I couldn't understand why she didn't want to go out with our friends and have fun, so after a while, I got angry and went on my own anyway. Stupid things like that."

"Did you cheat on her?"

"No," he said definitively.

"I knew I liked you," Alex said. "And...and it's never too late, is it?"

"Too late for me, but maybe you should ask yourself that question."

Alex peeled his eyes from Kit, who was animatedly telling a story, to focus on Nick, who was eyeing him with a loaded look. "What is it now?"

"Look, I just want to say something, and you can take it or leave it, okay?"

"Okaaay," Alex said hesitantly, "but you're scaring me. You're reminding me of the way my abuela used to look right before she started giving me advice."

"Well, if you'd talk to me more, maybe I'd really know what was going on with you instead of having to guess."

"Maybe you *are* my abuela. Reincarnated." He signaled for more drinks.

"I'm just a friend. Trying to help you." Nick suddenly swiveled on the bar stool and turned to him. "Look, Alex.

I was two years behind you in school, and I didn't hang with you and Carson like Cam did. But I remembered something that I can't get out of my mind."

"Okay, now you're *really* scaring me." The back of his neck prickled.

"It was homecoming, and I was a geeky sophomore watching popular senior guys."

"Wait a minute. You're talking, like, when we were in high school?"

"Hear me out. You were a big shot, and I was watching your every move. You were carrying two glasses of punch across the gym floor when some idiot plowed through the crowd and spilled it all over you. And Carson got to her first. Didn't he?" Nick paused. "You were headed to talk to Kit, but he got there first."

Alex cursed inside. "Why would you remember that?" Such an insignificant thing. To most people.

But the start of a special kind of misery for him.

That awful moment struck him again in the gut. Punch had seeped through his pressed shirt as he stood in the middle of that dazzling, disco ball–lit gym floor and watched his best friend go after the girl he'd wanted.

"I remember how you looked," Nick continued. "Angry. Sad. Maybe even heartbroken."

Words caught in Alex's throat.

"Carson talked to her for the rest of the night," Nick said. "I'm not sure where you went. With punch all over you, probably home."

Alex twirled his bottle, debating on whether or not he should deny it all. But Nick was reaching out. Being a friend. And he'd closed himself off for quite a while to those. So he pushed the bottle away and looked Nick in the eye. "I did go home," was all he managed.

"Maybe you weren't allowed to be in love with her before." Nick sat back and relaxed his posture. "But what's stopping you now?"

Alex couldn't put his feelings into words. He'd kept them inside for too long.

"I know you've been through a lot," Nick said quietly. "All I'm saying is, it's okay to be...human."

"She's not ready for anything serious."

"Maybe not, but she's ready for something, right? And maybe she will be someday. I mean, you already slept with her, right?"

Alex narrowed his eyes in warning.

Nick shrugged. "I might have heard that from Darla. I was over at her house working, and I accidentally overheard her talking to Hadley."

Women's friendships were...dangerous.

"I'm pretty sure you can trust me to keep quiet about this." The corner of his mouth tipped upward. "After all, I haven't said anything in seventeen years. Besides, maybe now we can really be friends."

"Hey, guys," Darla said, suddenly at their side, signaling the bartender for another round of drinks.

Her presence threw Alex. How long had she been standing there? Probably not long, he convinced himself. Plus she seemed really excited about her date and probably wasn't paying them any attention. "How's it going?"

"Oh, pretty fun," she said. "I think Sam knows my books better than I do. What's up with you two?"

"Just hanging out," Alex said.

"Waiting for Lauren," Nick said. Alex saw them look at each other for a beat or two before Darla reached for her beers.

"Oh. Well, have a good night." She smiled, gathering up the beers and heading back.

"Thanks for...the talk," Alex said, "but Lauren's not really meeting you, is she?" He took a swig of his own beer and gave him the side-eye. "Also, if you're Dear Abby, why don't you and Darla talk it out? Tell her she's the one who matters."

"Too much water under that bridge. And I've got to go." He nodded to where Lauren stood at the door, waving enthusiastically. "But...thanks."

Nick said his goodbyes, leaving Alex sitting there, looking over at the table where Darla had rejoined the others. In a very strange way, it felt like high school all over again.

Sitting back and letting another guy get a chance.

What *was* stopping him?

Carson. That's who.

A little while later, Kit came up to the bar, ordering another round of beers. "I thought you were leaving?" she asked.

"No, just hanging out for a while. You seem like you're having fun over there," he couldn't resist saying. Judging by the rounds of beer at least, the conversation must be amazing.

"Yes, I am," she said. "A *lot* of fun. Huge amounts. Thanks."

"I'd be careful with those guys. They're not from town, and you don't know them very well."

"Wait a minute." She put her hands on her hips and faced him. "You're not sitting here waiting for us, are you? To...make sure those guys are normal guys? Because that would be really...insulting."

Busted. "Of course I'm not doing that."

When she faced him, her color was high. "Go home, Alex. Okay? You may think you're some kind of super-protector, but you know what? I don't need a guardian angel. I'm doing just fine by myself. And having you watch over me is really annoying."

The bartender set the beers on the bar. She took them and left without another word.

Chapter 21

KIT PULLED UP to the bungalow a little later with her
head pounding, wondering how she managed to fit trail
mix, wipes, and the equivalent of a mini first-aid kit in
her purse but not have any pain relief.

Tylenol might help her headache but would definitely
not take away the major pain in the butt Alex de la Cruz
was coming to be in her life.

She locked her car and headed to the side door, her
worries about Ollie and her new babysitter temporarily
displacing thoughts of Alex. Her heart started to race in
unison with the throb in her head as she imagined worst-
case scenarios. What if the babysitter was making out
with her boyfriend on the couch, music cranked up, while
Ollie was MIA somewhere, left to wander off alone down
the beach?

As she walked in, the babysitter, sixteen-year-old
Catherine, was reading a paperback on the couch with the

TV on low. Which lowered Kit's blood pressure a little. Even though, between the throbbing beats of her headache, she was still seeing visions of a certain ex–air force captain whose neck she wanted to wring.

"Oh, Mrs. Blakemore." The babysitter closed her book. "Ollie's fine, but I have to tell you something."

Up, up skyrocketed her blood pressure. "What is it?" she asked with forced cheer.

"Hoot lost an eye, probably somewhere in the front yard. Ollie set him down on that big rock next to the seagrass while we were playing tag. We walked down to the beach for a while, but then it was getting dark and he went to collect Hoot and…no eye. I found some flashlights in the kitchen drawer, and we looked for about a half hour before Ollie went to bed but no luck."

Kit set her keys and purse down on the counter. "How did Ollie take that?"

"He was a little upset, but I promised you'd look again in the morning. And I read him, like, five books until he finally fell asleep." She scrolled through her cell. "The only trouble is, Hoot has unusual button eyes. The black button is rimmed with mother-of-pearl." She held out her phone so Kit could look at it. "Did you know that there are rare button companies? They say no button is too hard for them to find."

Kit glanced at the website. "Well. Who knew?"

"Also, your cat's really sweet."

"You actually saw him?"

She nodded. "More than that. He came and sat on the couch with me for a while. I should say on the other end of the couch, not exactly with me. Until Rex started sniffing him."

As she thanked Catherine and walked her to the door,

she said what was on her mind. Which was, "Would you want to come back and sit for Ollie again?" She would check with Ollie first, of course, but anyone who could read him five books and then search online for button companies was a win in her book.

"I'd love to," Catherine said. "Ollie's really sweet. Just give me some notice so I can check my work schedule. I do a few shifts a week at Burger Palace."

Wow, babysitting and a job too? *Okay, that wasn't so bad*, Kit thought as she closed the door. She'd survived hiring a sitter, and Cat seemed really responsible and nice. Now to find Hoot's eye before dawn.

She might need some wine for that. And for the fact that she was still fuming inside at Alex. Annoying, irritating man. How could he be so warm and loving and funny and then...go cold? She didn't get it.

Kit found Ollie tucked in, his sweet, angelic face reminding her how lucky she was to be his mom. When he was asleep, she always saw vestiges of Carson in him. The lip line, the arch of his brow. The same pang hit her as always, but it was tempered a little.

Maybe because she was doing her best to dig herself out of the rut. Maybe because this time she heard Carson's voice telling her, *You're doing it. Keep doing it.*

So she kicked off her heels, put on flip-flops, grabbed a sweater and a flashlight, and, on impulse, the leftover wine bottle from the fridge from when her friends were here last.

And went to find a needle in a haystack. In the dark.

"What are you doing?" a voice asked a few minutes later.

She startled. And looked up to find Mr. Crankenstein himself standing there, arms folded, watching her intently as she bent over, canvassing every blade of grass and every grain of sand for an inch-wide button.

"What does it look like I'm doing?" she asked, unable to contain the snark. But she was too mad to care. Her sweater slid off her shoulder, and she hiked it up and went back to business.

"Drinking again in your front yard?" The corner of his mouth turned up.

She rolled her eyes and did her best to ignore him.

He reached into his pocket for something. Why did he have to be so tall and broad-shouldered and...hot? "Here you go," he said, handing the object to her. One glance told her it was Darla's ring. Ugh. Just what she didn't want, but she slipped it on because losing Hoot's eye was awful but losing a family heirloom would be catastrophic. "Darla wanted you to have it earlier, but I forgot after our...er...discussion."

"You mean our *argument*," she said, narrowing her eyes at him.

He didn't respond. Finally he said, "You looked like you were having so much fun tonight with your date that I'm surprised to see you home this early."

That set off a flare of anger. She unfolded herself and accidentally shone the flashlight in his eyes. Which she didn't really feel sorry for. "I didn't have a date. And also, you don't get to comment on how much fun I do or don't have." She stood up straight. "Also, why did you wait around like that? It was...embarrassing. Sam's friend asked if you were my brother."

"What did you say?"

"I told him yes. My obsessively protective brother."

He made a strange sound in his throat. "I'm definitely not your brother."

"I just don't get you." Frustration leaked into her voice. "You're the one who suggested that I meet other people, but when I do, you seem to hate it—yet you don't do anything about it. Only act like a stalker and watch me."

Unless...unless he was jealous. Unless he still wanted her. In spite of herself, her heart sped up a little.

"You can spend time with whomever you want." He kicked some gravel from the driveway with his foot. "What are you looking for? A contact lens?"

"See?" She stabbed the air with her finger. "You should never sleep with anyone unless they know things about you. Like whether or not you wear contacts."

He walked into the grass and started looking himself. "Okay, so it's not your contact. Why don't you tell me what you're canvassing your yard for?"

"Be careful where you walk. There's a one-inch black button somewhere in this sandbox that I have to find before Ollie wakes up."

He arched a brow. "Hoot's eye?"

Did he have to spear her heart Every. Single. Time? How could that possibly be his first guess?

And how could she possibly resist a man who knew that?

"Yes," she said, staying focused. "It's black with a greenish mother-of-pearl rim. Which makes it nearly impossible to see at night."

"Just a sec." He ran to the garage and disappeared, giving her a few moments to get it together. She twisted the ring on her finger.

No games. If she could handle moving out, surviving her first class, and hiring babysitters, she could handle the simple truth. She just had to find the courage to try to get it out of him. But he'd already shown he didn't want to talk about it.

Why was he here, anyway?

They had an agreement. Platonic only. But that wasn't working.

At least not for her.

But did she engage him or tell him to leave?

Alex came jogging back with the world's largest flashlight, which was bright silver and half an arm long. He turned it on high beam, and it lit up the entire neighborhood.

Next door, a light flicked on.

Kit glanced up to see Maddy's next-door neighbor, Irene McGregor, standing at her door in a flowered muumuu and rollers. She gave her what she hoped was a reassuring wave. To Alex, she said, "Okay, well, thanks for the spotlight, but you can leave. I'm fine on my own."

"I know you're fine on your own. I *want* to help. If you'll let me."

She poked him in the chest. Her finger practically bounced off all that hard muscle. "I don't need you baby-sitting me on dates"—*poke, poke*—"and I don't need your help with this." *Poke.* "And this has nothing to do with your payback to Carson so you're officially free. *Absolved.*" She flicked her hand in a shooing gesture. "You can go home."

Too bad home was fifty feet away. Not far enough—times a million.

Instead of leaving, he planted himself in front of her, solid as a statue. "Is that what you think?" he asked. "That I only help you because of Carson?"

"Why wouldn't I think that, Alex?" She was waving her arms about and talking too loud, but she couldn't seem to stop. "You're taking two months out of your life to work on that stupid house. It's clear that you two were closer than blood brothers. I know you'd do anything for Carson."

"Except save him," he blurted.

She jerked her head up. "What?"

He cursed silently and turned away.

"Yoo-hoo," Mrs. McGregor called from across the way, now standing outside in her driveway. "Is everything all right over there?"

"Sorry, Mrs. M," Kit called, then dropped her voice. "Look, I need to go inside and check on Ollie. Meet me on the back patio?"

Kit was glad to escape to collect her whirling thoughts. *Except save him?*

What did that mean? Most of her didn't want to know. She didn't want to relive anything about Carson's dying, something she'd finally managed to not do anymore, except sometimes against her will in the middle of sleepless nights.

A fast check on Ollie revealed he was softly snoring, a one-eyed Hoot tucked tightly under his chin, and Rex sprawled on his back at the foot of the bed, also snoring softly. But Kit barely registered anything over the uncomfortable pounding of her heart. It took every ounce of courage to walk out onto her patio.

Which was empty.

"Ollie okay?" Alex asked from beyond. He'd dragged two foldable beach chairs into the sand.

"Sound asleep," she said.

He gestured for her to sit down. He, however, was standing, looking out over the sea. The waves were crashing loudly, a sure sign of high tide. Above their heads, every star in the universe shone brightly against an endless velvet sky. Powerful and calm. That's what she needed to be.

She was too tense to sit. So she stood before him, wrapping her arms around herself tightly. "Please explain what you just said."

He cast her a glance she could only describe as troubled. Pain flickered in his eyes, which drove up her pulse even more. She wished she could escape down that beach, arms wide, hair flying. Like Ollie, carefree and happy on a hot, sunny day.

"I should've been the one to fly that day," Alex said.

That day. Every muscle in Kit's body tensed because she knew exactly what day he meant. She curled her hands into fists under her folded arms, nails digging into her palms, bracing for the worst.

"It was my turn," he continued, sounding far away. "But the day before, we'd had training exercises in a river. Parachuting in, doing rescue and recovery maneuvers. My foot got caught in some brush on the riverbed, and I was late surfacing. I got air hungry, took a breath too soon, and ended up swallowing a few gulps of rank water. By the next morning, I had the chills and couldn't keep anything down. That's when our squadron leader decided to send Carson on the mission instead."

She gasped, and a hand flew to her throat. And she felt like she was going to be sick herself.

"Carson loved flying." Alex looked far, far out over the water. "But he hated combat. I knew he was counting down the days before we could get home. The stress of having to fly a real mission was hanging over all of us. Carson didn't take anything about that lightly. He...he came and saw me in the infirmary before he left. He saw me lying there, hooked into an IV, and he said, 'Look at you, de la Cruz. You're a sorry sight.' "

Alex chuckled softly. He seemed far away, lost in his memories. "I can't explain it, but I had this feeling—a dark dread, deep in my belly—that wasn't from retching my guts out. The terror of it made me try to sit up. I was desperate to get to the lieutenant colonel, to tell him I was fine. Anything to get my turn back. I begged the nurse to take out my IV, and she thought I was delirious. But Carson took my hand . . ." Alex took her hand, reenacting some kind of a complicated guy ritual, sliding it against hers and snapping his thumb. "And he said . . ."

His voice trailed off, unable to continue, which made Kit instantly tear up. She squeezed her eyes shut, trying to get a grip. She didn't want to know the last thing Carson said to Alex. And yet she couldn't not know. "Tell me," she finally said, her voice barely a whisper.

Alex swallowed so hard Kit saw his Adam's apple move. "Carson said, 'Sometimes you can't control every-thing, Cruz. So behave and I'll catch you on the other side, man.' Then he walked to the door of the infirmary and turned around one last time. And he said, 'You know I love you, right? And I know you'll always have my back.' He didn't say 'in case anything happens,' but he didn't have to. I understood what he meant."

Kit let out a sob and covered her mouth with her hand. Carson had told Alex to take care of her and Ollie in case something happened. They were his concern.

Of course they were.

Pain laced Alex's face as he forced out his words in the barest whisper. "I should have told you from the beginning. I failed him. I failed you." Alex's eyes darted up to her face. "I'm sorry, Kit." His voice broke. "I'm so sorry."

* * *

Alex held his breath, waiting for Kit to turn away. His impulse was to comfort her, but his feet were lead weights in the sand. And he felt...ashamed. Not worthy to comfort her. He hadn't expected telling the truth to be freeing, and by God, it wasn't. It had ripped his heart out. Kit had every right to be repulsed by his words. By *him*.

He backed away, but she stepped forward and wrapped him up in her arms with an intensity that nearly caused him to lose his balance. He was suddenly engulfed by her warmth and her sweet scent, the silky strands of her hair brushing his neck.

Her sobs reverberated against his chest. "Don't cry," he whispered. Tears formed in his own eyes. "Please don't cry." He raised his hand. But like before, he hesitated. He wanted to hold her but he also didn't because, once he touched her, his feelings would rush out, unstoppable as a broken dam.

"Alex." She backed up, gathering his hands in hers, forcing him to meet her gaze. "You're one of the kindest and most selfless people I've ever met," she said slowly and deliberately. "You care for everyone—except yourself. This is something you couldn't possibly be responsible for."

There was no blame. No accusation. Just the soothing tone of her voice, the steady grip of her hands, and the caring in her eyes. All of it hit him like a rock.

You couldn't be responsible.

She reached out and touched his cheek. "It just... happened. It wasn't your fault."

He swallowed hard, too aware of her touch, featherlight and gentle.

It wasn't your fault.

"It wasn't your job to be Carson's protector," she continued. "You were his colleague. What happened was out of anyone's control. He wouldn't have wanted you to think this way."

Kit didn't hold him responsible, even now that she knew the truth. A small feeling of relief washed over him, giving him a small bit of solace.

But he wanted—needed—her to know the whole truth. "I tried to stay away from you. I tried to pretend that I wasn't attracted to you. But I couldn't resist. I couldn't resist you, Kit. Even though I know I betrayed Carson even more by sleeping with you."

Kit shook her head adamantly. "You didn't sleep with me. We slept *together*. You were comforting *me*, remember? If anyone overstepped, it was me. I...I took advantage of your kindness."

He sucked in a sudden breath.

"What was that for?"

"Let me make one thing clear." He cleared his throat. "There was *nothing* kind about making love with you."

Her blush radiated to the roots of her hair. He saw it even in the dim light from the porch. "I was just as turned on and eager," he continued. "And the whole thing may have started out as sharing grief and comforting each other, but for me...for me it turned into something else entirely." He paused. Very quietly, he said, "It turned into me and you." No Carson, no grief. Just being with her, holding her, using their lovemaking to express the things he could never say.

"I'm not sorry for what happened," Kit said firmly.

Emotions rolled through him—grief, sadness, regret, *hope*. "My therapist is the one who told me to come here and work on the house. She said that in the process of doing something positive, I'd have to somehow figure out how to forgive myself."

"Oh, Alex." She shook her head solemnly. "You don't have to forgive yourself for surviving." She stood there, twisting her ring on her finger as she looked out at the darkened sea and sky. After a little while, she spoke. "I don't have my life sorted out. But I've been figuring out what I want." She spun around to face him. "I want you. For reasons that have nothing to do with Carson. You make me feel like myself again." She released a heavy sigh. "I was afraid that would never happen." She paused before continuing. "But you know I'm not in a good position for a relationship. I have a long way to go."

He placed his hand over hers. "Kit, I...I like you a lot." Which was the understatement of the century. "But I'm in no shape to give you what you need. And I don't want to hurt you."

"You've given me your friendship. That's what I needed—what I *need*." She paused and then broke out in a slow smile. "We can keep things loose and light. How about we just take it a half day at a time?"

He cracked a smile right back. "Actually, the expression in Spanish is a little different. *Vive un media dia a la vez.* It means to *live* one half day at a time."

"Yes. Better. Much better in Spanish." She drew close and wound her arms around him, flooding his senses with her sweetness. It was as if her touch were pulling out all his pain, taking it away.

He bent and kissed her. Savoring her lips, the taste of her, and the way she fit perfectly in his arms. Which, he thought, was natural and just right. And much different from before, when their hunger for each other left no room for taking their time. She opened to him, kissing him deeply, each stroke of their tongues deeper and more consuming.

He drew back, breathing heavily, a sense of amazement overtaking him. She stood before him, her eyes heavy lidded, reaching for him, her hands skimming along his arms, his chest, his back. His pulse beat strongly at his temple, and every muscle tensed as his hunger for her built and flamed. Finally, he held her to him, cradling her body against his, running his hands through her hair and down the smooth curves of her back.

This time, he didn't have to taste the bitterness of secrets. Or drown in guilt. Instead, he relished every moment, her softness, her constant willingness to give, and the way she arched her neck and softly murmured his name as he planted a trail of slow, thorough kisses on her warm, flushed skin.

It was totally different from the first time, when he hadn't been thinking at all.

Chapter 22

THIS TIME, KIT made love to Alex as if every kiss would heal him. She willed every touch, every stroke, to take away his pain, wash away his guilt. She couldn't bear his suffering.

Somehow they'd made it to her bed, where, much later, she lifted herself up on an elbow and looked at him as he lay there, resting his head on a pillow. His brow was unfurrowed, and he seemed relaxed and at ease.

"What can I do to make you know that you're... amazing?" she asked.

"*Querida*," he said, tracing her cheek with his finger, "you have no idea what you do to me."

"Tell me more about that," she said. She rested her hand on his chest. He covered it with his own. Underneath her hand, she felt his heartbeat, steady and strong.

"I'd rather show you."

With that, he rolled them over so that she was on her

back. His face was close, his eyes full of feeling. A feeling she read as just as excited to be here as she was.

Her own pulse sped up as desire flooded through her. She tried to separate it from every other feeling, to tell herself that this was just something she needed for now. Something that made her feel alive—and proved she was among the living again.

She tried not to see in her mind the adoring way Ollie looked up at Alex and how Alex ruffled Ollie's hair and laughed out loud as they walked together in the yard.

Or how he always treated her with kindness and compassion. How he seemed to know when she was nervous or alone or...just needed a friend.

And how he knew when *not* to agree with her. Telling her to relax about Ollie or not get uptight about the small stuff, and encouraging her when she had her doubts, to keep pressing onward to do what she thought was right for herself.

She shoved all those thoughts aside and focused on kissing him, his lips smooth and warm. His touch made her shiver, sending sensation reverberating all the way through to her bones.

He kissed her, carefully at first, taking his time. Then his arms wrapped around her and drew her to him, into his warm, sun-kissed body, hard with muscle, soft with tenderness.

As he angled his head, kissing her deeper and more thoroughly, an uncontrollable whimper rose from her throat. His kisses became more urgent, whole-mouthed and hungry, the taste of him sweet, the rough bristle of his jaw scraping satisfyingly rough against her skin. Heat rose everywhere, the liquid sensation of floating, of being swept far away from her cares and sufferings and the weight of grief that constantly kept her back pressed to the ground.

* * *

Sometime long after midnight, the moon showed up as a giant bluish orb right outside the bedroom window, the likes of which Alex had never seen before.

For a minute, he lay there, mesmerized by the big, glowing ball casting a trail of brilliant sparkles on the dark ocean. Kit had fallen asleep, her soft cheek on his chest, her hair draping over him in strands of silk. From the deep, even rhythm of her breathing, he could tell she was out cold, something that pleased him, the evidence of thorough lovemaking, but also made him envious because he was the one awake and thinking.

This hadn't exactly gone the way he'd planned.

He'd told himself over and over that the romantic fantasy he'd harbored was just that, a fantasy. That the reality couldn't ever match it. That being with her would prove that and he'd get her out of his mind for good.

And instead... *this* had happened.

He felt fiercely protective of her. Not just because she looked especially vulnerable asleep, but simply because he had the inexplicable urge to shield her from everything bad. He'd told her the truth and she hadn't turned away. Instead, she'd embraced him. Held him. Tried to take away his pain. He wanted to protect her from pain too.

He willed himself back to the present. He wanted to bottle up this moment and make it last, certain he'd remember it forever. The salt-tinged breeze blowing the curtains, the gentle roll of the waves, Kit's slow, quiet breathing. And a feeling inside of him that was increasingly lighter for the first time in a very long time.

He wondered if this summer would be a collection of memories like that, each one like a piece of chocolate you hoard away in a drawer to pull out when you need a candy fix.

But for right now, Kit was here in his arms, and that was the biggest damn moon he'd ever seen.

"Kit," he whispered. She was sleeping like the dead. He moved his shoulder a little until she finally stirred. Maybe he shouldn't disturb her but... hey, once in a lifetime.

"What is it?" she asked, sleep lacing her voice.

"Look out the window."

She rubbed her eyes sleepily and lifted her head. "Oh my. What is that?"

"It's a blue moon," he said.

"Because it's really blue or because it's really rare?" she asked, sounding more awake now.

"Well," he said, "it's actually a *double* blue moon. A blue moon is a moon that occurs twice in one month. And a moon that is the color blue is an atmospheric phenomenon, due to some kind of particles in the air."

She nodded toward the phone in his hands. "Maybe you're not very satisfied if you're lying there googling things."

"You're right," he said solemnly. "I'm not satisfied at all. Maybe we'd better do that again."

"Do what again?" Her sleep-tousled hair and mischievous grin were adorable. She wrapped a slender arm around his waist and snuggled a little closer, all of which had the unfortunate effect of making him want her all over again.

He tried to focus on reading his phone but the words merged into a mindless blur. She reached over and tugged it out of his fingers and set it down on the bedside table.

"Are you angry that I woke you up for that?" he asked.

She propped herself up on an elbow. The tiny strap of her nightgown fell off her shoulder. He reached over and kissed it.

She pressed a hand to her chest. "I can feel the beauty of that moon deep inside. And I can smell the sea air. And feel the breeze. And hear the tide. It seems that since you've been here, I've woken up to life again." Then she turned to him, her eyes soft and lit up by the moonlight. "Not to mention that I marvel about how I got such a beautiful man in my bed."

He let out a little chuckle. "I know what you mean."

She arched a brow. "That you're handsome?"

"Well, I am," he said with a grin, "but I was thinking more about the other stuff you said." He took her hand. "I feel a sense of calm with you. And I don't have to fill that space with words. That sounds . . . weird, huh?"

"Maybe. But I'd say it's accurate."

"And you are beautiful, Kit. Inside and out." As their eyes met, he realized that she had this uncanny ability to make him spill all his secrets, and he'd better stop now before he got into even worse trouble. He glanced at the nightstand, where the old-fashioned digital clock with extra large numbers, clearly Maddy's, told him it was 3:00 a.m. "It's late. I should probably go."

He started to get up, but she stopped him with a hand on his arm. "I was just going to say, don't go. I mean, unless you want to. And I do appreciate that you are okay leaving before Ollie wakes up."

"I'll definitely leave before Ollie wakes up, of course."

She smiled. A wide, sure smile that made his heart swell. "Stay. If you want to."

"I want to." He leaned back against the headboard and patted his chest. "Come here."

"Over there? Like, next to you?"

He indicated for her to lean back against his chest. "Right here."

She did. And he tucked her into his side, wrapping her arm around his waist like before.

They lay like that a long time, staring at the moon. It felt like she was made to lie there, fitting perfectly. He wasn't even too surprised when they heard a sudden *poof* as the cat came out of nowhere and landed on the down comforter at the bottom of the bed.

"Hey there, buddy," Alex said as Kit lifted her head to look. "He's getting a little bolder."

"Yes. Little by little. Hey, Seymour," Kit said. The cat answered with a loud meow before turning a few circles and settling in. "Okay if he stays?"

"Of course." He could relate because something similar was happening to him. Some kind of…loosening. A letting go. Maybe that's what Kit had been trying to express. But whatever it was, it felt like a two-ton weight had finally fallen off his chest. And he could finally breathe.

Chapter 23

THE NEXT MORNING, Kit woke with a start. Light streamed through the window, strong, steady, and direct, definitely not the hallmark of a slanted 7:00 a.m. sun. She'd slept great...again. Well, at least from the time they'd finally fallen asleep.

Which led her back to thinking of that first morning after. Except that today there wasn't a baseball game. *Was there?* A sudden sense of panic made her go in search of her phone. She thought she'd tossed it on the chest of drawers but it was gone.

As she got out of bed and passed the window facing the yard, laughter rang out.

Ollie's laughter.

Kit used the bathroom, threw on some clothes, and ran to the kitchen to find her phone once again placed tidily on the charging pad and the wonderful smell of strong coffee in the air. More voices drifted in through the kitchen, Ollie's and Alex's. And a happy scream.

She walked over to the door, ready to pull it open, but she hesitated when she saw Ollie flying through the air in some kind of airplane maneuver that she'd rather not have seen. But he landed safely on the ground, clutching his belly and giggling as Alex, who was now on his hands and knees, apparently continuing to comb through every blade of grass in her front yard. Rexy, never one to be ignored, rolled in the grass next to Ollie, his long leash weighted down by a rock.

Wow.

"Alex," Ollie said, sitting near him on the grass and examining Hoot carefully, "Hoot says he likes the eye patch you brought him."

Kit's heart caught in her throat. *Eye patch?*

Alex stopped what he was doing to assess the owl. "Tell him he looks sharp."

"Yeah, but Hoot says he can't see good with only one eye."

Alex held out his hand. "May I have him?"

Ollie handed the stoic little owl over, an impressive feat because Ollie was usually very picky about who got to hold Hoot. Alex put the owl to his ear. "Hmm. Uh-huh. Yes. Well, Mr. Hoot, I have just the thing." He reached into his pocket and handed Ollie something blue from his pocket. "Ollie," Alex said, "you only need one eye to see with a telescope."

Ollie held the small plastic tube up to his own eye. "Wow! You look really big!"

Alex turned Ollie toward the ocean. "You'll be able to see ships way out on the horizon. When Hoot's not using it, of course."

Before Kit could worry about Ollie forgetting his manners, he ran to Alex, catching his legs in a stranglehold. "Thank you, Alex! Hoot loves it. Me too!"

Alex hugged her kid back with what seemed to be just as much enthusiasm. "Okay, back to work. We have an eyeball to find."

"An eyeball?" That made Ollie dissolve into giggles again.

"Hi," Kit said, walking up. Fighting past a huge lump in her throat.

She was just recovering when Alex straightened and looked her over in a way that sent her stomach fluttering. She offered him her coffee, which he took a big gulp of before handing it back. "Good morning," she said to Ollie, greeting him with a hug.

"Mommy, look." Ollie held out Hoot so she could see his eye patch.

"My goodness," she said to Hoot, bending to plant a kiss on his head. "I'm sorry about your lost eye, but you look very handsome today."

"This too, Mommy." Ollie held up the little telescope. "It's to help Hoot see. Until we find his eye."

Ollie wandered off into the yard to check out the ocean through the telescope.

Kit was left to stand there and try to contain all the feelings that were tumbling through her. "A pirate patch *and* a telescope?" was the best she could do.

Alex gave a good, hearty laugh that made Kit's stomach flip even more. "God bless the dollar store."

He'd gone shopping. So her son wouldn't be upset. He'd turned this calamity of sorts into something funny and wonderful. "You have quite an imagination."

The way he lifted a brow and slowly tilted up his

mouth made her realize he was thinking of something else entirely.

"What are you staring at?" she asked under his intense gaze.

"You have an amazing smile," he said. "It lights up a room—or anyplace—just like the sun. Like, it takes my breath away."

She laughed. But his comment had jogged a memory. Carson had written that to her once. *Your beautiful smile lights up a room like the sun.*

Well, not like it was an original or unique expression. Alex looked so sincere, so earnest, she had to laugh and accept it for what it was. A very nice thing to say.

"You're ridiculous," she said. But she couldn't help smiling. She couldn't help it. "Thank you for the compliment. And for making coffee. And for charging my phone—again. I have a bad habit of forgetting to do that."

"It was nothing." He shook his head and shrugged it off, but his heightened color told Kit he was pleased. "Well, I wanted your phone to be charged when I send you heart emojis."

"You're going to send me heart emojis?" she asked.

"If your phone's charged, I will."

She rolled her eyes but their gazes collided in the snap of electricity that so often passed between them. "All kidding aside, thank you."

He gave a little nod. Which made his dark hair fall across his forehead. "Anytime."

Then she realized the two of them were standing in her front yard grinning like two teenagers. "I hope you're hungry," she said. "I'm going to make breakfast. And do you have sunblock on?"

"Yes on the hungry part. No on the sunblock. You're

not saying that because I'm going to be out here all day, are you?"

Just then, two cars pulled up. One with Darla and Sam. The other with Nick and Hadley and Cam.

"Reinforcements?" he asked.

She smiled and shrugged.

"Your friends stop what they're doing to find a button in your yard?"

She grinned. "If there's food involved, they do."

"Well, then. Hope you have a great breakfast planned. Not to mention some gallon-size sunblock."

The guys got into a huddle to strategize a plan while Darla and Hadley followed Kit into the house.

"So an eye patch? Cute," Darla said, looking out the window where the guys were laughing and talking—and crawling around in the grass. "Oh, someone else is pulling up."

Kit ran up behind her to look. Lauren got out of a beige Toyota sedan and immediately ran to give Nick an enthusiastic hug.

"I see that's still going strong," Darla said.

Kit acknowledged that with a shrug. "It was nice of her to want to help us look. She's gotten to know Ollie better because she's the director of the play he tried out for."

They watched as Lauren continued with lots of PDA, kissing Nick and playfully messing up his hair.

Hadley sighed. "That's so over the top."

"I know you said she doesn't feel threatened by you," Kit said, "but I think she does. I mean, she's clearly staking a claim."

"That's between her and Nick." Darla put her hands up defensively. "No threat here." She pointed to where Ollie was kneeling on the ground next to Alex as they both sifted through the sand. "Looks like someone's enchanted with Alex."

"Ollie hasn't left his side all morning," Kit said as she pulled out a lemonade pitcher from the cabinet over her fridge.

"I was talking about you," Darla said pointedly.

"I just...I don't want to make a big deal about this. It's not anything serious. And Alex is on board about being very discreet in front of Ollie. I don't want Ollie to get too attached."

"You worry about Ollie not getting too attached, which I'm sure is legit," Hadley said, "but what about you?"

Kit pressed her lips together tightly. "I can't think beyond right now. I just...can't."

"But you really like him, don't you?" Darla asked.

"It's not just how he is with Ollie," Kit confessed. "He reads me pretty well. Like, he always tries to make me laugh when he sees I'm getting too serious. And he's just so levelheaded and calming, which I really love. But he's still torn up over Carson's death too. I can't...I can't let myself fall too hard, you know?"

Hadley gave her a side hug. "Promise me you'll stay open to the possibilities."

Kit shrugged. "I'll do my best. But enough about me." She addressed Darla. "How are things with you and Sam?"

"He's cute and nice," she said. Which sounded like the way you'd describe your new college roommate.

"And?" Hadley took the pitcher from Kit and filled it with water.

"And things were nice." Darla sat at the little table, tidying the napkins, which were standing in a daisy napkin holder.

"Nice?" Hadley said. "That's two *nice*s in a row."

"I don't know." Darla seemed to really concentrate on straightening out those napkins. "I'm still thinking about it."

Darla was her usual unflappable self. But the fact that she fidgeted instead of making eye contact gave Kit a clue to the truth. "It's okay if it doesn't work out," Kit said softly.

Darla stopped playing with the napkins. "Sam's very sweet. And funny. And he treats me very well. I mean, he remembers the minor characters in my books better than I do. It's just...I don't know. The first time can be a little awkward." She paused. "It's just been a while since I've had a first time with anyone. Things don't mesh right away sometimes, right? It can take a little while."

Hadley set down glasses of lemonade and then took a seat. "You're essentially telling us you faked it."

Kit, sitting down next to Darla, sent Hadley a *Did you really have to say it that way?* look.

Darla didn't seem put off. "Did either of you have an...I don't know...awkward time at first—in bed?"

"I don't think that's uncommon. *At all*," Hadley said emphatically. "It takes time to get to know someone and—"

"Absolutely." Kit nodded her confirmation. "Everything is so new and—"

Darla assessed them both. "I can tell by your faces that you're just trying to make me feel better."

"I don't think there's a right or a wrong," Kit said.

"You're being really harsh on yourself," Hadley said. "You just started dating him."

"Nick is *not* my gold standard." Now Darla was twisting a napkin between her hands.

Kit glanced again at Hadley. Neither of them said anything for a while.

"We never said he was," Hadley finally said.

"No, but I can tell you're thinking it," Darla said, heaving a sigh. "Well, things with Sam are not the way they were with Nick. But honestly, nothing could be. I mean, we were young and crazy in love, and chemistry was never one of our problems."

"Just give it time," Kit said with more conviction than she felt. She didn't know how Stalker Sam was in bed, but in her opinion, he was way too enthusiastic about book characters. Maybe more enthusiastic than about Darla.

"Besides," Hadley added, "you can have explosive chemistry in bed and still argue about petty things like wedding details." She took a big gulp of lemonade. "Honestly, I just wish we were married already. The guest list keeps growing and growing. The dinner choices keep expanding. There are seventeen million choices for the cake, and they *all* taste good."

"It will be a beautiful wedding, and it will all come together," Kit said.

"Marriage is about compromise, right?" Hadley asked. "Cam is really famous, and a lot of people want to wish him well. I'm trying to understand that."

"But compromise means you have a say in things too," Darla said.

"Yoo-hoo!" They all turned as Kit's mom poked her head through the door.

"We heard you girls were in here making breakfast," the Admiral said, following behind his wife. His razor-sharp gaze focused on the half-empty pitcher. And the three of them sitting around drinking lemonade. Not a pancake flipper in sight.

"We got to talking," Kit said a little guiltily.

The Admiral rolled up his sleeves. "Your yard is a little small for all those people to be walking around pell-mell in it. You need someone to organize everyone and divide the yard into quadrants." At this point, Kit's mom gave her dad a look that Kit knew meant to curb his natural order-giving instincts. "And your neighbor keeps opening her door and peeking out. Maybe you could ask her to come help."

"Speaking of help, why don't you three go out there?" her mom said. "We've got breakfast covered."

"Yay," Kit said, throwing up her hands. She thanked her parents and left them to what they did best.

Outside, everyone was still searching.

"How many adults does it take to find a button in a yard the size of a postage stamp?" Kit asked with a chuckle.

"There are six of us," Nick said. "And we still haven't found it yet. And the grass is more sand than grass. Does that tell you something?"

"That maybe I better get on that button site my sitter recommended?" Kit said.

"It might mean that Ollie might have to accept that Hoot is a little...special," Alex said.

"Judging by the way he loves the eye patch," Kit said, "that might not be such a terrible thing."

"Hey, I found it," Sam said suddenly. Everyone stopped what they were doing and turned.

"Oh, never mind." He examined an object in his palm. "It's just a black shell. Sorry, everybody."

Okaaay. Back to work they all went. Lauren hooked her phone up to a speaker and turned on some music. The smell of soon-to-be-ready pancakes drifted out the windows, which lured Ollie in to hang out with his grandparents.

"It's kind of fun not to be stressing out about the wedding," Hadley said.

Cam smiled. "I was thinking that too. We've been so busy. It's been a long time since we got together with everyone to just hang out."

Hadley nodded her agreement. "We haven't done this in too long."

Sam stopped looking and said, "This reminds me of a scene in *Die, My Love, Die*."

Kit exchanged a glance with Alex, who looked a little amused. But if Sam fake-found Hoot's eye again, someone else was going to kick the bucket. And not a fake-someone in Darla's book.

"That book was so scary," Kit said. "I almost couldn't finish it. Except it was so good I had to."

Sam looked up from the lawn. "I was thinking about the scene where the killer dropped the dead woman's ring in the grass."

"Actually," Nick said, straightening out, "the heroine threw it into the woods so the killer wouldn't get it. Then he shot her. But she lived to get her ring back. Not to mention revenge as well."

Darla snapped to attention. "You read that book?" she asked Nick, who actually looked a little pleased with himself.

"Yeah, really," Lauren said. "Nicky doesn't read thrillers."

"Actually," Nick said, "I read *all* your books, Dar."

Darla looked flabbergasted. "When did you do that?"

"I'm sorry to say just in the past few months." He was standing in the middle of the lawn, speaking to her like she was the only one there. "They're good, Darla. Like, really good."

"I know, aren't they?" Sam said. "I love how there are so many twists and turns." He gestured with his hands. "And I always stay up half the night reading because I can't wait to find out what happens. Even though I know the killer always gets his due."

Darla tossed Nick a sweet smile and a shrug. "That's what happens when you envision each killer as your ex."

"Ha-ha." Nick shook his head as he got back to work.

"Are you saying you used Nick as a model for your villains?" Sam asked. "You must've hated him."

"Not anymore," Darla said. "Seriously, Nick," she said as they all resumed the search again. "Thanks. For reading."

"Well," he said quietly, "when we were married, I didn't appreciate all the time you spent trying to get published."

"She's really dedicated, isn't she?" Sam said. "I admire that." He came up behind her and nuzzled her neck. Kit couldn't speak for Darla, but this guy was definitely making *her* uncomfortable.

"Well, live and learn," Nick said.

As they all got back to sifting through the sandy soil, Kit thought that Nick had definitely caused his share of heartache. But he was also funny, always there in a pinch, and basically impossible not to like. And the way he looked at Darla when she didn't know it seemed to say something, although she wasn't sure exactly what.

A little while later, Alex found Kit in the shade between the house and the garage, taking a break from the heat. "What are you doing?" he asked, making her look up from her phone.

"Scrolling a button site." She held out her phone. "I

think I found one that's close. I figured I could buy two and give Hoot two new eyes that match, but they only have one in stock."

He took her hand and gently lowered it so she couldn't look at her phone anymore.

"I'm sorry about the button. But you have nice friends. They haven't given up yet, and it's getting hot."

She laughed. "I do have wonderful friends. And also, they think you're wonderful. In fact, ever since the lawn trimmer, so do my parents. And Ollie thinks you're practically better than Santa."

"I'm flattered. But how do *you* feel about me?"

She gave him the side-eye. "I don't want to like you."

He gave a big, hearty laugh. It was resonant and spontaneous and rumbled straight through her in a really pleasant way.

Kit tried to frown. "Is that your usual reaction when someone says they don't like you?"

"You like me," he said confidently. He took up both of her hands and looked in her eyes. "Have a little faith."

Was he talking about the button or about...them?

She didn't want to tell Alex it was hard to let herself believe in anything when the entire life she'd built had suddenly disappeared into thin air. Or that the scary thing about him was that he was filling her with hope, breaking through her resistance.

"Actually," he said, "I came over here because I didn't want you to miss the big moment."

"What big moment?" A quick glance revealed everyone working just as diligently as before.

He dug into his pocket. "Does it look like this?"

There, in his open palm, a little round owl eye glinted in the afternoon light. "Wait. You *found* it?"

"I left no blade of grass unturned. No grain of sand unsifted." He looked very pleased with himself.

"You're...crazy."

He shrugged. "Crazy for you, *querida*."

She folded herself into his arms and gave him a squeeze. "That's incredible."

"Big things happen when you believe," he said, still milking his feat for all it was worth.

She held him at arm's length. "Seriously, where did you find it?"

"If I tell you, I'll have to..." Instead of finishing the sentence, he bent and whispered something in her ear that made her blush.

"You still haven't told me wh-where you found it," she managed. But it was so hard when her knees were suddenly turning into Jell-O.

"Under Ollie's bed. I went to the bathroom, and on the way back, I checked his sheets, under his pillow; then I bent down and...there it was."

"Maybe we shouldn't tell our friends that you found it inside," she said as she tapped her lips in thought. "Everyone's sweaty."

"Once we feed everyone, they'll be okay," he said definitively. "Do I get to collect a reward?"

"What kind of reward?"

He held out his cheek and tapped it. "I'll take a kiss for now."

She reached up on tiptoe and went to kiss him, but he turned, giving her a good, thorough kiss that made her dizzy and caused her to grip his shoulders for balance. His mouth was warm and wonderful, and he tasted like lemonade. As his strong arms wound around her with a sort of calm, careful reverence that made her feel carefree and mindless and young, Kit couldn't help feeling that in the shade, with a warm breeze off the ocean, it was just about a perfect day.

"Mmm," he said, kissing her again quickly on the lips. "Nice reward."

"Alex," a little voice said, "are you kissing my mommy?" Kit broke off in time to see Ollie tugging on Alex's shirt. "Hey, Mommy," he continued, sounding unfazed, "does that mean Alex is going to be my dad?" He turned and yelled, "Hey, everybody, come see! Alex and my mom just kissed!"

Turns out, Ollie's announcement wasn't necessary because everyone was already watching from the front yard. Which paralyzed Kit with fear. But it didn't seem to faze Alex at all. He reached down and scooped Ollie up and kissed him on the head and said, "I really like your mom. And I really like you too. Would that be okay if I got to know both of you better?"

Ollie, beaming, nodded his enthusiastic approval.

"And, Oliver, look what I found." Alex uncurled his hand.

Ollie's eyes went wide. "You found it!" He curled his arms tightly around Alex's neck.

Everyone cheered. While Kit kept swiping her eyes. Because... *this man*.

"Pancakes are ready on the back patio," her mom announced from the front door.

"Kit, do you have champagne?" Hadley asked. "If you do, I'll make us mimosas."

"No champagne," Kit said.

"C'mon, Had, ride with me," Cam said. "We'll run and get some from the restaurant."

They took off together, looking happier than Kit had seen them in a while.

Alex met her gaze, his eyes full of amusement, which made her worry disintegrate, just like that. "Hiding's no fun anyway." He nodded toward everyone gathering on the patio. Then he held out his hand.

She took it without hesitation and then went with him to join their friends.

Chapter 24

"I'M NERVOUS ABOUT the color," Kit said a week later, standing back and assessing the large test patch of paint Alex had just rolled onto the dining room wall. "I think it's too...bluey."

"Isn't it white paint?" Alex asked in the innocent way that males clueless about decorating do.

"There are hundreds of shades of white," she said. "I'm just not sure I picked the right one."

"We bought four gallons of it," he said, looking around at all the painting supplies scattered on the floor. "I think it would be best if..." He must have seen her expression because he quickly reversed course. "What I mean is, how about we paint a wall and sleep on it? If you really hate it tomorrow, we'll go back to the drawing board."

She smiled. "I love it when you speak my language."

They worked for a while. Kit stood on a ladder, painting beneath the top molding while Alex stood below using a roller on large swaths of wall. Until a spider crept into her paint field and made her startle and drop the brush she'd just dipped in fresh paint.

The startled noise Alex made indicated that the brush hadn't landed on the floor. He stopped rolling and looked up at her. Sure enough, the brush had landed like a target on the top of his head, leaving a huge, wet, whitish-blue streak in his hair.

Kit balanced on the ladder, clasping her hand over her mouth. "I'm so sorry," she said. Half of her was horrified, but the other half was biting down hard on her cheeks so she didn't laugh. "It was a spider. I swear it. A big, black, treacherous spider."

He bent his head so she could see the awful, thick paint coating his dark hair like a stripe. Without saying anything, he walked over to where she stood, halfway up the ladder. The gleam in his eye told her that he was about to get her back. She promptly jumped down.

But he moved closer, his expression focused and purposeful, as he bit back a smile.

"Your eyes are funny," she said. "Like, full of revenge." She circled her index finger in front of his eyes. "And here I thought you were a nice guy. Not one to hold a grudge."

"I'm not a nice guy." He gave her a slow, wolfish grin, picked up the paint roller, and waved it at her. "I'm very, very vengeful."

"The streak looks kind of nice, by the way," she said, backing up with him following her every step. "Very...Cruella de Vil. Or"—she stood back and examined it critically—"a skunk."

With that he sped up and full-blown chased her. She gave a squeal and ran into the dining room, where she darted around the long table they'd found in the room upstairs, now in its rightful place but still draped with plastic sheeting.

"You stay away from me with that roller, Alex," she cried. "I mean it." She splayed out her hands, but he kept advancing slowly forward, a mischievous twinkle in his eyes. She ducked behind the ladder. "I . . . I have my good T-shirt on." She held out the bottom of the old shirt.

"It says LED ZEPPELIN SUMMER NIGHTS 1983," he said from the other side of the table. "You weren't even born then."

"It was my mom's. A real classic. I'd hate to ruin it."

"Somehow, I have difficulty imagining your mother at a Led Zeppelin concert."

"Okay, it might have come from the thrift shop." She appealed to his decency. "Spare me because it's the right thing to do."

"You're pretty funny when you're trying to distract me, you know that?"

She was in the corner of the room. Either way she moved, he would get her. "Okay, fine. I surrender." She stepped toward him and flung out her arms. "Get me back if you must." She closed her eyes and waited, tilting up her face.

She had a feeling he wouldn't be able to resist, and she was right. Just as Alex was about to kiss her, she ducked beneath his arms and ran out of the room, down the hall to the back door, and into the yard.

She was halfway to the water when she stopped in her tracks. Alex almost ran into her from behind. The amazing sight before her sucked all the fight—and the breath—right out of her. There, hanging from the giant tree, was a wooden swing. It was sturdy, with thickly coiled ropes that rose up, up, up to wrap around a long, fat branch.

She turned to face him. "You...you put up a swing?"

He looked at his handiwork and shrugged. "I had to."

"You had to?" she heard herself repeating dumbly.

From behind her, he rested his hands on her shoulders. "That tree was just begging for one. And I thought it might give Ollie something to do when he's here. And...I know Carson used to talk about it. So even though you're selling the house, I guess this sort of completes his vision."

"It's perfect." It was more than the fact that he'd honored Carson. It was that he'd added this finishing touch that was perfect for the tree, perfect for the house, perfect for a family.

For the first time, Kit thought about the house as something other than Carson's inheritance. Other than the financial suck it had been. With all their hard work and effort, it had turned into a project that she and Alex had made their own.

"Thank you for doing this," she said, facing him. "It's perfect. But I have to tell you, if Ollie discovers this, I'm probably going to have to include him with the house sale because he won't ever want to leave." She wrapped her arms around Alex's neck and kissed him.

"Glad you like it," he said, as his arms curved around her and he kissed her back. Which made her forget the spider and the paint and everything else but Alex's clever lips.

"Want to try out the swing?" he finally asked between a few slow, soft kisses.

"Sure," she said, sounding a little breathy. But she didn't mean it. Instead, she jumped into his arms and wrapped herself around him. "Is a little later okay?"

"Later is good," he said as he carried her into the house, holding her in his strong arms. "Really good." He kissed her thoroughly with his warm, skillful lips until she lost track of where she was and who she was, and it was a good thing she was holding on tight, because otherwise she'd be a swoony puddle on the ground. They made it through the doorway and into the main room, which now contained a sheet-covered couch right where Alex once spent the night rolled in a sheet on the floor.

He deposited her on it and then joined her.

"Is it wise to let that paint dry?" she asked, patting his hair around the paint streak.

He looked down at her like he was about to devour her in the best way. "Probably not, but who cares?"

"You're really kind of..."

He cocked a brow. "Yes?"

"...fun."

"You couldn't have said sexy, hot, something like that?"

"Well, the white streak, you know? It sort of lends a comical air to..."

He shut her up with a kiss. Then he kissed her until she couldn't think of any more jokes, until her breath became ragged and the rest of the world rolled away. He was playful, spontaneous, and fun, and Kit's heart was bursting with joy.

And she supposed that meant the final joke was on her.

* * *

The next two weeks were productive. Alex painted the walls and woodwork in the upstairs bedrooms. As soon as the kitchen was finished, he painted that, too, and then completed the rooms downstairs. Nick had helped him sand the floors and they'd had a professional flooring company stain them. The house was almost done at T-minus one week before the home tour. But when he knocked on Kit's door on a Monday evening, he sensed that something unusual was going on.

The first sign was that Ollie's blue bike with red training wheels was parked in the front yard. Kit was a stickler about making him put it in the garage. A quick peek through the screen showed dishes piled on the counter. A children's program played on the TV in the background.

Kit came to the door with circles under her eyes, hair in disarray, and a harried look on her face. Ollie, engrossed in the show, laughed at something while he ate, sitting cross-legged on the floor.

"Everything okay?" Alex asked. He was going to ask *What happened in there?* but decided he better not.

"Now's probably not the best time to ask that question," Kit said.

"Mommy," Ollie called, his eyes still riveted to the television, "can I please have another peanut butter sandwich? With more grape jelly. Rexy ate mine."

Kit slapped the heel of her hand on her forehead and closed her eyes. "That dog..."

"Now I *know* something's wrong," Alex said.

"Why's that?" Kit asked, still not opening the door.

He frowned. "Because you're letting Rex and Ollie eat PB and J for dinner."

"That's a perfectly acceptable dinner," she said. "Nutritious and filling."

He shot her an *I'm not buying that* look.

She sighed. "Okay, I have my first exam in an hour. And I had extra reports to take home from work this weekend. I left work a little early today, but I got a flat tire on the way home and barely got Ollie picked up from day care before it closed." She glanced at her watch. "And I have to get him to play practice in fifteen minutes. Which works great for my exam, but my sitter just texted me that she can't pick him up tonight, and my mom hasn't texted me back yet."

"Well," he said, giving her his best grin, "I make a mean PB and J."

"Thanks, but you didn't sign up for this. I'll be okay."

He frowned. "What do you mean I didn't sign up for this?"

"Well"—she leaned a little closer to the screen and lowered her voice—"we've never talked about...us. I mean, we've been keeping things light and fun. This"—she looked around at the disorder—"doesn't exactly fall into that category." She straightened up. "It's okay. I'm fine."

"Hey, I get to decide what's fun. And peanut butter is almost always fun. So open the door." Actually, he'd been meaning to talk to her about that keep-things-light part.

"Mommy! I'm hungry!" Ollie's voice was more urgent and a little whiny.

"Just a minute, Oliver!" she called.

"Let me in," he said. He meant more than in the door, though.

She opened the door. Reluctantly.

"You go get what you need for class. I'll take Ollie to practice, okay? And pick him up."

"Okay." He saw surrender in her eyes as she breathed a sigh. "Thank you."

She ran out from the kitchen but suddenly reversed course, picking up something big and yellow from the countertop.

"What is that?" he asked.

"This is the head to Ollie's costume. I'm sewing the rest but it's not ready yet. Please make sure it goes with him to practice."

"You made that?"

"Is it that bad?"

It was big and yellow and had clearly required a lot of work and effort. Whatever it was, he decided now was not the time for a critique. "No—I mean, I'm just not sure what it is."

"It's a papier-mâché lemon head."

"He's a...lemon?"

She nodded. "The play is about nutrition. He sings a song about vitamin C and eating healthy."

Alex examined the...thing. "Are lemons supposed to be a little flat on one side?"

She sent him a look of death.

He raised his arms in surrender. "Bad joke. I'm just trying to get you to laugh."

She dropped her voice again. "Ollie hasn't seen it. If you say it's okay, he'll think it is too. Because frankly, this is as good as it gets."

"I'm sure he'll be proud to wear it." He tried to remember at what age the good sense to be embarrassed kicked in. Hopefully not at age five.

He marveled that Kit was doing work reports, studying, and making lemon heads. Not to mention taking care of Ollie.

Whew. "I have everything covered," he said. "Just get ready for class."

"Thank you," she whispered, and ran down the hall to her bedroom.

Five minutes later, her hair was brushed back into

a ponytail and her book bag was slung over her shoulder.

"I want to give you a good-luck kiss," Ollie said from his new seat at the table, grape jelly smeared around his mouth from the second PB&J that Alex had made.

Kit kissed him on the forehead, avoiding the sticky zones. "Thank you, Ollie." She glanced at the table and then at Alex. "Are those carrots?"

"Well, healthy eating is what the play's about, right?" Alex said. "We're just practicing what we preach." She barely laughed, suddenly combing the countertops, lifting up chair pillows, and tossing up displaced clothes in a frantic search.

"What are you looking for?" Alex asked.

"My car keys."

He dug into his pocket. "Why don't you take my truck?"

She found her keys under a pile of mail on the counter. "Got them." She faced him. "Thank you. For...everything."

"You forgot one more thing."

She looked pained. "What's that?"

He leveled his most charming smile at her. "I want to give you a good-luck kiss too."

Her pretty mouth hitched up in a smile. "Do you have grape jelly on your face too?"

Ollie thought that was hysterical. Alex playfully ruffled his hair and then gave Kit a solid kiss. Giving her arm a little squeeze, he said, "Good luck. You got this."

Tiny frown lines appeared between her brows. "I think I might've forgotten everything I just crammed into my head."

"You already know it all. Now go out there and get an A."

"You got this, Mommy," Ollie said, licking the inside of the jelly jar and getting jelly on his fingers as well as his entire face. *Yikes.*

"Okay, guys. See you later." She cast a dubious glance in Ollie's direction.

Alex steered her toward the door. "No worries. Soap and water work every time." He hoped.

Fifteen minutes later, Alex pulled up to the grade school with a grape-jelly-less Ollie, lemon head in tow, and made their way to the gym.

"The daddies are here today," Ollie noted as Alex opened the door and followed him in.

"The what?" A cursory look around the grade-school gym confirmed that there was a handful of men clustered in a group talking. He recognized a few from Tee ball. "Why are all the dads here?"

"Because they're helping to build the set." Oh. "I didn't tell Mommy because I didn't want her to worry."

"Why would she worry?"

"She'd worry because I don't have a daddy. And she would be sad."

This kid. He bent down and placed a hand on his little shoulder. "Ollie, I'm not your dad but I'm here. And I know how to build stuff. You go get ready for rehearsal, and I'll go talk with the dads."

"Okay," Ollie said, wearing a hopeful expression. "Are you going to watch me?"

Well, Alex hadn't actually planned on that but since he was here... "Sure. I'll watch."

"I have to sing the Lemon song."

"That sounds fun."

"I sang it at home but now I have to sing it in front of everybody."

That would suck. For him, but maybe not for Ollie. "Well, you love singing."

"I know, but at home it's just me and Mommy." The little boy stood there, still and quiet.

Alex wasn't sure what to say, so he tried something basic. "Ollie, what's wrong?"

Ollie looked down and shuffled his feet. "What if the kids laugh at me because I sing funny?"

"Well, I've heard you sing, and you *don't* sing funny."

"Yes, I do. I lisp." Except it came out "lithp."

Alex looked at the five-year-old in front of him wearing such a worried expression on his face. The one whose head of curls reminded him so much of his life-long friend.

He had no idea what he was doing. He wasn't a father. But he had to do something. So he squatted down to Ollie's level and said, "People don't love us because we're perfect. They like us because we're fun and upbeat. We don't focus on the things we don't do perfectly. We just do them with joy."

Ollie didn't look like he was buying that.

Alex tried again. "Just be big and yellow and really excited to be a lemon. That's what's so much fun about being in a play. If you're happy and excited, you'll make everybody else happy too."

Alex tapped on Ollie's chest. "Every happy feeling you keep in here, belt it out. Do you know what that means?"

Ollie nodded. "It means let all your feelings out when you sing."

"That's right," Alex replied. "Let everybody know what it means to...be a lemon. Go out there and be the best singing lemon ever."

Suddenly he was being tackle-hugged by a five-year-old who'd wrapped himself around him and squeezed tight. "I love you, Alex."

Alex froze, even as his heart melted. Fumbling a little, he wrapped his arms tightly around the little boy. "I love you, too, Ollie," he managed through the sudden frog in his throat.

Then Ollie caught sight of his friend Corey and clambered to stand up. "I gotta go. Bye, Alex. Don't forget to watch me sing!"

As Ollie ran off to practice and Alex headed to volunteer for extra work that he clearly did not need, a thought occurred to him.

He'd come to Seashell Harbor on a mission, to take care of the house. But somehow the mission had become about taking care of Kit and Ollie. Like Ollie, maybe Alex was afraid too. Of falling all the way. Of letting Kit know how he felt. And maybe he needed to practice what he preached.

* * *

When Kit walked into the house after her class, the kitchen was tidy, the dishes put away. Ollie's clothes were carefully folded and placed on the arm of the couch. Looking out the front window, she could see Ollie and Alex, running into the surf, Ollie's arms open wide and laughing. Rex was beside himself, leaping right along with them.

Kit sat down on Maddy's stuffed yellow floral chair and took a breath. She felt a little...overwhelmed. Exhausted.

Proud that she probably nailed the exam. But upset

because her life was chaos. This proved that she was unprepared for a life that included a full-time job, classes, and a kid to care for.

Why did she move out of her parents' again?

Alex had been so kind and so patient on every level. But it wasn't his job to bail her out. Even though he was the type who rushed in to help—just look at why he'd come back to town. He was a natural rescuer.

What was she doing, allowing him to help her?

She didn't want to lean on him—she'd spent two years leaning on people. But he was always there for her, rain or shine, and that was comforting...and disturbing. He felt fine showing their friends that they were together. Their relationship was turning into something much more complicated than a summer fling.

But they *weren't* a couple. Alex was a comfort, a distraction, a nice guy who understood what she was going through because he was grieving too. But she could barely handle her life. She hardly knew what she wanted, or what she could handle.

Her phone rang. It was Carol Drake.

"Kit, you're not going to believe this," the Realtor said. "I have great news. A family is interested in the house."

Kit's head spun. "Someone wants to... You're kidding." A potential buyer—now? "But it's not even on the tour yet."

"It's a nice young couple with a cute kid. They went on and on about it. They peeked through the windows and fell in love with the kitchen and the big fireplace in the great room and the woodwork. And of course the water view. And they want a formal showing."

Kit's first thought was *Oh no*. Followed by a sinking in the pit of her stomach, which she immediately pushed away. It was probably because everything was happening so fast.

This is what she'd dreamed of. An end to her financial problems. The cutting of a noose around her neck.

Maybe it was just the stressful day, feeling more unsettled than happy. She should be thrilled to be rid of Carson's house. She would finally be able to move forward. But now it would be time to say goodbye for good.

And then Alex would leave, mission accomplished.

Good thing they weren't serious. And she'd be sure to keep it that way.

Because she was not going to mourn the loss of another man.

Chapter 25

KIT WANDERED OUT to the beach, where she found Alex and Ollie sitting side by side, leaning back in the sand. Once again, her heart was touched by Alex's loving way with Ollie. Between the breeze blowing off the sea and the low rumble of the surf, they didn't hear her approach.

"Let me see your shells, Ollie," Alex was saying.

Ollie dumped a whole handful onto the sand. "I got a slipper shell, a scallop, and an angelwing. And this!"

Alex took a red bit of sea glass from Ollie and held it up to the sky. "Red is rare," Alex said.

"What's *rare* mean?"

"It means hard to find." Alex handed the bit of glass back. "That's a keeper."

"I'm going to add it to my collection," Ollie said. "I have a special jar. It was my dad's."

"Your dad collected sea glass too?"

"Yep. He found a red piece too." Ollie lined up his shells in rows. "What else did my daddy like?"

"Besides sea glass? Um, let's see. Chocolate ice cream. Flying way up there." He pointed up to the sky. "He loved everything about the ocean—swimming in it, running along the beach, watching the sunrise and the sunset, just being near it. But there was one most important thing he loved most of all."

At Ollie's puzzled expression, Alex shot him a big grin. "You."

Her boy looked raptly up at Alex, absorbing every word. Kit knew she should make her presence known, but she stood there, feet riveted in the warm sand, on the verge of tears. Because the way Alex spoke to her son was tender and beautiful. It made her happy and heart-breakingly sad at the same time.

"He was so proud to be your dad," Alex continued. "After you were born, he showed all us guys in the squadron a photo of you. You were wearing a little baby shirt that said WINGMAN. Do you know what that is?"

She remembered that wingman onesie. Alex's gift to Ollie.

"A wingman is a pilot who flies his jet close to the lead pilot and protects him and watches his back. Your blue eyes matched the shirt, and your hair was, like, sticking up all over. You were a super-cute baby."

Ollie swept his hand through the sand, covering all his shells and then dusting them off. "I wish my daddy was here."

There was a long pause. "Me too, buddy." Alex ruffled Ollie's hair. "Me too." He sighed. "You know, your dad wanted you to know that he'd always watch over you.

Just like the ocean is always there, big and wide, and when you walk into it, it surrounds you like a hug. That's like your dad. He will always be with you, and he'll always be a part of you. Your dad loved you bigger than the ocean."

Kit's blood froze, the words echoing in her head.

A lovely analogy for Ollie. Beautiful words that were so familiar to her because they were *Carson's* words.

But why had they come out of Alex's mouth?

Take things a half day at a time. Okay, Alex's abuela was full of sayings. It was easy to see how Carson could have put that in a letter just from hanging around with Alex.

Your beautiful smile lights up the room like the sun. A little bit cliché, a little cheesy. Anyone could have said something like that, right?

Tell Ollie I love him bigger than the ocean, Carson had said often in his letters. *I'll always be there, always be with you, always be a part of you.* How many times had she read that sentence over? The similarity to what Alex had just told Ollie was...spot on.

Alex turned his head and saw her. "Oh, hey. How long have you been standing there?"

"Mommy!" Ollie ran to her. "We dove into the waves. And Rex did too. And we cleaned up for you. Did you see? So when you came back you'd be so happy."

"I am so happy, sweetheart." She hugged her wet son. "Thank you both for cleaning up."

"How was your test?" Alex asked as Ollie took off a little way down the beach with Rex.

"I think I did okay. Thanks for all you did. And for spending time with Ollie. I'm sorry you had to walk into all that chaos."

"I was happy to help." He must have seen her skeptical expression. "Things were a little bumpy today but it was just your first exam. I can tell you're being hard on yourself."

Geez. Did this guy ever run out of patience? Or support?

"I'm going to put Ollie to bed," Kit said. "And then... could we talk?"

Because those beautiful words that would have been so touching... were far too similar to Carson's to be a coincidence.

* * *

Kit's head reeled as she put Ollie to bed. After she tucked him in, she stopped at the little writing desk in her room and riffled through Carson's letters until she found a particular one. Like all his letters, it was the slightest bit yellowed, bent from being read so many times, and stained by countless tears. She skipped to the exact spot she wanted, finding it immediately. *You and I, we grew up with the ocean. We understand how much the ocean is part of us, part of our souls. Our son will grow up like this too.*

She went on to read the rest. There was no denying it. It was eerily similar to what Alex had just said to Ollie.

Alex sat on the couch, patting the cushion next to him. "Come tell me how you did."

Alex was a good man. He'd been nothing but kind. She was overstressed and exhausted. But something about his exchange with Ollie had hit her at her core, and she had to ask him about it.

Her feelings about Carson and Alex, about the house,

about Alex leaving, about her own life—it was all over-whelming. She took a deep breath and a sip of some water she'd brought from the kitchen.

"I have a good feeling," Kit said. "But if I think about it too much, I start doubting myself."

"Bet you did better than you think," Alex said. "You've worked too hard to just pass."

"I hope I did well," Kit said. "But everything it took to do that was…too much. The life disruption, the lack of sleep, the stress…I'm sorry I dragged you into all of this."

Alex assessed her carefully. "You didn't drag me any-where. Ollie and I had a great time."

"Maybe it's not such a great idea for you to spend so much time with him." Yikes, had she just said that? Yes, she did. Ollie was getting too close to Alex. *She* was getting too close.

He looked perplexed and hurt. "What do you mean?"

"This is a temporary arrangement, and he really likes you." She felt…upset. Confused. How had he known those lines, straight out of Carson's letter?

"Well, I really like Ollie too." He took her hand and smiled. "And I really like you too. I was thinking that maybe we should reassess this no-strings policy."

She couldn't hear those words right now. She held up a hand to keep his words at bay. To not *feel* them. "Alex, I have to ask you something."

"I can tell something's bothering you. What is it?"

"I heard what you said to Ollie on the beach. It was a beautiful sentiment. But it struck me as familiar. Very familiar." She handed him Carson's letter, tapping on a certain place on the page. Then she said out loud the lines she'd memorized years ago.

*Tell Ollie to think of me when he sees our
ocean, and tell him I'm right there, surrounding
him like a hug, wrapping my arms around him.
I will always be with him and always be a part
of him. And tell him I love him even bigger
than the sea.*

Kit set the letter down on the coffee table, her hand
shaking. She forced herself to look Alex in the eye.
"That...that's almost word for word what I heard you
say just now. How...how do you explain that? The coincidence is unusual enough that I have to ask." Because
these were her memories. This was Carson. All she had
left of him.

* * *

Alex sank deeper into the couch. He'd vowed never to
tell Kit anything about the letters, even though his part in
them was minor and reluctant. He would never interfere
with something that meant so much to her, the memory
of her husband. But somehow, with the best of intentions,
he'd gone and betrayed himself with his own words.

He faced her, speaking slowly and carefully. "Sometimes Carson and I would sit around the barracks at
night when he was writing to you, and he'd ask me for
something—something more poetic to say."

Kit's puzzled gaze flicked from the letter to Alex's face,
making his heartbeat accelerate. "You mean he asked you
for help?" she asked.

There was nothing to do but continue. "Not exactly.
What I mean is, he'd describe a feeling, and he'd ask me
to make it more...I don't know...He would just ask me

to help him say it better. Because he was trying to give you support. To show his love. To express himself in a way that sometimes wasn't easy for him."

"Okaay..." She was looking at him in disbelief and confusion.

He took a deep breath. "Carson was a straight shooter. He was big on actions, not words."

"I understand that," she said. She pushed back her hair with a shaky hand. "I'm still not certain I understand. How... how much of these letters are... you?"

Alex reached out to comfort her and touched her arm, but she drew away. "Please don't be upset. I was only trying to help him."

She stared at the paper. "I thought these were *his* words."

"Most of them are," he said honestly. "And they're *all* his sentiments. I just—"

"You just what?" Kit cut him off. Her color was high, her eyes flashing with anger. "Embellished them? Made them sound better?"

He hadn't wanted to hear the emotional things Carson had wanted to tell Kit. Alex didn't want to know about her worries and concerns either, and he didn't want to feel her pain, because all of it had made it impossible for him to forget about her.

"I have to know," she continued. "What else did he ask for help to write?" She sat before him with her arms crossed, looking upset.

"Nothing personal," he said honestly. "He would just be worried about you. It was important to him to give you the gift of a letter to hold in your hands. To express his love and to bring you some kind of comfort when he was so far away. I knew the two of you exchanged daily emails but he struggled to get words down on paper."

She shot him an accusatory look. "So *you* gave him those words."

He looked her in the eye. "Sometimes."

Kit waved the letter until the paper practically snapped. "I have every line of every letter memorized. I've read them over and over as if Carson were speaking to me himself. He told me how much he loved me, told me how he couldn't wait to come back home. The idea that a third person was involved in any of that—"

"They were *his* letters," Alex interrupted. "*His* feelings. He didn't ask me about the personal parts. Just adages, sayings, things he wanted to make sound more thoughtful. Poetic."

Alex could not shake a sense of impending dread. Because he was coming to see that nothing he could say would make this better.

Kit stood up from the couch. "I...I have to think about this."

His heart sped up in his chest. "Think about what?" he asked cautiously.

"How come you never told me any of this?" She looked hurt and confused. "I'm just trying to understand."

"I didn't think my contribution was important." As soon as he said that, he knew it was the wrong thing to say. But he couldn't tell her that his feelings for her had been long-standing and painful, and that being involved in any way with those letters was the last thing he'd wanted. He didn't want to make this about him at all.

He saw what was happening. His intrusion into the letters was a dealbreaker. Something that had ruined the memories she clung to.

And she *was* clinging to them. And why wouldn't she? Carson was her husband. This thing between the two of them was supposed to be...light. After all, they'd fallen into bed because they shared the mutual pain of losing him. "I'm sorry," Alex said. "I had no intention of interfering with your memories."

He would never call her out for still loving her husband. For not being ready to move on. But what hurt was that she was nowhere near ready to love *him*.

He'd known she was struggling. Yet he'd gotten involved with her anyway.

"I appreciate everything you've done for Ollie and me." She kept her arms crossed tightly over her chest. "But I've said this from the beginning—I'm not ready for anything serious."

He stood up from the couch, preparing to leave. He didn't want to interfere with her feelings for Carson. He'd been excellent at stepping aside from his own feelings since the day after that stupid dance, when Carson was smitten.

Anger and hurt welled up inside of him. He'd foolishly told himself that they'd managed to create a relationship apart from Carson. "Maybe part of you doesn't *want* to believe me when I say I had very little to do with Carson's letters."

"What are you talking about?"

"Maybe this isn't about the letters at all. Maybe it's about finding a reason to avoid having a relationship with me."

The look on her face confirmed his worst fear. She looked set and determined, shaking her head vehemently. "Look, Alex, I— The past few months have been a whirlwind of changes."

He held up a hand. "No need to say more." He'd hoped against hope that she could give him a chance. But the reality was that there would always be three people in this relationship. And he was no match for Carson. He never had been. He had no right to try for a place in her heart. "We agreed this was just a summer thing." He had to stop himself from flinching as he said it. Because he knew that it was anything but.

She averted her gaze from his face. "I think it's better if we stop seeing each other." Her voice was almost a whisper.

"Agreed." Sadness overwhelmed him. Still, he kept his voice steady. "I'll move out of the garage as soon as I can."

He'd come to fix up the house, not to have a summer fling with his friend's wife.

Except he'd gone and fallen in love with her for good.

* * *

"I love this place," Kit said the next day, trying desperately to close her eyes and relax on Darla's deck as the three of them laid out in their swimsuits on lounge chairs.

Her parents had taken Ollie to the annual Seashell Harbor fishing tournament, so she had an entire afternoon to herself. Except her heart ached with dread and sadness. And she hadn't slept a wink last night.

Alex should have told her about his hand in the letters. Shouldn't he? She was right, breaking things off. Wasn't she?

"Kit?" Hadley was saying. "You okay?"

On the beach in the distance, families and friends gathered under beach tents and umbrellas, enjoying a carefree day. "If I lived here," she said, "I wouldn't get a page written. I'd just sit on this deck and stare at the ocean all day." She hoped that sounded like a normal thing to say.

"Well, then, for the next year," Darla said, "you can come and use my house as an escape whenever you like. In fact, I'm looking for a long-term renter for the next year. I'd give you a great price."

Kit blinked and sat up. Rex, whom she'd brought along to enjoy the sunny day, also bolted upright at her side, his tags clinking from the sudden movement. "Wait. What did you just say?"

"I've decided to rent out my house," Darla said, "for a year."

"You can't leave." Hadley also sat up. "It feels like you just got here."

Darla shrugged. "I got offered a writer-in-residence spot in San Diego. So I'll have a new coast to look at as I write my next book. It will be something different. I'm excited to go."

Too bad she didn't sound very enthusiastic.

"For a whole year?" Hadley asked.

"San Diego is too far," Kit said, then immediately regretted it. "What I mean is—"

"We think you might be running away from your problems," Hadley interjected, looking to Kit for support. "Right?"

"If my *problem* is Nick, you're exactly right," Darla said before Kit could weigh in. "But I'm not running away. I just can't stay. It's only for a year. Enough time for me to clear my head and see if I can get over him for good." She walked over to the edge of the deck, which was surrounded by contemporary metal fencing.

The ocean was cheery and beckoning, the waves split by the sun into thousands of points of bright light.

It had all the makings of a perfect day. If it didn't happen to be the worst day ever.

"I can't stay here and watch Nick date woman after woman," Darla continued, "because it appears that I still have a thing for him. I've thought about this for a long time. He's so charming, and when we're together, we fall back into our old ways, you know? The back-and-forth, the chemistry. But that's all it is. Chemistry. I have to break the spell. That means going away for a while, putting some time and space between us. Seeing him every day is preventing me from moving forward with my life."

"Your mom is going to hate this," Hadley said.

"*We're* going to hate this," Kit added.

"That goes without saying," Hadley agreed.

Darla sighed. "I moved home to be closer to my mom, but she understands. Although she's always had a soft spot for Nick."

"Darla, are you sure?" Kit asked. "Can't you just stay and work through these feelings?" She couldn't imagine, now that they were all finally back together, having her friends split up.

"I see the future," Darla said. "Nick will date, but one day he'll find someone. And he's sure to settle down here and raise a family. I don't want to be the person watching from the sidelines, never able to move on."

"Before you go, you owe it to yourself to talk with him," Kit said, feeling like she probably shouldn't be allowed to give advice.

"He's made it clear what he wants," Darla said, shaking her head. "Besides, the reasons we divorced are still there. He's still hanging out with his friends all the time.

He didn't want to settle down when we were married, and he still doesn't. Why would I go back to my old mistakes?"

"Because your old mistake is hot?" Hadley said. "Sorry, that was really tacky. I hate to see you go, but it's a brave decision."

"Thanks, Hadley." Darla gave a little smile. "I'll have to fly back for your wedding."

Hadley gave an awkward pause. "We're just exhausted trying to figure out this wedding stuff. And we realized the other day when we were with everyone that planning the wedding's taken away all our fun. Our friends. We've lost our priorities. So we've put it on hold. And we're both okay with that for now."

Darla leaving. Hadley's wedding on hold. Soaking up the sun was apparently not having the effect of making any of them forget their troubles. "I have something to say too," Kit admitted. "I broke things off with Alex."

"Oh no." Hadley brought a hand to her mouth.

"But you two are so cute together," Darla said.

"I heard Alex talking to Ollie," Kit began, "saying something that sounded almost identical to a few lines in one of Carson's letters."

Her friends exchanged puzzled glances.

"I've had this déjà vu feeling before, but this time it was almost word for word. Turns out Alex admitted to helping Carson write his letters."

"Wait a minute," Darla said. "Are you saying Alex wrote the letters, Cyrano de Bergerac style?"

"Not like that." On the beach, a family played a carefree game of bocci ball. Two golden retrievers chased a Frisbee into the waves. "Alex said Carson asked him to help because Carson was terrible at that stuff. And Alex said he didn't have a hand in any of the really personal stuff. I just feel...I feel that those letters were my last piece of Carson. The words that kept me going through those desperate times turned out to be...a collaboration. I...I don't know what to think."

"Alex didn't say anything about this before?" Hadley asked. "That's really awkward."

"I think I might get that," Darla said. "I mean, Kit, you've been carrying those letters with you since Carson died. I'm sure Alex didn't want to spoil any of your feelings about Carson."

Kit shook her head. "He should have told me."

"Maybe Alex is right, Kit," Hadley said softly. "Maybe he really didn't have that much of a hand in them. He seems genuinely smitten with you—and Ollie."

A flurry of confusion and sadness welled up inside. "He started to say he wants a real relationship," she confessed. "But I can't." Her voice dropped to a whisper. "I just...can't. I'm not ready to love anyone else."

"Kit"—Darla reached out and squeezed her hand—"I'm sorry that what Alex told you about the letters upset you. But I have to say something honest. You might not like it."

Kit rolled her eyes. "That's never stopped you before."

"I'm just wondering if maybe you're a little frightened."

"I'm *angry*."

"What I mean is," Darla continued, "maybe you sensed you were getting a little too close to Alex. And maybe you told yourself all along that your relationship didn't mean much because that was a low-pressure way for you to give yourself permission to get to know him. But now you're sort of being forced to make a decision, and it's scary to love someone again."

Hadley nodded her agreement. "It's easy to push Alex away by holding on to Carson."

Push Alex away by holding on to Carson.

The words jarred her. "That's not true," Kit said quickly. She'd just started dating again. She needed more time to get her life together—a *lot* more. "I feel betrayed," she said stubbornly. Didn't her friends get it?

Darla looked at her sympathetically. But her words were firm. "It sounds like the real question is, how do you really feel about Alex?"

Kit brushed away tears and sniffed, suddenly over-whelmed. As she struggled to speak, Rex walked over and placed his head on her thigh.

"I have no idea what you want," she said, petting him. "Your water's over there." She pointed to the deck rail. "Do you have to pee?"

Darla got up and got his leash. "I'll take him. C'mon, Rexy." But the dog stayed with Kit, refusing to lift his head from her leg.

She looked into the dog's big, dark eyes as he looked steadily at her. He continued to wag his tail expectantly. Kit glanced from her friends to Rex, a little incredulously.

"He's worried about you," Hadley said.

Kit stroked Rex's soft ears and kissed his head. "I'm okay." She stroked the dog's fur. "Thanks for being my friend," she whispered. "Better late than never, huh, Rexy?" Maybe it was her more upbeat tone, or the fact that she stopped crying, or maybe Rex just sensed that she needed it, but the dog gave her a massive, full-faced lick.

Which actually made Kit laugh a little—and reach for her towel.

"My experience with love has to do with dogs," Hadley

said. "I remember the yellow Lab we had growing up, Maggie. She was the best dog, and we had her for fifteen years. And I swore, after she left us, that I'd never love another dog as much."

"But then you got Milo," Kit said.

"He was an awesome dog too. The point is, love is strange. It...expands. We don't just have enough love for one dog—or one person."

"I'm not ready to love anyone," Kit said. "I'm just...not."

They all turned to the sound of footsteps walking up the deck stairs. Nick appeared, wearing work boots and a tool belt. He looked surprised to see all three of them there. "Hey, Darla. Ladies," he said, giving them a cordial nod.

"What are you doing here?" Darla asked, sounding just as surprised.

"Hey, I just got a part in to fix that ceiling fan motor on your porch." He held up a small square box. "Mind if I replace it real quick?"

Darla ran into the house to unlock the porch door for Nick, and Hadley went to grab a call.

"I just swung by the garage apartment to talk to Alex," Nick said, "and I saw he's packing up."

Kit met his assessing gaze. "Already?" was what slipped out.

Nick nodded. "I'm sorry, Kit." He gave her a hug.

"Thank you," she whispered, hugging him back.

Nick left to do his job, leaving her alone on the deck to gather her stuff and think of life and Alex and the letters. Those letters that she'd clung to had seen her through so much. And she'd clung to them hard, like a stranded swimmer to a lifeline.

But they were only letters. And Carson was gone.

And the idea of loving someone like that again truly was...terrifying.

As Kit squinted out into the bright, relentless sunshine, she couldn't deny that maybe her friends were right. It was a lot easier to hang on to her memories of Carson than risk loving someone again.

Chapter 26

THAT FRIDAY WAS the final day before the tour. When Kit got to the house early that afternoon, Carol Drake was walking out the front door. As the door clicked shut with a little thud, the pretty wreath Hadley had added bounced a little. The grain of the dark wood and all the clusters of grapes practically gleamed from the fresh restaining she'd done herself.

It was a beautiful door. But that wasn't all. From the gray-floored porch that now held wicker furniture adorned with pretty pillows to the windows trimmed like the period in red and green against the tan boards of the house, the house was, plain and simple, the overachiever on the block. Who would've ever believed that it was possible to create such a beautiful thing out of such a train wreck?

But then, Alex had always believed the train wreck could be so much more.

"Oh, hi, Kit." Carol shut the door behind her. "Stopping by to put on some finishing touches?"

Kit held up the bouquet of fresh flowers she'd just bought. "I'm just going to put these in the kitchen." That was mostly true.

"You and Alex have done an amazing job. And I have great news." She walked down the brand-new concrete steps. "The family I told you about wants to put in a bid as soon as possible. Isn't that wonderful? Mission accomplished." She pumped her fist and mouthed *Yes!*

"We have a buyer?" Kit asked as the meaning finally sunk in. She'd been waiting over two years to hear those words. To get this behemoth off her hands. Related phrases like *pay for college*—hers and Ollie's—or *buy a house* or even *get a reliable car that works* should've had her jumping for joy.

But she just felt sad. Hollow. *Lonely.*

"You *are* okay with that, right?" Carol looked at her expectantly.

"Absolutely," Kit said as firmly as possible. But every syllable felt wrong.

"All right, then. I'll get the bid paperwork moving." Carol turned and looked at the house one last time. "What an amazing transformation. You should be very proud of all the work you've done."

Kit thanked Carol, said her goodbyes, and let herself into the house. Bright afternoon light streamed in, and every room looked like a page from a magazine. The wood floors were polished and the paned windows spotless, showcasing the deep blue bay outside. The furniture they'd cobbled together from all their various sources somehow looked just right. And despite the red velvet seats and intricate carving, Mr. Rochester's enormous table also looked somehow just right.

She smoothed her hand along the fireplace mantel as she looked out at the sparkling water. "Honey, we did what you wanted," she said out loud. "We made this into a beautiful home." She hadn't talked out loud to Carson in a while. But doing so now brought her to tears.

She didn't see Carson inhabiting the rooms anymore as she walked from one to another. She kept seeing *Alex*. Rolled up in a tarp by the fireplace. Laughing as he stood on a ladder handling the lights. Using a putty knife to put tile adhesive on the kitchen wall tile. Threatening to headbutt her with his skunk streak, full of paint and mischief.

How had this place stopped being the sad manifestation of a dream that could never be and instead become a bright, sunny, beautiful place filled with laughter and love and potential?

With a sigh, Kit placed the bright flowers in a vase on the kitchen counter and then...it was done. Two months of labor. So much had changed since the first day Alex had walked into her life.

And without him here, it was so *quiet*.

She missed him. His brilliant smile, his warm brown eyes. How he encouraged her and challenged her and called her out on what she needed to be called out on.

Yet he'd never accused her of pushing him away. He'd never pressured her to sort out her feelings for Carson and move on. But he'd known what was going on when she'd made the letters a dealbreaker. His face had told her everything.

Kit walked out into the backyard and stood near the water, dropping her shoulder bag on the grass. "Honey," she said, addressing the heavens, "I want you to know that I think I understand now what you were trying to do." Maybe it was hearing her own voice crack or the fact that she was addressing her dead husband, but the tears were flowing freely now. "You wanted me to have a record of your love for me. One that would last in case...in case you never made it back. Maybe that's why it wasn't good enough for you to just write those stupid letters. Like normal people." She smiled at that. She knew her husband's desire to do things not just *right* but to be the absolute *best*. "You wrote them with love and care, and I want you to know, I felt all of that so much."

She pulled the little bundle out of the bag, her heart accelerating. "But I don't need these anymore to get me through. I figured out how to be all right again." She let out an ironic chuckle. "At least, most of the time. But if I'm really going to be all right, I've got to let you go."

She looked out at the sea. It was so calm, the waves lapping gently at the low embankment where the lawn ended, that even the birdsong seemed loud.

Carson would never see this house. Or stand here again with her, looking over the harbor, dreaming of their life.

She'd have to go on and make a different life. And that's why the letters had to go.

She wasn't going to choose them over a chance at really living. Even though she'd hurt Alex over them. Probably permanently.

She was crying harder as she untied the ribboned bundle, pulled out the bottom letter, and read the last lines.

I love you, Kit. I always will, and my hope every single day is that we make it to 100 together like Alex's little abuelo and abuelita in Puerto

*Rico. But if I don't make it out of here, I want
you to live to the fullest. Don't let your grief for
me prevent you from leading a great life. With
love and laughter and everything good. Don't
let your memory of me hold you back from anything, okay?*

She got it. Carson wanted to express his feelings for
her in a beautiful, comforting way. But he'd never meant
for his letters to be a crutch. Or a shrine.

"I love you so much," she said out loud. "But I won't
remember you more because of these letters. I'll remember your spoken words and your touches and your great
laugh." She kissed the letters, her tears falling on them
like they'd done many times before, blurring the ink into
a fading gray. "I love you, Carson. I always will, but now
I have to say goodbye." She took the bundle, stepped over
to the bank, and set it on the grass. Picking up the top
letter, she started to rip it in two.

"Kit, my God, what are you doing?"

A voice from behind made her turn just in time to
see her mother running at a fast clip across the yard. Kit
hadn't seen her mom run with that much purpose since
their dog had eaten the entire handful of wild berries
she'd picked from the woods around their yard for her
sixth-grade science plant identification project, prompting
a fast trip to the vet hospital ER.

Her mom unceremoniously snatched the letter from her
hands and then scooped up the bundle from the ground.

"Mom! What the *hell*."

"The girls told me you'd probably be here," her mom
said. She looked put together as usual, in white ankle
jeans and a blue sleeveless blouse, except she was a little

out of breath and her hair was ruffled in the breeze. "They said you broke up with Alex, and you were upset." She reached over and picked something out of Kit's hair. "Is that peanut butter?"

"I'm fine." Kit was a little shaky and a little close to the edge of the lawn, where it ended before a brief sandy slope into the water. She attempted to wipe her eyes and her runny nose on her sleeveless T-shirt, not an easy feat.

Her mom took her by the elbow and steered her straight to the back porch, sitting her down on the now-brightly-painted blue and green Adirondack chairs.

Her mother turned her mom-vision onto her and swept her gaze up and down. "I can see you're not fine." She dug into her purse and pulled out a Kleenex, which Kit immediately used to blow her nose.

One look at her mom's concerned expression and the tears started to flow again. "You're right. I'm *not* fine. I pushed Alex away. And guess how I did it?" She nodded to the pile of letters. "I used these."

"I don't understand." Her mom dug through her bag for another Kleenex.

"Carson asked Alex for some help writing his letters," she said. "Alex said he added some sayings or made some things sound a little more poetic because the guys knew he had a way with words. But I...I overreacted. Because I was afraid. Afraid to let go. Afraid to love anyone else."

The truth hit her all at once, jarring as an anvil strike. It didn't matter that she was afraid to love Alex. Because she'd gone ahead and fallen in love with him anyway. "I love Alex, Mom. But it's too late. He's leaving."

Her mother held her hands. "Oh, Kit. My brave girl."

Kit hadn't heard her say those words since she was an angsty teenager. "It must be frightening to open your heart again. As your mother, I've certainly felt helpless watching you survive all that loss. I think that's why your father and I tried to do everything we knew to help you out of your pain. But what I'm learning is, sometimes we can't shield our kids. And sometimes we shouldn't."

"You and Dad have been the best." Kit hugged her mom. "I wouldn't have survived without you."

"I don't have any answers," her mom said, squeezing her tight. "I can just tell you that I think you're amazing. And I'm so proud of you, Kit."

"Mom, I'm a mess." She sniffled and wiped her eyes. "I was a mess before I moved out, and I'm an even worse mess now."

"You've taken a lot of risks lately." She stood up. "But if you really love Alex, you've got to take one more. And no matter what happens, you'll be okay." She picked up the bundle of letters from where they sat on the seat. "These shouldn't go in the water. One day, Ollie will want to hear his father's voice. His thoughts. And his feelings, which are real even if he asked Alex for a little help to express them. For Ollie's sake, let his father tell how much he loved you both. So keep them, Kit. Or let me keep them for Ollie. But don't toss them in the ocean."

Keep them for Ollie. Yes, Carson would want that, Kit felt sure. Ollie would one day look for ways to know what his dad had been like. What better way than through the letters?

Kit nodded toward the bundle. "You put them away for safekeeping, okay?" To which her mom breathed an enormous sigh of relief as she tucked them into her bag.

"Do me one more favor," her mom said.

"What's that?"

"Please resolve your love life. This is way too stressful." She gave Kit a wide smile.

"I'll do my best," Kit said, grinning back. "I love you, Mom."

* * *

"Are you okay?" Nick asked Alex that afternoon as they were doing one last walk-through of the house.

"Sure. Why?" Alex was going over the newly refinished wood floor in the kitchen with a dust mop in preparation for laying down plastic sheeting for all the foot traffic that would pass through in the next few days. The furniture was in place, and the house looked better than new.

Something he definitely couldn't say for himself.

Nick stood up from where he was applying a solvent to remove a paint splotch. Outside, a Bobcat whirred as workers dug the final holes for new landscaping. "Because you've gone over the same two feet about a dozen times. And you spent ten minutes looking for your phone but it's in your pocket. And...did you know your shirt's on backwards?"

Alex didn't even bother looking because it occurred to him that Nick had seen everything he'd been trying to hide all along. So he might as well be honest. "Look, I'm really proud of what we've done here. And I want to tell you how much I appreciate all your help and your expertise." He paused and sighed. "And your friendship." That part was hardest to say, but he meant it.

"Whoa there." Nick looked at him with concern. "This is sounding a little too much like goodbye."

"I've done what I came for, and now it's time to get back to my life."

"I thought you might stay because of Kit. And because you like us." Nick displayed the grin that... well, let's just say it coaxed a lot of women to go out with him. But Alex couldn't be so easily swayed.

"I do like you. But things haven't worked out with Kit."

The Bobcat working outside was making it hard to hear. So Nick walked around the kitchen island and stood right in front of him. "Why not?"

The persistence. Alex shook his head. "You know, you really could pinch-hit for my abuela."

"C'mon. Just tell me." Nick flashed another smile. "You know you want to, because I'm so easy to talk to."

Rolling his eyes, Alex said, "The bottom line is she's not over Carson. And I'm not sure she ever will be."

"None of my business but look how far she's come. She's gotten her own place, started classes, started dating *you...*"

"Ha-ha. You understand how complicated this is more than anyone. But I can't be involved in a relationship that's rooted in the past. That never works."

"First of all, maybe it's not as complicated as you think." Nick, who Alex was finding to be an eternal optimist, counted on his fingers. "And second, if you've loved her this long, maybe... maybe you just need to be patient a little while longer." He paused. "I want you to know I thought about what you said. I broke things off with Lauren."

Alex looked up in surprise. "Did I advise you to do that?"

"You got me to thinking that I need to tell Darla how I feel."

He set down the mop. "How *do* you feel?"

"Like things aren't right between us. I'm going to start by trying to get back to the kind of friends we used to be—the kind that don't tiptoe around each other like we're walking on broken glass."

"That's a start."

"Hey, guys, are you in there?" Darla's voice sounded from around the corner.

"And here's your chance." Alex shot him an ironic smile.

"Wow, this looks amazing." She looked around at the fresh paint, the gleaming countertops, and the bright light streaming in everywhere. "Did you know there's a whole crew digging up the landscaping? And a whole pickup truck bed full of bright pink flowers?"

"Finishing touches," Nick said. "What's up?"

"Actually, do you have a minute?" Her eyes darted between Alex and Nick. "I wanted to talk with you."

Alex hiked a thumb toward the dining room. "I'm going to start laying down that plastic sheeting," he said, trying to make himself scarce.

"It's okay, Alex," Darla said, making him stop in his tracks. "You can hear this too. Nick, I'm going out West to be a writer in residence. At the University of San Diego."

"Oh. Well, that's terrific." Nick ran a hand through his hair, sounding monotone and decidedly not enthusiastic. "Really terrific," he mumbled. "Congratulations." He forced a smile.

"Thanks," Darla said. "I'm excited about it." Interesting, Alex thought. Because she sounded just about as excited as Nick had.

"What are you doing with your house?" Nick asked.

Darla, looking thoughtful, leaned against the island. "I'm going to list it as a vacation rental, I think. That way it doesn't sit empty for a year."

Nick's eyes widened. "You'll be gone a whole year?"

"Yep," she said, confirming that with a nod. "That's how long the fellowship is."

"Right, right." Nick shifted into management mode. "Well, do you have someone to oversee it? Because I'd do that for you. Meet the renters at the beginning of their stay and again when they check out. Be on call for maintenance. That way you can rent it privately. The local rental company takes a big percentage of the rent, and when the season really kicks in, the oversight isn't so great."

"Oh." She sounded a little surprised as she considered his offer. "That sounds like a big commitment."

"No, I-I'd like to do it for you," Nick said, "I mean... I'd do anything for you, Dar."

"I know you would." They stared at each other. Alex really wished he was in the dining room putting down the plastic. "And I appreciate it," she said.

"Sure. Of course."

"I came over for another reason too. I wanted to ask you to run an errand with me. It's kind of important. I can pick you up in a half hour."

He gave a firm nod. "See you then."

Darla left, leaving Nick to pace the floor. "I'm too late."

"That's baloney," Alex said. "So you might have issues to work out. If you two have something good, don't let that stop you."

Somebody in the room should at least get some sense knocked into them. But the echoes of Alex's own voice ran through his head, as loud as the grating of the motor outside. It suddenly occurred to him that he was giving Nick advice he should be giving himself. He'd let everything—Carson's ghost, his own survivor guilt—stop him, not just from loving, but from living.

He'd been afraid to tell Kit how he really felt about her. Remind her of how good they were together. And tell her that, if she wasn't ready, he would wait.

Why wouldn't he wait? Why wouldn't he fight for her? He'd loved her forever.

* * *

"Okay," Darla said as she and Nick invaded Kit's kitchen that evening just as she was doing last-minute alterations on Ollie's lemon costume. "We have to tell you something."

Kit, who was struggling to thread a needle, looked up. "Now?"

Darla nodded. "It's important. I overheard something Nick said when we were in the Sand Bar a while ago. Something that I think you need to hear. *Nick.*"

She gave a nod to Nick, who looked like he'd rather be getting his prostate checked than standing here having to say whatever he was going to say. "Okay. Darla thinks you need to know this. I'm not so sure I should be—"

"Nick. Please tell her." Darla impatiently shifted her weight from one foot to another. "It's important."

Kit stabbed herself with the needle and jumped. "You have no idea how stressed I am right now. Just tell me." She *was* stressed, and not just because she had approximately a half hour to turn a round, yellow M&M costume into a lemon shape, something she'd been struggling badly with for the past hour and a half. But mostly, she was brokenhearted. *That's* what she was.

"Remember homecoming?" Nick asked. "Your senior year?"

"In high school?" Kit asked, incredulous. "And this is important *why*?"

Darla put a calming hand on her arm. "Honey, we've got you covered. Just listen, okay?"

Darla pushed aside the mess of yellow material and stuffing, and everyone sat down. Like it was teatime or something. But with T-minus twenty-eight minutes to go.

"You do realize I have to have Ollie dressed and backstage by seven, right?"

"Okay, Nick," Darla said, giving him an elbow nudge. "Talk."

Nick sighed and drummed his fingers on the table. "Okay, so homecoming."

"I remember homecoming," Kit said. "My date spent the whole time with Marcia Ledbetter. But Carson came up and started talking to me. We talked for most of the night."

"That's right." Nick stabbed the air with his finger. "Exactly. Well, do you remember the punch?"

She grabbed the mass of fabric and went back to weaving the needle in and out. "Someone got punched?"

"No."

"The spiked punch?" Kit asked, trying to remember. "The one the Carellis got suspended for?"

"Alex was walking over to talk to you," Nick said. "He was going to offer you a drink of punch."

She frowned. "I don't remember Alex that night at all."

"Of course you don't," Nick said. "Do you know why? Because someone plowed right into him and the punch spilled all over his shirt."

Kit pulled the thread tight. "Nick, I appreciate this

story, but I'm really freaking out right now. Could we maybe talk about this later?"

Nick grabbed her hand. "Alex wanted to talk with you. Alex had a crush on you." He spoke slowly and carefully, letting every word sink in. "Alex wanted to ask you out. But his best friend got to you first."

Kit froze. She shifted her gaze back and forth between Nick and Darla. "Wh-what are you saying?"

"We think Alex has loved you for a long time," Darla said quietly.

For a long time.

"I-I've never heard anything about this."

"Of course not," Darla said. "But it would explain…things. Like why he sort of gave you the cold shoulder for years."

"Homecoming was ages ago." But even as Kit said that, things began to click into place. How he'd barely spoken to her for years. His determination to fix up the house. And how hurt he must have been when she'd basically accused him of ruining Carson's letters for her.

"Maybe," Nick said. "But…we love who we love."

Darla looked away.

"Alex is a good guy," Nick said.

Kit gave Nick a hug. "I know," she said in a whisper. "Thank you for telling me that."

"So can I help?" Darla asked, sliding the bundle of yellow toward her.

Kit gave a dull laugh. "Only if you can turn something round into something oblong."

"Um, I can stay and offer moral support? Or else I'll see you tonight." Darla gave her a hug. "And whatever he looks like, Ollie will be the cutest little lemon M and M ever."

"Please don't mention that this was an M and M costume to Ollie," she said as they left her to her jumble of bright yellow thread. She cut the tangle of thread and started over for the third time.

Alex was a good guy, and she'd hurt him deeply.

He'd stepped aside for his best friend.

And all this time, he'd never said a word.

Chapter 27

*When life gives you lemons, make
lemonade.* —Julius Rosenwald

A LITTLE WHILE later, Kit stood backstage in the outdoor amphitheater helping Ollie get his lemon head on.

"You're the cutest little lemon, Oliver," she said, standing back and surveying her work. You couldn't even tell the costume used to be an M&M, except it did still look a little round versus oval. But the little white gloves were perfect and his bright green tights matched the little leaves she'd sewn around his neck and on his hat.

"Lemons are not just for lemonade," Ollie sang, barely holding still. "Mommy, where's Alex?"

That shot an arrow through her heart. "Alex had to do something important, sweetie," she said. "And I'm not sure if—"

"More important than my play? He won't miss it, will he, Mommy?" Ollie's large blue eyes looked concerned.

Kit tried to remember to breathe. And tell herself that every single thing she knew about Alex told her that he wouldn't abandon Ollie. Except that she'd pushed him away. She'd let him leave. And she had no idea how to answer her son.

"I'm sure Alex will do everything he can to be here for you." She gave her sweet boy a hug. "And in the meantime, Uncle Cam and Uncle Nick and Aunt Darla and Aunt Hadley and Grandma and Grandpa and I, we'll all be cheering you on."

Ollie seemed to accept that at face value and burst out singing, "Lemons aren't just for lemonaaaaaaade," as she gave him one last squeeze—ha—and watched him run to join his fruit and veggie colleagues.

She hoped she hadn't just lied to her son. She hoped Alex would find it in him to come tonight, for Ollie's sake.

Who was she kidding? For *her* sake too.

Kit jogged up into the audience seats and climbed over her mom and dad to settle in next to Hadley and Cam and Darla and Nick. A busload of seniors from the local independent living facility appeared to take up the rest of the row.

Her mom said, "I don't see Alex anywhere." Which only confirmed what she already knew. Alex wasn't here.

Then the lights dimmed, and Lauren came onstage to explain the farmers' market initiative to promote healthy eating. And out ran the dancing fruits and veggies. Parents were taking pictures. Grandparents were smiling. Everyone laughed when the little tomato, who was no more than three, waved sweetly to everyone.

She wanted Alex by her side, grinning with her at Ollie's antics as he danced and sang. She wanted to be holding his hand as he made a joke or whispered endearments in her ear.

Sharing...life.

Her life wasn't about mourning anymore. She wanted it to be about...joy.

"What's that green thing?" Darla asked.

"Cilantro?" Nick answered in a deadpan voice.

Darla shot him a *What the hell?* look, and he burst out laughing. "It's broccoli, Dar. See the little green bunches on his head?"

The apple sang. The cucumber sang.

And then her little lemon hopped out in front of everyone. A spotlight shone, and the music stopped, and all eyes were on Ollie.

Come on, Ollie, Kit rooted for him, her hands balled into fists in a manner very reminiscent of how it felt to be at Tee ball. She sat forward in her chair, full of nerves.

And then her heart stopped. Because Ollie...choked. His deer-in-the-headlights expression made her wince. *Come on, Ollie. You can do it*, she cheered and prayed at the same time.

"Do it, Ollie," Hadley whispered.

"Come on, little dude," Nick said, his jaw clenched.

Despite all the hundreds of times at home that Ollie burst out with his lemonade song, his enthusiasm had suddenly evaporated, and he was...paralyzed.

Kit didn't think. She just moved. Out of her chair, climbing over her friends' legs and all the seniors, who shuffled their bags and purses on the floor.

But it felt like she was crawling through pudding. She reached the side aisle as Ollie's expression turned from shell-shocked to panicked. She tried waving her arms, doing a thumbs-up, trying desperately to get him to see that she was there, that everything was okay, but it was too dark.

He couldn't see her. And she was so, so far away.

Where was Lauren? Couldn't somebody save this moment?

After an eternity, Kit reached the left side of the stage. She climbed the few stairs and whisked behind the curtain, hoping to talk to him from the wings.

"Hey, Oliver," a quiet, calm voice was saying, "channel the lemon." And singing softly, "Bright and sunny, round and funny, lemons aren't just for lemonaaaaade."

In front of her was a grown man, doing a lemon dance and singing about vitamin C.

Then Alex tapped his chest. And he said, "Belt it out, *mijo*. Just like Tee ball, Oliver. Knock it out of the ballpark!"

Mijo. Mi hijo. He'd just called Ollie *my son*.

Kit clutched her heart. Tears stung her eyes as she watched Ollie suddenly perk up. He looked at Alex, who nodded and smiled. Slowly, her son faced the audience, who all seemed to be holding their breath along with her.

Then Ollie began to sing. Not quietly. Not timidly. But like the Ollie who loved to sing. Enthusiastically, exuberantly, he waved his arms and legs and did his lemon dance and belted out the words to his song. As the audience cheered and clapped, he hammed it up even more. To the point where everyone was laughing and clapping and whistling and cheering.

Kit had to lean against a wooden beam for support until she finally started breathing again.

"He's got some *Boricua* spirit in him, that kid." Alex was beaming with pride. Smiling widely. Clearly overjoyed for her son, who was bowing and grinning widely and waving to the crowd.

"You talked him through his fear." Her heart was pounding over the noise of the crowd. And wondering— did he only love Ollie? Could he still love her, too, even if she'd pushed him away and made him feel that he was second best?

Alex's warm, dark eyes were full of feeling. She hoped some of that was for her. "I knew he could do it," he said. "He just needed to believe in himself."

"Alex, I—" Beyond the curtain, parents were snapping photos and gathering around the stage. Soon Ollie would be wondering where she was. Where *they* were.

She swallowed hard. "I love you."

It was noisy onstage, but behind the curtain, the silence surrounding them was deadening. Her pulse pounded in her ears, her heart clogged her throat.

Alex looked…shocked maybe. Or skeptical, she couldn't tell. But she kept going anyway.

"I was afraid—like Ollie. I saw us getting too close, and I…panicked. I used Carson's letters to push you away because I was afraid of loving someone so completely again. I used those letters like a crutch. I treated them as if Carson were really speaking to me, weighing in on all of life's decisions and moments. They made me feel like I wasn't alone."

She swiped at her eyes and continued, "But I kept them like some kind of sacred memory. So when you said you had a part in them, I got angry. It was like my memory of Carson was being tampered with."

There, she'd said everything. Put all her feelings out there. And scanned his face for a reaction.

His brows knit down into a frown. "Kit, I didn't want to contribute to those letters."

"I understand that now." She paused and looked into

his eyes. "Alex, you are the kindest person I know. And so, so kind to my son, who is blossoming right before my eyes." She swiped again at more tears. Because she understood now that he'd loved her. And she really hoped she hadn't blown this. "But that's not why I love you. You make me laugh, and you make me feel that I can achieve my dreams, and you've made me feel...alive again. And you get me in a way that...that no one has ever gotten me before. And you've helped me to find the courage to stand on my own."

She gripped his hands. "I'm still shaky on my legs. I still have a long way to go. But I love you. So much. And I'm so sorry I pushed you away. Please give me another chance."

"I've loved you for a long time," he said. "I tried not to. Believe me, I fought it as hard as I could. But I've come to realize that I'm never going to stop loving you. So if you need more time, take it. You're important enough for me to wait."

The parents were rushing onto the stage, hugging their little veggies. "Would you...would you meet me at the old house tonight? I have to get Ollie settled so...around ten or so? My parents already said they'd come over."

It was really noisy now, the stage overrun by photo-taking family members and enthusiastic fans, essentially everyone from the audience. Ollie was in his glory, prancing around with his fellow edible colleagues.

Alex cradled her face in his gentle hands. "I love you. I should have told you that. Because, Kit, I've loved you forever. And I finally feel like that's okay. If you'll have me."

Then he kissed her. A kiss full of joy, and relief, and of...beginnings.

Wonderful, exciting beginnings. Of new life. Of promise.

The noisy theater disappeared, and it was just Alex, his lips, his arms, him.

"Look, Ollie's still dancing," Alex said as they finally made their way onto the stage.

"I think that might be a different kind of dance," Kit said a little warily. "Maybe we better hurry."

Alex laughed. "I have a penknife on my key chain if we need to bust him out of that costume quick."

Then they ran out to celebrate with their happy little lemon.

* * *

The doorbell at the new/old house rang at ten precisely. But it made Kit jump anyway. Her heart lodged in her throat as she opened the heavy door to find Alex standing there on the brand-new stoop, in jeans and a black T-shirt, looking so handsome that she longed to touch him. But she didn't. She wanted to make sure they were okay.

"Thanks for coming," she said. "Tomorrow, the whole town will see what we've done. But for right now, I thought you and I could take a moment and enjoy it ourselves." She gestured him inside. "Come in."

Their footsteps fell softly on the polished floors. Kit had turned on all the lights and lit a bevy of candles in the fireplace. With the warm throw over the couch, more fresh flowers on the coffee table, and the soft gray-patterned rug, compliments of Apoorva, the house shone in the soft glow at its very best.

An image came to her mind of a rumpled Alex, just waking from sleep and smelling like mothballs, startled when she'd finally forced herself to enter the dark, dusty house.

A lot had changed since then.

She led him into the kitchen and gestured for him to sit down. The undercabinet lighting made the glass tile sparkle.

If he noticed the glass punch bowl full of orange fizzy liquid on the table and tiny-handled glasses scattered between more candles, he didn't say.

She used the ladle to fill a glass and pushed it toward him. "Want some?"

His brow lifted in a *strange but okay I'll just go with it* vibe. "Punch?"

"I heard that, a long time ago, you might've been on the way to bring me some." She took his hands in hers and looked straight into his eyes. "I'll always love Carson, but he's my past. I...I hope that we can be each other's future." She truly felt it. That Carson was a part of her, some of the best parts. But there was room to love Alex. And for once, she didn't hear Carson's voice in her head. But she didn't miss it. Because she felt his blessing, wanting her to be happy.

Alex gripped her hands tightly. "Well, *querida*, I suppose I have Nick to blame for telling you about the punch. But the truth is, I've tried every trick in the book to forget about you. I thought coming here would finally make me see that you were a fantasy." He softly touched her cheek. "But you were more than I'd ever dreamed."

She leaned her face into his hand. "I love you," she whispered.

"I love you right back." He prevented her from saying any more with a kiss. Then he drew something from his jeans pocket. "I brought something for you."

It was a plain white business envelope with his name written on it.

Kit examined it, flipping it over in her hands. Startled, she looked up at Alex. "That's Carson's handwriting."

"This is a letter from Carson. It's the kind of letter no one wants to read. I suppose that's why I never opened it."

Her hands were trembling. "You never opened it?"

Alex shrugged. "I already knew what he wanted me to do about you and Ollie. I just couldn't bring myself to hear his last words to me."

"Oh, Alex." Kit felt tears prick her eyes as she tried to hand it back.

"I wrote him one like it too. Mine said what a great friend he was, how much I loved him. I...I just couldn't bear reading stuff like that. I still can't."

She led him to the couch in front of the fireplace in the great room. "We'll read it together."

As Kit began to read the familiar script, her eyes were dry, her hands steady. That lasted for about one sentence, but she forced herself to continue.

Al, if you're reading this, I didn't make it. I don't have the words you do, but there's no other way to say it. The only request I have is one you already know—to make sure Kit and Ollie are okay. I don't trust anyone else to do it. They are my life. Kit will fight you, but I know you can get her to accept the help she needs. And eventually, if she finds someone to be with, I want you to give your blessing on my behalf. If you approve, I approve. Because I trust you with my life. One day, I want you both to stand in that beautiful yard and raise a glass to me as the sun sets over the harbor. I love you, man. Carson

As soon as she finished, Alex wrapped her up in his arms. His cheek was as wet as hers was.

"He says if you approve, he approves," she whispered.

"It's like a blessing from him," Alex said.

They sat quietly for a moment, thinking about that.

"Alex," Kit finally said, "I had an idea about the house, and I wondered if it would be all right with you."

He drew back, scanning her face. "What is it?"

"Would it be okay for you financially if I rented out the house instead of sold it? I'd give you three-fourths of the rent money every month until all your expenses were paid off."

"I could make that work. With everything going on, I forgot to tell you Mr. Cammareri offered me a job on his crew while I apply for law school. What are you thinking?"

"It's a beautiful house. You worked so hard to make it stand out."

"*We* worked so hard."

"Okay, *we*," she agreed. "I know Carson would be so proud of what we did. Somewhere along the line, I stopped working on it in honor of Carson and started thinking of it as a house that maybe one day we might live in. That might be thinking way too far ahead, but what would you think of that?" She wasn't sure what he would say. But if she'd learned one lesson, it was that life was way too short not to live every moment to the fullest.

Alex tugged her up off the couch and led her to the kitchen. "I have to show you something I found when I was painting." He opened the door to the old butler's pantry and pointed to it. There, on the old, grayish paint, were a series of pencil marks. Kit bent to examine them more carefully.

"These are ruler marks," she said, pointing.

"I didn't have the heart to paint over them," he said. "Look closer."

"Heights," she said, her voice choking up as she read the penciled names. "Of children. Rose, Louise, Edward, and Ellie."

"Yep. Maybe measured over the years by their proud parents. I thought you'd like to see this, since you were wondering about who lived here."

She straightened out. "A family."

"Yep," he said, leaning against the doorway, "I feel exactly the same way, Kit. I can see it being ours one day. But in the meantime, I'm okay with taking it slow for Ollie."

Aw. The perfect answer. "Also," she said, "I put in my notice."

He smiled widely. "No more Mr. Marfler?"

She pretend dusted off her hands. "No more Mr. Marfler. Your mom gave me a lead for a front desk position at the county mental health center, and they hired me. I was thinking it might lead to some other opportunities once I get my degree."

"Congratulations," he said. "But then I always knew you were headed for great things."

That made her blush a little. "I don't know about that, but a degree and a good job would be acceptable." The way he was looking at her touched her deeply. Like he knew she could achieve anything, and he'd be there with her all the way. And she vowed to do the same for him.

"One last thing," Kit said. "You don't mind two cats, do you?"

"The cat is now plural?"

"Yes. Turns out Seymour loves that little kitten Hadley brought over. I think, if it was two against one, he might be able to handle living with Rexy."

"Ollie and I will help Rexy handle his feline friends," he said.

"So," Kit said, "do you approve?"

"Of the cats?"

"Of us."

"Kit." Alex took her hands in his calloused, strong ones. "I've always felt honored that Carson would entrust you and Ollie into my care. And I swear to you now, I will honor that promise for the rest of my life."

As they stood close together, in the house that smelled of cut wood and fresh paint, every nook and cranny filled with the labor of love, she remembered a time when she felt alone and so burdened by memories that she had to force herself to enter it. Since then, everything had changed. They'd gone on a journey of healing and forgiveness, and in the process, love had crept in when she'd least expected it. "I can't wait to start the rest of our lives," she whispered, her voice filled with emotion. And then she kissed him.

Epilogue

EVERYONE WORKED THEIR stations on the day of the home tour, which was July 4. Kit was the greeter at the front door. She got to welcome everyone in, make sure they put on their paper booties before they trekked through, and got to tell them a little about the house. Like how they'd recently discovered the original family had four kids, and all of their heights were recorded on one side of the pantry door.

Kit's parents brought Ollie by in the late afternoon, and it didn't take more than thirty seconds for him to discover the swing in the back.

Then, when the tours were over for the day, all the friends gathered in the backyard to feast on picnic food, compliments of Cam and Hadley, and await the annual Seashell Harbor fireworks show.

Cam stood up and raised his glass of wine. "I'd like to propose a toast," he said. "Kit, Alex," he said, looking around. "Or should I say Chip and Joanna?" That got an eye roll from Kit and a belly laugh from Alex. "You both put heart and soul into this project. I think we can all say we did Carson proud. To our dear friend Carson, whom I'd like to think is looking down at us with a smile."

"To Carson," Alex seconded, touching Kit's glass and wrapping his arm around her. "To Carson," Kit whispered, nodding first to Alex and then to her friends. She smiled quietly to herself, watching her sweet, happy little boy as he pumped his legs on that swing.

It was not the life she'd imagined when she'd sat here with Carson so long ago. But she felt his love and, she was certain, his happiness for her.

"By the way," Kit said a little later, chowing down on a piece of Cam's fried chicken, "we got second place."

Darla frowned. "Who got first place?"

"The house with the kitchen that looks like a fifties diner," Kit said.

"Yours is more classy," Darla said.

"I agree," Hadley added. "The diner idea must've cost a fortune. We were on a shoestring budget. We got creative."

"It doesn't matter that we didn't win," Alex said, taking up Kit's hand.

"Because we love it and that's all that counts?" she asked.

"No," he said, grinning widely. "Because I won first place with you."

Everyone groaned—in the best way.

"You two are too cute," Hadley said.

"I'd like to propose another toast," Cam said. "To Kit and Alex." Everyone lifted their glasses as Cam continued. "Who would've guessed that this old house would help you find your way to each other?"

"I'm going to miss this," Darla said with a sigh after they'd all clinked glasses again.

Nick perked up at her comment. "Oh, I forgot. When are you leaving?"

"As soon as I can pack up," she said. "Classes start in two weeks, and I need some time to get settled."

"Does this have anything to do with me?" Nick asked in front of everybody.

He looked genuinely concerned. "I mean, you're not leaving because you don't think this town is big enough for the two of us, are you? Because I thought we were getting along pretty well." He sounded a little hurt, a little upset. Very unlike the usual easygoing Nick.

Darla rolled her eyes and said in a teasing tone, "The world doesn't revolve around you, Nick Cammareri. And to answer your question, I'm leaving because it's a great opportunity. One I couldn't pass up."

"What does Sam think about that?" Nick asked.

"I don't know," she said. "We broke up."

"Oh. Sorry to hear it." Nick tried to sound sorry, but to Kit, he looked visibly relieved. "I broke things off with Lauren," he blurted.

Kit caught Hadley's eye and knew she was thinking the exact same thing. That Nick and Darla didn't seem to notice everyone around them trying not to listen. Also, Kit thought, this was the first time in recent memory that neither of them was dating anyone else. Then she realized something she'd almost forgotten.

"Here you go," she said, taking Darla's ring from her pocket and handing it over. "Thanks for the ring, Dar. It's been quite a summer, but I think I'm done with adventures. Now it's your turn. Good luck in California."

Darla smiled, a little sadly, Kit thought, and hugged her tightly. "I'm so happy for you," she said, a little choked up.

"The fireworks are starting!" Ollie yelled, running over, pointing up at the sky as small explosions of red, white, and blue burst above the bay. Rex barked, and Alex tugged his leash and stroked his back reassuringly. "It's okay, buddy," Alex said. "Just a few *booms*. Nothing to get nervous about."

Ollie climbed onto Alex's lap. "I want to watch the fireworks with you, Alex," he said. Alex laughed and boosted him up.

Kit felt Rex's cold nose nudging her knee. "I know you don't care much for the loud noise, Rexy," she said, petting the dog. "You sort of look like you want to climb up on my lap, too, don't you?" In response, the dog placed his face on her leg and wiggled his butt.

She kissed the soft fur on top of his head. "I love you too."

There were plenty of ooohs and aaahs as the fireworks burst one after another in rapid succession over the bay, reflecting their magical colors in the dark water. Alex squeezed Kit's hand tightly. Her son was oblivious, mesmerized by the light show, pointing up at the sky while he cuddled against Alex. When Alex looked over at her and winked, Kit thought that life really couldn't get much better.

* * *

Shortly after ten, all of Kit's friends went home, and her parents stopped by to take Ollie with them for an overnight. That left Kit and Alex to lock up the house. And gave Alex time for one last little surprise.

"I'll be back bright and early," Kit said. "Apoorva's delivery people are coming at eight sharp to take all the furniture away."

"I'm glad that a lot of it sold," Alex said, tapping the manila SOLD tag on the couch.

Kit looked around. "Me too." She sounded a little melancholy.

But he had something to cheer her up. "Before we go, I have something to show you." She looked perplexed. "Close your eyes."

"Close my eyes?" she repeated.

He took her hand and led her to the bottom of the staircase. "Stay right here." He walked over to the wall and flipped a switch. "You can open them now."

He couldn't help but be pleased as Kit's eyes grew wide as the stained-glass window above the stair landing came alive with color. Alex was a little amazed himself on seeing the bright greens of the leaves, the vivid purple of the birds, and the wavy blue and green ocean, lit by a bold yellow sun.

Kit's breath caught. "How did you—"

He took her hand and led her up the stairs to the landing, where they admired the glowing artwork. "Nick talked me through installing the backlighting. I didn't want you to have to wait until the sun was beaming through to see the beauty of it. I wanted you to be able to enjoy it all the time."

He stood behind her as she took in the beautiful lit-up window that fit like it was made for the space. "I see what the woman at the salvage place told us," she said, "that your eye is lifted through the branches, through the tree, up to the sun and the water."

Through the shadows of the branches and the chaos of the birds. "Leaving the past behind, onto the future, right?"

"Which is exactly what happened to me," he said. "Because of you."

"Make that to both of us. With help from each other."

"I love you, Katherine," he said. "I've always loved you." With that, he took her into his arms.

"I love you too," she said as he planted a slow, careful trail of kisses down her neck. "But you're not admiring the window."

"I have all the beauty I need right here," was his answer. Which he could tell she liked, judging by the way she moved so he could get to more of her neck. And how she leaned back into him, molding to his body.

She gave a soft laugh. "Whatever you're planning next, the answer is yes."

"Whatever I'm planning?" He chuckled against her soft skin. "Whyever would you think that I'm planning something?"

Without waiting for an answer, he stepped back and scooped her up over his shoulder. She let out a squeal. "Where are you taking me?" she said from her upside-down position.

With one more glance at the beautiful window, with the sparkling, shining sea glass, he carried her up, up the grand staircase, which really did smell lemony now, right into their future.

Author's Note

Dear Readers,

I hope you enjoyed this story about how love lifted one couple out of loneliness and sadness when they least expected it.

As I was writing about Alex and Kit and her two lifelong best friends, I couldn't help but think about how the pandemic has challenged all of us in ways we never could have imagined. The potential for loneliness and isolation on a daily basis is overwhelming. Now more than ever, we need our family and friends. We need stories of hope and love.

Seashell Harbor is my little escape to a sunny beach town where the streets are lined with fragrant flowers and quaint old homes, where long friendships never fail, and where we can hopefully share a laugh or two.

Writing a book always takes a village. I wanted to thank my agent, Jill Marsal, and the fabulous team at Forever Romance—my editors, Amy Pierpont and Alex Logan, assistant editor Sam Brody, publicity and marketing associate

*director Estelle Hallick, senior production edi-
tor Mari Okuda, and Daniela Medina for the
gorgeous cover that I keep on my desk and stare
at because it's so beautiful. Thanks to my dear
writer friends Sandra Owens and AE Jones, who
always have my back, regardless of the time of
day or night. And also to Yvonne Cruz, who read
the book early and provided insight into Alex's
heritage. And lastly, to my husband Ed for all
the love and support and for always giving me a
daily dose of laughter.*

*And thank you, kind readers, for seeking out
my books. I couldn't do this without you!*

*I hope you reach out and give someone a hug
today. And never hesitate to drop me a line. I'd
love to hear from you.*

*Miranda Liasson
November 2021*

About the Author

Miranda Liasson is a bestselling author who writes about the important relationships in women's lives as well as the self-discovery and wisdom gained along the way. Her heartwarming and humorous romances have won numerous accolades and have been praised by *Entertainment Weekly* for the way she deals with "so much of what makes life hard...without ever losing the warmth and heart that characterize her writing." She believes that we can handle whatever life throws at us just a little bit better with a laugh.

A proud native of northeast Ohio, she and her husband live in a neighborhood of old homes that serves as inspiration for her books. She is very proud of her three young adult children. And though every day she thinks about getting a dog, she fears a writer's life may bore the poor animal to tears. When she's not writing or enjoying books herself, she can be found biking along the old Ohio and Erie Canal Towpath trails in the beautiful Ohio Metro Parks.

Miranda loves to hear from readers!

MirandaLiasson.com
Facebook.com/MirandaLiassonAuthor
@Miranda Liasson

Book your next trip to a charming small town—
and fall in love—with one of these swoony
Forever contemporary romances!!

THIRD TIME'S THE CHARM
by **Annie Sereno**

College professor Athena Murphy needs to make a big move to keep her job. Her plan: unveil the identity of an anonymous author living in her hometown. And while everyone at the local café is eager to help, no one has an answer. Including the owner, her exasperating ex-boyfriend whom she'd rather not see ever again. After all, they ended their relationship not just once but twice. There's no denying they still have chemistry. So it's going to be a long, hot summer...unless the third time really is the charm.

SEA GLASS SUMMER
by **Miranda Liasson**

After Kit Blakemore's husband died, she was in a haze of grief. Now she wants to live again and give their son the kind of unforgettable seaside summer she'd had growing up. When her husband's best friend returns to town, she doesn't expect her numb heart to begin thawing. Kit swore she wouldn't leave herself open to the pain of loss again. But if she's going to teach her son to be brave and move forward, Kit must first face her own fears.

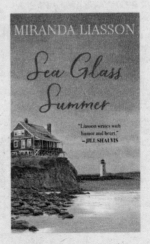

Connect with us at Facebook.com/ReadForeverPub

Discover bonus content and more on
read-forever.com

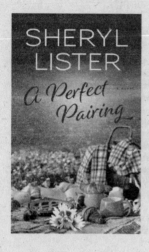

A PERFECT PAIRING
by Sheryl Lister

As a top Realtor in Firefly Lake, Natasha Baldwin can't complain and really has only two regrets: never pursuing her dream…and how she left Antonio Hayes years before. So when an opportunity arises to show off her passion for interior design, Tasha's excited…until she discovers Antonio is her partner on the project. Now is not the time to let her past impact her future, but working with Antonio immediately sparks undeniable chemistry. Just as a second chance at love is within reach, her big break comes around and she must decide what she truly wants…

FOUR WEDDINGS AND A PUPPY
by Lizzie Shane

When her Olympic dreams were crushed, Kendall Walsh retreated to Pine Hollow to help run the ski resort—while her childhood friend went on to dominate winter sports. Years later, Brody James is suddenly retired and back home. But he isn't the same daredevil Kendall once had a crush on. As the resort's events coordinator, she has no time for romance. Yet when Brody begins tailing her as eagerly as her foster puppy, she's reminded of why he's always been her kryptonite. Could this winter make them remember to be a little more daring…even in love?

Meet your next favorite book with @ReadForeverPub on TikTok

BALANCING ACT
by Emily March

After settling into life in Lake in the Clouds, Colorado, Genevieve Prentice is finally finding her balance. But her newfound steadiness is threatened when her daughter unexpectedly arrives with a mountain of emotional baggage. Willow Eldridge needs a fresh start, but that can't happen until she stops putting off the heart-to-heart with her mom. Yet when Willow grows close to her kind but standoffish neighbor keeping secrets of his own, she realizes there's no moving forward without facing the past…Can they all confront their fears to create the future they deserve?

FALLING FOR ALASKA
by Belle Calhoune

True Everett knows better than to let a handsome man distract her, especially when it's the same guy who stands between her and owning the tavern she manages in picturesque Moose Falls, Alaska. She didn't pour her soul into the restaurant just for former pro-football player Xavier Stone to swoop in and snatch away her dreams. But amid all the barbs—and sparks—flying, True glimpses the man beneath the swagger. That version of Xavier, the real one, might just steal True's heart.

CHANGE OF PLANS
by Dylan Newton

When chef Bryce Weatherford is given guardianship of her three young nieces, she knows she won't have time for a life outside of managing her family and her new job. It's been years since Ryker Matthews had his below-the-knee amputation, and he's lucky to be alive—but "lucky" feels more like "cursed" to his lonely heart. When Ryker literally sweeps Bryce off her feet in the grocery store, they both feel sparks. But is falling in love one more curveball…or exactly the change of plans they need?

FAKE IT TILL YOU MAKE IT
by Siera London

When Amarie Walker leaves her life behind, she lands in a small town with no plan and no money. An opening at the animal clinic is the only gig for miles, but the vet is a certified grump. At least his adorable dog appreciates her! When Eli Calvary took over the failing practice, he'd decided there was no time for social niceties. But when Eli needs help, it's Amarie's name that comes to his lips. Now Eli and Amarie need to hustle to save the clinic.